The Long Journey into a Life

A Novel
by H. H. Gorder

PublishAmerica
Baltimore

ISBN: 1-60813-140-8
PUBLISHED BY PUBLISHAMERICA, LLLP
www.publishamerica.com
Baltimore

Printed in the United States of America

This book is dedicated to my father, Harvey Harold Gorder. If it weren't for labors on his part, the miracle of life, and the will of God, I would not be here.

If his passing hadn't occurred at such a young age, both his and mine, I truly believe this book would not have come into existence.

I still miss you.

H. H. GORDER
09 April 2007

Kruser —
Thanks for being
a friend all of these years.

Preface

They say that for most people, the journey into a life begins at birth. But, for Patrick Raymond McCray, it began with death.

Part One

Summer 1970

Chapter 1

Pat moaned, softly, way back in his throat; then he rolled over. His eyes flickered rapidly behind his closed eyelids as he was deeply absorbed in his dream:

"You are so beautiful," Pat said to the beautiful woman in the red suit standing directly in front of him, her hands planted firmly on her subtle hips. She held a look on her stunning face that could have been a pout; or, she was upset with the fact that it was only Pat standing here with her. Pat couldn't be sure which it was, but he was positive about one thing: she was truly dazzling in that red suit.

"You know," Pat started to say to this woman as he walked slowly, carefully and deliberately towards her, "it is an amazing thing that you and I are here...all alone. One might even say that it was sheer coincidence that we are here together on a night such as this."

Pat looked around them at the night in question. It was absolutely still, there wasn't a cloud in the sky and that cloudless sky was filled with twinkling stars to numerous to count.

When he got within a few feet of her, she dropped her head and looked at the ground directly in front of them.

"Hey," Pat said softly, tipping his head to one side to look at her. He reached out his hand to her to lift her chin so he could look at her eyes. "I am thinking of kissing you; if, IF you don't mind."

Pat closed his eyes and began to lean forward, puckered lips leading the way. He had been waiting for this moment forever. He had been dreaming of this time, this woman, forever.

Once he got her to raise her head she opened her mouth and said,
"Tweet. Tweet, tweet; tweet."
Pat snapped his eyes open and jerked his head back from her.
"What did you say?" Pat asked her with a quizzical look on his surprised face.

Pat woke up quickly to the song of robins sitting and singing somewhere outside. Their songs trickled in through his open bedroom window.

He stared up at his bedroom ceiling trying to get his bearings at such an early hour.

Now that *was a strange dream*, Pat contemplated as he turned his head and looked towards his open window.

Must be around seven o'clock, he thought, as he tossed aside the covers and got ready for another day. His hair, tangled by the night's sleep by which he dreamt about chasing the assorted dragons, and saving damsels-in-distress, especially those in red suits, stuck out from his skull like auburn corkscrews. He wiped the sleep granules from his eyes, stretched and then slipped on his favorite moccasin slippers that he got from his Grandma for Christmas last year.

He shuffled his slipped feet slowly across his bedroom carpet towards the window in question.

Pat looked out the window at the world outside. He squinted against the reflection of the rising sun radiating from off the window on the walkout door on the front of their garage. He then spied two robins that sang so sweetly sitting on the top of the garage roof. They were singing so brightly while watching two other robins as they worked the yard for any stray worms that may have been excavated from the ground with the morning dew. It looked as though robins must always have guards posted while the others worked, Pat speculated. He recalled that he had observed that behavior before in most birds.

It must truly be something to have to live your life in constant fear, such as that of a song bird, or a squirrel or rabbit, Pat thought; always looking over your shoulder as you gathered what you could to eat and sustain your meager life. They were gathering food, or eating knowing that the predators were out there, just out of your sight, watching as you fed, waiting to pounce.

Although way too young to understand, completely, the stories he had read in the newspaper about Vietnam, he imagined those Vietnamese people were like so many scared rabbits, shivering every time they made a move to portage for food.

Pat couldn't imagine living a life like that.

I

The weather outside was absolutely gorgeous, as it always was in Wahkashen, North Dakota, in the summertime. The town, pronounced 'Wah-Cash-En' was an old city, established in 1878 by mostly German/ Norwegian immigrants tired of the ways of their own country and who hungered for the new world; they struck out to create a better life for their descendants who were sure to follow them—in time. The population was approximately seven thousand in August, 1970.

The area was held together mostly by the perfect farming soil that went all up and down the Red River Valley, housed the towns of Wahkashen, North Dakota, and Bulliford, which was located across the Red River in Minnesota. This farming rich soil was deposited there over ten thousand years ago by the glaciers that carved up most of Wisconsin, Minnesota and the Dakotas. Minnesota was the fortunate state to receive its "ten thousand lakes", and North Dakota was blest with soil that farmers could almost take to the bank like so much gold dust in a burlap bag.

Farming and a little industry (industry used to support the local farming community that is) was the principle economy for this area.

The weather was so unblemished this day that it caused one to stop and think that Mother Nature had sat down with God to have a cup of coffee, discuss topics of various nature (no pun intended) and then, when they finally agreed that they wished to create spectacular weather for a day, they definitely had Wahkashen in mind.

The mystical North Dakota fall colors of red, orange, and brown on the leaves, which may be the prettiest season of all in North Dakota, gave way to winter, the harshest of seasons in any area of the world; which in turn gave way to spring and then it stepped aside to the budding oaks, assorted elms and the various hardwood trees which lined the streets of the quiet, farming community.

A light breeze moved the leaves around, very slowly and quietly like the whisper of a lover's voice in your ear. The stirring of these leaves did nothing in changing the shadows created by the intermingling branches high above the street by these large, old trees; and it gave the street the appearance of a long and winding tunnel. The kind of tunnel one would have found only dug through ancient and large mountain ranges while riding on a train somewhere in Europe.

9th street north disappeared in a one point perspective towards Main Street, when looking south from 6th avenue. This morning the avenue was unbroken by any cars parked along its sides. The concrete gutters on both sides of the street held the color of archaic battleships that covered the South Pacific in search of the Japanese fleet.

Every now and again one could spot traces of the prior days grass cuttings as they lay quietly and untouched by wind, or man. There was an earthy smell of that cut grass, and it hung softly and thick in the still air of early morning. The only sound all up and down 9th street were the various song birds expressing their joy at such a wonderful and promising morning. It was absolutely gorgeous, as it always was.

9th street north was a one-way, going north; and the next street over, 8th street, was a one-way going south back towards Main Street. Patrick Raymond McCray lived on 9th street north. In fact, he lived at 523, 9th street north, with his family in an older two story house in which he was afforded the luxury of having his own room. Even at the tender age of thirteen, that was maybe the most important thing in a young man's life; when one had an older sister, and no brothers.

He loved his sister to death, but he cherished the serenity of being able to escape to the comfort, solitude, and secrecy of his own bedroom.

There was nothing spectacular or magnificent about Pat McCray himself. He was a typical boy of thirteen with a slight stature and a warm smile that revealed hidden dimples. When he received more than his share of ribbing about those dimples after they showed themselves, Pat would merely express that he got them from his mother, and then smile even more.

He was smallish, for a thirteen year old when compared to other boys his age, but what he did not possess in physique he more than made up in heart; Pat held the heart of a lion in his chest, and the will to survive was strong. His five foot four frame was slightly built, and he was representative of most teenage boys throughout the Midwest who were still growing into the frames God gave them.

There was also nothing exactly spectacular or magnificent about his room, except for the plain fact that it was his and his alone. Best of all, he didn't have to share with his older sister since Pat and Penny were three and five years old, respectively. The walls of Pat's bedroom had dark brown paneling and were adorned with posters of hockey players and various rock-n-roll singers thumb tacked to them; the floor was covered with a style of high traffic carpet of a color that was made specifically for rambunctious young men, and the ceiling was roofed with squares of white acoustic tiles that Pat had helped his dad staple to the ceiling joists.

Pat was fairly neat and orderly, which was considered quite rare in young boys, but he didn't mind picking up after himself. It gave him a strange sense of order, which made him feel good, and made his mother happy. Both of those outcomes were just fine by Pat.

Pat held high aspirations of becoming an astronaut, fireman, or even a hockey player like Lou Nanny. Anything would be good in the mind of a thirteen year old boy, as long as it held the imagination to the point where it was more spectacular and magnificent than the life currently being lived. Pat fancied it would be genuinely cool to be a Dragon slayer, if there *were* such mythological creatures.

The McCray house was furthermore nothing extravagant or superb. It blended in with the surroundings of all of the other houses on this street.

Most homes were two-story dwellings built around the turn of the century to the 1920's and 30's, and a few of the homes up and down this street, further north from Pat's home, were a bit newer as those were built in the 50's and 60's.

The darker brown lap siding that covered the outside of the McCray house kept the house indiscrete amongst the trees; and the silver shingles helped to radiate the heat away from the upstairs, according to his Dad. The double hung windows that were typical in the houses built during this period held curtains of various designs on the first floor, and mostly pull down shades on the second. The front lawn had a small fence on both sides of the walkway to their front door, and the yard was neatly trimmed.

It was a typical house in an archetypal town housing an atypical family with nothing to distinguish it from any other house in the area, or across North Dakota in the 1970's, for that matter.

II

He left his open window and the birds' beautiful morning music and walked the small hallway outside his bedroom towards the steps that eventually led downstairs. When he arrived at his parents' bedroom door, he began to tip-toe softly past so he could avoid waking his Mother at this early hour on a Tuesday. He looked towards their bedroom door with his deep green eyes tinted with flecks of robin egg blue.

Although tip-toeing was not completely necessary, as Pat weighed all of a buck and a quarter, and a stiff wind might topple him over at any time. Most people commented that Pat's stature was considerable, but promising. If Pat were a black lab puppy, the neighbors have always said, 'he will grow into those paws someday.'

Slipping as quietly as possible past the door of his parents' bedroom, he remembered the advice of his late Grandpa, *"Discretion is the better part of Valor."*

Now, Grandpa Alvin Timmerman was a wise man, and he gave Pat that advice when Pat came to him crying about being called a sissy for not fighting one of the toughest kids in his grade. Although taunted and teased almost to the brink of throwing a punch at the bully (who out weighed Pat by, at the very least, 25 pounds, and had a 3 inch height advantage), Pat absorbed the names and the instigating punches to his arms. When the 'gang' finally tired of taunting him, like a cat with its captured mouse before it would kill and devour it, Pat ran, in tears, all the way home to the safety of his bedroom.

He spoke to his Grandpa at length about the incident.

"Ray," his Grandpa started to say (his Grandpa always called him Ray, although his true, Christian name was Patrick Raymond McCray, named by his father Howard Raymond McCray, and his father before him, Raymond Howard McCray. Pat secretly wondered why his father decided to name him Pat instead of Raymond. He had trouble with the name Pat, as the many schoolyard brawls and bloody noses indicated).

"You don't need to get beaten up by any boy bigger and stronger than you because the other boys are teasing you to fight this bigger boy," his Grandpa continued. "Walking away in tears is better than being hauled into the doctor with a split skull or a broken nose.

"You see," he continued, "'Discretion is the better part of Valor'."

Now Pat had absolutely no idea what *discretion* was, or *valor*, for that matter; but he always chuckled when he talked to his Grandpa and his Grandpa called him Ray. When confronting his Grandpa about his nickname, Grandpa Al said that he always thought of Pat as his 'little ray of sunshine' ever since he was born, and looked at him with those big green eyes.

Mom told Pat it was because Grandpa Alvin thought Pat was a silly name, a girl's name; and Grandpa Al told Mom that the nickname of Ray, although named for a brazen bastard like Raymond Howard McCray; sounded better than Pat.

Once again, Pat had no idea what *brazen* meant, but he always chuckled when Grandpa called him Ray.

Pat did know, however, that he never got to meet his Grandpa Ray, as he passed away in '54, a year before Penny was even born.

Pat loved spending his time with Grandpa Al. He loved sitting on his lap, which was quite comfortable, and sucking in the soft, musky smell that radiated from his Grandpa's clothing from the pipe that he frequently smoked. It seemed that Grandpa had a billion stories to tell to Pat, at any time he wished. His stories varied from serving in 'The Big One' (WWII, Pat would later discover) to his tales about growing up on a little farm with his two brothers; the numerous chickens that he used to chase, and working the fields with his father.

Grandpa Al would delight Pat with his tales of sneaking behind the barn with his older brothers and smoking 'corn silk' cigarettes that they had rolled. Pat always found it hard to believe his Grandpa that he and his brothers would smoke corn silk, but he never said anything like that to his Grandpa. Alvin told him how they were good at making chickens fall asleep when you held them just right in your hands. And, when you had them, lying neatly in your hands, beak straight in the air they *would* actually fall asleep. He said that they would then walk over to the water trough for the horses and cows and without a sound, drop the sleeping chicken into the trough and watch as, "all Hell broke loose," Alvin would say with a burst of laughter.

So, tip-toeing past his sleeping Mother did seem like the better part of *whatever*, at this hour.

After Pat went past his sleeping mother, undetected, he reached the downstairs, went into the kitchen, and realized that he still had a couple of hours before his Little League practice. So he would have some cereal, watch some TV, and head to the park in plenty of time. Maybe he could catch "The Andy Griffith Show." That was one of Pat's favorites. He just loved the guy who played Barney Fife. Pat's humble opinion was that Barney Fife sure could use some of Grandpa Al's advice about discretion.

It didn't really matter if he got to ball practice on time anyway, as he was far from the 'star player', so the coach and most of the team wouldn't miss him if he didn't show up—but he felt an awkward sense of devotion to himself, as well as the team. It was hard for Pat to explain, but he just felt that if he didn't show up, somehow that would have an adverse affect on the team that never allowed him to play. Somehow he felt if he didn't stick to going to practices and always showing up for the games (even though he very rarely left the bench) that he was letting down the team and they would think even less of him than they do right now.

III

Walking to the park with his bat on his shoulder accompanying the sunshine that was also there, Pat felt at ease with the world this fine morning. Even though he would much rather be riding his bike to the ballpark for practice, he still felt really good this morning.

He'd better get that front tire fixed soon, as the fancy of walking would wear off quickly. Even at thirteen, seven blocks was seven blocks; and the trip would go much quicker with the aid of rolling tires beneath you.

He waved at Mr. Ferguson as he walked by. Mr. Ferguson was walking in a seemingly endless circle behind his lawnmower. He still had the old-fashioned push mowers without an engine. When asked, Mr. Ferguson said he liked the 'chickty-chick-chick' sound that the mower made when he pushed it around the yard. Mr. Ferguson said it reminded him of the mower that he used as a child and that made both Pat and Mr. Ferguson smile.

Mr. Ferguson had to be about seventy years old, and his wife passed away a couple of years earlier, but he still kept himself busy. Maybe, Pat thought; that was why Mr. Ferguson was still with us today. Maybe the exercise behind the antiquated mower, and the memories that remained strong in Mr. Ferguson's mind was all a person needed to stay alive at seventy.

He passed Mr. Ferguson's house and continued walking down 6th Avenue looking at the houses that lined the streets and avenues, admiring the yards that these houses held. Some were really nice, and some were in definite need of repair. Pat could tell which houses were occupied by the people who had a great deal of pride in the ownership of their property, and a strong sense of community.

As Pat admired these houses with their well-kept lawns, and as he got closer to the corner of 6th avenue and 4th street, he heard the approaching sounds of laughter and bicycle tires turning on the small pebbles and sand remaining in the gutters. The pebbles and sand were the remnants of the automobile aids from last year's snow and ice. North Dakota had to lay down sand and salt in certain areas for traction, mostly intersections.

Roads in the winter, in North Dakota, could be treacherous and fatal…even in towns, in the winter months.

Pat barely started getting his head turned to see if maybe it was some of his teammates on their way to the ball field, when one of the first riders stuck out his foot and caught Pat right behind the left knee. The force of the forward momentum of the rider on his bike striking the stationary left leg of Pat's caused Pat's left knee to buckle quickly.

Pat's bat and mitt went flying into the air as easily as pigeons released from one's hands, and he landed hard on his butt, with his hands out, palm down. Instinctively, he put out his hands to help absorb the shock of impact, and they were met by the pebbles in the gutter. After landing with a 'thud' and hearing his mitt and bat come crashing back down onto the ground, he gazed up with a surprised look on his face, staring straight into the face of Brian Osterman.

"Hi, Pat-ty," Brian said, with a high pitched, sing-song voice coming out of the scowl on his pimply face. "Did you have a nice trip?"

With that being said, Brian received a roar of approval in the form of laughter from his two cohorts, Ed Closterman and Pete Benningham.

"Did you have a nice trip," snickered Ed, one of the mindless followers of Brian's 'Clan of Idiots'. "That was a good one, Brian."

Pat had heard his name pronounced like that, mostly by the bullies and mindless thugs that are housed in every town in the modern world, since time out of mind; and to date, he still had not gotten used to it.

Now, Brian Osterman, quite affluent on brute strength, size, anger and pimples, but oh, so insolvent on intellect, commonsense, and compassion, as most bullies were, smiled at Ed, and then turned his pock-marked face back towards Pat, who was still sitting in the gutter.

"You gonna do something about that, Pat-ty?" Brian spit out in that same girlish sing-song voice that Pat despised over the years, "or are you just gonna sit there and bleed?" He threw his leg over his bike and threw the bike down on the ground…hard. He was dressed in his usual blue jeans and black biker boots. He had his t-shirt with the cut-off sleeves. The A-typical bully apparel, Pat thought.

Pat lifted his hands and noticed the pebbles stuck to his palms, and then he noticed the little beads of blood bubbling out from under quite a few of them.

"No," Pat stammered, quietly. "I'm all right."

He stood up, slowly, and carefully began wiping the pebbles from his hands onto the pant legs of his jeans. The blood smeared a little across the fabric. *Mom will kill me for that*, Pat thought with a sense of gloom that struck Pat as not as important as the peril facing him at the moment.

Pat began to reach for his fallen bat and glove lying on the ground at his feet. Brian, as quick as he was stupid, stepped over and kicked them aside before Pat could get to them. Once again, this action was met with tons of approval from 'The Three Stooges'.

"What's it gonna take to have you fight like a man," Brian said with a sneer on his face.

Pat thought three against one was never really going to happen. Hell, he didn't even like the thought of fighting Brian alone. So he just kept repeating to himself in his head, *'The better part of valor...the better part of valor...'*

He fought hard to stop the tears that were welling up in his eyes; more from the sting of the taunting than from the pain in his hands.

"Come on, Brian," Pat said staring down at the ground in front of him, and the he looked up at him. "I'm already late for baseball practice, and I don't want to fight you. You are way bigger than me. I know you'd kill me, you know you'd kill me, even your friends know you'd kill me; so why do we even bother with this?"

Brian came at Pat with both hands out and struck Pat in the shoulders and shoved him hard enough for him to land a couple of feet away on the grassy boulevard.

As Pat tried to roll over to get back on his feet again, Brian jumped on him and pinned him to the ground. He then reached into the back of Pat's jeans, found his underwear and pulled up fast and hard.

Pat felt his testicles as they were slammed against his body by the force of the pull, and he was lifted up off of the ground. Pat then heard a sickening *tearing* sound indicating bad news for his Fruit of the Looms.

"You just better stay out of my way, sissy boy," Brian snorted, as he let Pat fall back to the ground. He walked away and picked up his bike. "The next time I see you, I won't be asking for you to start swinging…you will have no choice. And, it won't just be a snuggy then."

They got on their bikes and with a roar of laughter and jeers, they left Pat there, lying on his chest on the grass. Pat fought hard against the stinging hot tears from the pain in his groin from the snuggy he just received; as well as the humiliation with the fact that he was lying on a boulevard somewhere on 6th Avenue with half of his underwear sticking out the back of his blue jeans.

Pat finally rolled over to his back and started to manipulate his underwear back into position, the best he could.

Why ME, God? Why was it always me? Pat thought, as he stared at the crystal blue sky above him, silent tears rolled from the outside corners of both eyes. *'You couldn't find anyone better to serve as victim here; it just had to be me?'*

I really need to get the front tire repaired on my bike, Pat thought, *so I won't have to go through this again. Maybe I could outrun them if I had my bike. It may not work; it may be that I would be trying to outrun the wind. Would be worth a try, anyway,* Pat figured.

So off they rode, the 'Three Stooges', Pat thought as he heard their departure. He'd better hurry if he was going to get to the ball field in time.

Pat stood up and wiggled his butt back and forth a couple of times, reached back and pulled out on the back of his crotch until he was sure that his mangled underwear were back in the proper location…again. He wiped a sleeve across both eyes, quickly. He smoothed down his ego, tried to straighten out his wrinkled self-esteem as he re-position his damaged underwear.

Pat then remembered how the robins outside his bedroom window were always on guard while trying to feed themselves, and he was beginning to feel the same way. He was going to have to stay on the alert from now on, because the predators were out there, and they now had the taste of Pat's fear and blood on their tongues.

And, they liked it.

He looked down at his hands and saw the small scratches that the pebbles left on both of his palms. They were not bleeding too badly, now, so he should be alright at practice.

He looked up and down the street to see if anyone had witnessed the disgraceful event that had just transpired. It was like a person who was walking down the street, hitting and slipping on a sheet of ice. After going down hard on their ass they spring to their feet quickly looking around to see if anyone noticed what had just happened to them.

Pat looked at his hands again. They really were not bleeding too badly now, so he should be able to get his mitt on without too much concern…or pain.

It didn't really matter one way or the other, Pat figured.

Hell, the coach probably won't even have him put on his glove today.

Chapter 2

In the months that followed the senseless killing of four young students at Kent State University at the hands of the Army National Guard while protesting the United States 'police action', things in Vietnam and Cambodia went spiraling down, and out of control. President Nixon and his administration's public reaction to the shootings was perceived by many in the anti-war movement as callous. Then National Security Advisor, Henry Kissinger, said the president was "pretending indifference."

Demonstrations escalated, more and more young men, and women, were hauled off to jail for sit-ins, hunger strikes and quiet protests. Howard McCray stated that most of those dope smokers belonged there anyway, as Delores, his wife, would *'shush'* him at the dinner table.

Those not hauled away, holed away out of sight, or made for the nearest border in quick fashion never to be seen in the United States ever again.

But none of that could touch or have any influence on the world that was Wahkashen. Baseball practice went as predicted. Pat didn't have to worry about his hands or put on his ball mitt, because he never left the bench.

Pat heard the other kids calling out for the ball as they assembled in the various positions that they played. Some of these kids, the really snotty ones, Pat thought, said things behind cupped hands as they slowly ambled by him while he occupied his position on the bench; derogatory stuff, aimed at him, and only him with the sole purpose of trying to inflict emotional damage. Pat paid them no mind as he watched the team doing their grass drills, having batting practice; observed their two pitchers they had, throwing on the third base side of the field to the catcher, and the coach; as they only had one catcher.

Pat always wished that he had had more friends on the baseball team. Guys he could hang out with and practice throwing to and catching from on a more constant basis. It wasn't as if Pat were shy…far from it; but he didn't really have anyone on the team that he would be able to chum around with, and most of the team was from a better 'class' of people, as he was always told by those *from* that other class.

Pat was sitting on the bench watching and listening, but after a little while he was not at all seeing or hearing anything that was happening in front of him.

However, Pat seemed to see and hear everything this morning with clarity that he never had before. The sky seemed so deep and so blue it was as if you could dive into it and swim to the clouds which looked like distant islands. Once reached, one could then lie back on the beach of those fluffy islands and listen to the steady ebb and flow of the imagined tide. Listen to the tropical birds cluck and call all day as they frolicked in the trees. Feel the tropical breeze as it rolled slowly, quietly up the shore to rustle the fronds of those trees. Not a care in the world. No 'Three Stooges' to worry about and one could eat bananas and fresh pineapple all day.

The grass infield appeared as rich and soft as the felt covering on the finest of billiards tables. Pat remembered he saw a beautiful billiard table with his Dad when they drove to the Twin Cities one year (the Twin Cities being Minneapolis/St Paul in Minnesota). Pat didn't recall the purpose of the trip. Could have been a planned visit, a trip to the Como Zoo, or something; but he did remember the billiards table.

It was one of the old-fashioned ones with the leather stitched cups hanging under each of the holes. The dark wood, mahogany, his Dad said, seemed to glow under its own power as it stood bold and beautiful below the green and red billiards light that hung directly over the table. Those billiards lights appeared to be almost as long as the table itself. The light from that fixture flooded the playing surface, creating no shadows on any piece of the table top; that Pat could see.

Pat could picture the players, bent at the waist, lining up their next shot; cigarette dangling loosely from the corner of their mouths as smoke filled the room and hung thick around the light, giving everything in the room a dreamy, nostalgic look. He could almost hear the faint sound of the jukebox as it played all the favorites; this music intermingled with the thunderous sound of the ivory balls as they struck each other on the break.

The smell of the freshly cut grass field hung in the air; air which seemed thicker now than when he first arrived at the park. Of course, it was fast approaching noon, and then the temperature and humidity would be competing with themselves to see who can be the most unbearable for the day. Temperatures in Wahkashen always seemed to soar this time of the year; this time of the day. The only way to obtain relief was to go to the Red River for a swim, or go to the pool when it opened for the day.

He heard the players' voices intermingle with the song birds sitting high up in distant trees and droning bees that flew past his ear in their search for more nectar. The sounds were just so much more vibrant today. He heard the remote sound of lawnmowers from the grounds keepers preparing the other fields here at the park. He saw women and children as they strolled by heading to the zoo that was just down the road from the ball fields, or maybe to feed the ducks or play in the huge playground that the park also housed.

Everything just seemed so much….brighter, today.

Practice was just about over. He heard the coach barking out one command or another. He tried to pay attention but his mind was still wandering. His mind seemed to be shifting from the brilliant sky, to the smell of the grass; to his worries about becoming a bird or rabbit because of the intimidation caused by Brian Osterman and his Stooges, to the women with their children in tow. He wondered what he was going to eat for lunch before he went to the swimming pool for the afternoon.

Mom and Dad had bought seasons passes for his sister and him, and they spent nearly every minute there as soon as the doors opened at noon, until they closed for supper at five o'clock.

He wondered if maybe he couldn't get his bike tire fixed so he wouldn't have to walk back down to the park after lunch. He didn't mind walking all that much, but at least riding the bike gave you a little relief from the heat with the passing air that accompanied the speed in which one peddled.

I

"Don't forget," his coached yelled out as the players were leaving the field. "We will leave at six o'clock sharp Saturday morning. So, don't be late."

That seemed to bring Pat out of his mental wandering, and as he watched most of the other players walking away from practice, he fixed his eyes on the coach.

"Six o'clock for what, Coach?" Pat said.

"Pat," his coach turned to face him and replied, "weren't you listening when I talked to the team? You always seem to be someplace else when we have practice."

This statement was met by snickers and comments like, *"what a moron"* and *"idiot"*; from some of the boys who were still in the general area. Pat paid them as much attention as a llama would in attendance of an opera.

"Keep it down, boys," the coach growled looking at them like he were a mean dog.

Pat thought that he would probably be more focused if the Coach actually *let* him practice, but he kept this thought to himself. Discretion and all…

"We are driving to Forester to play them on Saturday," the coach started in again. "You do want to go with the team and pound on the Flyers, don't you?"

Pat looked at his coach's old and worn face. It was lined with a great deal of wrinkles, and it was also quite tan. For only being about forty five years old, Pat thought Coach Unrich looked very old, very tired…and extremely frazzled. Maybe coaching a bunch of thirteen and fourteen year old boys wasn't at all as easy as people thought, Pat considered.

"Will I get to play, coach?" Pat whispered as he leaned a little closer to the coach.

"Well, we'll see how the team looks that morning," Coach Unrich replied patting Patrick on his knee. "You may get outfield for some of the game. But, you need to have your Dad work with you on catching and fielding the ball a little more. You are getting better, but you need to work on the basic skills a bit more. Talk to your Dad to work with you every night, and we'll see you bright and early Saturday morning."

Pat walked home slowly along the side of 6th Avenue, head down, contemplating what his coach had told him. There was no way Dad was going to play catch with him. His Dad worked way too hard all day, every day, *and* on weekends, to have any spare time for something like that. Not that his Dad didn't teach him things or spend time with him, baseball was just not in his Dad's world.

Howard McCray was a mechanic who worked at the local Shell station in Wahkashen. He has worked there for as long as Pat could remember. Howard had aspirations of someday owning his own shop, and he told Pat that he would someday reach that goal through dedication and hard work. He would work late into the nights sometimes, coming home haggard and worn out with knuckles scraped and bleeding, grease and dirt under his fingernails, sleep deprivation and despair in his beautiful eyes.

His hands were the typical mechanics hands: spent too long repairing engines and transmissions that the dirt and grease would forever be imbedded in the creases of them, and no soap known to man would ever be able to remove the antediluvian tarnish from those hands.

He would even do the odd jobs in his own garage on the weekends to try and save enough money to maybe some day open his own shop. His Dad even told him the name of the shop would be 'Knuckle Busters', and then he would laugh his deep and hearty laugh.

Howard was born with the same chestnut brown hair as Pat, except that Howard had a head full of natural curls that did not get passed onto Pat through his genes.

Although all the girls were in love with Howard and his luscious curls in high school, Howard chose not to sport them. So, he was known, even infamously, for the crew cut that he always wore. He was a towering man of six feet four inches and weighing in at about two hundred and fifty pounds, he had crystal clear blue eyes that lay behind black rimmed glasses, and a personality that people both respected, and feared, due to his stature. Gentle natured, he was also known for his honesty, integrity and his work ethic; and that he could put away a lion's share of beer, whenever called upon to do so.

Howard was the eldest of Raymond McCray's two children. He was born and raised in Hargrove, Minnesota. Hargrove was a typical Midwestern town the size of a postage stamp, and as picturesque as a Norman Rockwell painting. That is, a Norman Rockwell with a perverse sense of humor when it came to mid-western towns that were small and indifferent. It was mostly a farming town, like most mid-western towns were in the '30's and struggling to survive both the aftereffects of WW 1 and the depression; as there were more people than stores, or jobs. Hell, there were more cows than people and stores put together.

Howard was a city boy, without the city to live in. He was forever tinkering with old dilapidated cars when he got together with his buddies who all shared the same interest. Interest, or obsession, as Howard's dad humorously referred to it.

He actually started to get pretty good at engine and transmission rebuilding without the formal education. Howard and his father both agreed that experience and learning from your mistakes would far out shine any formal education anyway, but Howard knew if he was to ever get out of Hargrove, he would have to get an education. And, getting out of Hargrove to pursue that formal education, seemed like it would be the only way out of Hargrove period.

When Howard graduated high school he saw his opportunity to get out of Hargrove forever by going to the Trade School in the Twin Cities, taking Auto Maintenance, and starting out fresh in a new town. All of this, of course he did.

II

Pat came out of his cerebral drifting at the sound of bikes coming at him at a fast speed. He cringed. He slowed and waited for the blow that would surely come from one of the Stooges. Instead, a bike came to a 'screeching' halt, showering his pant legs with tiny pebbles.

"Hey, man," the familiar voice of Mike came to Pat's ears. "Where you headed?' Mike Said and then held his hand out for the customary 'five' that the gang shared.

Pat turned to meet them, gave Mike his 'five'; glad it was his friends.

Mike Schomer and Lenny Ermish were on their bikes, breathing heavy and both had beads of sweat on their foreheads. Pat figured they had been riding hard and fast when they pulled up behind him.

"Just heading home," Pat said with a sigh of relief. "Ball practice is over. I was going to eat and head back to the pool. Wanna go?"

"Sure," Mike replied. "I'll go home and grab my suit and meet you there."

"I'm going to see my Dad, first" Pat said, "he has my bike and maybe patched my front tire tube already, and then I'll be there."

It was agreed, all around, that they would meet at the pool.

"See ya later, Gator," Mike said over his shoulder as he rode away on his bike, with Lenny following.

Maybe, Pat thought as he continued walking home, just maybe, Karla was working this afternoon. That would be the coolest.

III

Karla

Just the sound of her name in his head gave him goose bumps. Karla was the prettiest lifeguard at the pool. Maybe even the prettiest lifeguard in the state, Pat reasoned. She was much prettier than another lifeguard, Candi, in Pat's opinion.

Although when it came to adolescent fantasies, Pat was confident that Candi showed up just as often as Karla did in the young minds of the gang.

The lifeguards had to be at least sixteen to work at the pool, but Karla was going to be a junior this year, so she had to be at least seventeen now, and she was the most popular girl at the pool. Damn, she was the most popular girl in school also. She definitely occupied a great deal of time of the male lifeguards, as well as those who were there to cool off from the summer heat.

Pat knew she occupied quite a few dreams of the boys in town, as well.

There were lots of fantasies floating around in the circle of boys Pat's age about Karla. About her breath: how they knew it would smell like Juicy Fruit, as that was the gum she constantly chewed. Whenever you saw Karla she was smiling and chewing gum. Just the movements of her silky jaw made the boys sigh inside. They speculated that her breath would be warm, like a kitten against your neck, as they had images of her whispering in their ear. They all dreamed the taste of her sultry lips would be the sweetest thing they had ever tasted; sweet, like a cherry, and maybe a bit tart like a fresh strawberry, and that the feel of her golden hair running through their fingers would be like a finely spun silk.

Mike, the oldest of his gang, even spoke about the how the firmness, yet softness of her full breasts would feel under their trembling grip. Pat always felt a little woozy at the very *thought* of actually touching her swelling bosom. Karla's swimsuit was definitely full at the top, Pat thought.

She was a goddess in Pat's eyes, as well as in the eyes of his gang. More times than he would *ever* dare talk about, even to his buddies, did Pat wake in the morning and found a little wet spot occupying his bed with him.

Every now and then Mike would bring around a copy of the new Playboy that he would 'borrow' from his Dad. Mike called it borrowing, which was accurate in the minds of the gang, because he would always replace it when the gang was done ogling over it. Mike, Pat and the gang would get together in the fort Pat had built in the rafters of his dad's garage, and the boys would hang out up there and page through the

Playboys that Mike would 'borrow'. Many times Mike, Pat, and Lenny would speculate how Karla might look in a layout in Playboy. That thought would also make Pat feel a bit woozy.

She had the nicest figure Pat had ever seen, except for those models in his mom's shopping magazines; and maybe Candi's. Although Karla was a little taller and fuller in the chest, Candi was pretty, shorter by at least 3 inches, and she had smaller breasts.

"More than a hand full is a waste, anyway," Mike would say, and the gang would break up in laughing fits.

Karla was better than Candi because Candi also had a snotty air about her, which Pat didn't like. She was just a sophomore, and although she came from a rich family, from *that* class of people that Pat was told he was not a part of, that didn't make *her* rich, in Pat's eye; so why did she have to act like the money her family made was money *she* had earned? Karla never acted like that.

Karla was always nice to their little circle. It was as if she knew she occupied their sleep at night; or better yet, their lack of sleep, as they dreamed about wonderful rendezvous' with her. She didn't flaunt the fact that she was a creature of their restless nights, but she seemed to take this as a fact she willingly accepted with an unassuming air.

Her beautiful smile, as she talked with the boys reflected the brilliance of the afternoon sun off of her teeth to the point that it almost hurt to look at her when she smiled. Actually, when she did talk to Pat and his group, Pat would drop his eyes from hers. Pat was always afraid he would be caught staring, which is impolite anyway, and if he was caught staring at her breasts, well then, it would be embarrassing as well.

IV

Pat came blasting into the house feeling warm from the thoughts of Karla, and Candi, he guessed, and ran straight to the fridge. As he broke open the door, he heard the familiar clearing of the voice behind him.

He turned and he spied his mother standing in the archway to the living room, her arms crossed in front of her chest, wearing that familiar smirk on her angelic face. Could she read his thoughts, Pat had always wondered? Did she know what he had been thinking about when he came charging into the house like a bull elephant?

"And just what are you looking for, young man," his mother asked him.

Pat, not knowing what to say for the fear that his mother knew what he was thinking about when he came into the house, held his frozen tongue.

"I need to have a quick sandwich," he finally spit out, "so I can run to Dad's shop and see if he patched my front bike tire. I'm meeting the guys at the pool at Noon."

"Well, if I were to make you some lunch, would that help?" his mother asked, not leaving her position in the doorway.

"Yeah, it sure would."

"Then slow down for just a second and put your bat and mitt away, I will make sandwiches and some soup.

"Go on, put your stuff away and then go get your suit. You and I will have some lunch, and then I will walk uptown with you to get your tube fixed."

Pat ran upstairs quickly so he could change his underwear, and put away his ball gear. He would throw the underwear away, of course, because he didn't want his mother to find them and face her with some type of an explanation. It was all too embarrassing the way it was, let alone having to explain something like that to his mother.

Chapter 3

Walking with his mom up to Main Street was cool with Pat. Most kids wouldn't be caught dead walking with their Mom anywhere, but Pat didn't mind. He liked talking with her about his summer days, ball practice (although he told her very little about what he actually did on the team), and about books that he was currently reading.

Pat's mom was wearing a pair of lime green culottes and a white blouse. She looked good for a mom, in Pat's opinion. She still had a tendency to turn a few heads while she was walking down the street.

Delores McCray was five feet six inches, and she had the light brown hair and green eyes, as did Pat. She was a happy woman, and her happiness was contagious around everyone in which she came into contact.

Delores, a petite woman in her early thirties, hailed from the same small town as her husband, Howard. In fact, Howard and Delores were quite the couple in their teens. Never really popular to the point of being Prom king and queen, or anything of that nature; they were, nonetheless, popular in their own little circle. They went to the small soda shop whenever Howard had a nickel or more, and spend hours holding hands and talking, sharing a soda, while staring dreamily into each others eyes.

They would drive the twenty five miles to Straton, MN, to go to the local roadhouse almost every weekend when the weather was good. Howard's dad would let him borrow the Desoto, sometimes, and they would go on a double date with Albert and Shirley, their two closest friends.

When Howard went away to study his mechanics classes, after he graduated from high school (Howard was a year ahead of Delores in school) Delores cried every night for two weeks thinking she would never see Howard again; and that Howard would *strand* her in Hargrove where she would either grow old, alone, or she would become a farmer's wife and live the rest of her days with the smell of cow manure and chicken feed in her nostrils.

She didn't even like cows. She cared even less for chickens.

Howard would write letters to her quite often, and would try to get back to Hargrove whenever the chances would arise, but trying to keep up with school work and working part-time at a local garage in the town while he attended college would fill almost every minute of every day of Howard's life for those two years. They were the longest two years of Delores' young life.

When Howard returned after two years and came to Delores' house to ask her father for her hand in marriage, it was the greatest day of her life. However, it did pale, slightly, to the day she gave birth to Penny, the older of her two children nine months later. The day Howard proposed became hardly a remnant in her mind after she gave birth to Pat, one and a half years after the birth of Penny. They would have no more children after that...it was mutually agreed.

I

While walking down the street towards the shop where Howard McCray spent his days earning the little money that he brought home, they passed the local clothing store. This store was not J C Penney's as they sold more 'radical' clothing than did the more conservative Penney's store, according to the locals. "Hippy clothes," was the most common termed used whenever the store's name was brought up in conversation.

The light sounds of Mick Jagger and the boys singing about his

"Brown Sugar" could be heard rolling (pardon the pun) out through the open front door, to intermingle with the bustle of shoppers' feet and passing cars.

This store, Jasper's, stocked everything and sold everything from used Army field jackets, to Storm Coats with the fur collars, to Dashiki's. It held tie-dyed t-shirts for the guys and the same style of wear in summer dresses for the young ladies bold enough to wear a thin, spaghetti string tie-dyed dress around town. Surprisingly, there were quite a few young people in town who would wear this radical style, much to the horror of the older residents in town, and much to the delight of the young men. They also sold the leather braided necklaces that became so popular over the past few months.

Jasper's was run by a young couple, supposedly from the west coast somewhere, who apparently decided to leave that life-style and come to North Dakota for a change of pace. That was the rumor, anyway.

Today, right there in the front window, displayed for every man, woman, and child to see (a bit early his mother would later say), was the CPO coat that Pat wanted so badly. Of course the price tag was not as prominently displayed as the coat itself, and Pat speculated that it wasn't going to be cheap.

"Mom," Pat screamed and started to pull on her hand. "Look, it's the coat I was telling you all about. It's even the right color that I wanted." The color combination in question was a dark hunter's green, with a light brown, and trimmed throughout with lines of jet black to pull everything together.

"Now why would they display a winter coat in the middle of summer?" his mother said with one finger on her chin. She said that to no one in particular.

"Well," Pat started with a slight air of confidence in his voice, which almost disappeared completely from view as he went along, "I suppose it's because they are so popular these days that if they don't show them now, other stores may sell more than Jasper's will. Maybe even Penney's up the street!"

Pat hoped that throwing in the phrase *'so popular these days'* might have a convincing effect on his mom, but he wouldn't hold his breath.

Sometimes, Pat thought, sometimes you had to throw caution to the wind and see what would happen.

They stopped to look at the coat. It was the coolest coat Pat had ever seen, or could have ever dreamed about and it was right there in front of his face. It seemed to be calling to him. It was right there, and still about a thousand miles out of reach.

As they stood there looking at the coat and quietly talking, the sounds coming from the open front door changed to "War" by Edwin Starr, and Pat thought to himself that that is just about perfect for this situation. He knew if he wanted that coat, it would, truly, be war. He straightened up a bit, and turned to face his mother with a look on his face that was both determined and filled with fear.

"Mom," he began with a slight tremble in his voice, so slight that maybe his mother would not pick up on it. "I really would like to have a coat like that. My winter coat is getting a bit small for me and worn out, and I will need something new this year."

Delores said nothing, just looked up and down, surveying the coat like it was a rare find while walking through the woods. Finally, without a word, she reached over, grabbed Pat's hand and turned.

Oh, man, Pat thought, he figured they were leaving the store without her saying a word about his chances of ever scoring a coat like that. With his head hung low like the six-shooter on a gunslingers hip, Pat followed his mothers lead…albeit with a sense of dejection and loss. I am never going to own one of those cool coats, Pat thought. No matter what I say, how long I plead; my folks will never succumb to me long enough for me to be able to wear a coat like that. Man, Pat thought, Mike and Lenny would really have been jealous if they saw me in *that* coat…

His disheartened thoughts were quickly dismissed as Delores turned into the open doorway of the store, instead of walking straight down the sidewalk, and walked directly to the only person in the store. It turned out that it was a young woman in one of those spaghetti string tie-dyed summer dresses of really wonderful colors that danced and twirled as she moved around a rack that contained numerous and various tie-dyed dresses of that style.

The dress she was wearing mesmerized Pat as the colors seemed to constantly move around the material.

She was a smallish woman, with long flowing blonde hair, about the same height as his mother, and about twenty or so pounds lighter than his mom. Not that his mom was fat, by any means; but that this woman was very slender.

She kind of resembled an older Candi from behind, Pat thought.

Pat noticed that her hair was very blonde, almost transparent. Her physique looked nice underneath the hippy dress she wore so well.

Although the hippy tie-dyed dress is designed to more or less hang on the frame of the wearer, she filled out the front of the dress quite nicely, 'thank you very much', Pat thought.

Pat came to a realization, after spending the first few moments he walked into this store gazing at how well this young woman made the front of her dress stand out, noticeably, that he had been spending a great deal of time fixating on women's breasts this summer. He thought about them; he speculated about the feel of them in his hands; he dreamed about them while he was both awake, and asleep. He began to wonder if this was the normal behavior of a thirteen year old boy, or if there was something truly mentally wrong with him. He felt okay, and he sure didn't mind looking, speculating, and dreaming about women's breasts at almost every waking minute...but wondered if this was a normal mental function of a budding young man.

He was fairly certain he was normal, and he was also fairly certain he felt normal; only later, of which he was also fairly certain, he would doubt his certainty.

"Good morning," Delores said, shaking Pat's mind back into focus.

The woman who turned to greet them was pretty, in an earthy kind of way, and she was a woman of mid-twenties, Pat suspected.

"Good morning to you," she replied with a smile that was not feigned, nor unattractive.

"How may I assist you this morning?"

"That coat in the window, my son said it's called a 'CPO'? How much is a coat like that?"

"Well, your son is right. That is what is called a CPO coat. CPO's are very popular these days. Follow me and let's take a look."

She began to move towards the front window display passing Delores and Pat as she walked, and Pat heard the soft whisper of the sundress as she flowed past him, as well as leaving a vapor trail of an amazing, amusing and unrecognizable aroma. It was a smell he had never witnessed before today.

Patchouli (Pat would later discover) was the scent the woman was wearing that morning. Pat always liked the soft smell of patchouli from that day on, and it reminded him of…something he couldn't quite place his finger on. Maybe from that day on, Patchouli would remind him of the young, blonde saleslady in a tie-dyed spaghetti string sundress, with small, pert breasts.

Her long blonde hair seemed to float around her like a hand-full of corn silk in a light breeze as she crossed the room past them. Pat also spied her round, perky breasts bobbed a little under the thin material. Of course, he thought; she isn't wearing a bra with the spaghetti string sundress she had covering her lithe body. He blushed a bit and then quickly turned his gaze away from her breasts for fear of getting caught…by either of the women in this room.

That would truly suck.

"This is a wonderful color combination," she said as she reached towards the half mannequin who was sporting the coat, "don't you agree?" Pat and his mother shook their heads 'yes' in response as they watched her lift the mannequin from out of the store window with hardly an effort on her part.

Pat kind of chuckled a bit when he saw the metal stand protruding from the lower cavity of the figure, that and the fact that it had no head on its shoulders.

"Let's see," she began to say as she looked at the back of the jacket's collar for the price tag that normally hung there, out of sight. "It looks like this coat is selling for…$21.95. That is, without tax, of course," she finished and then smiled at Delores.

"Of course," Delores replied.

Delores ran the skilled fingers of a woman who had checked the quality of workmanship, once or twice in her life, over the coat in question. She then studied the front, looked at how the buttons were sewn on to the coat; looked at the quality of the liner on the inside, and then ran her eyes up and down as many seams as humanly possible in a matter of seconds with the precision of a diamond cutter working in the finest of jewelry stores, on a very rare diamond.

"This looks like it was well made," she began to tell the patchouli basted saleslady.

"Oh, yes," the saleslady, (whose real name was Daisy, they discovered after the normal introductions were applied) replied. "We have in the past, received many articles of clothing from that particular company. We have had no complaints on any of their articles."

Daisy turned back towards the front window, and carefully placed the half mannequin back in its original place of honor.

"The price…does that seem a bit expensive to you?" Delores asked rather timidly.

"Well, the way I look at it," Daisy retorted, "this is a quality item from a fine company. And, as my mother always said, 'you always get what you pay for.'"

"I don't know," Delores mumbled. "Maybe we will look around some more first. It is, after all, only July."

As Delores and Pat said thank you to Daisy for her efforts and knowledge and started heading towards the front door, Delores stopped, turned and asked Daisy, "by the way, this *is* only July, but you have winter coats on display. Why is that?"

"Well, my man and I are from California," Daisy started to say, "and I wasn't sure when to put out the fall and winter wear. So, Duke, that's my man's name… Duke, said we shouldn't wait too long to let the people know that we will have these available when the weather finally does change. Is that crazy, or is it just me?"

"No, "Delores replied. "I don't find that too crazy to plan ahead…a little. I was just curious. Well, have a nice day."

"The same to the both of you," Daisy said and turned and immediately began walking towards the tie-dyed area racks once again.

Outside the store, Pat sneaked a peek back over his shoulder at the coat he would have died to wear this coming winter.

As they were leaving the vicinity of Jasper's, Pat heard the faint sounds of "Bridge over Troubled Waters" by Simon and Garfunkel as it came streaming out of the store. The song seemed fitting to Pat as they slowly strolled away from the store which housed Pat's prize; and Daisy, with her Patchouli overcoat.

II

About twenty minutes later they were standing in the musty, soiled waiting area of the Shell station where Howard worked. They wandered around in the waiting area a few moments waiting for Howard, afraid to sit down for fear of staining some article of clothing or, as his mother would say very quietly so as not to be heard, *sticking* to something.

"What did you think of the coat, mom?" Pat asked, looking at the floor in front of him, and trying to break the silence between them.

"It's a nice coat. Looked warm, I guess…oh, I don't know Pat; I don't know if we can afford something like that, though."

"I'll help save the money for it," Pat said very quickly and with a hint of excitement, "if I have to. I mean…if you'll help…a little bit."

Delores smiled at that, pulled on her earlobe (a nervous tick that Pat always thought was cute, and Howard always reminded her of the fact that she was doing it), and gazed out the dirty picture window at the front of the store, seemingly lost in her own thoughts.

"We'll have to see, Pat," his mom finally replied, and then walked over to him and placed her arm around his shoulders. "You know how badly your father wants to be done working here," she said and then turned her eyes all around the room with a hint of disgust very prominent in them, "with the long hours and the…lousy pay…so every nickel is so precious for him. He really needs to be done here and open his own business. That way the money he makes will be *his* money, and not just getting only a small portion for doing *all* of the work. Do you understand that?"

"I know that, mom," Pat replied, feeling somewhat guilty even asking for something like that coat, "but I promise I will save most of the money myself."

"We'll talk about it, honey," Delores said, and then walked back towards the grimy window that let in streaks of greasy sunshine.

Howard came into the waiting area about five minutes later, wearing a soft smile, and wiping his big hands with an old shop towel.

He came over and gently kissed his wife on the cheek. He then leaned down and accepted a hug from his son along with a firm handshake. His father always told him how important it was to present yourself well, and offer a firm handshake.

"So, what brings you two down here today?" he asked with a slight grin on his face.

Pat thought, at that time, by the look on his dad's face that his dad knew a great secret. A secret so immense and so wonderful that he had to restrain himself against the urge to utter this secret knowledge to them; and, therefore, this restraint created a secret smile on his dad's face as he withstood against the urge in a most amazing fashion.

Pat always wondered why, when his dad looked at his mother, at certain times, that his dad's face held that secret smile.

"Well," replied Delores, with a hint of a smile herself, "Pat needs to get his bicycle up and running again. So, we thought we would walk down here and see if you have fixed the tire yet."

"Oh, is that it? Well, it just so happens that I do have that front tire tube fixed, and we have to put the tire all back together, but I thought I would wait until Pat got here to actually put the tube back into the tire and then get that tire back on the bike. I thought maybe Pat would like to help me complete that task.

"What do you say, sport," Howard said as he turned his face away from his wife and towards Pat, "want to give me a hand so you can learn a little about maintenance on your bike?"

"You bet!" Pat explained.

"Maybe you'd like to lend a hand as well, my lady," Howard said with an exaggerated bow to Delores.

"Why, thank you kind Sir," Delores replied and then curtsied.

Pat laughed at the antics and then watched as his parents kissed.

"Uggh," Pat moaned and then made retching sounds.

"Careful, young man," Howard said to him. "Some day you will be in love, and then *you* will know what it feels like to be in love, and have someone return that love."

Pat looked at his mother's face and then back to his father's face and Pat knew that there wasn't any doubt…they were in love with each other.

All three of them went past the front counter which was plastered with bulletins and ads for garage sales; the top was littered with a clutter of maintenance magazines, and housed a dirty, ancient cash register. It also held antiquated, stained coffee mugs that appeared like they have been on this particular counter since the turn of the century.

Pat wondered if someone actually *drank* out of those mugs.

Pat liked going in the back after they passed the sign on the door that stated '*Employees Only Past this Point*'. He liked the greasy, dusty-dirty smell that hung in the air, thick and full, like the heavy smell of a strong, fragrant flower. The odors of oil, grease and dirt were intermingled with the ancient remnants of tobacco, of various types. The old, worn and wooden workbench covered the entire length of the south wall, and was a catch-all for everything from old fan belts to dirty rags, carburetors and cracked heads. There was a large selection of used, but seemingly never replaced, wrenches and other various tools.

Hanging on the wall above this workbench was a tool calendar. It had on it, for the month of August 1970, a picture of a large breasted woman, who was topless, you could tell, but you could only see the cleavage of those enormous breasts because she was bent over into the open engine compartment of a fully restored '34 Chevy coupe. The angle of the photo had hidden her nipples, for some sort of effect by a company named 'Snap-On', Pat guessed. She had short cropped red hair, a very nice smile (and, of course, very large boobs), as she gazed into the camera lens; and in one hand she held a socket wrench.

One was apparently led to believe, by this 'Snap-On' company, that this attractive, large breasted, red-headed model, was actually working on this beautifully restored classic car.

Pat didn't buy it.

III

He walked over to where his bike was sitting, upside down, on its seat and handlebars with the front tire out of its sprocket. Howard went over to the water tank where, standing against its side, was the front tire of Pat's bike. He picked it up and carried it back to where Pat and his mom were standing by the waiting bicycle.

His dad showed him how to make sure that the spacing between the bolts and nuts on both sides of the tire remained the same in order for the tire to spin freely without any rubbing against the fork of the bike which held the tire in place. Then he demonstrated to Pat that you had to torque the nuts in place by spinning them in directions opposite of each other.

"You see, Pat," Howard said to him while turning a wrench on the right side, while Pat turned the wrench on the left side of the threaded shaft in the opposite direction, "you have to apply the threads evenly in order to have the tire balanced between both sides of the fork.

"That way the tire will spin freely. Do you see?" he said as he spun the tire.

"That's pretty cool, Dad," Pat answered.

Smiling at the task completed, Pat helped his dad turn the bike upright.

Pat loved being able to do stuff like that with his dad. He would forever enjoy doing stuff like that with his dad.

After test driving it around in the cramped space of the garage, he waved at both of his parents, took one more look at the large breasted *mechanic* in the Snap-On calendar as he drove out the open overhead garage door and headed for the swimming pool…and, his pals.

Hopefully, Karla would be working.

Chapter 4

As Pat rode his bike down the shady tree-lined streets, he could hear the soft chirping sounds of the lazy grasshoppers; see the quick flight paths that the robins and sparrows made while darting in and out the trees above him. Beams of sunlight came through the tree tops, intermittently, and Pat felt better and better with every beam he drove through. He could hear the subtle stirring sounds in the leaves caused by a gentle breeze. Pat began to smile. He just couldn't help himself.

He thought about his dad and the work that they had just completed. Just like most boys of thirteen, Pat thought his dad was the smartest man on the entire planet. He so liked to be around him and learn the various skills that his dad possessed. He prayed, quietly in his mind, that his dad would soon have his own store and both his dad and he would be so much happier. His dad might even be home on time every night for supper, instead of coming home almost too tired to eat.

Pat was about three of four blocks from the city park when he could hear the weak sound of the radio being broadcast over the four loudspeakers that surrounded the swimming pool. Those big outdoor speakers were mounted on the tops of wooden utility poles that were located in the corners of the fifty meter long and twenty meter wide pool.

The lifeguards who ran the pool always played the radio station from Flagstone, ND. Flagstone was a largely populated city of over thirty five thousand people that laid about forty five miles north of Wahkashen, and they had *the* best radio station. They played all of the best new music, and

Pat had become quite a music expert with the aid of the play list from that station.

Closing the distance between him and the park, he could hear the faint sound of *'Cracklin' Rose'*. He could also hear the joyful sounds of the kids in the pool screaming over the sound of the radio. Pat figured it sounded fairly full there already, and it wasn't quite half past twelve.

Pat slid gracefully and easily down the big hill that entered the park. The wind was blowing hard past his ears as he gained speed without pedaling. Without any effort on his part, Pat felt refreshed as the wind cooled his skin, even though it was warm air that he was riding through. He spied the pool parking lot at the bottom of the hill and noticed that there were a good couple of dozen bikes of various shapes and sizes deposited into the racks that the city park provided. The sun shone down onto the tarmac of the parking lot and it cast the hallucinatory shimmering water effect that layered itself upon itself the nearer Pat came to the lot that contained the couple dozen bikes.

Pat came screeching into a slot that was ready to accept his bike, tossed a leg over and pushed the bike forward into the waiting slot. As his eyes scanned over the bikes, he set the kickstand of his bike down to the ground, and he recognized some. There was Mike's and Lenny's. He was glad they were here.

Over there was Brian Osterman's, and that means the rest of the Stooges were probably here as well.

Oh, well. He wouldn't let the fact that Brian was in the pool with his gang of idiots take away from the excitement of this day. Pat was ready to have some fun: play tag without getting yelled at by the lifeguards about running on the wet concrete that surrounded the pool, to lie in the shallow water at the far end of the pool with Mike and Lenny and gaze up at Karla and Candi. They would whisper secret intentions to one another, at the expense of those lifeguards.

He would even get to practice his diving later on in the day.

He walked up to the counter in the front office, and immediately the smell of heavy chlorine filled his nostrils. Candi was at the counter, and Dan Meyer was behind her.

Pat said 'Hi' and Dan raised his hand in response. Candi, well Candi merely looked down her nose at him.

"Number?" Candi asked stoically.

"137," Pat replied with a smile that she didn't even notice, or bother to take the time to even register.

Everyone who paid for the yearly membership had a certain membership number that they had to remember, or else they wouldn't be allowed in...unless they paid money.

Candi handed him a fishnet bag and a super large diaper pin after writing down his number into a records book. Pat went into the dressing room to change, and put all of his stuff into the bag and take it back out front where they would hang the bag on a numbered post. They would then give you a rubber band with a numbered brass circle on it so you could retrieve your stuff when you were done swimming.

Candi was talking to Dan when Pat came back with his belongings, and she only took his bag, gave him the numbered disc on the rubber band, and never once looked at him. Forget her...what a stuck up, Pat thought.

Pat went back into the dressing room where the showers were located. It was the number two rule at the pool that everyone had to take a shower before they were allowed into the pool. It wasn't a complete shower, but you had to be wet when you came out of the dressing room, or the lifeguards would not allow you to enter the swimming pool. You would be directed to go back in and shower off, if they didn't think you were wet enough.

The number one rule, of course, was 'No peeing in the pool." In fact, they had a sign hanging in the front office, off to one side, with the drawing of a man in a pool, and ripples of yellow fluid emitted from him and all around him. The caption below stated quite simply:

"We don't swim in your toilet...So please; don't pee in our pool."

The caricature man had this humbled look on his face that bordered between embarrassment and sorrow. Pat smiled every time he walked past that sign. He thought that the man should be embarrassed for peeing in the pool. What a moron...

I

Pat came out from taking his partial shower. Immediately he felt pain radiate across both cheeks of his butt, and then heard the very audible *'thwack'* from the wet towel that struck him.

Pat let out a scream of both surprise and pain, and then turned around to see Brian hold his towel in a manner which spoke of his intent to repeat the process that had just struck Pat in the butt.

"Damn, Brian!" Pat screamed. "That really hurt."

Pat stood there rubbing his backside and looking into the menacing eyes that were stuck so far back in Brian's forehead that they held a darkness; not only from the mean streak that ran through every fiber of Brian's body, but because those eyes held shadows from being set back so far in his rock-like forehead.

"Felt pretty good, didn't it Pat-ty," Brian said with a sneer as he reeled back for a second lashing with the towel.

Pat didn't waste any time waiting around to be struck again by Brian's towel, so he turned and bolted out of the dressing room at such a quick pace as to attract the attention of the lifeguard at that end of the pool.

"Hey," screamed the lifeguard. "No running in the pool area."

Once away from the screaming lifeguard and Brian's wet towel, he came upon his friends in the shallow end of the pool. They were getting ready for a game of tag, and were just waiting for one or more players. Pat so enjoyed playing tag with his friends. It was good for him to practice his swimming.

Out of all the things he enjoyed when he came here to the pool, save for being with his friends; was to play tag and to practice his dives on the boards at the deep end of the pool.

The only thing about playing tag in the public pool: there was NO running. You did everything by swimming. Not that you couldn't get out of the pool and make a break for it whenever you wanted, and if the situation dictated; but if you were not 'It', you had to make your way around the pool, for the most part, by swimming. It was a great time especially because Pat was a strong swimmer. He wasn't as strong as Mike, but could leave Lenny and the others in the dust, so to speak.

So, playing tag for the first couple of hours would get his heart racing, and then he would be set to do something else, as the vanity of the game would soon wear off as soon as Dennis was finally 'It'. Dennis, the boy who was part of the gang's game of tag, but wasn't really part of the gang as he was a year younger than the gang; Dennis in his infamous light blue shorts with bananas on them that the gang dubbed, *'banana boats'*, couldn't swim very well, would ultimately be 'It' until the remainder of the game.

Pat decided he wanted to practice the inside gainer that Dan Meyer, a lifeguard who was the same age as Karla, taught him last fall. Pat, being smaller in stature, had a fairly good center of balance, and was not really afraid of heights, so he did a lot of different things on the trampoline that the school had, as well as the one that the city police maintained at a Youth Center.

Wahkashen had a National Guard unit in their town, and the Armory that held this unit was opened for a period of time, in the evenings, by the local Police force so that the local children would have a place to go. That way, the city administrators and the police agreed, it would keep these kids off of the streets in the evening.

In the armory, the kids could roller skate around the large auditorium floor. There were basketball courts, wrestling mats lined two of the class room floors; you could play ping pong, or just hang out.

Pat found the trampoline that was always set-up a haven for him to practice. Getting serious height on the trampoline was cool, especially for the girls who watched, as their 'oohs' and 'ahhs' indicated, but being able to do forward and backward flips, double forward and one and a half backward flips, was so much better than just jumping up and down.

It was at the Armory where Dan Meyer had taught him the inside gainer, much to the delight of Mike and Lenny, as they watched him land awkwardly time and time again. All an inside gainer was on the tramp was a back flip, but when you are at the pool, standing at the very edge of the diving board, it was like a *forward* back flip. One had to jump out and away from the board, and then bring the knees to the chest as the diver's head went back towards the edge of the board, and the centrifugal force brought your body around until you landed in the water feet first.

The Wahkashen city pool had three diving boards. The lowest was three feet above the waters surface. The next board was five feet from the waters surface, and the high board was ten and a half feet high. Pat had practiced it quite a bit on the smaller diving board, and was starting to feel pretty confident about performing this feat on the other two boards before the end of the summer.

However, one time…

II

…around the beginning of this summer, while trying to show off, and show-off to Karla as she sat in the lifeguard chair at the deep end of the pool where the three diving boards were located, Pat had tried his gainer. The key word there would be: 'tried'.

He had been working so hard on getting it down just right. So he bided his time waiting for the right moment when he knew she would be sitting in the lifeguard chair…watching; Pat walked slowly, deliberately to the end of the board, stood very still for a second or two, and made his move.

After Pat jumped up and down twice on the board, he kicked his feet straight out and tucked his knees into his chest as he was taught, and the momentum was bringing his body around from the inside. When he was sure that he had made the revolution and was prepared to hit the water with the precision that he felt sure would earn him a score of a perfect ten from the Czechoslovakian judge, he felt a serious pain erupt from his feet as he entered the water.

Pat had made the revolution, but came out of it a split second too soon and struck the end of the diving board with all ten of his toes. As soon as he entered the water, and the chlorine in the water attacked the abrasions of his open skin on the tops of his toes with the ferocity of ravenous piranha fish, Pat knew there was a God.

He broke the surface of the water as quickly as he could trying to stifle the scream that was slowing building up from his toes, and swam to the edge of the pool. Slight traces of red were following him as he made his way to the edge of the pool.

Karla came quickly down from her chair to check on him; apparently, she had watched him perform his perfect 'ten' disaster dive.

"Are you OK," she asked with true conviction in her voice. "Come on out and let's take a look at your toes. I can see you are bleeding a bit."

"I'm alright…I think," Pat replied, sheepishly, trying not to wince from the pain he was feeling, or show any of it in his voice; or the embarrassment he was trying hard not to display.

Pat could not wait to get out of the water and away from the chlorine that seemed to be chewing away what was left of his toes.

Karla held out her hand and helped Pat get out of the water. As she bent down to reach for him, Pat could smell the Juicy Fruit on her breath.

She sat him on the edge of the pool where she could get a better look.

"Oh, boy," Karla exclaimed when she finally did get a good look at Pat's toes. "Let's get you up and away from the edge here."

She helped Pat up and walked him back by where the sunbathers had laid out towels of various sizes and bright colors. The smell of Hawaiian Tropics' sun tanning lotion was cloying in the air of the sunbather's area, and immediately he felt a bazillion eyes on him.

"You wait here and I'll go get the first-aid kit from the office." She said.

Pat looked down at his toes. It wasn't as bad as it felt, that's for sure. Every toe had an abrasion on them from the rough material that was painted onto the tops of the diving boards to give the divers traction when the boards were wet. Every toe…save for the pinky toe on his left foot had been damaged. That one appeared to have been spared, for whatever reason.

Pat looked up just as Karla was walking away.

Not a bad view, he thought, as she sauntered away from him with quickness in her step.

Her firm body moved gracefully, like that of a skilled, graceful dancer, as she walked across the sunbathers' area until she reached the walkway to go to the office over by the dressing rooms.

She looked terrific in red, he thought, and then looked back down at his damaged toes.

Speaking of red, he reflected, when looked back down at what remained of his toes.

Man, he swore in his mind throwing his head back and closing his eyes against the brightness of the sun; that was the worst thing that could have happened to him in front of her. He must have looked like a complete idiot to her. She's probably in the office laughing with all of her lifeguard friends to the point of producing tears as she recapped the story of his dive.

Pat looked down again at his mangled toes and then once again felt a bazillion eyes on him. He raised his eyes from his toes and looked around at all of the sunbathers. Most of them were looking at him with the curiosity of an Entomologist observing a bug after he pinned it to a display board.

The heat of embarrassment was rising, slowly, up from the center of his stomach until he felt hot and flushed. He hoped he wasn't turning red in front of everyone.

Karla came back much quicker than he thought she would, carrying a bag with a large red plus sign on it. She must not have been in there telling the story and gaining the hearty laughter from it as Pat suspected.

She kneeled down next to him and afforded Pat a nice view of the front of her suit.

If he wasn't red and flushed from embarrassment, he certainly would be if he kept his eyes were they were: locked on the cleavage she presented to him in the front of her suit.

"This may sting a bit," Karla said as she pulled out a bottle of hydrogen peroxide. She poured some of the peroxide onto a large cotton swab and then slowly, carefully began to dab the toes on his right foot.

Pat winced a bit, but said nothing. He was embarrassed enough the way it was without making it worse by acting like a baby.

"Did that hurt?" Karla asked him and lifted her hand away from his toes.

"No, it's just the anticipation of it, I guess. I didn't mean to jump."

"You don't have to apologize, Pat. Try to relax."

That is easy for you to say, Pat thought to himself. You don't have mangled toes, nor have to suffer the humiliation of screwing up a dive in front of the woman who you wanted to impress…and then sit here while that very same woman is cleaning up your mess. All of this happening while giving you an eyeful of beautiful cleavage at the same time.

While Karla was working so diligently on his toes, Pat raised his head again and noticed that other lifeguards were now coming around to get a first hand glimpse at the 'Amazing Diving Fool'.

Dan was one of them…and so was Candi.

Dan shot him a wink as he must have heard Pat was attempting…attempting being the key word here, an inside gainer that Dan himself had taught him.

"That doesn't look too bad," Dan stated as he took a knee beside Pat. "What hurts more, Pat; the toes…or the ego?"

"Both," Pat said sheepishly as slowly his head began to rise from those injured toes until he looked up at Dan. He then turned his head to face the girl playing nursemaid, as she spoke.

"Don't listen to him," Karla told Pat as she looked directly into his eyes and smiled.

Pat noticed her eyes were a hazel color; dark with little flecks in them. They were beautiful, just like she was, he thought.

With that, Dan patted Pat's shoulder and walked slowly back to the office with Candi in tow. Candi never said a word. In fact, Pat didn't think she even glanced his way as she slowly scanned the swimming area.

"I thought you had made it," Karla finally spoke still working diligently on his toes. "Until, that is, until I heard you strike the board and then I saw the blood from behind you as you were swimming over to the side."

"Yeah," Pat replied very quietly. "I thought I did too."

She did a little more patching of his toes while affording Pat the most wonderful view for any budding, hot-blooded thirteen year old boy.

Pat did wonder how those beautiful breasts might feel as they met his shaking hands. Would they be firm like fresh tomatoes? Soft and smooth to the touch, yet when one started to gently squeeze them, would there be some resistance? Would they feel like so much Play-Do or Silly Putty in your hands?

They were truly amazing things: breasts. Pat thought they were pretty much just flesh, muscle and fat. He didn't think there was any bone inside a woman's breast, so there had to be muscle in them to make them stand out like they did.

There was nothing really magical or mythical about them, Pat didn't think, but they sure did occupy a great deal of man's imaginations, anticipations…and, frustrations.

"Well," Karla said with a huge grin on her face breaking Pat out of his voyeuristic mental wanderings, "you have to let these toes heal a bit before you make another attempt. OK?"

"Alright," Pat replied, smiling back at her; his heart just racing as he did. Would she hear his hammering heart, he wondered?

She packed up the belongings of the first-aid case, and policed up the cotton balls used. She gave him a nice smile, stood up, and started to walk back to the lifeguard's office.

Just as she got up from her crouch and started to slowly walk away from him, 'American Woman' began to play over the loudspeakers.

That was fitting, Pat thought.

51

He watched as she walked away from him back to the lifeguard's area of the pool. God…she looked really good in that red suit.

Pat forgot all about his injured toes…for a fraction of a minute, anyway.

Chapter 5

Pat finally arrived at the deep end of the pool where the diving boards were located, as well as the sunbather's area after getting tired of staying away from Dennis wearing his banana boats, who was 'It', and forever and a day will always be 'It'. He sat for a while watching the older kids doing their fancy dives while he contemplated his 'infamous dive' from earlier this summer. Unconsciously, he looked down at his toes, which had healed up very nicely, thank you very much.

Some of the divers up there today were pretty good, Pat thought; while others caused him pain in just watching. Pat thought he'd sit here and watch for awhile, and then he would probably join them. Start with the lower board, first; and then maybe work his way up.

There were a couple of nice looking young women here bathing in the abundant sun that Pat knew from school. He knew of them, but didn't think they had the same thoughts about him. If they did, they would never let it show...not in public, that's for sure.

There were also a few girls that Pat had never seen before, and they seemed to be about the same age as Pat. One was really cute, he thought as she sat there looking out at the pool. She was wearing a bright yellow two piece suit, and she was pretty tan.

Mike and Lenny came by and sat with him for a while. Mike would nudge Pat every now and then and give him the 'look over there' move with a flick of his head indicating the nice tanned bodies lying right behind them.

Pat would slowly, carefully glance their way, and then give Mike his patented *'I know what you mean, Pal'* smile. There was a small group of girls who Pat knew were in his grade in school, but they were from *that* social class; which meant that none of them would urinate on any of the gang if they were ever found rolling on the ground completely engulfed in flames.

The boys had small talk about some of the divers, how slow Dennis was as a swimmer, how they would like to sit on a grassy hill with so-and-so who was sunbathing behind them. Pat brought up how nice Karla was looking this afternoon, which was met by a huge sigh of approval from the others.

Lenny asked if they wanted to get another game of tag started, and when Pat said he might consider it, Mike said he'd much rather 'tag' the girl who was lying behind them right now.

Pat snorted a little with a chocked-back snicker, which caused Lenny to breakout in a serious belly-laugh. Before you knew it, all three were rolling around on the hot, wet concrete that was the home of the sunbathers, holding onto their stomachs as laughter poured out of them.

Some of the bathers even looked up from their towels to see just what was so funny.

"Stop it," Pat cried when the joviality started to subside. "It's not that funny."

"I don't know which is funnier," Mike whispered, wiping tears from his eyes, "you snorting, or playing tag with the rich snotty bitches behind us."

Pat punched Mike in the shoulder, and then began to laugh himself as the punch did nothing to deter Mike from rolling around on the ground with merriment.

When the laughter began to subside, they sat there a while longer, each wrapped in their own thoughts.

"Hey, if you guys don't want to get another game going, let's get out of here and grab a cone," Lenny said. He apparently had had enough laughter to last him awhile. "I'm kinda hungry from swimming."

"Yeah, we may as well," Mike replied and looked over to Pat. "I don't think any of these girls want to play with us, either."

"Man," Pat said. "You got that right."

So all three boys went to get into their street clothes, and then walked across the street in the front of the swimming pool to the Tasty Freeze that sat on the same corner, right next to the Putt-Putt Golf, for as long as anyone of them could remember.

The boys sat down at one of the few wooden picnic tables that the park board had provided, and ate their cones while they continued watching the divers from over the top of the tall chain link fence that surrounded the entire pool area, as the divers were going off of all three of the boards. They murmured their points awarded as each diver attempted one stunt or another.

They could hear the kids at the Putt-Putt behind them as their clubs made contact with the pink and yellow balls that the course offered its participants. Pat even heard one participant swear, and quickly shot a glance over his shoulder to see Craig Wynter with his girlfriend, Julie Fisher.

Julie was really nice, easy on the eyes and was three years older than Pat and his gang. Craig was a prick, and he was truly, amazingly good at it. He was much better at that than he was at Putt-Putt, Pat thought, and snickered a bit to himself.

Julie was dressed in tight blue jean cut-offs and a white halter top. Her tanned skin glowed under the light of the sun. She was wearing those big round white plastic sunglasses that seemed to get more and more popular as the summer months rolled by. She looked great.

However, Julie didn't look like she was having much fun. Being Craig's girlfriend for the past 2 years, it seemed she became more and more stoic, as most of the girls seemed to get when they became serious with one guy or another. Pat wondered why that happened. It amazed Pat to watch girls who were extroverted and jovial become so introverted after they hung out with a certain guy for a while.

He didn't know the answer to that, but he was sure that it was wrong to change that way.

"Hey," Mike finally said after he took another lick from his cone, 'M*A*S*H' is playing at the Kashen Theatre starting tonight. You guys wanna go tomorrow night? I heard it's a great movie. They have nudity and everything."

Nudity?

Well, then of course it *had* to be a great movie, Pat thought. Pat hadn't been to a movie for awhile where there actually *was* nudity, and having some this Friday night would be fine with him.

"That means it's probably rated 'R'," Lenny said in a dismal tone, "and then we won't be able to get into it by ourselves. We'd have to have a parent with us. No way am I going to a movie with my mom, OR my dad, when there's boobs sticking out all over the place. They'd pitch a fit, for sure!"

They all agreed that watching a movie as cool as one that would show bare boobs would not be as much fun if you were sitting next to your parents.

"I could probably talk my sister Lisa into taking us," Mike finally said. "She's seventeen now. We won't have to sit by her or nothin'. She gets us in, and we go hang out some place together and watch the movie. You got any money?"

"I should have enough for the show and some popcorn," Lenny replied.

"Pat?" Mike asked.

"I'd have to ask for some money," Pat said, sheepishly. "I spent all of mine the other day."

"So ask, nimrod," Mike snorted.

All three erupted in laughter again.

"I'll ask," Pat said, "but my mom isn't going to let me go to an 'R' rated movie. There's no way she'd let me go even if I were going with you guys, or not. Not even if Lisa decided to take us there."

The boys sat and pondered the situation before them, while watching the divers, while eating their ice cream, and enjoying the sun-filled day.

"Well, 'Two Mules for Sister Sara' is still playing at the Bijou in Bulliford," Mike replied after contemplating for awhile. "We've already seen that. Tell her we're going to see that movie instead."

"Yeah," Lenny chimed in, smiling. "Your mom won't remember that we've already seen that movie."

Pat thought he could probably get away with that little white lie.

Actually, he didn't even think of it as lying. They *were* going to a movie, even though it was not the one he would plan on telling his parents.

It sure was good to have friends, Pat thought.

Making friends was pretty easy, but to keep friends one had to work at it. Pat always subscribed to the notion that friends are easily made, and good friends are hard to keep.

I

Pat said goodbye to his friends at the pool, and hopped onto this bike for the trip home, which would be a great deal faster that walking. He secretly hoped he wouldn't run into any of the Three Stooges, and after looking back at the bike rack as he began to pull away from the pool, he saw that Brian's bike was still in its slot. That's a good thing, he thought.

Pat got home about a quarter to five, and came dashing into the house like his hair was on fire and his ass was catching; just like he always did these days. He blasted straight into the living room where he caught his mom ironing some clothes. Mostly Penny's he observed.

Typical, he thought.

"Mom," Pat asked after he caught his breath, a little, anyway. "Do you think I could go to the movie with Mike and Lenny on Friday?"

"Ummm," was the reply from his distracted mother.

"Mom?" Pat asked again after waiting for a second or two, and to Pat, it seemed like ten minutes or more.

"What?" she replied, coming out of her ironing induced daze. "I'm sorry, honey…what did you say?"

"Do you think I could go to the movie with Mike and Lenny?"

"Yes, I'm quite certain that you could go to the movie with your friends," his mother replied with an air of sarcasm in her voice.

She would do that every time one of the children would use improper English when they spoke. It irritated Pat to no end, but it did seem to improve on his speaking aloud, and his thinking *before* speaking aloud. He must have slipped, and of course, his mother caught it.

"Mom, may I go to the movie with Mike and Lenny on Friday…please?"

"I don't see why not," she replied with a smile. "What movie are you boys planning to see?" she asked him after a slight pause.

"That Clint Eastwood movie about a mule…and some woman," Pat replied looking over at the television. The television was on, and it was showing a soap opera. No wonder she was distracted when I came in to the house, Pat thought.

"Oh, do you mean 'Two Mules for Sister Sara'?"

"Yeah, that's it," Pat replied and turned his eyes back to his mother.

"Didn't you go see that one last weekend?"

The question caught Pat by surprise. He did not fully expect to be questioned about the movie. He was not fully prepared to answer a question like that.

He swallowed hard.

"No," he lied. "We went to 'The Aristocrats', remember?"

"Was that the movie?" she said with a distant voice, as her eyes went back and forth from her ironing to a very handsome man without a shirt on, that was engaged in some conversation with a pretty lady on the TV.

Man, soap operas…

II

Supper was just the three of them, again. Mom, Penny and Pat sat at the chrome kitchen table with matching high back chairs and ate one of Pat's all-time favorite meals: grilled cheese sandwiches with catsup, and tomato soup with crackers. Dad called about a half an hour ago and told them to save him some as he would be home in about an hour or two. He had a lube job come in late that just *had* to be done, according to the boss…and the customer.

As his boss would always say, *'The customer comes first, and the customer is always right.'*

So, it was just the three of them eating quietly.

Delores asked her children about their day, as they were out of the house all day.

Penny began spinning her tales of adventure here in Wahkashen which affected her, and everyone else. You see, the world spun around Penny and her friends, and so anything and everything they touched or attempted to touch, or did affected the whole, like it or not. Mostly it involved walking around town, up and down the streets and window shopping; talking trash about the girls in her age group, as there was a great deal of competition that existed between all of the girls in her grade; and speaking about who was dating whom these days.

Pat often wondered how any of this crap affected him, but kept a civil tongue, as once again Grandpa Alvin came to mind about 'Discretion…'.

"Didn't you go to the swimming pool today?" Delores asked Penny. "It was a beautiful day for lounging around with your girlfriends."

Or, Pat thought, ironing your own clothes for a change, but he only thought that…did not blurt it out.

"No," Penny replied after a long pause, as her mind must have been someplace else, "there are just *too many* kids at the pool these days."

Kids, Pat thought? You are only a year and a half older than me, for cryin' out loud. Kids? Pl-ease.

"I went to ball practice," Pat finally interjected when Penny was finished bashing everyone, "and then came home and walked uptown with you."

"I know, sweetheart," Delores said, and ruffled his hair.

Pat hated it when she did stuff like that, especially when it was in public. He didn't really care much for it when she did it in front of Penny either, because when he glanced over to see the effect her mannerisms had on Penny, Pat could see that smirk on her face that he really, truly hated.

Pat had to be cautious even *thinking* the word 'hate'. That word was not allowed in the McCray house. His mom said a word like 'hate' should be stricken from the English language as it was the most common root of all evil.

It was, according to his mother, the word 'hate' that had caused all of the problems in the world today, and in its past. All of the hatred was what made the world a dangerous place, and therefore, the word should be stricken from the English language.

"One may dislike something, tremendously," his mother said time and time again, "but one will never, ever use the word 'hate' to describe the level of dislike that they possess. You are not allowed to even hate broccoli. You may dislike it, Penny…but you will not hate it. Do you understand?"

Both children understood, tremendously.

"Then I spent the day at the pool, with the guys," Pat finished and went back to his sandwich.

Pat waited for his father to come home by watching a little TV with his mom. Penny set off to conquer the universe as soon as dishes were completed (she *always* had to wash, Pat *always* had to dry. Something about being the youngest in the order of things, Pat figured). Carol Burnett was on, and he so enjoyed Tim Conroy. Pat thought he was probably *the* funniest man on TV these days.

However, tonight he wasn't watching it so much as he was just sitting in front of the TV staring at it. His mind seemed to be a million miles away as thoughts of Karla entered his mind.

Karla, Julie Fisher from the Putt-Putt place, looking very sexy in her tight jean shorts, the girls lying on their towels behind him in the sunbather's area at the pool. The sunshine made their skin glow in a very wonderful way, Pat thought.

It seemed to Pat that he was daydreaming a great deal about girls these past few weeks, about girls and their secrets; their soft skin and silky hair; their curves and the way some of them had dimples that would spring to life whenever they smiled.

He dreamed about what it would be like to be alone with a girl, to discover what their secrets really were. Sometimes, Pat thought, all girls were from a completely different planet. He had no idea what made them tick…at all. He would like to know what it felt like to be with a girl like those he saw in the Playboy magazines that Mike would bring up into the garage fort.

Those girls, well, actually women, in the Playboy's were simply beautiful. But to actually see them lie there without any clothes on, in *real* life, was way too much to even imagine....

His dad came in the back door and snapped Pat out of his trance. Pat ran to him with the intention of asking for money for the movie on Friday night, but stopped short when he saw the utter exhaustion in his dad's eyes.

Instead, he grabbed his dad's lunchbox from the floor in front of him and carried it over to the kitchen counter, by the sink, so mom could rinse it out. His dad groaned ever so lightly as he made it to the closest kitchen chair and sat down to take his work boots off his feet.

Howard slowly raised his head after he placed his tired butt in the chair and looked long and hard at Pat. He lit up a Camel. After what seemed like an eternity to Pat, he smiled at Pat after Pat returned from taking his lunchbox to the sink.

Howard took off his black rimmed glasses that he constantly wore and rubbed at the bridge of his nose. His glasses had left a permanent mark on the bridge of his nose. That mark would probably remain there forever, Pat suspected.

Howard set his glasses down on the table and looked down at his boots.

He struggled with the laces of his boots, and finally prevailed over a battle that should not have taken more than a couple of seconds. First the right foot became boot free, with a sigh...and then the left, with an even heavier sigh.

Pat took a seat across from his Dad; saw the smoke trickling out of his dad's mouth as the Camel dangled from its corner. He watched as his dad carefully set his boots aside, closer to the back door so that Mom wouldn't yell about having the boots in the way. Observed his dad sit back in the chair, blow a huge puff of smoke towards the ceiling, and stare straight out in front of him for a few seconds.

"And, how was your day?" Howard finally asked when he was situated to the point of a little comfort.

"OK, I guess."

"How's the tire holding out, Buddy?"

"Good. It's not leaking, anyway," Pat replied with a smile.

His dad shared a laugh with Pat, and then set his cigarette down in the ashtray.

"You look really tired, Dad," Pat started.

"It was a tough day today. I'll be OK now that I got those damned boots off."

Pat was chewing on the bit to ask for money; but thought better of it. Maybe, just maybe after his dad had something to eat, first.

Chapter 6

Pat lay on his back in his bed that night, looking at his ceiling, thinking about nothing and everything all at the same time.

He thought about baseball and the way the players all seemed to mock him, despise him; he thought about the game of tag that they played this afternoon and then about poor Dennis who was *always* the last player because he just doesn't swim very well.

He thought about the movie that he and his friends wanted to go see on Friday night. He remembered that he failed to ask for the money tonight, but he would have plenty of chances later on, and he would do it then. Maybe it was best to ask for the money from his Dad while he was at work.

He considered this for a minute or two and then decided that that was probably the best course of action in obtaining the required funds. It seemed to Pat that it was harder to say no to a child when you were at work.

He even thought about the Three Stooges; God, how Pat tired of being tormented by those guys. If only Pat were bigger, maybe Brian and his group of bullies would leave him alone for once.

But mostly he thought about the CPO coat that he saw this afternoon. He could almost imagine himself walking down the street this fall wearing the CPO. Mike and Lenny would be green with envy, Pat was almost positive.

Just before he dozed off to sleep, Pat thought about Karla. Before he even knew it, REM overtook his conscious mind...

…He was walking along a trail cut deep in the trees just outside town. The boys always called this trail 'The Hobo Path' due to the fact that it was located close to the BN Railroad line that skirted town, and the boys always found the remnants of camp fires scattered along the path. Mike had even talked with a hobo, at length, one time, he told Pat. If Mike's mom ever found out, Mike wouldn't be able to sit down for well over a week, Pat suspected; as Mike's mom was notorious for tanning Mike's hide when called upon to do so. Mike had even talked the hobo into buying some cheap whiskey for the gang, and they drank that retched stuff right there in those trees.

They also dubbed these woods 'Sleepy Hollow' after the book they read as little kids. It was a great hangout for the gang, next to Pat's fort that he had built in the rafters of his garage. Mostly, the reason they labeled their favorite hangout such was to instill a sense of fear of these woods in an attempt to keep the little kids out of it.

The gang would go to these woods when the time was just right; which was, normally, all of the time. There they would watch the wildlife that lived there forever. Rabbits and gophers galore, intermingled with red and gray squirrels, lived in these woods. The trees were filled with robins, swallows and finches. Finches were Pat's favorite bird, next to the green-throated hummingbird.

More times than not the gang would bring their BB guns and .22s with them and shoot at pretty much anything that moved. As they got better with their shooting skills, they got better with taking home animals for their mothers to clean and cook.

They knew an older man in town who would pay them $1.50 per red squirrel if they brought that freshly killed squirrel to him, at his apartment, which he shared with his handicapped wife. She loved squirrel…and so did he. The boys would be able to collect $2.50 per squirrel if they took the time to skin them before hand. They could add an extra dollar, skinned on not skinned, for all gray squirrels.

The gang had also been quite skilled at nailing a few snowshoe and jack rabbits in these woods in the winter. The snow was a perfect way to zero the .22's, especially the semi-automatic one that Mike owned. You just adjusted up and down according to the flying snow where the bullet struck it. One would watch as the rabbit would haul ass away from you, and the shooter would move the barrel up and down until the target was struck.

In the center of Sleepy Hollow, which covered a good couple of acres, there was a vast ocean-field of nothing but grass. Wild native grass of North Dakota was beautiful, and when the August winds blew, it rippled just like waves of water. In fact, the sound of the winds moving the grasses around mimicked the sounds of the pine trees as they felt the same motion of the winds.

Smack dab in the middle of this field was one lone oak tree well over a hundred years old and surrounded by large field rocks. The gang gave this area the title 'Eagle's Nest'. It was an anomaly, Eagle's Nest; as no one really knew how or why or how long that tree was in the middle of that ocean of grass with field stone around it in a nice tight circle. Inside this circle the boys could hold small camp fires, which they did on occasion.

Pat looked up at the moon and then down the trail upon which he had found himself walking. How Pat got here he did not know. What time it was he was not completely sure of either, but when he looked down at himself he noticed he was wearing his good shoes; his good shoes and his best corduroys. Mom was definitely going to kill him for wearing his good clothes out here in the woods, and in the middle of the night. He thinks it's the middle of the night, anyway.

Pat lifted his left arm up in front of his face and turned his palm out so he could get a good look at his wristwatch. The moon was full, and the light filtering down from the sky was so fine that he could make out even the tiniest details. He then noticed that he wasn't wearing his watch at all; however, he did notice that he was wearing his good blue shirt with the button down collar that his aunt Betti bought him two years ago.

"What the hell was going on?" he thought uneasily.

He looked up at the moon, which was incredibly full this evening, and marveled at how well it illuminated everything around him.

He walked along the trail with absolutely no idea where he was going, or why he was going there. He was pretty sure he would find out when he got there as to the where's and the why's of his midnight stroll. Well, then again, he was pretty sure, anyway.

The moonlight really illuminated the trail so he had no problem walking in the darkness of the trees, while staying on the trail, that is. He could hear the small creatures of the night rummaging through the undergrowth, but he was not able to distinguish the type of critter that was moving around.

"Pa-at," a voice singing his name came from back in the tress, soft and subtle, almost to the point of being nonexistent.

Pat spun his head in the direction of the voice. His heart rate immediately increased twofold. Squinting, trying to actually see into these dark woods, even with the moons help was an act of desperation. What did he think he was going to see amongst these dark trees?

He waited as long as he could for the voice to repeat. Did it actually say his name, *or was that a trick of the breeze through the trees? He waited for his heart rate to slow down, just a bit. He thought he may not hear that voice again over the imagined cacophony of his beating heart. He even stopped breathing all together just in case it would aid in locating the source of the voice.*

"Pa-at," the strange, but fairly familiar voice spoke again after what seemed like five minutes, and in all actuality was more like ten seconds. It traveled through the trees easy like wisps of smoke from a distant fire.

Pat stared back into the area where he thought the voice was coming from, but in the woods, in the darkness of night with no real breeze apparent, made sounds come from every direction, he thought. He did not move. He felt that if he did move, he would lose any bearing on the direction of that strange voice.

It felt like it was coming from the vicinity of Eagle's Nest, but out here, surrounded by trees in the middle of the night made it so hard to pinpoint its origin.

With a weird sense of confidence on why he should be walking that direction, he started off on a bearing to Eagle's Nest.

As he made his way easily through the shadows of the trees, knowing all conduits that led away from main path like the wristwatch on his left hand (which of course he was not wearing at this time), he headed towards the destination of the lone tree in the field of native grass.

When he cleared the last of the dense trees, he could make out the faint detail of Eagle's Nest in the clearing. There was a fine mist crawling slowly across the ground as if the very grass itself were smoldering from an ancient fire.

He moved further from the tree line and into the grass field. The fog engulfed his legs from the calf down, and as he walked further into the grass and fog, the clearer the Eagle's Nest became.

His heart was beating quicker now than ever with trepidation he had never felt before.

He spied a figure standing along side the tree, as he got nearer to Eagle's Nest. He didn't feel panicked and threatened by this lone figure, but for some reason he couldn't put his finger on he felt a strange sense of calm. He would not know why until he actually got to the tree itself and discovered that Karla was standing there, plain as day in the moonlight.

"Karla?" Pat said with a hint of apprehension and jubilation. "What are you doing out here at this hour?" Pat looked around to make sure that he was really out here in the middle of the night with, of all people, Karla.

"I've been waiting for you," she replied, and there was a warm glow that covered her face, which had to have been radiated by the moon's light.

Pat noticed that Karla had a blanket of dark colors and an even darker pattern spread at the base of the tree. It looked as though that blanket had been there for awhile as it was fairly trampled down and not as fluffy as when one lays out a blanket in tall grass. As he got closer, he discovered that the pattern of the blanket was the same colors as that of the CPO coat hanging on the mannequin in Jasper's front window.

Pat also noticed that Karla was wearing nothing but her red lifeguard swimsuit…and a wonderfully full smile.

"What are we doing…out here?" Pat asked her, with confusion tinting his voice as he surveyed his surroundings with a quick turning of his head.

"We are having the rendezvous that you have been waiting for, for such a long time now. Are you surprised?"

"How did you now that I was waiting for this?" Pat asked.

Karla smiled, said nothing and walked slowly, sensually towards Pat. She held her hand out for him, enticing him forward to the waiting blanket.

As Pat grasped her hand, he noticed how smooth, soft and warm it was in his. Her delicate fingers overlapped his as she drew him close to her. He could feel the heat radiating from her body as she narrowed the distance between them. She placed her left arm around his waist and drew him closer to her body. She reached forward with her right hand and slowly ran her fingers through his hair.

She leaned, oh so slowly, towards his face. She was parting her lips in preparation for the kiss that Pat had waited for, dreamed about forever.

Their lips met like they were meant to be together. Their kiss was everything Pat dreamt about. Her lips were soft like warm taffy to the touch. They held a flavor that Pat couldn't quite disseminate, but he thought if he were to keep on kissing her for the next, say, two to six hours, he just might figure it out.

He was willing to take that chance.

While they were caught in their embrace he slowly reached up towards her. And just as his right hand was directly below the roundness of her left breast, and just when he thought he would get the chance…the one chance in hell, that he would finally know what secrets lie in the fullness of Karla's breasts when they were in the grip of a trembling thirteen year old boy, Karla stopped his hand from its final destination.

She stopped his hand short, smiled her beautiful smile and then motioned that he sit down on the waiting blanket.

Pat sat down feeling flushed and alive; confused and excited.

"You have to remember, Pat," Karla spoke in a voice that seemed to come from nowhere, and everywhere, as Pat made it to the blanket and sat down, "discretion **is** *the better part of valor."*

Pat gave her a perplexed look after hearing her repeating his Grandpa's words of wisdom. Karla just stood there, smiling in her red swimsuit.

"I have something for us in the basket," she said with a voice that sounded like silk upon silk to Pat's ears. She nodded towards a wicker picnic basket just off of the edge of the blanket.

"Why don't you grab it for us, while I make myself more comfortable..."

With that, Pat started to crawl towards the basket. The blanket was velvety soft and felt warm under his hands, as if it were placed over an old fire pit which still held the remains of coals from the last fire. The smile plastered across his face felt like it had been there forever, and probably would remain there for just as long.

Right before he reached the edge of that soft blanket that looked so much like the CPO coat that he wanted so badly, he chanced a look over his shoulder to spy Karla beginning to slowly and carefully slide the strap of her swimsuit down from one of her satiny shoulders.

She caught his eyes upon her and smiled at him. And then, with even more deliberation, she continued to take her strap down from off of her other shoulder.

Pat's heart rate just went up another 3 notches, even though something like that was not exactly possible. The pounding of his heart was so loud in his ears, it muffled out all of the nights sounds. Pat was sure that the sound of his beating heart would scare away any and all small animals from the immediate vicinity.

Pat reached towards the old-fashioned picnic basket and opened one end...

*"*Peek-a-Boo, Nimrod, *" said the severed head that held Brian Osterman's face.*

I

Pat awoke with a scream stuck in his throat like a piece of dry toast. He looked around his dark room to fix on anything familiar; anything he could focus on to slow down the maddening pace of his heart. With a parched throat from the panic and pure surprise of what he discovered in the picnic basket, he spun his feet out of bed to go to the bathroom to splash water on his face, and then take a drink.

Under the bright light of the bathroom, Pat ran cold water into the sink's basin, and then began throwing that water up into his face. He did this four times, and then finally took some in his hand and fed his parched throat. After this task was completed, he chanced a look into the mirror above the sink and saw the look in his eyes.

Wide-eyed, he looked like a man who had been under some terrible duress. His hair was all askew and he felt it wasn't just due to being asleep. It looked liked someone who had just had a tussle in bed…or on a blanket.

Anxiety…that's all it was, he thought.

He turned to face the waiting toilet.

After he voided himself, he turned off the bathroom light and carefully and quietly went back to his room.

Strange shadows filled the familiar corners of his room at two thirty in the morning. Pat's bed held a macabre feel to it as he lay back down on sheets that were slightly damp from his perspiration. Immediately, the images that he had from the dream came flooding back into his mind as clear as the dream itself.

Would he get back to sleep, he wondered? If, and when he did, would Karla and her basket of amusement be there waiting for him?

And, why in the hell was Brian Osterman in his dream? Karla he could figure out her being in his dreams as she normally held a place of honor there…but Brian Osterman? No way did he belong there.

Pat lay there for what seemed to be a couple of hours twisting and turning trying to get comfortable enough to fall back to sleep. Finally, around four in the morning, sleep came.

It was fitful.

Chapter 7

The morning came on like the past few mornings did for Pat. The sun was bouncing off of the window in the walkout door of their garage and the robins were singing their familiar phrases for the start of a new day.

Pat so loved the song those robins sang for him in the mornings. He felt like they were singing for him, and only him.

He crawled out of bed, got dressed and headed downstairs to start another typical day.

Pat met his sister downstairs. She was already dressed and had just finished her cereal. It was strange to see her downstairs so early in the morning...especially on a Wednesday morning.

"Good morning, sleepy-head," Penny said with a hint of sarcasm in her voice.

"What are *you* doing up so early?" Pat replied. "The department store having a huge sale today, or what?"

"Ha ha; not funny. Lori and I are meeting with Beth and we are going to Fairfield this morning to do some early school shopping. Beth's mom is going to drive."

"Man, am I glad I am not in *that* car!"

With that, Penny headed out the door to meet Lori out in the front of the house. From there they would walk together over to Beth's house, and then off to conquer their own little piece of the universe.

Good riddance, thought Pat. He loved his sister a great deal, but no where near as much as she loved herself, he was quite certain.

Pat headed for the cupboard that held the huge variety of cereals. It seemed that both Pat and Penny would open a box, have a bowl or two, and then not completely finish the box. They would then wait for the next shopping day so they could petition to get a different cereal, and the whole cycle would begin again. Therefore, the outcome was approximately no less than four to six different cereals that were forced to remain forever in the unfinished stage of their existence, deep in the confines of the McCray cupboard.

News of this cycle, of course, was the chagrin of Delores McCray.

Pat grabbed one box, held it out and shook it, and then placed it back. It sounded like it was almost empty, so it needed to go back into the cupboard. Not only did he not think about throwing the box away, he didn't think about anything else but the next box of cereal.

He settled on a half-full box of Sugar Crisps.

As he headed in the general direction of the other cupboard that housed the bowls, plates and coffee cups, he shuffled along on feet that seemed to him to be still asleep.

As Pat sat there slowly eating his cereal, his mind began to wander back to the dream from last night. It was beautiful in the sense that it housed images of Karla that seemed so real he could still feel the softness of her lips on his. He could still sense the silky feel of her skin under his hands. He could still feel the heat that radiated from her body as he got closer to her; could still sense the warmth of her breath before their kiss. Everything seemed so perfect…until, that is, Brian showed up to ruin the day. Brian's severed head, that is.

Brian Osterman. He was the anti-thesis of Under Dog, for sure.

I

Pat finished his cereal, dropped the spoon and bowl into the kitchen sick and walked over to pick up the phone. He dialed 642-5757.

"Hello," the voice at the other end said after a couple of rings.

"Is Mike up yet, Mrs. Schomer?" Pat asked.

"Yes…yes he is, dear…hold on," Pat could hear Mrs. Schomer set the phone down with a 'clunk'. Pat knew by his memory that the phone now rested on the solid oak table in their dining room.

"Mike," Mrs. Schomer yelled out to her son from back in the distance, "Telephone. I think it's Pat."

As Pat waited, he took a mental trip around the Schomer's dining room. The room was about fourteen by twenty feet across and it had a darker color mahogany wainscoting. The new wallpaper that Mrs. Schomer just put up last fall to match her new drapes blended in well with everything in the room. The oversized dining room table was made of oak. It sat on a huge pedestal that had claw feet on it to support the tremendous weight. The tall back oak chairs that accented the oak dining room table were trimmed with seat covers of a color similar to the background of the wallpaper and it also fit well with the new drapes.

There were pictures and paintings hanging on the walls that covered both family photos and landscapes artfully created. It was a magnificent, handsome room.

Pat then heard the footsteps of Mike approaching.

"Hey," Mike said when he picked up the phone.

"What's happenin' my man?" Pat said in a different voice.

"Oh, nothing," was Mike's reply. Pat could still sense a bit of 'I just woke up' in his voice. Also, he wouldn't be fooled by Pat's masqueraded voice. "I was thinking of heading down to the park in a bit. You?"

"I was thinking of going fishing down at the Red. You wanna go?"

"Yeah. Good idea. I'll call Lenny and see what's up with him. Let's meet in about twenty minutes."

"OK. I'll make some sandwiches. I'll meet you at 'The Hill' in 20."

Pat set the phone down in its cradle and began making some sandwiches for him, Mike and Lenny. He found bologna, cheese and wheat bread, and that was all; so that was what they would be having for lunch this afternoon. He also found a new double bag box of Old Dutch potato chips in the cupboard that also held the infamous cereal selections, so he grabbed a bag and put it in the paper bag with the three bologna sandwiches, just for good measure.

All through the sandwich making process, Pat could not rid his mind of the dream. It came to him in stages: the walk down the moonlit trail; the voice coming to him through the trees; the soft feel of Karla's skin and lips against his; and finally Brian Osterman's severed head in a wicker picnic basket.

Why did Brian have to show up and ruin what could have quite possibly been the absolute best dream Pat ever had…or could ever have?

What did Pat ever do to deserve a person like Brian always hovering over his every move? Why do the Brian Osterman's exist in this world anyway? Pests were all they were, in Pat's mind.

Didn't they already have mosquitoes?

Pat yelled up to his mom that he was going fishing. He only did that instead of leaving a note because he heard her footsteps about ten minutes earlier.

"Be careful," was her response as it drifted down the stairwell.

II

Pat sat waiting at 'The Hill' for about four minutes before he saw Mike and Lenny coming towards him down 3rd Avenue with their fishing poles in tow.

'The Hill' was the name the boys called the approach going downhill entering into Cetanmila Park, Wahkashen's city park. The paved road going into Cetanmila Park (pronounced "See-tan-Mi-la") started at the top of 'The Hill'. Cetanmila Park was named so by the Lakota Sioux, and it stood for, literally, *'Hawk Knife'*, Pat thought he heard once. He wasn't positive, but he was pretty sure that someone told him that was the meaning behind Cetanmila.

Cetanmila Park was probably the greatest most naturally preserved city park Pat had ever seen. Thousands of large oaks and elms filled the city park and gave it an unpretentious setting unlike anything Pat had ever seen before. Although Pat had been to Fairfield once in awhile with his dad, he didn't remember seeing too many city parks in that large city; certainly none that would warrant the praise for such a park as this. But for a town the size of Wahkashen, Cetanmila Park was the greatest place on earth. Pat and his friends spent literally hundreds of hours in the park doing everything, and nothing all at the same time.

There were two roads that accessed the park from 2nd Street. One road called the Snake road, (for obvious reasons as it wound through hundreds of trees and the sides of the road were protected by large boulders. These boulders were probably used for two reasons: to keep the traffic slow and to keep the traffic on the road) went through a small wooded area behind the duck pond and past a playground as it flowed past a couple of beautifully maintained picnic shelters. It would eventually meet up with the main road coming down from 'The Hill' that went past the Putt-Putt course and the swimming pool. One of the shelters the Snake road went past had a stone fireplace and the other one had a couple of fire pits that sat along side the shelter.

The road down from 'The Hill' curved through more ancient solemn trees and past yet another split log shelter that held the most beautiful stone fireplace, and the shelter itself would be able to accommodate thirty or forty picnickers. There were hundreds of picnic tables that were scattered about, and some surrounded these shelters. There was a large well kept playground for the children that was located close to the largest split log shelter in the park, and was just south of the softball fields and the small Snake road. The playground itself was covered with pea rock for the base and held numerous swings, slides and merry-go-rounds.

It was a park that maintained a public swimming pool at the bottom of the road, a couple of tennis courts off to the right of the main road, the Putt-Putt golf course behind them and across from the swimming pool, and all of this could be seen from the top of 'The Hill'. There was also a well-maintained baseball field where the city league would play just to the right of the tennis courts, and it ran along side 2nd Street.

Also, off to the left of 'The Hill' was another grassy hill that was used in the winter months as children would slide down that snow covered hill towards the frozen duck pond at the bottom. The duck pond became the skating rink in the winter. The Park Board even put up a hockey rink for the kids right along side the warming house, to the west of the parking lot for the swimming pool.

If one followed the main winding road down the hill and through the park, one would also find numerous softball fields, a city zoo with a wide selection of animals and plant life that that was built along side, and followed the curves of, the Red River. This road eventually led to the public golf course at the end of the park, and the road, which finally dumped out on 4ᵗʰ Street. The golf course was unique in a way that the front nine holes were on the North Dakota side in Wahkashen, and the back nine holes were on the Minnesota side in Buliford, just across the Red River.

More time than not come spring of the year, the Red River would flood, and most of the area of Cetanmila Park at the bottom of 'The Hill' would be under water for a few months. The worst flooding Pat and his family had seen was in 1965 when the waters of the Red were so high, all one could see of the warming house that sat before the duck pond was about two inches of the peak of the roof. Pat's dad told him there had to be about sixteen to twenty feet of water at its deepest.

Pat waited for the gang to get to him, and they all headed down 'The Hill' in order to get to their favorite fishing spot.

All three boys headed down the hill without pedaling their bikes at all. They could always generate enough speed just coasting down the hill to take them almost all the way past the swimming pool at the bottom.

"What did you make for sandwiches?" Mike yelled while trying to catch up his buddies as they got close to the swimming pool. He glanced over at the pool to see the little kids participating in their swimming lessons.

Man, I bet that water is really cold at this early hour, Mike thought. Surely the sun had not been out long enough to take the evenings chill out of it yet, Mike maintained.

"Bologna," Pat replied with a smile. "Lenny's favorite."

"I hate bologna," Lenny said with a scowl coming up along side Pat as the road finally evened out…a little, and their speed began to decrease.

This was met by a roar of laughter from both Pat and Mike as they knew that would be Lenny's response.

"I know…that's why I made it," Pat answered. "Besides, it was all we had. But relax, I also found a bag of Old Dutch to help wash them down."

"How in the hell do you wash down bologna sandwiches with salty potato chips?" Lenny shot back.

This was also met by a roar of laughter from both Pat and Mike.

"Just take a drink of the Red to wash ALL of it down," Mike said, while he and Pat were still laughing.

After riding along quietly for the next five minutes watching the scenery, the boys finally arrived at their favorite fishing spot. There was a nice slope of sandy beach along the Red which was at least thirty feet long and fifteen feet deep. The boys could still see the marks of their shoes from their last visit, as well as the holes in the beach were they had stuck their poles into the sand so they would not have to hold onto their poles.

There were even three strategically placed large stones that they had moved into the positions on a previous visit that satisfied each of them for them to sit upon while fishing for small fish and spinning tall tales.

"OK," Pat said after he got settled onto his rock and cast his line into the water, "I brought the sandwiches and chips. What did you guys bring along with you?"

"I brought a bag of gumdrops and a package of firecrackers," Lenny replied.

"I didn't grab anything...except for these," Mike replied, and then produced a half a pack of Camel no-filter cigarettes from the back pocket of his faded blue jeans. Pat and Lenny's eyes got real wide at the sight of the stash that Mike pilfered from his dad.

"I knew you'd come through," Lenny said and slapped Mike on the shoulder. "Give me one, will ya?"

"Yeah," Pat said. "Toss one to me as well."

"Yeah, yeah," Mike said with feigned anger in his voice. "You'll both get one as soon as I am ready to give them out.

"Right...about....now will do" Mike said, and with that he shook out three cigarettes and threw one to Pat, and handed one over to Lenny. "You got any matches for those firecrackers, Lenny?" Mike asked while he was placing his cigarette into his mouth.

"Well, yeah, shitbird," Lenny answered. "What, you think I'm stupid, or what?"

"That question does not even qualify for a response," Mike replied.

Pat snickered, and looked out at his line in the water.

Lenny passed out the matchbook after he lit his smoke. Finally all three lit up, sat back to enjoy their first cigarette of the day, and soak in the sun's early morning rays while they looked out at the slow flowing Red River. Pat watched the water as it manipulated his fishing line; he watched as his line in the water created an eddy, with a quiet resolve.

There was a very slight breeze in the trees and it was a wonderful sound, Pat thought. There is really no other place I would rather be right now, Pat imagined as he took another drag from his smoke, exhaled, and looked over at his two best friends.

No place at all.

Pat doesn't remember when he started smoking cigarettes, or even *why* he started, but he did remember that he started with both Mike and Lenny. Peer pressure, all the way, that's for sure. He doesn't remember really enjoying a cigarette, but he smoked them anyway. After awhile, they did start to taste pretty good, and now he had the habit that would follow him for many years after.

The boys finished their smokes and flicked them into the river. They watched as the slow moving current grabbed hold of them and shuttled them down and out of sight.

After a few minutes, Pat said, "Hey…let me tell you guys about the crazy dream that *I* had last night…"

Chapter 8

The river flowed by the gang without a single care in the world. Nothing could stop its journey, even if it tried; and the muddy water swirled and eddied by the bank where the boys sat on their special rocks. The water flowed by them easily, undemonstratively.

As Pat began his tale about the moonlight stroll, the rendezvous with the lovely Karla, with all of the details, the boys didn't see Brian, Ed and Pete looking over the river bank spying the three fisher boys. Had they done that, they would have more than likely reeled in their lines and headed someplace else. As it were, though, they were going to be in for a surprise. A surprise none of the boys was prepared to face.

"So, here I am," Pat continues on, "lying on the blanket waiting to find out what's going to happen next, when I reach over to open the basket...and what do I find?"

Pat hesitated just long enough for Lenny to get antsy, as Pat knew he would.

"What...what did you find?" Lenny finally spurted out.

"Brian Osterman's head," Pat replied, quietly. "That's what I found. Brian Osterman's head, which looked like it was severed off as it was all jagged at the neck. I stared at it for a couple of seconds, in shock, I guess. Then he opened his eyes and said 'Peek-a-Boo' to me. Can you believe that shit?"

"No," said the voice from behind them. "No, I can't."

Pat finally realized without looking that that voice belonged to the severed head he spied in the basket last night. However, he figured it out a just a tish too late.

All three boys turned their heads just in time to see the Three Stooges descend upon them.

Mike got to his feet quickly and was immediately met by Ed, who was at least two inches taller, two years older, and about ten pounds lighter than Mike, yet Ed was quite gangly in his body shape. Ed reached for Mike and got hold of him. As quick as a snake he stepped behind Mike and wrapped his long lanky arms around Mike's arms, and pinned them against his sides. Ed may have been skinny and tall, but he was pretty strong as well. Mike could not move his arms at all.

Lenny got to his feet during Mike's scuffle with Ed. Pat rose quickly as well. Lenny was face-to-face with Pete before Pat even knew what was going on. Lenny stood staring into the eyes of Pete, who was about the same size as Lenny.

"What the hell do you guys want?" Lenny asked Pete, his eyes never leaving Pete's eyes at all.

"Shut up, dickface," Brian spat out at him. "If I want any lip from you, I'll scrap it off of my zipper."

That statement was met, of course, by a bray of laughter from the 'Clan of Idiots'.

Brian turned his face towards Pat.

"Hello, Pat-ty," Brian said in his sickening sing-song voice.

"Hey, Brian," Pat stammered out. Pat's eyes shifted back and forth from Ed and Lenny to Brain's pimpled face in front of him. Pat tried not to show any fear, but just like a snared rabbit, his eyes reflected the apprehension that he now was feeling. He could see the hatred in Brian's pale eyes, and he just knew he was in serious trouble today; grave trouble that he would not be able to escape from, no matter how hard he tried.

Brian moved his eyes from Pat's and looked over at their fishing poles. Smiling his well documented devilish grin, he went over and started to pull their fishing poles out of the sand that held them in place. One by one he walked down the shoreline and jerked their poles and threw them to the ground.

"How they bitin', boys?" Brian said with a sneer.

Ed and Pete laughed at this. Pat stood staring at Brian with eyes wide, not knowing what to say or do next.

"Brian," Pat finally said with a light, but slightly jittery voice. "What do you want?"

"You know what I want, sissy-boy," Brian sneered as he walked back to stand toe to toe with Pat. Brian smiled at Pat and his retched breath came at Pat like a wave of nauseating gas from a very old septic tank. "It's what I have wanted all along."

"Brian, I am not going to fight you. You are way bigger than me. I have told you that befo…."

"I don't give a shit," Brian said and came at Pat fast and hard, left fist leading the way, and struck Pat dead center of his chest.

"Uff," Pat gasped as the air was pushed out of his lungs and he went down hard. He landed, hard, on the sandy beach after absorbing the blow Brian delivered to him.

"Hey," Mike said straining in Ed's grasp. "Why don't you leave him alone? Why are you always messing with Pat? He's no where near your size, Brian." He struggled against Ed's long arms, but to no avail. "Is that what it is? Knowing that Pat is smaller than you makes you look bigger…is that it?"

As quick as the snake that he was, Brian turned his face towards Mike and spat, "Maybe I should be messin' with you…you want that, Mike?"

Mike stared at Brian for a second or two and then slowly dropped his eyes from that beady stare Brian had laid upon him. It was like trying to stare down a snake, Mike thought; a snake with coal-black, dead eyes. Ed tightened the grip he held around Mike's waist with a giggle in his voice.

At the same time Mike was speaking up to Brian, Lenny made a move to go forward and Pete stopped him by delivering a blow to the solar plexus.

Lenny went down to one knee holding onto his stomach, fighting to get some much needed air back into his body.

Brian looked down at Lenny holding his stomach trying to catch his breath. Brian snorted out a laugh that was a mixture of humor and hatred. He then turned back to Pat who was still lying in the sand.

"On your feet, sissy-boy," Brian ordered him.

Pat, barely able to breath from the blow he received from Brian, only lay there fighting back the scorching tears that were welling up behind his eyes. He was rubbing the area of his chest where Brian punched him. He didn't know quite yet what he should do next.

"I said get up, Pat-ty," Brian said again, and reached down and grabbed Pat by his shirt collar. The brute strength Brian possessed was quite apparent as he lifted Pat straight up in the air. Then, as easy as you please, set him down on Pat's slightly unsteady feet. Brian got his face real close to Pat's and Pat could smell the decay that had already started to form in Brian's mouth. Pat thought Brian probably wouldn't have any of his own teeth by the time he reached forty.

"So, you dream of having my head in a basket, ehhh?"

"That was only a dream, Brian," Pat whispered out with the little air left in his lungs. "It was only a dream. It doesn't mean anything."

"Maybe it does...maybe it doesn't. Put your hands up...I want you to try and defend yourself...boy," Brian hissed softly in his face.

With that said, Brian let go of Pat's shirt collar and swung his fist. The uppercut caught Pat squarely on the chin. Pat felt his teeth clack together with an audible 'crunch'. Pat immediately saw all the stars of heaven appear to him in a split second, and heard the proverbial bells of St Mary's ringing in his head as his knees buckled, and he went down to the ground; unconscious before he even fully hit it.

I

"Jesus Christ," Mike screamed and tore himself free from Ed's grip.

Ed actually loosened his grip when he saw Brian was really going to hit the McCray kid. What the hell was Brian thinking, Ed thought? He is going to kill that kid if he hits him too hard...and then we'll *all* be in trouble.

"What the hell is wrong with you, Brian?" Mike yelled at him. "Pat is half your size."

"You want to go a round with me, then," Brian sneered.

"No…no, I don't, Brian," Mike replied as he reached Pat's limp body on the ground. "And you know what, neither did Pat."

Mike started to tap Pat softly on the side of his face to try and wake him. Mike thought, feared, as hard as Brian hit him, he may have really hurt Pat. He did not like the way Pat collapsed to the ground after being hit.

"What do you know, guys…the kid can't take a punch," Brian said and started to laugh.

Ed and Pete laughed a little at that, but Lenny could hear the uncertainty in the laughter.

He turned to walk away and Mike called out, "You are such a prick, Brian."

"You watch your mouth, homo," Brian said with a fury in his voice that none of them had heard before, "or you'll get worse than what I just gave to the sissy-boy over there, sleeping in the sand." He laughed loudly, turned and headed for the bank from which he had earlier appeared.

"Enjoy your fishing, homos," Pete said.

They turned their backs and started back up the slope from which they jumped what felt like an hour ago, and only a mere ten minutes had passed.

Ed and Pete joined Brian at the top of the bank and then they disappeared over the slope and out of sight, still throwing sarcasm and threats over their shoulders. The boys heard the intermingled laughter, as they strolled away from the gang and out of earshot.

Lenny got to his feet, still slightly bent over from the blow from Pete on which he was on the receiving end. He took a knee beside Mike and started talking to Pat to see if he would respond.

"God, those guys are such bastards," Lenny finally spoke.

"I hear ya," Mike replied still tapping Pat lightly on the cheek in an effort to revive him. "I hear ya," and he looked over to the slope where they vacated the area.

After a few minutes, Pat started to come around. His eyes were slightly glazed over when they first opened up and looked around, unsure of where or what they were seeing.

"Can you hear me, Pat?" Mike asked him, gently and fearful of the answer.

"Yeah," Pat replied, his voice sounding distant and disconnected. "Is that you, Mike?"

"Yeah, it's me. Who'd ya think it was…Karla?"

Lenny spit out a bray of laughter with that, and looked at the expression on Pat's face. He saw that it went from dazed and confused, to one of humor that Lenny was used to seeing.

"Karla?" Pat said, shyly and reached out for the front of Mike's shirt. He was reaching for an imagined Karla breast.

"Hey," Mike started knocking Pat's hand away. "What the hell? Are you, you…a homo or something? Good Lord, maybe Brian was right!"

"Do you think you can sit up…homo?"

Lenny started laughing at that.

"I think so," Pat replied as he tried, with the aid of Lenny's shoulder and Mike's arm.

Once upright, the glaze finally broke up a little and Pat's eyes became much clearer. The boys noticed a blooming red mark on the underside of Pat's chin and wondered how Pat was going to explain that to his folks.

"That prick hit me," Pat said rubbing his chin, "didn't he?"

"Oh, yeah," Lenny replied.

"Yes, he really did," Mike retorted. "I wouldn't have believed it had I not seen it with my own eyes. The bastard actually hit you."

"You know," Pat started to say, "I have never done anything to him. Why does he always want to kick the shit out of me?"

"I don't know," Mike replied and patted Pat on the shoulder. "Maybe because he can…I just don't know."

"The stars are starting to leave me," Pat said to no one in particular and with a slight shake of his head, "and the bells have tapered off a little."

Mike and Lenny exchanged a glance over the top of Pat's head and they shared a smile at that.

"Come on," Lenny said, "let's get you on your feet. You can sit down on your rock until the birds and bells are gone completely. Hell, we still have some fishing to do."

"It was stars and bells, Lenny," Pat replied, with a shaky voice.

The boys walked slowly back to their rocks and took a seat as Mike fished out three more Camels. They all lit up and with the first drag off of his smoke, Pat felt a great deal better. His jaw was sore as he moved it back and forth, very tentatively.

"Man, I still can't believe Brian just hauled off and hit you," Lenny said. "He is the biggest prick in Wahkashen…no, in all of North Dakota."

"He did warn me yesterday," Pat said to both of the boys, "right before baseball practice, and then before I met you guys. He told me the next time I was going to have to defend myself."

Lenny and Mike looked at each other, unsure of what to say to Pat. Finally Mike spoke to break the silence.

"I think it was a good thing that he knocked you out, Pat," Mike started, "cuz if you would have gotten to your feet, he probably would have beaten on you a great deal more than just with the one punch."

They all stared at each other for a few seconds. Mike and Lenny watched Pat move around on his 'sea legs' trying to get them under control a little more with each fleeting second.

"Let's get those lines back into the water," Lenny said and flicked away his spent cigarette.

About an hour later, after more than a few tentative worried glances over at Pat by both Mike and Lenny, and with no caught fish, yet, the boys broke out the sandwiches and chips. They ate in silence watching their lines in the water. Chewing kind of hurt Pat with the sore jaw, but he didn't say anything about it.

II

When Pat finished his lunch he pulled his pole out from the sand and reeled in his line. He noticed immediately that there wasn't a trace of bait remaining on his hook. He got up from his rock and went over to the can to check the limited supply of worms; he discovered that they were all gone.

"What the hell," Pat said out loud, to no one in particular. "What am I going to use for bait now?"

No one said anything as Pat stood looking out at the river slowly rolling by him with nary a sound. No bait, he thought. That's just great. I guess fishing is over for me...

"I have some lemon gumdrops," Lenny said, not taking his eyes off of his line in the water.

Mike immediately started laughing, quietly at first, and louder and louder the longer he thought about fishing with lemon gumdrops as bait.

Pat, hearing the good belly laughter by Mike, soon joined in. Before too long, Lenny had also jumped onto the wagon, and all three were having a good laugh.

After the laughter subsided to the point where the boys could actually breathe again, Pat said he would take one of Lenny's gumdrops.

"Ahh, what the hell," Pat said. "It's better than not fishing at all. Who knows...?"

So Pat fit his hook with a lemon gumdrop. It looked as much out of place as a straight, white tooth in Brian Osterman's mouth.

Pat cast his line and sat down on his rock and waited.

They fished in silence for awhile until Pat had a strike on his line after it was in the water for no more than a minute.

Enthusiastically, Pat grabbed the pole from out of the sand and very carefully and quickly pulled back on the pole to set the hook. He then tried his hardest to calm his heart down enough to slowly start reeling in the fish. He fought with his catch for about five minutes letting the fish take the line out slowly and then reeling it in again.

Pat was grinning from ear to ear even though his chin hurt when he did grin.

"Reel it in slow and steady," Mike advised.

A moment later all three boys were looking down at the eleven and a half inch walleye that Pat had just caught...using a lemon gumdrop as bait.

A stupid lemon gumdrop...who would have thought it possible?

It certainly was not any of the gang looking down at it in disbelief.

Despite the pain radiating around that area where Brian punched him, he had caught a beautiful fish...with a gumdrop, nonetheless.

How weird can this day get, anyway?

After a few pats on the back to Pat delivered by Lenny and Mike in a congratulatory effort, they decided to let the fish go back into the river.

Chapter 9

Nobody would have ever guessed that Earth Shoes would have even taken off with the worldwide fashion frenzy that they did with the younger generation, and while they did, the trend for an environmentally conscious society was born as the very first 'Earth Day' was celebrated on 22 April of 1970. Society, as a whole, began to start to appreciate what they had, more or less, as the consciousness levels were raised up to the height of the hem of the young women's dresses as mini skirts were also introduced.

People everywhere were hugging more trees, tuning in and dropping out; bras were burning at an alarming rate in stiff competition with draft notices. It would be eight more years before the world would be forced to turn their attention to a small, little know community called Love Canal in New York, and only then would they have to face the dilemma of succumbing to another pseudo-environmentally friendly source of energy.

Even before the world began to be worried about the toxicity of high levels of lead and mercury in the fish caught from the rivers and lakes of the United States, Pat and the gang decided not to take the fish home to eat.

Face it; these boys just did not want to take home only one fish.

So they packed up what remained of their gear, and walked over to their waiting bikes.

"Let me look at your chin again," Mike said to Pat before they reached their bikes.

"It doesn't feel too bad, anymore," Pat told him, stopping to face him, "but I have no idea what it looks like."

Pat lifted his chin to a level where both Mike and Lenny could survey the damage left behind by the fury of Brian. They saw redness, and it was sore to the touch as indicated when they did touch it by the grimace on Pat's face.

"You'll live," Mike concluded, with a slap on Pat's shoulder. "I don't think your folks will even notice it. If they do, tell them your foot slipped off of your bike pedal and you hit your chin on the handlebars.

"Thanks, guys," Pat said to them. "I really wish I could figure out why Brian is so set on beating me up. I don't know what I ever did to have him so focused on me."

"I think it's because you are the smallest of the gang," Mike said, finally. "It gives him a strange sense of power being able to better you, if you know what I mean."

"Yeah, you're probably right" Pat replied and then looked down at his feet. "I guess I will never know."

They walked along in silence for the remainder of the trip to the bike holding area, each absorbed in their own thoughts about the day's events.

"Don't forget, guys," Mike said, "we are going to see 'M*A*S*H' tonight. Lisa said she would be our *chaperone*, as she put it. But, she will ditch us as soon as we get our popcorn and go sit with her gaggle of friends."

Lenny and Pat giggled at that. Pat could picture in his head a group of seventeen year old girls squawking away like so many chickens.

"I'm going to stop by dad's work and ask for money for the movie,' Pat told the gang. "I think I will have better results if I ask for the money from him while he is at work."

"A fine plan, Stan," Lenny said. "May I call you Stan?"

"You can call me anything you want…" Pat replied.

"But don't call me *late for dinner,"* all three said at the very same time. Then they laughed.

They split up after they climbed back up the hill, with Lenny and Mike heading west on 3rd Avenue, and Pat heading down 4th Street to the Shell station on Main.

"Later 'gator," Mike cried over his shoulder as he and Lenny disappeared from view.

Pat rode down the shady street enjoying the late afternoon sounds: a sprinkler off his right shoulder working a front lawn as it tried to keep up with the blistering sun of the day; laughter of little children as they splashed around in an inflatable pool trying to accomplish the same mission as the sprinkler.

He watched the leaves of the elms fluttering back and forth on the stems alternating from the green side on the front to the silver side on the back. The rapid movement of these leaves gave the huge tree a shimmering appearance like so many appliqués had been attached to its branches. The effect was quite appealing, and mesmerizing.

He was close to passing a lemonade stand that the Haskin's girls were maintaining at the corner of 4th and 3rd.

"Do you want a glass of lemonade, Pat?" the oldest yelled out to him as he was about to pass. Her name was Julie, Pat thought…but wasn't sure.

"Sure," Pat replied coming to a stop in front of their makeshift stand, "why not."

The youngest Haskin girl was about four or five, cute as a button with little pigtails lying on both sides of her head. The ends of the tails held a pink ribbon.

"Is it any good?" Pat asked with a smile on his face and a wink at the youngest.

He dropped the kickstand of his bike and walked over to their stand which was comprised of a small wooden table with a white dish towel covering it. The handmade sign leaning against the front of this table announced that the girls had: 'Lemon-Aid for sale. 10 cents.'

"Why, of course it's good," the oldest, Julie, her name was Julie, Pat thought, replied with a roll of her eyes. "We wouldn't sell anything bad."

They poured a Dixie cup with lemonade, handed it to Pat as he handed them a dime. Pat swallowed the entire contents down in three gulps, dropped the cup into the trash can that was placed beside their little stand, and then turned to face them.

"Buuuurrp," Pat belched as loud as he intentionally could.

"Eewww!," they both screamed at the same time. "That's gross!"

"My humblest of apologizes, my ladies," Pat said and did a slight bow at the waist while extending his right arm out in a graceful sweeping gesture like only D'Artagnan would do.

He stood, offered the youngest one another light wink, threw his leg over his bike and off he went.

"Thank you," they yelled at him as he rode off to the Shell station just a few blocks ahead.

Pat returned their thanks with a wave of his hand over his shoulder.

Pat pulled into the lot of the Shell station a couple of minutes later and set his kickstand down. He walked to the open garage bay and peered into its dark surroundings. Surely his dad was in there somewhere.

I

He stepped over the threshold and walked past an older Chevrolet up on the lift stands, oil dripping from the pan. He watched the dripping oil for a second or two and noticed how much the time between the drips had increased. He saw the old oil filter in the drip pan as well, and then looked over to the workbench and noticed the new filter along side quarts of oil ready to be installed into the car to complete the change.

Without even thinking about it, his eyes moved up the wall behind the workbench and came to rest upon the red headed, large breasted 'Snap-On' girl with the nice smile emblazoned on the August 1970 calendar.

Nope, he thought. There was no way that the 'Snap-On' people were ever going to convince Pat that this large breasted beauty was actually working on the '34 coup.

She was nice on the eyes, but he had his doubts on her maintenance abilities.

He walked slowly past the workbench towards the door that led into the front lobby. As he got closer to the door, he could hear his father's voice while he was talking to someone.

"Like I said before, Ralph," Howard was saying with a little exasperation in his voice to the man standing before him with his hands on his hips, "the cost to do the brakes and a front end alignment is going to be $35.75. It may come to a little more if we have to turn the front drums. That's the cost of the brake pads and the alignment, with my labor.

"I'll do a fine job for you, Ralph," Howard said with a wide smile.

"Howard," Ralph replied, "I don't doubt your abilities, but the costs seem a bit extreme, don't you think?"

"My costs are minimal. It's the brake pads and the alignment which are most of the costs. But I will do the best job for the money, Ralph."

"As I said earlier, I don't doubt your abilities. Do you have a breakdown of the costs that I can look at?"

"Sure, Ralph...its right over here."

Howard turned around to walk behind the front counter, and he saw Pat coming through the Employees Only door that separated the front from the shop.

"Hi, son," Howard said to Pat in passing.

"Hi, dad," Pat replied, and then looked over to see Ralph Wilson, still standing with his hands on his hips, and with a look on his face like he just had a huge glass of the Haskin girls' lemonade, but with a touch more bitter lemon added.

"Hi, Mr. Wilson," Pat said and offered a hand wave.

"Hello there, young man," Ralph replied. "Are you enjoying your summer vacation?"

"Yes, Sir," Pat told him, "very much so."

"Very polite boy," Ralph told Howard when he looked up from Pat's face.

"Thank you...he sure is," Howard said and looked down at Pat with a smile on his face and gave him a wink.

After a few moments went by, Howard found the paperwork estimate that Ralph had requested, and he motioned for Ralph to join him at the front counter. Pat walked over to the grease streaked front window and peered out at the moving three-thirty traffic.

He watched as the cars drove by and all of those people who had a million places to go, and no where to be at this particular time.

He saw a few people walking down the street past the American Legion club, and stop to go into the furniture store next door.

The Main Street was a constant bustle of cars and people, even for a small town like Wahkashen. Both sides of the street were lined with the old-fashioned hanging triple globe street lights that Pat had seen in magazines. He liked that style of lights, and at night when they came on automatically, their glow was soft, yet bright enough for the traffic of people, both on foot and in their cars, to navigate with little problem.

The city had redone parts of Main over the past few years and added left turn lanes at most every intersection. This seemed to alleviate most, if not all, of the traffic problems and kept the flow of traffic constant.

He could see the Jasper's store from here, if he craned his neck enough and almost plastered his face to the grease-coated front window. He wondered if that CPO coat was still in the window. He wondered what the cute salesgirl was wearing today.

What was her name again? He tried to think about her name and all that came to his mind was her flowing past his mother and him that day they visited the store. Watching her breasts sway, slightly, under the thin tie-dyed gypsy dress that she was wearing, and that she was also selling.

What *was* her name?

He remembered how her perfume followed her movements like unseen wisps of smoke. He could almost smell that enchanting aroma in his mind. He could see in his mind how gracefully she lifted the mannequin from the front window display to show his mother the coat. How easily she picked that mannequin up amazed him, as she was such a smallish woman…almost petite, one could say.

He could see her face surrounded by that beautiful blond hair.

What was her name? Rachel? Robin?

No, not a bird. More like a flower, like she was…a delicate flower. Rose? No…that's not it.

What was it…?

II

"Pat?" his dad said again, and bent a little in front of his face to see if he were awake.

"Huh," Pat replied, and looked at his dad. The glassiness of the salesgirl (whatever the hell her name was) daydream dissipating quickly from his eyes.

"You OK, buddy?" his dad asked.

"Oh, yeah, sorry…I was, daydreaming I guess," and he felt the redness of embarrassment start to creep from inside the collar of his shirt in preparation to take up residency all over his face.

"What brings you around today?" Howard asked as he started to walk towards the *'Employees Only'* door.

Pat spun on his heels and followed his dad through the door which led to the best part of this building; the serious business portion of the building; the part of the building that had the best smells in the world, next to the perfume that, *what's her name*, was wearing.

What *WAS* her name….?

"So, what's up, Bud?"

"Well," Pat started out, "the guys and I were just out fishing today. I caught a nice sized walleye. He was eleven and a half inches. Had to go about five pounds, if I had to guess. You'll never guess how I caught him, Dad."

Pat waited, just like he did with Lenny and Mike, but his father was not as quick to bite as Lenny was.

"It was on a lemon gumdrop," Pat finally said after his father did *not* bite.

"Oh, you're kidding me, aren't you," Howard replied without looking at Pat. He was looking at the Chevy on the lift stand, and contemplating his next move. "A lemon gumdrop?"

"Yeah! We ran out of bait and that was all we had left. He hit it almost immediately."

"Where is he? Out by your bike?"

"Nah, we decided to throw him back in. Nobody wanted to carry him home or clean him when we got there."

Howard walked under the Chevy and grabbed for the drain plug, pulled the ratchet out from his back pocket and started to replace the oil drain plug, and tighten it.

"Good call. Your mother wouldn't clean it for you, and I wouldn't want to by the time I got home. You almost have to clean them right away if you want to enjoy the meat, I've been told. Besides, one walleye isn't much of a meal, is it?"

"No, not really," Pat replied.

"Oh, by the way, there is another thing I wanted to talk to you about," Pat said, in a off-handed way. "The guys want to go to the movie at the Kashen tonight. Do you think I could go with them?"

"What's playing?"

"Something called 'M*A*S*H'. It's supposed to be an army movie, I guess."

Howard stepped out from under the car to retrieve the new oil filter, and then turned back towards the waiting car. Pat often wondered how his dad seemed to be able to locate whatever he needed, whenever he needed it from that cluttered bench. It just seemed like such an impossible and improbable task when you really took a good look at the bench.

"You have any money?" Howard asked and turned to face Pat.

"Well..." Pat began, and slowly turned his face away from his dad.

"So, this isn't just asking for my permission," Howard started with a hint of a smile on his face, "this is asking for the funds to actually attend the movie. Is that about right?"

"Well, I had the money the other day..."

"The other day?" Howard answered. "Well, the other day doesn't count if you don't have the money today; now does it?"

"No, I guess not."

His dad started spinning on the new oil filter, reached for the filter wrench to finish the job.

"So...how much *do* you need?"

"Well...the admission is $1.65, and popcorn, which is really a luxury, but a necessity to sit and watch a movie is..."

"Alright, alright...I'll give you three dollars, but don't you *dare* say anything to your mother OR Penny, or it will be the last three dollars you get from me for awhile. However, you will need to pay this back. So, I will expect you to do the tasks that I throw at you for the weekend. Agreed?"

"Yes…yes, anything you say, dad." was Pat's ambitious reply.

Howard reached back for his wallet, opened it and found he only had two ones, a couple of fives and a ten. After contemplating, he pulled out a five.

"You owe me big time for this one," Howard said as he handed the five over to Pat's waiting, yet trembling hand.

"Wow, thanks dad. I will get the change back to you tomorrow morning for sure."

"No, that's alright. You just try to make that last as long as you possibly can. I know with Penny it would be five to ten minutes…tops. But I expect it to be in your pocket a few days longer. Right?"

"Right."

Pat came forward and gave his dad a huge hug.

"Thanks, dad."

"You are more than welcome, Bud. Now run along. I sill have this oil change to finish, and then I have to get Ralph's Olds in for a brake job and alignment before closing, or I will be here until after supper time. I don't think your mother would like me working late on a Friday night. She wants to go to the VFW for a couple of drinks and dancing tonight, so I better be at home at a decent time."

Pat started towards the open overhead door, turned and said, "Thanks, again, dad. You're the best."

"You're welcome. See you at home for supper…I hope."

Pat got on his bike, lifted up the kickstand, and started down the driveway towards Main Street.

Pat thought he had the best dad in the world, and the money in his pocket was not the only reason.

Life was good, he thought, as he stepped up his speed and headed for home.

Chapter 10

Pat ate a quick supper without Penny, and said bye to his mom and hopped on his bike to meet the guys.

The gang met at the top of The Hill and then headed to the movie and parked their bikes in the rack that was provided by the theater. They stood outside and waited for Mike's sister, Lisa, while they talked quietly and watched the traffic as it rolled by them.

They recognized some of the '*motorheads*' that cruised in their muscle cars every single night. They were pretty nice guys, Pat always thought, and they were never mean to Pat. Every one of those muscle cars that drove by the gang was incredible. The gang had all agreed that they would give up their left testicle to be the actual owner of one of those cars.

Lisa finally showed up at the front door about five minutes later as she pulled in with a car full of girls. Every one of them was gorgeous, Pat thought; but they could be blind, deaf and dumb, and as long as they had a pretty face, breasts and they were still breathing, they were gorgeous in Pat's mind.

Lisa walked to the ticket window with the boys (after she gathered all of their money for the tickets, that is) and asked for four tickets. The ticket lady looked at the boys a couple of times, said nothing, and handed Lisa four tickets of admission. The four of them walked in, Lisa gave the ticket custodian the four tickets and he let them in. No problem at all.

Hell, that was easy, Pat thought.

Lisa left them without a word at the concessions stand, met up with her three friends, and off they went to sit down inside the theater.

The boys ordered popcorn and a soda, and then went and found three seats towards the front of the theater. There were always seats in the front, as most people liked to sit towards the back to neck instead of watching the movie.

Pat looked over his shoulder and spied two or three couples in the way back. He didn't see a single face on any of the couples which meant they were not paying too much attention to the giant screen in front of them, which was pure white at the moment, but would be showing the film before too long.

They didn't seem to notice anything in the theater except for each other. He thought he knew one of the couples, but sitting way up front and them way in back made it hard to distinguish who was who.

Maybe when I get older, Pat thought, it would be me sitting way in the back, copping a feel and doing some heavy kissing with someone instead of sitting up front where the kids go.

Someday...

The movie was great. And, it did have nudity!
The boys were very delighted.

I

They were heading back home after the movie riding their bikes and discussing the Film: what were the best parts, besides the nudity, of course, and what they really liked about the movie...besides the nudity, of course.

They decided to head down to the park before going home to see who was out and about. It seemed that there always was someone down in the park, sitting around, smoking and joking.

The boys rode past one of the shelters where it sat back in the trees.

They saw a car parked in the front of it, and it was just as murky as the pavilion that a couple of people were sitting in. Pat could make out the dark silhouettes of two people sitting on a picnic table back in the shadows. To confirm this fact Pat spied the red-orange glow of the cherry end of a cigarette as someone drew from it.

They rode past slowly in case they knew who was sitting in the dark…and who with? Pat didn't recognize the car, anyway, so why would he know who was sitting in the dark necking?

They drove down the winding roads that wove through the park in the semi-darkness with the confidence of a race driver on a course that he has driven more than once before. They arrived by one of the many shelters that the park contained, and stopped to have a cigarette. They listened to the cars in the background, and the sounds of the ducks on the pond.

"Sounds like the ducks are getting a little horny tonight, doesn't it?" Mike asked the gang.

"Yeah," Lenny replied. "At least we know someone…or something is getting a little action."

All three laughed at that. After a while they got back on their bikes and headed further down the road.

They went towards the zoo and got off of their bikes to take a quick walk through. Maybe they could get the Llama to spit again. Usually, Lenny could get the Llama riled up so much that it would spit. However, if that projectile hit you, it stuck like the dickens…but was funny, nonetheless.

They then rode past the darkened ball fields and golf course on their way out of the park.

Pat and Lenny dropped Mike off at his house, and then Pat said good night to Lenny as they split up at 7th street and 6th avenue.

Pat came into the house to see his dad still up and watching Johnny Carson. He had a huge bowl of popcorn in his lap and the rich smell of buttered popcorn hung in the air. Mom was sleeping gently on the couch.

Apparently, Johnny was not too interesting for her tonight, for she enjoyed watching him as much as dad did.

"How was the movie, Buddy?" Howard asked his son.

As his voice traveled across the room, Delores woke and looked at her son.

"Hi, honey," his mom said in a sleepy voice.

"Hey, mom, Pat said. "It was OK," he told his dad in response to his question.

"Good," his dad replied. His eyes never left the TV.

Pat turned and looked at the TV for a second and looked at a pretty woman who Pat didn't know was talking with Johnny and Ed.

I can see why dad never turned his attention away from the TV, Pat thought. He smiled a little. I guess all guys will look at pretty women, he thought.

"How was the VFW?" Pat asked his dad. "You guys are home kinda early, aren't you?"

Howard put his finger to his lips to indicate the 'be quiet' sign and then turned to look at his sleeping wife…but too late as Delores rolled over and explained, as gently as possible (with a slight hint of sarcasm in her voice that she is known for, occasionally) that his father worked late again tonight, so they were not afforded the *luxury* of going out together…for fun.

"I'm going to brush my teeth and go to bed," Pat said looking at his dad but giving his mom a side-ward glance. Then he smiled at his dad as his dad just shrugged his shoulders, and grabbed another handful of popcorn.

Pat left the room, went to the bathroom and closed the door behind him.

He reached for the light and immediately it filled the room with a soft white light. He went to the medicine cabinet above the sink, and grabbed what he needed to complete the task at hand.

He stared at his reflection in the mirror as he brushed his teeth. He thought about Sally Kellerman who was long-legged, blond and fairly large busted. She was very pretty and really provocative to a young boy. Probably to most men too, Pat thought.

He thought that someday he would be older and sitting in the back seats of a movie theater with a woman like Sally Kellerman.

He liked that idea very much.

He finished up and went out to the living room again. His mother had fallen asleep again. He sat in a chair next to his dad.

Don Rickles was now on answering questions of Johnny with his patented sarcasm that Pat and Howard both found amusing.

When the next commercial came on Pat got up and kissed and hugged his father and said 'good night'.

He then went over and gave his mom a kiss on the cheek. She stirred a little but didn't wake up.

He walked up the stairs to his room with visions of Sally Kellerman's wet and naked body in his mind…

II

It was a touch stifling with the shade down and the window closed in his bedroom when he arrived. Pat pulled up the shade, opened the window, and a cool evening breeze began to fill his room.

Pat stripped down and crawled into his bed. He picked up his copy of "The Catcher in the Rye" and began to read where he last left off. After reading only a few pages, Pat slowly drifted off to sleep…

…He was standing in a room he doesn't recognize right away. It was not a very well lit area and there was only one tiny shaded window. As he turned around in a three sixty and examined his surroundings, he realized that he was in some sort of hotel room, or something. Cheap furniture sat against walls that had torn wallpaper covering them. There were two small antique-looking table lamps in this indiscrete room; one on the nightstand next to the bed, and one on top of a smallish dresser.

The room almost looked to him like the hotel room his mind's eye depicted in his book "The Catcher in the Rye."

The room was warm, tepid. It held the faint smells of former tenants. Pat could make out stale smoke from too many cigarettes, cheap perfume and what could maybe be the faded, slightly pungent smell of very old, sour urine.

There was a pull string hanging from the main light fixture on the ceiling in the center of this small room.

He spied a young girl sitting alone on the bed, and walked over to her. She had her head down looking at the floor which was covered in a worn out carpet that looked like it was from the thirties.

"What are you doing in here?" Pat asked her.

The girl lifted her head to face him and Pat saw it was Sally Kellerman's face that she wore. She looked at him and smiled.

"Maurice, the elevator boy sent me to you," she said to him.

She stood, and said, "My name is Sunny." She held out her hand to him.

"You must be Jim, and Maurice was right…you are attractive," she said and started to walk towards him.

Sunny had a very nice body, and was dressed rather like a whore, Pat thought, even though he wouldn't know a whore from a hoot owl. Even if a whore came up and kicked him, right square in the ass.

Pat looked at this attractive young woman with Sally Kellerman's face. What was she doing here…and where was here?

Pat took a timid uncertain step backwards.

"Don't be afraid, Jim. I was sent to you, for you," she said and took another step towards him, her smile widened.

"By Maurice…right," Pat said to this attractive, prostitute? He looked around the room for a way out. But did he really want to leave.

Why did this attractive woman scare him so?

"Yes, by Maurice. So, what shall we do, now, Jim?" she asked him as she stood in the middle of the room, hands on her hips.

Pat did not know what to say.

He wanted badly to reach out and touch this Sunny who wore Sally Kellerman's face.

Tentatively, Pat took a step forward…

Pat woke up and looked around a dark bedroom. His copy of "The Catcher in the Rye" lay on his bed next to him. He picked the book up and placed it on the nightstand next to the head of his bed. He then rolled over and went back to sleep.

He felt the start of sweat as it was building on his brow. Must still be fairly warm in his room, he figured.

Pat rolled over to his side and closed his eyes again, waiting for sleep to overtake him once more. He sure had been having some really bazaar dreams these past few days.

It seemed that they were dreams that, when mentioned out loud, got him beat up by Brian and everything.

What the hell was going on in his mind these days, Pat considered.

Secretly, he wanted that dream to come back and visit him, but it did not, and for the rest of the night his sleep was dreamless.

Chapter 11

Pat rode with the coach and the rest of the team on one of the Wahkashen school buses to Forester to play them on Saturday morning. He never got to go out onto the field at all that day. He didn't expect to, anyway. It didn't break Pat's heart, or his spirit, and the team got pounded.

Pat watched as the more powerful Forester team simply out hit, out pitched, and out ran the entire Wahkashen baseball team. Even when they were down by ten runs, Coach Unrich never called his name to take the field.

Pat listened to the guys bitch and complain at each other about the lack of attention on certain plays, or as they criticized one another on the apparent lack of hustle.

All the while, Pat tried not to smile as the team bickered amongst themselves for the entire nine innings.

The ride back was a long one, and the coach didn't have much to say.

Pat rode in silence, sitting alone on one of the bench seats.

He quit the team the following Monday.

I

The rest of the summer of nineteen seventy droned on lazily like a bee flying from one flower to another. Pat would pretend to go to baseball practice and never told anyone that he had actually quit the team when he went to practice Monday. He didn't have the heart to tell anyone…not his friends, and especially not his parents.

Pat wasn't sure why he didn't tell anyone that he decided to quit the baseball team. Maybe, he thought, it was all too embarrassing to admit. His parents knew, like Pat did, that he was not the 'star' of the team, but always told him how proud they were of him for his commitment to the team.

So every day he would pretend to show up for practice, because you just never know if someone was watching. He would hate to be caught by anyone not going to the park in the morning with his bat and glove.

He needed to be ready.

The boys met up at the pool nearly every day for swimming and playing tag, of course. Poor Dennis is all Pat could think. It sucked for him, but then again, he was also like the eager little puppy that never tired playing fetch. So, they would out swim Dennis and his banana boats, and he would stay 'it' for an hour or more until the gang got tired of the game.

At least Dennis was getting in more and more practice in his swimming, so that was a good thing for him; and it also made Pat feel a little better about playing tag with the poor kid.

Pat would practice his gainers and finally attempted one off of the high board after a few encouraging words from Dan Meyer.

His first couple of attempts were total fiascos, but they did not injure him, which was good. He tried one last time before school started and the pool closed down for the summer. He got to the top of the board, waited in line, concentrated and completed it in fine fashion. He figured he would truly be prepared for the next summer.

He'd sit in the sunbather's area and watch the divers, and the girls bathing in the sun. There always seemed to be the same group of girls from *that* class who wouldn't waste urine…laying out there every afternoon, but they sure were attractive, and Pat thought they knew it all along, as well.

He daydreamed about them while he was there beside them. Their lean tanned bodies glistened in the sun from the Hawaiian Tropics suntan lotion that they applied to their bodies.

He dreamed that some day, some day, he would be older and would quite possibly have a girl that attractive with him all the time. He would be the one who would be able to apply a coating of Hawaiian Tropic to their bodies.

That would be like, way cool, Pat thought.

He avoided Brian and the Three Stooges as much as possible. He would run into Brian a couple of times and take the taunting and name calling. Brian would push him around, Ed and/or Pete would trip him when Brian pushed him backwards, stuff like that, much to their delight.

It seemed to Pat that the simple things really amused the simple-minded.

He started to feel like a timid rabbit or one of those robins he always observed sitting on the garage maintaining vigil for oncoming problems. If Pat knew how to defend himself, and was of a build where he *could* defend himself, he wouldn't have to live looking over his shoulder all the time. But, that seemed to be the way of the world: eat or be eaten. He pretty much figured that he *was* living his life like a robin, or a timid rabbit, always looking over his shoulder before he made an attempt to do anything.

He didn't like it much, but sometimes life handed you lemons...

One day, Pat was riding home from the park and he had a run in with Brian.

"Hi, Pa-ty," Brian said to him as he pulled up along side of him and kicked his leg out hard enough to knock Pat from off of his bike onto the cruel waiting street below him.

Pat crashed hard and his legs were tangled up in the bike as it came down on top of him. He had also torn open a huge gash in his jeans and the knee below.

Brian got off of his bike and came at Pat lying on the ground under his bike.

"Get on your feet, pussy-boy," Brian hissed at him as he grabbed a couple of hands full of Pat's t-shirt.

"God DAMN it, Brian," Pat yelled at him as he was being jerked to his feet. He looked down to assess the damage to both his pants and his knee. "What the HELL is wrong with you? Why do you have to be such a big prick all of the time?"

"What did you just say to me?" Brian spit out and when he asked, spittle flew from his foul breathed mouth.

"Why are you always picking on me, you fat prick?" Pat spat back to him while wiping the spit from his face, knowing full well that he was about to get his ass handed to him.

"You are going to die for that, sissy boy," Brian growled and pulled his right arm back to deliver a blow that Pat would not soon forget.

Pat closed his eyes and braced for the impact.

He even began to say a little prayer to God to make it quick. Pat didn't feel like suffering today.

Just before Brian could bring forward the punch that would definitely put out all of Pat's lights, Pat heard a scream that came from behind Brian.

Pat opened his eyes just enough to see Mike jump onto Brian's back screaming vulgarities and punching Brian on the side of his head.

"HEY!!" Brian screamed and let go of Pat's shirt for a second as he struggled with Mike who was hanging onto Brian with one arm around his neck, while the other hand was hitting him as rapidly as possible.

That was all the time Pat needed.

Pat curled up his fist and punched Brian as hard as he could.

The blow struck Brian dead on the end of his nose.

Pat heard, and felt, the sickening 'crunch' of the cartilage that made up the structure of one's nose.

Blood splattered and flew, then immediately began to pour from Brian's nose as Brian's knees buckled, and down to the pavement he went.

Mike rode him all the way down to the ground like a bulldog on a bear hunt.

Brian put his hands to his broken nose and said, through his hands, "You broke my nose, Pat." The sound of Brian's voice through his hands and through his busted nose almost caused Pat to laugh aloud. But he didn't.

Mike finally let go of the death grip he held around Brian's neck, and walked over to stand next to Pat.

They gave each other 'five', and when he got his breathing under control, Mike spoke to Brian.

"We've had enough of your shit, Brian. We are not going to take it anymore."

Brian muttered something (probably derogatory, Pat suspected) although the boys really couldn't understand what he said through his hands.

"The next time you have anything to say, or want to do to Pat," Mike continued, and gave Brian a light kick with the side of his foot, "you say or do to me. Do you understand?"

Brian lay on the ground with blood pouring from his hands and said nothing.

Mike gave him another kick and asked him again, "Do you understand me, Brian?"

"Yes," Brian screamed. "I understand."

It sounded like, *"Die dundetand."*

"Good. Let's get out of here, Pat and leave him alone," Mike said to Pat and they walked over to where Pat's bike lie waiting.

Pat looked over his shoulder and watched as Brian finally sat up in the street and was amazed at how much blood was still flowing through his fingers.

"Where the hell did you come from?" Pat asked Mike as he slowly picked up his bike.

"I forgot to tell you something really important," Mike answered him and then looked back at Brian. "I jumped on my bike and rode as fast as I could to catch you. I just happened to see Brian kick you off of your bike. So, as quietly as I could I snuck up behind him. Just in time, too."

"Man, you got that right," Pat said and looked down at his damaged knee. "So, what was it you wanted to tell me, anyway?" Pat asked when he looked back up at Mike.

"Shit," Mike answered him with a slight smile on his face, "I don't know. I can't remember now."

The boys laughed, gave each other another 'five' and Pat headed home once again.

II

The only other fun thing the gang did between the times of Pat quitting the baseball team (much to the approval of the guys, after he spilled his guts…Lenny said Pat wasn't much of a ball player, anyway) and the first day of school was to hang out at their other favorite swimming spot on the Otter Tail River just outside Bulliford, MN. The Otter Tail and the Bois de Sioux rivers joined to form the Red River.

The Red River was the only river in North America that flowed north, instead of south. Most people did not know this fact that The Red River was the only river in North America that flowed north, instead of south; then ended its journey at Lake Winnipeg.

The gang would ride their bikes out about 3 miles to the Otter Tail. There they would hang out, play grab ass in the water and smoke cigarettes. They would lie in the sun and bask like spoiled pedigree dogs. They would play another version of tag, albeit without Dennis, in the slow moving river.

The river was only about four and a half feet deep, for the most part, and it was only about twenty five feet across. There was a slight current, and it wasn't heavy enough to worry about being swept away at any given time. Their swimming spot was right on an oxbow and the sand would accumulate on the curved side of the river. At max, the depth of the river was no more than six feet. It was a dark muddy brown river, but it held fairly clean water for the boys to swim.

Pat's mother really didn't like him swimming in the Otter Tail because there were no lifeguards, or adults, for the most part, in case there was trouble. But, all three boys were strong swimmers and so they would watch out for each other.

Pat really enjoyed being out here at the river, more so than the swimming pool only because it was a natural setting. There weren't any attractive young girls to look at and daydream about out here, but he was with his best friends and that more than made up for it.

The day was beautiful with a clear blue sky uninterrupted by even the most minuscule of clouds. There was a light breeze that moved the short native grass around, and was just strong enough to keep the majority of bugs away from you as you lie on the banks and dream about Karla, Candi and red-headed, large breasted mechanics.

Pat just crawled out of the water to grab a cigarette just in time to watch Mike and Lenny as Mike was throwing Lenny up over his shoulder in an attempt to aid Lenny in doing a forward flip.

It didn't work so well.

Pat sure enjoyed being friends with Mike and Lenny, and he was quite sure that their friendship would last a long time.

Later that afternoon, a good friend of Lenny's (her name was Ann, and she graduated from Wahkashen about a year ago) brought two of her friends, Ben and his girlfriend Alice, who were visiting from Alaska, out to the river.

She also brought with her a couple of cases of Old Mil. The boys didn't mind when she joined them, as long as she was willing to spread the wealth with her Old Mil. Which she was, Pat discovered.

All of them were all very nice to the boys. They didn't act like they were older, and therefore better than Pat and the gang, and that was cool with the gang.

When Ann, Ben and Alice showed up with all of that beer, Pat, Mike and Lenny knew it was going to be a great day. Everyone sat back and drank beer, suntanned, smoked cigarettes and Ben and Alice answered a great deal of questions pertaining to living in Alaska.

Ben, who was originally from somewhere in Minnesota, knew Ann from a time out of mind, but had been in Alaska working for the past five years as a guide for a huge guided hunting service. He had some great tales about the wilderness in which he would escort people on hunts that had no more business in the wilderness than a chicken would have on Wall Street. The boys laughed really hard at that. Pat really liked Ben. He was as funny as he was tall, powerfully built and good looking, for a guy. But Pat especially liked the fact that he was full of really cool tales and adventures in which he had participated.

"So how long *have* you lived in Alaska now, Ben?" Pat asked him after taking a swallow of beer.

"Let's see….I think it's been five years now…right Alice?" Ben asked.

"Yeah," she answered him. "I'm pretty sure it's been five years."

The boys continued to ask lots of questions, and also kept staring at Alice who was blond, about six feet tall and all legs. She was very well built; very well built and very easy on the boys' eyes.

They would ask Ben questions about the wild life, and about the scenery (which was real good right now, Pat thought as he would sneak another peek at Alice who was sitting cross-legged and looking really fine) and how a person was able to try to get a job like that, where and who would he talk to.

"If you are interested when you finish school," Ben told them "you just get a hold of me and I will give you the advice that you need. We are always looking for good people who know their way around in the woods to help guide these people."

The day was turning out to be a great one, indeed. What with Ben spinning his yarns, Alice looking quite delectable, and all of this Old Mil to drink...what more could a hot-blooded thirteen year old male want out of life?

Pat was also starting to feel the affects of the Old Mil...with the help of the sun beating down on them.

Yes, it was turning out to be a *great* day.

What made the day even better was the fact that, after sitting in the hot Minnesota sun for a couple of hours drinking beer, Alice commented that she was hot (all puns intended) and wanted to go swimming. Ben told her to go right ahead, and he would join her later. However, she commented that she forgot to bring her suit with her. That didn't seem to bother her at all. She didn't even think twice about it as she began to take off all of her clothing right there in front of God and everyone.

And when she started to take off her clothing, she took off everything! This was all completed very much to the delight of the gang.

Alice was very well developed (Mike and Lenny speculated later when they were alone that she was at the very least a 36 to 38, double D...although Pat had really no clue what any of that meant, he was positive that she had some extremely large tits) and nicely tanned. Her breasts held the faint tan lines of a slinky swimsuit; although the tan line was discernable, it was still quite pale as if she did a great deal of sun tanning, sans swimsuits.

The gang sat there, wide-eyed, feeling a little drunk. All of them were staring at Alice (much to the enjoyment of Ben who couldn't help but snicker as he witnessed the gap-mouthed thirteen year old boys staring at his Alice) and tried so hard not to show it. They tried very hard, but Pat didn't think they were fooling anyone but themselves.

The one thing that Pat saw that really threw him for a loop was the fact that Alaskan women, apparently, did not shave under their arms.

It was either that, or Alice was a true Hippy woman, Pat thought. Most hippies, Pat had heard, were a little lax in their personal hygiene; and, therefore, Alice must a true hippy?

Now to some people this would be a complete turn-off, but with the way Alice was built, Pat didn't think the boys noticed. And if they did, they could have really given two shits about that.

Pat wasn't quite sure if she were a hippy or that Alaskan women were just like hippies, but she did have some nice tits…and THAT'S a fact, Pat thought in his alcohol induced mind.

Pat noticed her hairy armpits when she lifted her arms up and removed the t-shirt she was wearing. She was fairly full of hair under her arms, like a man, Pat thought. Pat really didn't care, and cared even less when she actually reached behind her back to unhook her bra to set those massive creatures free.

Pat and the gang were very attentive when she got the clasp of her bra undone.

Pat felt like screaming, "*Set them* FREE!" and then getting up, clapping his hands and stomping his feet cheering, but thought that would not go over very well with her boyfriend; and so once again, discretion raised its head in front of Pat's eyes.

The boys simply watched her and 'what's-his-name' swimming in the water. They stayed in the water for about an hour, and even the boys went in after a while, but gave Alice and 'what's-his-name' a wide berth.

What the hell was his name? Pat thought as he stared drunkenly and directly at Alice. The only thing he seemed to remember extremely at that time was the large set of nicely tanned breasts that accompanied the gang and him in the water.

She appeared very buoyant for some reason, Pat thought.

The boys finally got out of the water so they could watch her better. A 'bird's eye view', as it were.

They sat there and sun-dried, smoked cigarettes and tried to hide their growing hard-on's, all while they drank beer watching Alice play grab ass with...Ben; that was his name.

Pat thought, his mind swirled with the aid of the beer, that the gang would have gladly given their left foot to have the ability to play a little grab ass with Alice...lovely Alice.

After her swim with her boyfriend, she pretty much just laid around naked for the rest of the time she was there along side Otter Tail River, sipping beer, teasing the young boys to no end, near the end of August in nineteen seventy.

The boys didn't mind at all.

In fact, the boys would dream about Alice for years later, which they didn't mind either.

Part Two

October 1970

Chapter 1

School is a school is a school, to jokingly quote Gertrude Stein (as she had been misquoted and misinterpreted for decades since the publishing of "Sacred Emily" in 1922); but in the case of the Wahkashen public school district, it was a truism that: school is a school...

At least in the junior high school, it was true. Wahkashen junior high school was typical of most schools, junior high or not, in the nineteen seventies that they all had a look to them like early colonial penal system buildings built during the turn-of-the-century: two stories, red and brown brick which housed large, two pane, penal looking square windows (sans bars, of course) that never seemed to open correctly. No matter how hard one would try, those windows never seemed to open more than an inch or two, at *the* very least. Then, they would not close after you were able to squeeze out an inch or two of fresh air from them.

The school year started off without a major hitch for Pat and the boys. They had been talking about pheasant hunting along the Red River and the deer hunting season that was coming up, quickly, and how their favorite football teams were or were not going to play this year. This was an almost constant topic from the beginning of the school year until well into the spring of the following year.

Pat never did make much of a ball player on the baseball team during the summer, and hoped to maybe make the wrestling team as a feather weight. He had to work a little harder than most boys as his stature was a tish more on the slight side. He planned to spend a little more time in the weight room amid the laughter of the older boys who were so much larger than Pat. Maybe if I keep at it, Pat thought, those boys would not be laughing for long…but he had his reservations about all of that.

He spent most of his time with Mike and Lenny both in and out of school. They were his gang, after all; or at least he was a part of that gang, anyway. He liked the idea of being a part of that gang. It fit him to know that he belonged with those two guys. They accepted him, and he was way cool with that.

Pat could be himself around Lenny and Mike. He knew he would never be laughed at, unless Pat said or did something so lame that he deserved it. He would even laugh at himself as the gang would tease him about it.

Yes, Pat enjoyed being a part of the gang.

On October 2nd Billy Martin was named manager of the Detroit Tigers after a hitch with the Minnesota Twins. His brashness would cause him to only manager the Tigers for two years before moving on to a more infamous career. That career would live and die so many times over the next two decades that the only ones who could keep up with it were Billy Martin, and the sportswriters who made a living off of him.

On that very same day, a plane carrying Wichita State University football team to a game in Utah crashed in the Rocky Mountains after the plane clipped the treetops, killing 31 of the 40 people on board. It was the worst college sports team tragedy in history at that time.

These incidents had no affect on Pat's life; but still, there was something ominous hanging in the crisp autumn North Dakota air. It was something dark and destructive that no one could see coming. But nonetheless, it *was* coming, and quickly; and there was nothing anyone could do about it. It was on the move like a freight train bearing down on the hapless maiden lying tied and vulnerable on the railroad tracks.

It was foreboding and sinister. It moved like a rapid, secret shadow in the gloomiest corner of the scariest house on the block.

Mindless, senseless, merciless and so unnecessary; it had been described in so many different ways. It was so definite and final. It was ancient and ever changing in its destructive force. It was going to turn the world completely upside down for many people whether they liked it or not.

It was unavoidable, unstoppable and unpredictable.

It was insensitive and could not be bartered with, nor could it be convinced to take its business elsewhere.

Its business was here and now, and it was futile to try to and ignore the fact that it was on the move, and its next stop…was Wahkashen, ND.

It seemed like October was going to be a tough month for Pat in nineteen seventy…

I

Pat had a couple of run-ins with Brian Osterman and his Stooges this month alone. Although Brian never really did anything more than taunt Pat in front of his cronies, Pat didn't think much of the run-ins. God how he hated Brian and his cronies (may his mother forgive him his thoughts), but he knew Brian would be too afraid to do anything to him now ever since the day Mike and him had broken Brian's nose.

Pat was sitting in band practice at around 1:50 pm on Wednesday, 28 October, 1970, when the practice was interrupted by the principal, Mr. Taylor. He knocked on the door, opened it without waiting for a response from the Band Director, Mr. Pearson, and gestured for Mr. Pearson to follow him into the hallway where they could have a short conversation.

Pat set his instrument down on his leg and immediately began talking to Scott Winston next to him. The autumn sun was shining through the second story windows and it reflected off of the bright brass cymbals that were hanging on the southeast corner of the band room, right behind the tympanis and drum kits. The reflected light from those cymbals was warm even though the outside temperature was not.

Pat turned his eyes towards the door every now and then to see what was going on. He saw the two men talking, he saw Mr. Pearson turn his face towards the small window in the double doors that led back into the band room. He could see that there was a troubled, poignant look on Mr. Pearson's face. And, Pat swore that when Mr. Pearson did look back through the window, he was looking directly at him.

Pat turned back towards Scott and continued the small talk that they started earlier...only to be interrupted.

"Pat," Mr. Pearson said looking directly at him after he re-entered the room again with Mr. Taylor in tow.

"Pat McCray," Mr. Pearson said again when no one answered him.

Pat turned away from the conversation he was holding with Scott when he heard his name mentioned, and looked directly at Mr. Pearson.

Pat raised his hand and pointed at himself as if to say, "me?"

"Yes, Pat, you," Mr. Pearson said to him. "Leave your instrument and come down here, please."

Pat turned one more time to look at Scott and see if there may be an answer there somewhere on his face as to why he was being called down in front of class.

Mr. Pearson turned and whispered something into Mr. Taylor's ear as Pat stood up, and Pat was dying...just dying to know what he was saying to him. It had to be something very terrible or something so appalling as to cause Mr. Taylor's face to sag into a slight frown that was either disgust or pain. It was as if Mr. Pearson had stuck something awful tasting into Mr. Taylor's mouth.

Pat set his instrument down on his chair immediately after he vacated it, and began the tumultuous task off climbing over and around the other students in the row. It was a slow task as his area of concern was more in the middle of the row than on the outside.

A deep furrow had appeared on Pat's forehead as he checked his index card file in his mind as to why he would be singled out of class like this. He had done nothing in the past few days to warrant any reprisals. There was no reason that he could think of...at this time. He was quite sure that whatever it was, the memory would come flooding back into his mind at the very first mention by either of these men who waited for him at the front of the class.

After what felt like a half an hour and getting past a gazillion staring eyes of Pat's classmates, he finally came to rest in front of the man who had called for him.

Mr. Pearson leaned down towards him and said "Pat," and then, placed his hand on Pat's shoulder, "I want you to go with Mr. Taylor, please."

Pat turned his face towards the waiting principal, Mr. Taylor, as a hard lump of fear settled in his throat. He tried to swallow, and found that this hard object of fear which lodged itself in his throat would not allow that to happen. It felt as though he had swallowed the world's largest jaw breaker, and it stuck there like Benny Swanson's head did when he tried to stick his head through the opening in the back of the classroom chairs in English last week.

Benny's antics were funny; this thing stuck in Pat's throat was anything but funny. It was a full, yet empty *something* lodged tightly in his throat. All the swallowing in the world would not dislodge it.

He turned back to Mr. Pearson who simply smiled, a half-hearted smile, and then he stood and turned to face the class once more.

Pat turned back to Mr. Taylor who was now holding one side of the double doors open for him. As Pat headed towards the open door and the hallway just beyond it, he heard Mr. Pearson say, "OK, sorry for the interruption…now, where were we…?"

Pat entered the hallway with Mr. Taylor who did not talk but merely motioned with his right hand that Pat should take the lead for their walk to wherever they were going. Pat figured it was down to the office, but still, for the life of him he could not figure out why.

"You know whatever this is, Mr. Taylor," Pat said to him while trying to keep up Mr. Taylor's tall long-legged gait on his own young thirteen year old legs, "I didn't do it; and I have witnesses," Pat said to him with a tone of humor in his voice.

"Humm, I don't doubt that, Pat," Mr. Taylor said with a slight, sort of choked-up chuckle. "I don't doubt that at all."

Pat looked up at the principal as they walked down the long hallway to places unknown to see why he had produced such a strange chuckle. They walked the hallway together; Pat and the principal, for the next few minutes and neither said a word.

Pat and his escort finally reached their objective: the main office, after a few minutes in which that lump of fear would not, could not be passed down the throat by a simple gulp. Pat had swallowed numerous times on the way to their destination, but that lump would not dissolve or dissipate.

They entered the main lobby of the office.

There was a large 'L' shaped counter behind which all of the daily work to keep the school functioning happened. It also kept all of the secretaries in check to the rear of it; as well as it served to keep the school children in check in front of it.

The principal's office was to the left of the counter, and its door was open. Mr. Taylor motioned for Pat to enter his office in front of him. As Pat crossed the threshold of the office, he noticed with the aid of his peripheral vision that there was someone else in his office already. That someone else was sitting in a chair off to the left of the doorway.

II

Pat turned to see who was already here and noticed it was his sister, Penny, and she was crying…and by the looks of it, had been crying for some time. Penny was wearing her gym clothes as if she were in pulled out of Gym class, which of course she had at this hour.

"Penny!" Pat cried out and went to her. He got down on one knee in front of her to find out what had happened to make her cry. "Are you hurt?"

Pat began to look for blood, abrasions or anything to cause her to be crying so. "Why are you crying…Penny?"

Penny was crying and sobbing way too hard for her to answer him.

Pat turned and looked up at the principal and asked, "What's the matter with her, Mr. Taylor?"

He noticed that a secondary door between the principal's office and the main office behind the counter where the secretaries worked was standing open as well, and there were two of the school's secretaries staring in at him with a look of pain, sorrow and sympathy on their faces.

Mr. Taylor straightforwardly reached over and slowly, deliberately and quietly closed that door to keep the rubberneckers out of his office. Then he went to the main door and closed that one in the same fashion.

Penny was still weeping a little but it was more like sobbing, uncontrollably now. Pat watched as Mr. Taylor walked slowly back past him towards his desk, where he calmly sat down, clasped his hands together before him on the top of his desk, looked at Pat directly and said, "Pat, would you please take the seat next to your sister," in a voice that was void of all emotion. It was either that or else his voice was filled with way too much emotion that it sounded dead and buried to Pat's ears.

Pat looked at Mr. Taylor. And although he understood his request, getting up off of his knee was one of the hardest things Pat ever had to do. The tone of Mr. Taylor's voice filled Pat with a sense of dread that he had never, ever felt before. He was about two seconds away from telling Mr. Taylor, "*...with all due respect, Sir, I really don't want to do that right now. I think it would be best if I stay right here in front of my weeping sister. I think I would like to say 'No', and be done with it, thank you very much.*"

But instead, Pat wordlessly rose to his feet, and slowly turned to sit in the chair next to Penny and face Mr. Taylor and whatever terrible news he was holding inside like so many bad dreams.

Pat looked at his sobbing sister and back at Mr. Taylor as his knees started to bend and he found the waiting seat next to Penny.

"Mr. Taylor, I don't think I want to hear what you..." Pat began but was cut off by Mr. Taylor's solemn voice.

"Pat," he started, stopped for a second to clear his throat and then continued, "I have some terrible news," and then he paused again for what felt like three hours.

Pat continued to stare directly at Mr. Taylor. He could not take his eyes away from Mr. Taylor's face, even if he wanted to.

"*I have some terrible news.*" Those words hung in the air in front of his desk like a dark cloud all charged with rain. Pat wanted with all of his might to reach out and squash that cloud so he would not have to hear the *terrible news* that it carried.

Pat stared at Mr. Taylor and then turned his head back to his sister. *What could be so terrible that it was a cause for all of this? Pat thought.*

"Pat…" Mr. Taylor said and looked down at his hands for a second. Pat's eyes joined him and he noticed that Mr. Taylor's hands were trembling a little.

"Pat, this is very difficult for me to say, so I am just going to say it. Pat, your father passed away today."

Pat sat there for a second letting his mind chew on what it had been fed by his ears. Penny immediately began crying harder.

"I am so…so, very sorry, Pat, Penny," Mr. Taylor said with all the humility he could muster. It sounded very sincere to Pat, and in fact it was sincere; Pat knew in his heart that Mr. Taylor was truly sorry for having to be the bearer of bad news. He was positive that Mr. Taylor was also sincere in the fact that it was a terrible thing to have happen to his father.

Pat just stared. He was unsure of just what he was to do next.

He can't be dead, Pat thought. I was just there to see him yesterday before he had to close the shop. I saw him last night and said 'good night' to him before I went upstairs to bed.

"Your mother called," Mr. Taylor said to both Pat and Penny, and which broke Pat out of his trance, "there are some friends of your family on their way here to pick you and Penny up and take you home. OK?" Mr. Taylor finished.

Pat nodded, slowly, and then sat there with his hands in his lap and stared out the window directly behind Mr. Taylor's desk.

Mr. Taylor couldn't be fibbing about something like that, could he, Pat wondered? Is my father really dead?

He didn't respond to Mr. Taylor after that, even if he wanted to. He felt like he was just anesthetized and was slowly coming out of it; and he figured that strange sensation of regaining your wits after the anesthesia started to wear off would stay with him…well, probably, forever.

He heard Mr. Taylor as he got up from his chair and came around the front of his desk. He heard Mr. Taylor ask Penny if she was ready to go change into her street clothes now, but he registered what he heard as well as a deaf dog would if asked to fetch a stick that had just been tossed. Pat did not move his head or blink an eye.

Pat sat there starred straight over the top of Mr. Taylor's desk and out the window that was behind his desk. He saw the leaves of the trees and the various colors that they had been turning. For autumn was here and not far behind winter was approaching. The leaves were accepting the fact that their time had come, and they were dying. These leaves had succumbed to their fate with no resistance other than to show their possible disappointment that summer was over by conveying their displeasure in their various shades of expiration.

It seemed so easy for a leaf to yield to its fate: that with the changing of the seasons, they must die in order to have a re-birth in the spring. It seemed so perfectly natural for leaves to die.

It appeared to Pat to be so *unnatural* to have his father die.

His father was not a dying leaf. He would not be reappearing in the spring like the leaves would be.

Pat was so lost in thoughts concerning death that he did not realize that he was still sitting in the Mr. Taylor's office; however, after he witnessed several of those dead leaves fall impassibly from one of the large oaks that surrounded the school while he was staring out the window of the principal's office, he become conscious of the fact that he was all alone.

All alone.

That's just fitting, Pat thought, watching those dead leaves.

It was then the tears began to well up behind his young green eyes.

Chapter 2

Pat walked out of the school's front doors after it was confirmed that people were coming to pick Penny and him up in front of the school. Penny left the principal's office so she could change clothes, and Pat simply walked out the front door like a zombie on valium.

He heard the obligatory words of sympathy coming from behind him as he left the main office. He heard them, but his brain simply did not register what or who had spoken to him.

He wasn't even sure if he responded to their sympathetic words or not.

He was empty. He had no thoughts running through his head what so ever. His brain was still chewing on what it was fed, but it seemed that his mind was having trouble interpreting the information that he himself had just been given.

He walked out the front door with no more ambition than a man on death row walking to his ultimate fate. If a loose brick would have, at that particular time, came free and fell from the second story above the front door and hit Pat directly on the head, it was doubtful Pat would have even flinched.

Numb.

That's what it was. He was completely numb.

He made it to the street in the front of the school and found one of the benches that the school had installed. They had them installed for the students and faculty, and then they bolted them to the ground; apparently to deter criminals from stealing and furnishing their homes with ugly black wrought iron park benches with wooden slates for seats and back rests.

He sat on one of the benches out front and felt the cool autumn breeze blowing all around him. The leaves on the sidewalk were swirling around his feet. He watched them as a few blew up and over his shoes, and then they would haphazardly blow out into the gutter. He heard the dry, scratchy, scruffy sound they made as they fluttered away from him with little resistance.

He sat there on that cold bench, quietly and alone with his head hung low and his eyes open and fixed to the ground in front of him. He knew he was waiting for something, but for the life of him he couldn't remember what it was. Hell, he wasn't even sure why he was sitting out on this cold bench in front of his school watching dead leaves dance all around him.

So, until he could figure out why he was here in the first place, he continued to watch the dead leaves as they did the foxtrot in the region of his feet.

Why was he so cold? He did a quick survey of his clothing and discovered he didn't even have his jacket on. What the hell was wrong with him, he wondered? No wonder he was cold.

Where *was* his coat, he wondered? How come he was not wearing it right now in this cold air, he also questioned? His mother would be yelling at him right now had she seen him sitting out here without his coat.

'*Catch yourself a cold*', he could hear his mother saying to him.

How stupid was he for sitting outside the school on one of their bolted black iron benches in October without wearing his coat.

He thought he should probably get up and go get his coat out of the locker that was assigned to him by the school.

As Pat questioned himself about his actions, an older car pulled up and parked a little past him in the designated school parking slots, but Pat didn't register it anymore than he would have thought that there were even things *like* cars in this world.

Pat continued to watch as the leaves danced their ballet of death for him. He was amazed that he could be as mesmerized by something as simple as dancing leaves, but he was unable to turn his eyes away from the show.

What was I just thinking about, Pat wondered? It was important, I'm sure of it...

"Pat," a voice called to him from a million miles away.

He didn't answer. He thought that maybe he had imagined his name being called...and why in the world would anyone want to call him now when he was busy watching the dancing dead leaves, and freezing his ass off?

I should really get up and go get my coat...I'm freezing, Pat thought, but he could not take his eyes off of those leaves as they skipped and swirled at his feet.

"Pat."

He heard his name being called again, but it still sounded like it was coming from a different dimension.

Pat finally raised his head and turned his eyes away from the mesmerizing dead leaves that held his attention so well long enough to see Elmer and Janet West were walking towards him. They both looked as if they had been crying and each held a sympathetic look on their face.

Elmer and Janet were Howard and Delores' oldest, and dearest friends from the day when the McCray's had first moved to Wahkashen after they were married.

Janet came over and sat down next to Pat. She placed her hand on his leg and tapped it twice and then gave it a good squeeze.

"How are you doing, kiddo?" she asked him.

Pat only had to look up at her and all of his silent tears came flooding out. He threw himself at her.

"It's going to be alright, Pat," she said to him and pulled him to her as tears began to stream down her cheeks once more. She turned her face up to her husband who simply stood there with his hands stuffed deep into his pockets.

Elmer really had no idea what to say or do for the boy, so he succumbed to let Janet take care of it. He could only stand there and unconsciously kick at loose pebbles at his feet that had so suddenly earned his interest.

Pat buried his face into Janet's side as the sobs began to shake his body.

All Janet could do was hold him, rock him a bit making the customary *'shushing'* sounds and drop huge tears onto the top of Pat's head as they sat there and waited for Penny to emerge from the school.

I

After Janet and Elmer brought the children home, they slipped into the kitchen to get a cup of coffee as Pat and Penny joined their mother on the living room couch. The wailing soon filled the room and spilled into the kitchen so much, Janet thought she would never be able to make it. However, she knew she had to remain strong for her best friend, and so she grabbed her cup of coffee and stepped outside to get a breath of fresh air.

Elmer, as stoic as most men were, continued to sit at the kitchen table and sip his coffee. He knew the best thing for him to do at this time was to stay out of everyone's way, and that is just what he was going to do.

Elmer sat there and reflected on Howard, and the friendship that the two had maintained for almost fifteen years. He thought about all of the projects they had worked on together; all of the hunting trips they had taken together, the numerous beers that they consumed well into the night while solving all of the world's problems standing in Howard's garage.

It was definitely going to be quite different with his best friend, a man he'd known for the past fifteen years, now gone. Elmer would not have a companion like Howard in his life anymore, he didn't think.

Amazing, Elmer thought, how quickly things like this can change in a person's life. How short and precious life was, and how quickly it can be taken from you.

The phone started ringing, and Elmer jumped up to answer it before it could ring twice.

"Hello," Elmer said, "the McCray residence." He stood there and listened for a second and then looked up to see Janet coming back in from outside. Apparently she had heard the phone ring as well.

"No, this is Elmer West," Elmer answered to whoever was on the other side of the line. "Yes, of course. I will see to it…thank you. Yes…no, I understand. OK. Good by."

Janet didn't have to ask; her eyes did all of the asking.

"That was the funeral home," Elmer said quietly to his wife so Delores wouldn't hear. "They talked with the coroner and he has begun his autopsy. They figured they would be able to talk business tomorrow morning."

Elmer took a small step backwards to look in at Delores and the kids, in the living room, and then he continued. "They said they spoke with the police chief as well and that the cause of death, by the chief's estimation was natural causes; but they won't know for sure until the coroner completes his autopsy. I guess it's because he was found in the garage, and so it needs to be done."

Janet looked at him and nodded her head. She looked very tired, Elmer thought, and we just got the news a couple of hours ago.

"They asked if we were going to stay with them for a while and if they should call the Bethel church and send the minister over. I told them I would call him."

Janet nodded her head again and lifted her cup with a very shaky hand to take a sip of her coffee. Her eyes felt as if they were burning, and for some reason hot coffee seemed to be the fix that she needed to cure the burning affect.

"What was the minister's name again, honey?" Elmer asked her.

"Pastor Hartman, I believe is Bethel's minister. In fact, I'm quite sure of it."

"I'll look in the book for his number. You want to go in and check on them?" he said with a nod of his head towards the living room. "Maybe they could use something to drink, or more Kleenex…or something…I don't know."

Elmer dug in the drawer below where the phone sat to look up the phone number as Janet slipped past him and into the living room.

Just as Elmer was going to pick-up the phone to dial the number that he had found, the phone rang and caused him to jump a bit and clutch at the front of his chest.

Shit, he thought, I sure wish the phone would quit doing that. That scared the hell out of me.

He picked it up again real quick and almost dropped it in his haste.

"Hello, McCray residence," he said in a voice that felt slightly harried, but he tried to disguise it.

"Is Pat there?" the voice on the other side of the line spoke.

"Well, yes he is; however, I don't think he is prepared to take any phone calls just yet," and then Elmer leaned back to see Janet kneeling in front of Delores and hugging her and the kids all at the same time. The sobbing and weeping began again in earnest.

"In fact," Elmer told the person on the phone after he witnessed the event going on in the living room, "I'm quite sure he isn't. Who is this…maybe I can take a message for him?"

"Yeah? Oh, yeah. Tell him that Mike called would ya? And he can call me, whenever he gets a chance; or when he feels up to it…or whatever…"

"OK, Mike, I will give him the message. And, Mike…"

"Yeah?"

"Thanks for calling your friend. He'll be glad to hear it."

"Yeah…OK. Thanks."

Elmer thought he heard a stifled sob from Mike before he hung up the phone at his end. Elmer quietly replaced the phone and then thought: Pat was going to need every friend he had now, for sure.

Elmer started to go to the table to get his coffee, and then stopped and turned back because he remembered he was going to call the minister…Pastor…what's-his-name.

II

Pastor Hartman showed up at a little past five. Janet was making soup and sandwiches and trying to convince the McCray's that they needed to eat something. People would start to bring over covered dishes as news of Howard's demise would spread like wild fire.

Delores came into the kitchen over an hour ago and had simply sat at the table and was continually moving the salt-n-pepper shakers around. Apparently, things were out of whack in her world right now, and it all started with those *damned* salt-n-pepper shakers.

Pastor Hartman was in the living room consoling the children, one by one. When he first arrived, he had spoken with Delores, and then he sent her into the kitchen for a cup of her own coffee. He then went back into the living room and spoke with Penny, and now he was talking with Pat.

"You know son," Pastor Hartman began, "there is just no telling when God is going to call you up into Heaven to be with him through all of eternity, so we all need to be prepared for that day…every day of our lives. I remember back when you were confirmed how proud your mom and dad were of your accomplishment."

"I remember that day, too," Pat said, not lifting his head.

"Your baptism and confirmation were just a couple of small steps to the passage right for you to join God in Heaven…when your time comes."

"That's what they said in class, all right." Pat replied.

"That's right," the Pastor said. "And for God to call on your father at such a young age…well; there must have been a good reason for it. Perhaps God needed a good mechanic in Heaven, and so he wanted the very best mechanic that he could find. Therefore, he chose your father.

"You see son, there comes a time in everyone's life when one must except the mysteries of God's will," Pastor Hartman continued. "In the time of death, I have always found comfort in knowing that when people that I know and that I love, die, they are in a far better place than they were here on earth…and that alone gives me comfort to defeat the sorrow that I feel."

Or maybe, Pat thought to himself, *maybe God was really just a spoiled, childish, selfish punk who would actually take a man, as young as his father, away from his wife and children who loved him and needed him far more than God ever could, and ever would. Maybe that's why he took my Father away from me. Did you stop to think about THAT…Pastor Hartman?*

As soon as he thought that, he felt bad and wished he could take that thought back, because he knew it was not fair to think that way. He could no more change things out of his control any more than he could bench press a '57 Chevy.

"Yeah, maybe that was God's intentions," was what Pat really said. "I will try to find comfort thinking my dad IS in a better place," Pat continued.

"My door is always open to you, Pat," Pastor Hartman said rising to his feet. "Don't be afraid to come and see me when things get confusing in your life. Don't try to deal with all of this grief by yourself, Pat. Grief will eat at you like a cancer…"

Then he stopped, very abruptly, highly noticeably, and turned his face towards Pat. Pat noticed that the Pastor was beginning to show a light shade of red creeping up slowly from his collar.

Pat wondered why he stopped so suddenly.

"I'm sorry, Pat," he said to him. "I shouldn't have used an analogy 'like cancer'. We are not sure quite yet how your father passed away, but it was so sudden that it couldn't have possibly been from cancer, but that is not the analogy that I should have used. I should be more careful in my choice of words."

"That's OK, Pastor," Pat told him. "It was a good talk. I feel better already."

"You are going to be just fine, young man," Pastor Hartman said and stuck out his hand.

Pat reached out and grabbed the Pastor's hand and gave a firm shake, just like his dad taught him. Then his eyes began to swell with tears again thinking about how his dad taught him how important it was to have a firm grip for a handshake.

The Pastor reached over and gave Pat a couple of soft pats on his shoulder and turned around and headed for the kitchen.

Pat sat down on the couch again and overheard Pastor Hartman talking to his mom in the kitchen.

His mom thanked him over and over for coming to their house while she was walking him to the door for him to leave.

The house became very quiet after the Pastor left and the door closed behind him. Elmer, Janet and his mom were still in the kitchen, but were either not talking, or were talking very quietly. Penny was up in her room, and more than likely had cried herself to sleep.

Pat lay back on the couch and stared at the ceiling for a while. He enjoyed the quiet for the time being. He knew that this quiet would not last for very long as relatives were probably already packed and surely on the move.

Pat very much wanted to see his dad. He asked his mom if he could see his dad when he got up tomorrow morning, but she told him that the city had taken their father away. She said that Pat would have to wait until the day of the funeral before he would get to see his dad again.

III

Funeral...
It's just a word, but it sounded so ominous and sinister to Pat.
Funeral.
It sounded so final.
Funeral.
He would have to wait until the *funeral* to see his dad again, she said.

Pat had only been to one funeral in his life and that was when they buried his Grandpa Timmerman last year. He remembered going into the funeral home with his parents...and his sister, of course.

It was full of flowers, he remembered. Even if those flowers were not in full view, they were well represented in olfactory capacity.

The carpet was worn when you crossed the threshold, Pat noticed. The weave was very different, he thought. It was dark and foreboding, when you would think that carpet in a funeral home would be a color meant to contrast the sorrow, the disappoint that filled this room with people.

That was Pat's thought, anyway.

There were lots of people there, he recalled; aunts, uncles and a great deal of cousins. Then there were the people he didn't know who more than likely felt like Pat did at this time of mourning: confused, and disoriented.

Who were these people of Grandpa's age? Certainly friends and fellow farmers from down the road. Some were probably merely slight acquaintances here to get a good meal, out of respect, mind you; as Pat noticed that those people never talked to any of Grandpa Al's family or the group that Pat knew.

He remembered he saw Grandpa lying in that open coffin. He was walking up the aisle next to his mom and...there he was!

He could only see a small the portion of his face hovering just above the lip of that box that held him prisoner; when seeing him from a floor view walking forward up the aisle. He remembered how his mother squeezed his hand harder at that time. She must have seen him at the same moment, Pat reasoned.

They took a seat in one of the front pews that had "Reserved for Family" written on a brass plate and laid over the aisle end of that pew.

The sermon was long, and Pat didn't recall most of it. Random words like: 'peace', 'hope' and 'better life' floated by him like so many butterflies that Pat ambiguously flicked away with the back of his mind's hand.

He only stared at the face that he knew lying very quietly in the box in front of him.

He turned and surveyed the faces in the crowd. Who were they anyway...? He didn't know any of them at this time. Why where they really here? He knew why HE was here; he was here because he was Grandpa Al's grandson!

The sermon over, they headed to the cemetery where Grandpa Al would spend his eternity.

He asked his mom while they were standing at his grave site who would he be able to talk to when bullies were picking on him now that Grandpa Al was dead? Grandpa Al had the world's best lap to sit in and hear war stories. Grandpa Al had the world's best smells on him when you got to sit in his lap.

Delores did not have an answer for her son. She simply squeezed his hand a little harder and looked back to the box that held her father.

Funeral.

Pat had only experienced death once before with Grandpa Al.

He had never buried a dog, or a family pet of any type.

He did remember, however, watching a squirrel as it slowly died after being struck by a car. It was late in the summer and the squirrels, busy as usual at that time of the year, were making ready for the winter months. Pat was looking down the street at the time when this squirrel tried to make it across a busy street.

The squirrel just didn't make it.

Pat noticed that the driver didn't even stop. The man just kept driving after he struck that poor animal. However, the squirrel had still managed to crawl out of the street and up onto the boulevard before it finally succumbed to its death. Pat saw it get hit (more like run over) and its back legs were crushed. How it managed to crawl away and up onto the grassy boulevard, Pat would never know.

Maybe it was in the squirrel's fate that it should die in grass, and not on asphalt or in the middle of a street.

Pat got off of his bike and hunkered down next to the dying animal. There was a look in its eyes that would have appeared to be fear; but what kind of fear?

Maybe fear of a human being that just happened to be hunkered down and staring at it as it lay dying? More than likely it was just the plain old fear of dying that the squirrel was realizing. Or, it could be that it was just the pain and suffering that the squirrel's eyes were registering.

Either way, the squirrel just laid there, its last labored breaths getting shorter and shorter. The look in its eyes never wavered or faded from what was there when Pat got off of his bike to witness this death.

Pat had heard, or read somewhere, that the *'eyes are the windows of the soul'*. Was that expression strictly for human beings, or did that ring true for squirrels as well?

The squirrel's eyes never left those of Pat's, either.

After a few minutes, it was over.

The look in the eyes of the squirrel never changed. Yet, it was dead. Pat watched it for just a little longer; not to see if the squirrel was faking it, by any means; but for some...other reason.

Even though this squirrel had been crushed (which had to have been painful as hell, Pat figured) the eyes never gave way to what fear this squirrel had surrendered.

Was it the fear of dying, Pat thought? Do animals have the fear of death like human beings do? Perhaps it was the fear of the '*other world*' that waits for dead squirrels; or maybe it *was* simply the fear of some curious human being that just happened to come along and get close enough to witness the death.

Pat sat there a little while longer occasionally looking back at the dead squirrel as he watched cars cruise by, their drivers indifferent to the dead squirrel that lay on the boulevard.

Pat finally rose from the couch and headed upstairs to lie down, and perhaps get some sleep...if possible.

Chapter 3

Pat's sleep was like his mother's and his sister's...sporadic and unfulfilling. When he woke up, he didn't think he had dreamed, and then contemplated again that that was about all he did last night. He seemed to recall very vivid dreams about everything dealing with his father. That's probably why he felt so tired after being in bed for eight hours. He didn't really sleep, but floated in and out of REM which, in Pat's opinion, isn't very satisfying.

Pat woke up with some sort of a crust that was dried on both sides of his face. As he wiped it off, he looked at it. He couldn't figure out what it was. He walked into the bathroom, turned on the light and looked in the mirror.

It looked like he had been crying all night, yet he didn't remember any of it. He looked down at his hands and the collection of what could have been dried tears that he had wiped from off of his face, and it looked like so much fine sand in the palms of his hands.

He turned towards the toilet and lifted the lid. After he voided himself, he washed both his hands and his face with no more attention to the task than a crow would have pecking away on the remnants of a rabbit corpse lying in a ditch on the side of a deserted road.

It just had to be done.

He looked again at his face in the mirror. He looked tired, and he felt that way. He had not slept well, and he saw the onset of little black circles under both eyes.

What was it his mother said, *"The extra baggage without handles carried under the eyes?"*

Pat also woke up angry, hurt; wild, scared and confused all at the same time. If he were an adult with all of these feelings coursing through his body at one time, he would more than likely be spending thousands of dollars and countless hours at a psychiatrist.

However, he was a child. Thirteen years old could be construed as a young adult, being that it was now in the teens; however, during times like this, he was no more than a child. It was apparent to Pat that children were able to hold their emotions in check better than adults did and probably always would.

He looked up at his face in the mirror once more, and then before exiting the bathroom he slammed his fists down on the top of the sink; hard...twice.

That hurt like hell, Pat grimaced, but it made him feel a little better...for a little while, anyway. He was livid with the thought that his father was dead; that his father was gone, never to return again. He would not return like the leaves and plants would come spring.

He flushed the toilet and walked slowly out of the bathroom. He turned to head towards his bedroom as his eyes looked towards his parents' bedroom.

No more would he be able to knock, walk in and wrestle with his dad on their huge bed. No more would he hear the loud and thunderous snoring sliding out under, and through the door.

His father used to joke to Pat when Pat talked to him about the noise from his snoring that he had tried out and had made the Olympic Snoring Team for the '60 Olympics, but was later held to an alternate.

He walked back into his bedroom to change out of the clothes he apparently slept in all night.

What had he done to deserve this? Pat sat down on his bed and thought hard about what he possibly could have done for God to punish him so.

What possible acts of a thirteen year old child would evoke a punishment as terrible as this?

Pat thought of himself as a good guy; he helped his mom around the house, he obeyed the orders and directives of his parents, he truly loved his sister even though there were times when it didn't show. He was conscientious of other people feelings, and would always help his neighbors if they asked for his help.

So what could it have been?

Wasn't Pat the one who was always being persecuted by Brian and the Clan of Idiots? Pat wasn't the victimizer…he was the victim. Pat could see being punished if he were a bully like Brian, Ed and Pete; but he wasn't, nor did he have the heart to become a person who took to browbeating smaller, weaker kids.

Was it the lewd thoughts he seemed to be having at a greater frequency lately regarding women; and sex? Was it the fact that he had been exposed to a woman's naked body a couple of months ago along the Otter Tail river, seeing her at such a young age, was it that, was it that which pissed God off enough to punish Pat in such a fashion?

Could it be the fact that he, occasionally, manipulated himself with the images of Karla and, most recently, Alice, the lovely Alice, in his young vivid memory? Was that so bad to warrant this…this…horrible outcome?

Just being a hot-blooded thirteen year old boy couldn't be the reason God would punish him, Pat didn't think. Could it? The world was full of hot-blooded thirteen year old boys, wasn't it? Why then would God chose Pat to set as an example of what could happen if you entertained lewd and lascivious thoughts?

Pat admitted he had lied before. He remembered telling the little lies to his mom regarding homework being completed, when it wasn't…completely, so that he could go out with Mike and Lenny. His grades never really suffered because of that, so was it that bad? He remembered lying to his mom about going to the movie 'M*A*S*H' a few months ago.

He remembered telling his father that he wasn't the one who used his tools, and then left them outside in the rain only to be discovered by an enraged Howard the next morning.

But was telling little white lies to his parents or friends so worthy a sin to be chastised in such a manner? Pat didn't think it was.

Pat had stolen before, when he was younger; stupid stuff, like candy from the five and dime store. He had taken other things that didn't belong to him mostly on a dare. But when he said his prayers at night, he had always asked Jesus to forgive him his little indiscretions. Wasn't that how it was supposed to work? You did something bad, simple bad like stealing some candy, and then you asked for forgiveness, and everything was to be absolved. Wasn't that how it was supposed to work?

Could it have been that Pat did nothing for that injured squirrel that he watched dying on the boulevard? Pat didn't think there would have been anything he could have possibly done for that pitiful creature…save for burying it. For that, he was remorseful, anyway.

So if it were any of these things Pat did, unconsciously or not, why did God punish him by taking his father away from him? Why do those things to his father, when it was Pat's doing…? Why take his father's life for the sins that Pat had committed?

And if any of these reasons were enough to cause God to strike his father down in the prime of his life, taking away everything he had and everything he would ever have; if any of these reasons were true, would any form of apology even change the outcome? Pat would get on his knees right here and right now and he would pray, he would have *begged* God to forgive him; give him another chance to redeem himself and spare his father for the good of himself, his family, and for his father life.

Why was he being singled out, Pat wondered? He was no better or worse than Brian Osterman and his cronies, so why take Pat's father and not the father of a prick like Brian Osterman? Pat then felt bad for having that thought about Brian's dad.

It wasn't fair, damn it…it just wasn't fair. Pat's dad was a good man. He cared for his family the best he could at all times. Why punish him AND his family by taking away his life?

Was there more to it than that? Was it really, truly something Pat did…or didn't do, that had such a crushing affect on Pat's life. Pat wondered why God hated him so. He seemed to hate him and his family. He was punishing him, his father, and his entire family for reasons unbeknown to Pat.

Maybe, just maybe when Pat was older, he may figure this whole thing out, but as it stands right now, he was befuddled and mystified.

Or, Pat thought again, as he started to look at this outcome in a different direction; was it his father that had done something so terrible that the after effects were rocking Pat's world down to its very core? Did it all come to what his father had done in his life that caused this vicious outcome?

Pat started to go through the Ten Commandments in his head to see if there were any that his father could have actually committed without Pat and his family ever knowing about it.

What commandments being broken would be worthy enough to warrant death?

His dad would never have killed anyone. Pat was at least one hundred percent sure of that fact. His dad was way too gentle and kind to take the life of another human. Besides, Pat was also sure that he would have been captured if he had done such a thing. He thought his dad was gentle and kind, but would never be able to live with the guilt of taking away another human being's life. He would never be able to live on the lamb, one step away from the law, as it were. Hell, his father would not have been here had he committed such an audacious crime.

Stealing? Could his father have been capable of doing that to himself, and his family? Would God actually strike you down dead if you actually stole something? To have taken something that didn't belong to you is truly a sin, and is against the law as well; but, was it so bad in God's view to take your life away from you?

How about coveting your neighbor's property? He didn't think his dad did any of that, but how much about his father did he really know at the tender age of thirteen? Coveting…was that the same as stealing? Pat didn't know.

He knew his father worked quite often on Sunday and didn't attend church like Penny and he did, but to not go to church on Sunday when you were working instead to help support your family, to give your family a better life than what they currently had, was THAT enough to justify the outcome that God bestowed upon Pat and his family?

How about…wait a minute, what about his mother, Pat thought?

Could it have been something his mother did? Could she have committed a crime against man and God so enormously horrible to warrant this effect? Would she have willingly executed this act against God knowing full well that God would smite her and take her husband away from her...from her and her family?

Pat thought long and hard about all of these things: the sins that he had perpetrated, with or without conscience; the actions of his father, and or his mother, which could have had such a blatant effect upon him and his family.

Could any of this been true?

Or was it just as the Pastor had said, *"Perhaps God needed a good mechanic in Heaven, and so he wanted the very best mechanic that he could find. Therefore, he chose your father."*

Pat also considered the old cliché about how, *'God works in mysterious ways'.* He had never really considered this saying before today, and maybe it was true. We are simply mortal beings and should not be allowed to question the reasoning behind those actions of a God...right?

He may never get any answers to any of these questions for as long as he lived, he thought. However, Pat was sure of one thing and one thing only; God took his father away from him, way before his time.

And for that, Pat would never forgive God.

Never.

I

Pat went quietly downstairs and saw his mother sitting alone at the kitchen table staring absently at the salt-n-pepper shakers. It looked to Pat like she had not slept at all last night. The dark circles under her eyes made her look thirty years older.

"Mom?" Pat asked softly.

She slowly turned her head to face him t the sound of his voice.

"Good morning, sweetheart," she replied, and then she stared to cry again, very delicately. Pat watched her for a second, not knowing what he should do. She then stood up and pulled him into her arms and squeezed him so hard Pat thought she might break a rib…or two.

Pat could feel her hot tears on the back of his neck.

"It's going to be alright, mom," is all Pat could think of to say to her. *Hard consolation, at the very least,* Pat thought; but it was all he could think of to say.

His mother released him, and pushed him out to arms length and said to him, "I…don't…know what….to do….Pat. I sit here thinking…thinking, that everything would be different…if I just had….had been here…"

"Mom," Pat said, his own tears now streaming down his cheeks with no confrontation, in tracks that had been laid previously. "It wasn't your fault, Mom…" And then he threw himself into her waiting arms again. He did not want her to ever release him from the safety and solitude of her arms, ever again.

"I know, dear," his mother sobbed, barely able to catch her breath, "it was not my fault; but I should have been here for him."

"No, mom," Pat replied, crying harder now that his words were almost unintelligible coming from the side of her body where he hid his face. "This was all my fault. God is punishing me for something I did…I know it."

Delores stopped crying, and stopped crying immediately.

She released him, stepped back and lifted his face up to hers so she could look directly into his eyes. "Pat," she said, her voice was terse, concise; angry and calm all at the same time; "none of this was your fault. Do you understand me? None of this was *your* fault." She wiped away her tears with the back of her hand, sniffed a couple of times and continued to look very carefully at her son. "Now I want to hear you say it, Pat. I want to hear you say it to me…right now."

Pat stood there sobbing and looked directly at his mother.

"But, mom" Pat started to say, "it WAS my fault. God is punishing me for something I did."

Delores got down on her knees so she could be directly in front of her son.

"Honey," she said using the same tone she had used earlier, "I don't want to hear you talking like that. God is *not* punishing you. God is not punishing Penny, or me. God is not *punishing* us, sweetheart. Your father died, and if that was God's will to..." she stifled back a sob that had been brimming in the back of her throat since she started this discussion, "...to, take your father from us, then it was God's will.

"We cannot change things that are not in our control. We can only accept the things that do happen in our lives, but it is not a punishment. It is God's will, and that's all. It is not a punishment. God would never do that to us, honey. Never. Do you understand me?"

Pat stood there, negated of everything. All he could do was sob and stare at his mother through tear stained eyes. He reached forward and wrapped his arms around her neck and laid his head down on her shoulder as the shuddering began to take hold of him.

Delores held him close and cried with him.

"It will be alright, some day, Pat," his mother assured him as best as she could. "It will be alright...someday..."

They stood there in the middle of the kitchen for minutes, holding onto each other like drowning victims clinging onto one another for safety and comfort before they go under the water, never to be seen again.

Penny came downstairs and joined them right before lunch. She had slept for about fourteen hours, Delores thought. She didn't look well.

She sat down at the table without a word, and began to stare at the same salt-n-pepper shakers that seemed to control so much of Delores' concentration these last twenty four hours.

"Honey," Delores said to her, "would you like something to eat?"

Penny continued to sit there with her hands in her lap and her back hunched forward.

"Penny," Delores said and walked slowly towards her daughter. "Sweetheart, please sit up straight, you know how I so dislike it when you do that." She reached Penny's side and knelt down beside her, took her right hand and gently pulled Penny's hair out of her eyes and placed it back behind Penny's left ear. "Would you like to have me make something for you to eat?"

Penny did not answer her but began to slowly, as if in a drug induced daze, move her head in a fashion that represented the answer 'yes'.

Delores leaned forward and placed a kiss on Penny's temple, reached around her and gave her a strong and steady hug. Then she got to her feet looked at Pat who sat at the other side of the table not saying a word, and moved towards the refrigerator to fetch a couple of eggs.

Delores was moving around her all familiar kitchen like a person who had never been there before, but still knew, through some outside influence, exactly where everything was, and began to make Penny some breakfast.

"Penny," Delores said facing the stove with spatula in hand and with her back to Penny, "right after breakfast I want for you to get cleaned up and dressed. We will be getting quite a few visitors today. OK, honey?"

Delores turned around after receiving no response to find Penny slumped even further over in her chair; her forehead merely inches from the table top, and sobbing quietly. The sobs were raking her body like she were convulsing ever so slightly.

Delores dropped the spatula to the floor of the kitchen without even thinking twice and ran over to her daughter's side.

Penny immediately sprang to her feet to meet her mother's waiting embrace. The two women stood embraced, crying loudly and riding out the sobs that had enveloped both of their bodies.

Pat watched them for a minute or so simply sitting there and crying himself until his mother looked his way, opened her arms for him to find a refuge deep inside the waiting hug of the only two people left in his world.

Chapter 4

Relatives, friends and people began showing up around lunch. They all seemed to be carrying some type of covered dish when they entered the house. They carried dishes and plates with Saran wrap on them to keep the insects from the food that lay on the plates.

No one came to their house empty handed, or dry-eyed.

Delores had laid down for a couple of hours before they arrived. When she woke, she still looked older than ever, in Pat's opinion, but he didn't say anything to that affect.

Pat's whole house was nothing but a blur for the entire day. Old women with tears in their eyes and lacy handkerchiefs in their hands were constantly grabbing him and hugging him. Most of these older women were quite large in stature and colossal in the chest. They murmured sweet nothings into his ear ever so lightly that it almost tickled. Pat could smell their sorrow as they embraced him into their mammoth chests. Pat almost broke out in a chuckle with one woman, whom Pat didn't know, when she clutched him and began that soft uttering into his ear. It tickled him. It would have been appalling had he not fought back the laughter that wanted so desperately to break out from his chest.

Old men would merely walk by and pat him on the back. Or, they would simply stand next to him and give him solace without speaking a word. They never really said anything more than a simple nod of their heads; produced a smile so thin it looked like they drew it on with a pencil. Some even shook his hand. Pat returned their shake while looking down at their shoes. He noticed that old men seemed to wear the same style shoe; as if it were an unwritten law that when you reached a certain age, you were awarded that style of shoe, and you had to wear them the rest of your days.

Everyone he met that day was sympathetic. It was only human nature to feel sympathy, Pat thought, for those who had this unimaginable tragedy thrust upon them. You had to have been a heartless animal with no idea what it meant to *'feel'* if you never sympathized with those who suffered the tragic loss of a loved one.

Everywhere in his house today was sympathy; but not much for empathy. Unless you yourself had lost your father at the tender age of thirteen could you even try to empathize with Pat.

The house was a mixture of various smells: coffee and cigarette smoke was in the forefront. Then it was the odors of hot dishes too numerous to mention intermingled with the scents of potato salads, coleslaws and pickles; various desserts like Jello, with and without the fruit and raw fresh vegetables; fruit cocktail dishes made with whipped cream, and at least a dozen different pies, all home made.

There were buns and loaves of fresh bread, also home made, of course; and competing with all of these wonderful, sad, funeral-sy smells was that of the perfume that old ladies generally buy by the bucket…and then marinate themselves in it.

Pat swore that these old ladies could literally leave vapor trails when they moved about the house.

Everyone was walking around the house talking quietly and carrying little plates with a mixture of a little bit of everything for food on them. Some people were content to stand in the back, looking at the family pictures that hung on the walls, and not talking to anyone.

Pat wondered if these were the same people that attended his Grandpa Al's funeral. How did they find out about his dad dying? He almost felt like walking up and asking them their business here. Did they even know his father?

Was it somewhere in the Wahkashen newspaper already? Was there an article in the obituary section already to indicate that there was a death in the McCray family, so these people could come here, stand here, not say a word to anyone and eat his mother's food and the food brought in to their house covered with Saran wrap?

Could the people at the newspaper be that quick as to have his father's name in the obituary section of the paper the very next day after he died? Pat didn't think that they were that resourceful…or could they be?

Who are you people? Why are you here in my house?

Pat wandered around, smiled sheepishly to all of those who noticed him and gave him the patented sorrowful look. Most of these people he didn't even know and he didn't think that they had ever been in his house before.

He had heard the murmured whispers of death amongst the living here in his house: *'so did you hear that he died in their garage',* and *'he was so young…way too young'; must be hard on the children'…*

Were these people so ignorant to think that Pat couldn't hear their muffled whispers to one another? Sure, they held their hands up to their mouths and spoke to each other very closely, but he could still make out most of their conversations even when they quit in mid-sentence as he came into the little circle that surrounded them.

How impolite could they be, Pat thought?

Delores had introduced so many different people to Pat over an four hour period that Pat's head was spinning.

She had him meet Aunts from Washington and from all over Minnesota; Uncles from *this* side of the family and more uncles from *that* side of the family.

Cousins once, twice and thrice removed…what ever the hell that meant?

He met friends from his father's childhood. He met friends from his mother's childhood.

He met people from this side of the tracks, from the wrong side of town and, apparently, from the state of confusion.

Pat couldn't recall one of their names after he was introduced anymore than he could recite the Declaration of Independence…verbatim.

He saw the owner of the Shell station was here.

What was his name again, Pat couldn't remember? Pat really didn't care at this time, either.

Faces floated by Pat like so many balloons on a string held by a man with clown white on his face. They were vivid at first, and then without any warning began to blur into one long, steady stream of noses, glasses and different hair colors. The old men shoes were the only constant in this never ending steam of bodies, tears and handkerchiefs.

There were ties and suit coats of various colors intermingled with dresses of a darker color. Everything went swirling by him at a considerable pace.

It was as if he were riding on a merry-go-round and all of the relatives and well-wishers were standing in a deep circle around him, and they were spinning him faster and faster on this merry-go-round until Pat thought he was going to throw up.

Intermingled with all of these balloon faces was that putrid smell of old women perfume...mixed with the faint odor of Old Spice.

Pat finally couldn't take it anymore, and he bolted outside to get some fresh air. Once there, he saw more people standing around and smoking. Some were drinking a beer and they all stopped the conversation and turned their attention to him when he walked out the door.

Pat smiled faintly and politely, looked down at the ground in front of his feet, and headed towards the garage...and then past it.

The next thing Pat knew, he was running.

I

Pat ran and ran, not looking at anything and seeing just that...nothing. He ran without having any idea where he was heading. He figured he would know where he was, or where he was headed as soon as he arrived there and after he ran out of air.

He could hear someone was calling his name from behind him. He ran even harder.

He ran west past the Olson's and then across the railroad tracks. He heard the Olson's TV was on, but didn't register what program it was. He stopped for a split second, then turned and followed the tracks past the Thimpkin's. After he reached the Weaver's, he turned again.

He crossed Eleventh Street and was running past the cemetery on the outskirts of town. It was ironic that he was crossing by a cemetery. He was trying his hardest to run away from a cemetery, but the irony of the situation he did not register in his empty mind as on he ran.

His foot steps were slightly muffled and yet slightly crunchy in the fallen autumn leaves that littered the path on which he ran. The smell of the dead and decaying leaves filled his nostrils as the odor that they emitted was suspended in the air by the crisp autumn air that held no trace of a breeze.

Pat felt like he was running blindly down an indistinctly lit tunnel. He could not reach out and touch the sides of this tunnel as down it he ran, and he didn't exactly know where this passageway was leading. He was simply running full speed, blind, down an unknown channel.

He also had the strange, sinking feeling that he was descending, not exactly running in a parallel fashion along the curvature of the earth. He couldn't explain why he was feeling this, but he felt that the faster he ran the deeper down into the earth's core he was going.

So on he ran...undiscerning and weeping; unheedingly aware that he was sinking into the earth with every step, yet unable to stop his forward, and *downward*, progression.

The passing October air was cool against the skin of his face as down this tunnel he ran. His cheeks felt a little cold with the autumn air brushing past the tears on his cheeks.

He heard the stiff snapping of small branches below his feet; he felt and heard the soft, muffled impact of each and every step that he took.

Recollection of just where in the blue hell he was suddenly began to fill his empty head.

As he hit a more familiar area and ran a couple of hundred feet, he came to a slow walk so he could catch his breath a little as he had a huge hitch in his left side. He finally stopped, bent at the waist and placed his hands upon his knees as the air that was so desperately needed in his aching lungs was sucked in and expelled out at an alarmingly quick rate.

He watched as the tears dripped from his face onto the brown dead leaves at his feet.

He looked up into the trees and noticed that most of the leaves had fallen from their branches. Those that had not fallen hopelessly to the ground earlier in the month maintained their color array of decay that arrived every year.

He stood that way, breathing heavily and staring up into the tree line like he had never seen a tree before in his life.

He finally knew exactly where he was headed all along. He finally was made aware that this was where he needed to be all along; not with those people back at his house who all wore the same grief-stricken masks.

He made it. He made it to Eagle's Nest.

II

He finally made it to the place where he could be alone with his grief; alone with his misery and loss, with no one looking over his shoulder every waking moment, no one questioning how he was feeling at this time and that time.

He was in his own personal nirvana; he had arrived at his Valhalla.

Now he could breathe the fresh air that his whole body had fought so hard to acquire while walking around his home full of familiar strangers. Now he could sit, by himself, and try to come to grips with what had happened to his world in a matter of twenty four hours.

Now he could cry and release all the emotional turmoil that had been building inside him for so long.

He walked slowly, languidly to an area where he could sit and quietly reflect upon what had transpired to him…and his family. He walked through the field of tall native grasses. He stuck his hands out, palm down at waist level and let the grass play with the palms of his hands as he ambled towards the lone tree with an empty heart and a quiet, yet troubled mind.

As he reached the lone tree, he looked up at the familiar sight with different eyes. It seemed that something was out of place here at Eagle's Nest; things just did not look the same for some reason. Something was definitely awry here at Eagle's Nest, and after considering this for awhile, he finally came to the realization that Eagle's Nest had not changed at all.

It was him that had become distorted.

Echoes of distant voices began to load his head like his mind were a vacant wash basin being filled by the associated pitcher that sat with it on the antiquated commode. Visions accompanied these echoes and swirled around in his mind like so much used waste water going down a drain.

He could hear his father's laughter, and he cried.

He could see his father's face before his eyes, and he sobbed.

He could recall everything about his father and nothing about his father at the same time.

He remembered the Christmas last year when he got the Apollo 11 plastic scale model that he had wished for over three months. He recalled that he had left subtle little hints all over their house indicating his desire for such a model for Christmas. It must have paid off to be persistent, Pat thought.

He remembered the look of surprise…albeit, mock surprise; on his father's face when Pat ripped open the gift. He could see very clearly in his memory running toward his father as he wrapped his arms around his thick neck and hugged him as hard as he could. Pat actually felt his arms tighten as the memory was so vivid; he almost felt that he was there again, right now.

He reminisced about watching his father change the flat tire on the front of the Chevy pick-up that they owned, and was so happy when his dad asked him if he would like to give him a hand. Listened very carefully as his dad explained how to use the lug wrench. Howard placed the foreign feeling lug wrench into Pat's smaller hands and told him how all bolts and nuts were, *'lefty loosey, righty tighty'*.

He remembered the first time his father put that .410 single-shot Springfield shotgun in his hands when he was nine years old, much to the chagrin of his mother, of course; and then realized that this shotgun was the very first one his father had been given as a child himself.

Pat knew that that shotgun was his and was always going to be his until he was able to give it to *his* son…someday.

He could recall when his dad built that small scale wooden paddleboat with the wind-up rubber band paddle in the back. They took it to the lake outside his home town, Pebble Lake, Pat recalled it was named; and they watched as it floated along the shoreline with speed generated by the wound rubber band.

Pat could feel the rough texture of his father's face against his own skin because he did not shave one morning. It felt as if there were a million tiny soft and prickly thorns on his dad's face that did not hold the ability to draw blood when touched, even if they wanted to do that upon stroking them.

Pat could smell the heavy odor of smoke on his father's breath when he leaned closer to him to reveal an amazing tidbit of information. His father's breath was always smoky, and usually held the scent of faint beer at the end of the day. He could see his father's face behind the flame of his Zippo lighter as he set fire to yet another Camel cigarette. He saw how the yellow-red flame radiated across his face, and caused the blue tint of his eyes to become more of a darker color when viewed from behind that flame.

Pat remembered all of those things with clarity, as if they were happening to him right at that time. He could hear his father's voice as he called out to him from somewhere far away, but it was only in his mind. He could see his father's brilliant smile, and Pat absently smiled with the thought as he brushed away forgotten tears.

Pat sat there and contemplated all of these things. He thought about all of the good times that they had shared from the youngest memories to the memory of yesterday at his father's shop.

He thought about what he was supposed to do now that his father was no longer there. Who would he turn to for answers? Who would be there for Pat when he got his kite stuck in a tree, again (like he did a couple of weeks ago); retrieve the red rubber balls from off of the grade school roof across the street when the gang would kick them too high...and too hard.

Would those balls remain forever a captive on that roof like his kites would be in the trees of the neighborhood?

He looked up into the sky above him. It was a gray like he had never seen before. The sky looked like the belly of the PT-109 model that Pat and his father had recently built...together.

He looked at this sky and he silently cursed God for taking his father away from him.

Pat swore at the tree he was leaning against; he swore and screamed at the winter wheat in the field. He cursed at the sky and shook his fists with anger. He clenched his hands so hard when he made the fists that he left little half moon imprints in his palms from his fingernails.

What was it that God didn't see in His infinite wisdom when He chose to take Pat's father from him? Didn't He realize how deeply He would scar this boy of thirteen years of age? Didn't He even think about that, Pat screamed in his head and shook his fists at the gray sky above him?

Wasn't God listening to him when he prayed that his father be allowed to succeed and have his own shop? Didn't God understand that if his father had his own shop, that he would be home on a regular basis to have time for his family?

Wasn't he watching him and his family as they interacted together? Did he not see the love that this family shared...as a family? How was he supposed to feel from this day on knowing that his prayers were never going to be answered; that God apparently had no time for him, or his family?

How was Pat ever going to forgive God for this tragedy beset upon him and his family?

Was Pat ever *going* to forgive God?

Pat may forgive, as he was taught, both in his home and in the confirmation classes he attended at Bethel Lutheran church; but Pat knew deep in his heart, buried way down in his very soul that he would never, ever forget.

There would be no forgetting. He would commit to memory this day for as long as he lived, and he would never fail to remember the hurt; the frustration and anger that he never even knew he could hold inside him. Pat never felt so alone, so alienated before in his short life. He was not sure just what in the hell he was supposed to do.

Pat felt as though his entire spirit and soul had been ripped savagely from his body. He felt void, empty of all fortitude. Is this how he was supposed to feel? Is this what God had in mind for a boy of thirteen, to experience an absolute emptiness inside?

Was he going to feel like this for the rest of his life? Was he destined to hold this awful, sickening empty feeling in the pit of his stomach forever?

Pat thought that it was the worst feeling he had ever experienced. He thought he would never ever have this sensation again. Or would he?

Would he suffer this way when his mother passed on later in Pat's life, or did he only feel this way because of his young age?

Pat got to the point where he maybe negated God.

Pat questioned why a God, *if* He existed, one as powerful as his God, would do this...*could* do this to him. Did his God really exist? Could a God be real that would willingly inflict this kind of spiritual and emotional damage to a person?

Inflict this upon a young boy of thirteen?

Pat thought about all of the tragic happenings in the world; all of the tragedy in the world, both past and present and wondered if God truly existed.

Would Pat ever discover the truth? Would he ever find the answers concerning his God?

Was there any truth waiting in the dark for Pat?

Was there even a God? Could there be an entity called God? And if one truly existed, why in the world would He choose to do this?

Was it possible that God had no feeling for human beings as Pat was taught? Was it possible that God really hated the whole human race, and therefore did whatever he could to make life miserable for the living?

Could a God live to inflict so much pain and damage with no more thought to it than, say, plucking the wings from off of a defenseless fly?

Was God really so pissed at Adam and Eve that He created as much misery, despair and turmoil for the entire planet in the form of floods, hurricanes, tornadoes and other natural disasters, to include and *not* include the death of father's; as He sat back and watched with a sad and weird sense of merriment?

Could God really have taken his father away as a form of sad entertainment for His own personal pleasure?

Was Pat losing faith in God?

Pat thought hard about these things.

But mostly, he sat down against that lone tree, and cried quietly in his hands.

Chapter 5

Pat sat there with his back against the tree and listened to the breeze move the leaves around. He heard the breeze as it softly stirred the deep winter wheat that surrounded Eagle's Nest. He watched as the wheat moved like the ebb and flow of an ocean's water being manipulated by the earth's gravitation pull.

There was something sad about the sound of the leaves being influenced by the soft autumn breeze, Pat thought; but just what it was Pat could not quite put his finger on it. Maybe it was the sound of the dead leaves rustling about on dormant branches in the late of the year that gave the affect of sadness.

Pat listened to the leaves lost in his thoughts.

He was happy that he was able to be lost in his own thoughts without having to explain himself to someone who he was, or wasn't related to, about what he thought, and why he thought what he was thinking.

He was also content in knowing that he didn't have to elucidate how he felt at this time, or why he felt that way. He could sit here by himself and just think…about everything…and nothing, all at the same time.

Pat could see his dad's face in his mind. He remembered going to the shop and meeting with his dad. They talked about anything while Pat watched him work, amazed at the skill that his dad possessed.

He thought about how his dad wanted to open his own shop. How his dad was bound and determined to work for himself so he could come home and have suppers with his family, like any ordinary father and husband.

Now he wouldn't be able to come home anymore.

Pat thought about his father: his smile, the way he would push his glasses up on his nose, the absent way he rubbed the side of his face with the back of his hand. He thought about how blue his dad's eyes were, how they would seemingly sparkle whenever he was happy about something.

Pat felt his thoughts were bouncing aimlessly around in his mind like so many leaves caught in a whirlwind. He felt the emptiness inside him; the feeling of something missing in the pit of his stomach. The feeling deep inside that he knew would never be filled again. He was forced to be walking this earth with emptiness in his soul for all eternity.

The sky remained a gun metal gray this afternoon, and if he remembered right, there was a slight chance of rain in the next day or two.

That was just great, Pat thought. It would make for such a memorable funeral burying his dad in the rain.

He would be *'burying his dad in the rain'*. Pat ran those words through his head. They just didn't sound right no matter how many times he repeated them.

He would be *'burying his dad in the rain'*. For some reason, that statement just seemed so out of place in his world right now.

Silent tears were once again running unheedingly down his smooth cheeks. He had had so many tears these past twenty four hours that he didn't even register that he had been crying the whole time he sat there thinking about *'burying his dad in the rain'*.

Pat continued to sit there until it started to get darker, and then he decided he'd better head back home. He had no idea just how long he had sat there. His mom would probably be getting worried about him, and she had enough on her plate right this minute. He didn't to give her more to worry about on top of everything else.

He was about to get back on his feet when he saw a figure coming out of the trees and off of the path, walking directly towards him. He strained his eyes to try and see just who was walking out here, out here to his sacred place.

This was *his* place and *his* place alone. He needed this place more than ever today to reflect, to be left alone until he was ready to return to the upside down world that he was forced to call home.

Who was that person bold enough to be walking on the sacred ground of Patrick Howard McCray?

I

Pat thought about just getting up and walking off in the opposite direction to avoid whoever was walking out here to desecrate his sacred area. He would take the long way around to get back home again. He really didn't feel like getting into a confrontation, or God forbid, a conversation with anyone at this time.

He waited a few more seconds, and then the figure became clearer.

It was Mike. Mike was walking towards him and Pat did not know whether he should stay and talk with his best friend, or if he should turn and run. Pat was still crying, quietly, as the tears just came with no resistance.

Pat decided that he could probably talk with his friend for a minute before he had to walk back home again, so he stood up to meet Mike.

After a couple of minutes, Mike made it to Eagle's Nest; he had his hands stuffed deep in his pockets, and was more or less staring at his feet as he spoke to Pat.

"Hey," Mike said in a timid fashion.

It had suddenly occurred to Pat that everyone who spoke to him and to his family lately, had this timid sense to their voices, as if they really had nothing to say; and yet by the sheer influence, the sheer force that death placed on everything and everyone, they felt this peculiar, this abnormal sense of obligation to utter...anything. Simple words became complex sentences to these people in the shadow of death.

Death apparently had a way to change even the most effortless of daily routines into difficult arrangements.

"Hey," Pat responded, as he looked away from his friend and absently wiped away the tracks of his tears with the backs of both hands. He didn't know why, but he felt he had to turn away from the view of his best friend.

"How'd you know I would be out here," Pat asked with his back to his friend.

"It really wasn't too hard to figure out," Mike replied, "when I went to your house and your mom said that you had run out of the back yard about four hours ago.

"I figured," he continued as he took a step closer to Pat and then placed a warm and reassuring hand on his best friend's shoulder, "that you would come out here to get away from…all of that," then he swept his hand back towards Pat's house.

About four hours ago? Pat thought. Had he been out here that long? Could he have really spent that much time out here? It didn't seem like that long ago since he'd run out here and sat down, lost in his emotions and thoughts.

Pat turned to meet his friend. He felt ashamed that he'd been crying out here at Eagle's Nest, but then he noticed that Mike had tears rolling down his cheeks as well.

"I'm really sorry, Pat," Mike told him.

They stood there looking at each other, two good friends who didn't know what to say to each other, but were fighting to figure it all out the best they could.

"This really sucks, Man" Mike finally said. "I mean, I don't know what I'd do if my old man died…you know?"

"Yeah," Pat agreed. "I just can't believe that this is true, you know?" Pat sat back down, hard, at the base of the tree and looked up at Mike. He finally said, "It all seems like a stupid dream, and I just can't seem to wake up…even though I really want to."

"I hear ya, man," Mike said to him. He came over and stood next to Pat. Mike stuffed his hands back into his pockets. He looked down at Pat and didn't know what to say. Sometimes, Mike figured, saying nothing to a friend, but just being there is the best; so he simply stood there and felt sorry for Pat.

"I keep asking myself if I told my dad that I loved him before I went to bed the night…the night, he died," Pat spoke so softly Mike almost didn't hear him. "I have been racking my brain to remember if I did or not. It probably isn't that important, but right now it seems to be the most important thing in my life."

Pat turned his face up to Mike with fresh tears streaming down his face, he felt no shame and said to him, "To know that I had the one final chance to say '*I love you*' to my dad, before he actually died. You know what I mean?

"It just seems really…really, *damned* important right now," Pat screamed so loud he felt certain Heaven would hear his plea for an answer.

Pat also thought he would really be in trouble if his mom heard him talking like that…and God forbid his dad heard him use that kind of language.

Right after he had that thought about his dad, Pat cried even harder.

Mike watched as his friend was slowly falling apart, and he felt helpless to do anything but witness the act with his own heart breaking.

"If I knew that I had told him that I loved him," Pat continued with his head hanging so low his chin almost touched his heaving chest, "and was positive that he was sure that I loved him, and then maybe all of this might be easier to take…I think."

"I'm sure you did, Pat," Mike told him. "I know I say it to my folks every night, and you are better at all of that than I am."

"Yeah, maybe," Pat replied wiping away the tears with the sleeve of his dress shirt, "maybe."

They sat in silence for a couple of minutes, save for the sniffles that Pat was fighting.

"I suppose I better be getting on home or Mom will kill me, no pun intended." Pat looked up at Mike and gave him a faint, patented Pat McCray smile.

"Yeah, you probably should" Mike said to him and then walked over and extended his hand to help his buddy up from off of the ground. "I'll walk with you. OK?"

"OK…thanks" Pat replied, reached out to grab his friend's helping hand and they left Eagle's Nest together.

II

They arrived back at Pat's house after walking away from Eagle's Nest and out of Sleepy Hollow. Pat opened the back door, and then hesitated and turned around to face Mike.

"You wanna come in and have something to eat?" Pat asked Mike. "We could go upstairs and eat in my room?"

"Nah," Mike replied after he stood on his tip-toes and looked past Pat's shoulder at all of the relatives and people in the house. "I'd better be getting home myself. I'll call you later, OK? We'll hook up and go for a bike ride, or something, alright?"

"Alright," Pat said. "Give me a call. As he turned around to go through the back door he stopped and said over his shoulder, "Thanks for coming by, Mike. It meant a lot to me."

"No prob, my man," Mike told him and then walked down the driveway towards his house.

Pat's mom came up to him and pulled him aside in the kitchen.

"Where have you been, Pat?" she asked him with genuine concern and a touch of anger in her voice.

"I couldn't take it in here anymore, mom," Pat told her, "I mean all of the people, the smells and no fresh air. I felt like I just couldn't breathe. I just had to get out for a walk."

Pat couldn't bring himself to tell her that he went to Eagle's Nest. He didn't know why, but he just couldn't.

"You should have told me before you go running off like that. You nearly scared me to deat…well, you scared me very badly, Pat."

"I'm sorry, mom," Pat told her and then dropped his eyes to the floor.

Delores reached out and tenderly lifted the trembling chin of her son. She looked him directly in eye. "It's OK," she said to him, "I was just scared for you is all. I don't mean to upset you."

"Have you had anything to eat?" she asked him and led him, slowly, to the tables filled with food.

Immediately Pat's nostrils were viciously attacked with all of those various smells that he ran from earlier in the day and he realized that he really was hungry.

"No, not yet" he told her, and she grabbed a plate and began to fill it with everything that Pat liked. The nice thing about mother's at times like this: they would fill your plate with only the foods you liked. It was different than times where they were guests at someone's house and she would insist that you at least 'try' everything. *"You must be polite, Patrick,"* his mother would say. *"If you don't like it after you've tried it, then so be it; but you must at least give everything a chance."*

Pat took the plate and a soft gentle kiss to the forehead from his mother, walked into the other room where he found an empty step on their stairway that led upstairs, sat down, and ate with more enthusiasm than he thought he had

All through the time had sat down to eat, he felt a billion eyes on him by the people in the house absently milling about from room to room. He knew they were looking at him like some strange specimen found on a deserted island, or a newly discovered virus spread on a glass slide and looked at through the power of the Micron microscope, so much more powerful than the one Pat had in his bedroom.

He hated that feeling...and then absently looked around for his mother to make sure she hadn't psychically picked up on him using that word in her house. Even though this was a time of mourning, she would still be willing to administer a sound whack on his head for even thinking the word...in *her* house.

Pat also continued to hear the mindless banter while he was eating. Did these people think that Pat was deaf? He heard their whispered conversations bouncing all around the room from behind their cupped hands: *'...what do you think that Delores will do now?'; 'Did Howard have adequate insurance for the family?'...I heard that he may have, committed suicide, but I just can't believe that'... I just can't help but feel so sorry for the children...'*

He had all of the plate down in a matter of minutes. He didn't realize that he was so hungry. I guess crying your eyes out consumes a great deal of energy, Pat thought.

He did notice one thing about the food that he had just inhaled...it all seemed to taste like old lady perfume.

He sat there staring at his empty plate, and that trance was only broken by the ringing phone.

Pat answered the phone after a couple of rings.

"Hey, Pat, it's Mike" as the familiar voice came over the wire. "You want to go for a bike ride down to the park, or something?"

"Yeah," Pat replied, "hold on and I'll ask my mom." Mike heard the phone get laid down on the phone shelf that the McCray's had; he heard the faint conversation in the background from all of the people who filled their house.

Pat returned after a minute or so. "Yeah, I will go upstairs and change clothes, and then I'll ride over to your house."

"Alright," Mike replied "I will be outside waiting for you."

"Cool. See you in a bit," Pat said and hung up the phone.

Pat rode his bike towards Mike's and tried not to think about anything as he rode there. He tried; however, he fell short of completing that task.

It seemed that everywhere he looked, he saw something that reminded him of his father: Mr. Ferguson's Chevy sitting in his driveway. It was a car that his dad had worked on before…many times, Pat recalled. Up the street was the Johnson's old Dodge pick-up that had seen the light of the Shell garage more than one time.

Pat drove his bike past houses where dads and moms were outside raking leaves with their children; these people not really knowing the mortality of any one of the members of their own family was so short, and final. It would just hit you between the eyes with no prior warning.

And, it hurt like hell.

Chapter 6

Mycoplasma pneumonia was the cause of death. So read the coroners report.

Mycoplasma pneumonia; a.k.a., Streptococcus pneumoniae; a.k.a., Walking pneumonia, was the killer of Howard Raymond McCray.

Delores listened to this line in the report that she had just received over and over in her head.

She was sitting at the kitchen table with the last of the day's coffee in her cup.

The house had pretty much cleared out about a half an hour ago, and she actually cherished the little silence that was there for her; for awhile.

My husband died from pneumonia, Delores thought? How could that be? My husband was healthy. He didn't complain that his chest was causing him any discomfort, and all along his lungs were filling up with fluids produced by his own body? How could this be?

My husband was only thirty five years old!

She had just received the report over the phone from the coroner.

She sat there at the kitchen table, alone, at eight o'clock in the evening contemplating those salt-n-pepper shakers' place on her table…in her world.

My husband of fifteen years, the man who shared my bed for fifteen years, who shared all of my dreams, faced all of my nightmares and slaughtered all of my demons…was dead.

The man who helped conceive our two children, who have now been left behind, was dead.

He died outside in our garage.

There was nothing I could have done for him.

He died from walking pneumonia.

And, there was nothing I could have done for him.

So, what was I to do now, Delores thought to herself? How do I care for and raise my children all alone? How does a person lose a spouse at such a young age and still maintain their sanity?

Who am I going to go to when I need answers? Where do I run when things get out of control?

Why is this happening to me…?

Delores picked up the salt shaker and threw it across the kitchen where it crashed against the far wall, and then she laid her head down on the table and cried.

with words when you were comfortable enough to sit in the calm and simply enjoy each others company. You are able to communicate without words when you are with a true friend; and Pat thought that he really had two true, blue friends for the rest of his life.

Mike reached into his pocket and pulled out a crumpled pack of cigarettes.

Wordlessly he handed one to Pat and then to Lenny.

Lenny produced a pack of matches and lit his, held the match to Pat who lit his, and then Lenny still had enough for Mike's as well.

"Three on a match," Lenny said to the gang while shaking his hand to extinguish what remained of the match. "That's good luck, you know."

"Yeah," Mike replied and then exhaled a puff of smoke that slowly rose to the ceiling of the pavilion, "In Tahiti."

Pat snorted out wisps of smoke when he heard that and then began choking on what was left in his lungs.

"Don't do that when I have smoke in my mouth," Pat said, and the boys began to laugh.

The boys sat and smoked in the easy silence for a few minutes.

"So when is the funeral, Pat?" Mike asked him, cautiously, not trying to inflict any more emotional pain on Pat than necessary. "Do you know?"

"It's in a couple of days, I guess," Pat replied and ground out his cigarette on the concrete floor of the pavilion. He walked forward towards the doorway of the pavilion, and facing the duck pond he stood there with his hands in his pockets and his back to his friends.

"It all feels like a dream, ya know? I keep thinking I will wake up and see my dad's truck slowly backing down the driveway as he heads to work.

"I keep thinking that I'll come home from school, do my homework, and when dad gets home, we'll all sit down and have supper...if he didn't have to stay at the shop for one reason or another.

"I can still hear his voice in my head. I can still smell his stinky feet in the house..." Pat continued, but his voice began to trail off a bit and the last of it was swallowed up in a muffled sob.

Mike and Lenny sat there, not talking and staring at the back of their grieving friend, helpless and unsure what move they *should* make; if there even was one *to* make.

"Sorry," Pat said and turned around to face his friends.

"There's no need to apologize, Pat," Mike said, and Lenny confirmed.

"It just seems so weird, ya know?" Pat started up again once his sobbing subsided to the point where it diminished all together. "I feel like someone has punched me, hard, right in the center of my stomach. It feels like Brian Osterman ran at me hard and fast and slammed me right in the pit of my stomach.

"So then, when I did wake up this morning and nothing had changed," Pat said as he looked at his two best friends, "it was then I knew that it was really true. He's dead. There is nothing anyone can do to change that fact. My father died, and I will never see him again."

Tears simply rolled down Pat's cheeks, and they did so with no resistance and no shame.

Mike and Lenny had no words to ease their friend's pain.

"This really sucks," was all Mike could think of to say. He got up and walked slowly towards his friend and put an arm around his shoulder. "I wish there was something I could do for you, my man…but all I can do is give you a shoulder to lean on, if you need it."

Lenny came walking up to the boys and gave the same advice.

"You know," Lenny said after he reached the guys, "when I lost my Grandmother a couple of years ago, I felt the same way. I know that if I were to lose my dad, that feeling would be back…about ten fold, I figure."

"Is the funeral in town?" Mike asked.

"No," Pat said and then walked back towards the picnic table. He asked for another cigarette. "It's going to be in Hargrove, 'cuz dad still has lots of family in that area.

"It's going to be hard not to be able to go to the cemetery whenever I want to because he is going to be buried over seventy five miles away."

Mike produced another smoke for Pat. Then the two stared down at the concrete for awhile.

"Maybe we should go pheasant hunting tomorrow," Lenny said looking at the ducks on the pond water swimming easily. "Maybe that would help take your mind off of all of this…for a little while, anyway."

"You know…that's not a bad idea," Mike said and then looked at Pat. "What do ya say, Pal…you want to walk the Red and shoot some roosters in the morning?"

Pat looked at Lenny, then turned and looked at Mike. "That sounds like a *great* idea. A nice long walk hunting roosters just might work."

"We'll just skip school for the day," Mike said to the guys. "It wouldn't break my heart to miss a day of school, anyway."

"Yeah," Lenny replied and walked over to Pat and put his arm around Pat's shoulders. "Besides, what's more fun then watching Pat try to hit a pheasant on the wing…right, Mike?"

Pat turned his head and replied, "Me? You must be talking about someone else, Lenny. I can take 'em on the flush. I don't ground pound them like *some* people I know," and then nodded his head towards Mike.

"Ahhh, bullshit," Mike said with feigned anger in his voice. "I don't ground pound…but, if it's flyin', it's dyin'.'"

That statement was met by laughter, and high fives were given all around.

It was getting darker as the night came on, so the boys climbed aboard their bikes and proceeded to head back home for the night.

I

Pat came in the back door, saw his mother sitting by herself in the kitchen, and walked slowly and quietly up to her.

He gave her a kiss on her cheek.

She looked up at her son. Her eyes looked heavy and sad. It was hard for Pat to see his mother looking like this.

"Where were you, Pat?" his mother inquired.

"I went to Mike's, remember?" Pat replied with concern for his mother's sanity in his voice. "Do you remember when the phone call came; I told you I was going to meet Mike?"

"Oh…yeah," his mother replied with a heavy sigh. "I guess I recall the phone call."

Pat watched his mother for a couple of seconds, concern etched all over his face. What would Penny and I do if something would happen to our mother, Pat wondered?

Pat looked over at the far wall and saw the salt shaker lying on the floor. It had spilled some of its contents as it lay askew on the floor by the sink. Pat walked over, picked it up and walked back to the kitchen table where he placed it along side the pepper shaker.

"I'm going to go to bed, mom," Pat told her after he replaced the salt shaker and he made his way out of the kitchen.

"I love you, Pat," his mother said to him as he started to leave. Her eyes never left the table in front of her, but Pat could hear the emotion in those words.

"I love you, too…mom," Pat turned and replied.

She lifted her head up from the table and he saw the smile on his mom's face and it made him feel better…for a little while, anyway.

"Mike and Lenny and I are going to go pheasant hunting in the morning, for a little while," Pat said to his mom. "Is that OK?"

"Where are you going to go?"

"We'll just walk the Red along Paul Bunyan's piss line…, ahhh, sorry, Mom."

Delores turned her head to look at Pat. "What did you say?"

"It's a grassy strip on the south side of town along the river." Pat said looking at his mother. He then finished his sentence a bit more timidly, as he looked down at the kitchen floor, "The guy's call it…'Paul Bunyan's…piss line.'"

Delores sat there dumbfounded and looked at her son. She then spat out a burst of laughter that was like music to Pat's ears. He had not heard that sound in this house for quite some time.

"Did you say, *'piss line'*?" she asked him between breaths of needed air from the laughing. "Did I hear you say, 'Paul Bunyan's…*piss line?'*"

Pat, now snickering himself, not really afraid to laugh, but not sure if what he said was as funny as his mother thought it was, replied, "Yes, yes I did."

Delores laughed even harder and bent over at the waist in her chair.

"That is the funniest thing…I think I have ever heard you say…to me, Pat" she stammered out in between fits of uncontrollable laughter.

Pat grabbed a chair next to his mother where they laughed looking at each other. It seemed the more they looked at each while they were laughing, the harder they laughed. They were both bent over and hanging onto the stomachs as the laughter took control of their bodies.

"Where in the world did you get that term?" she asked him as her fits tapered off a little.

Pat laughed a little and replied, "I'm not sure, mom…we've always called it that."

"It's just a strip of native grass," Delores asked, "that someone decided looked like a large piss line?"

"That's all it is," Pat replied.

"How big is this strip of land?"

"Oh, I suppose it's about thirty to forty feet across and about two to three hundred feet long."

"That is hilarious, Pat," Delores said looking at her son. She then leaned over and placed a soft kiss on his cheek.

"Just don't ever say that in front of anyone else but me, OK?"

"OK, mom" Pat replied and sat back in the chair looking at the tabletop and actually felt good there, for a while. A good hearty laugh felt amazing to Pat.

He wondered if his mom felt the same way.

Chapter 8

The funeral that Pat so dreaded was to take place three days after his family was notified of Howard's passing was finally upon them.

It was scheduled to rain, according to the weather guy, as Pat had also dreaded. It was scheduled, and it looked as if it were going to come true.

The one hour drive to the town where his dad had lived his first eighteen years of his short life was a quiet ride. There were the slight, quiet murmurs by his mom and his aunt in the front seat of the car, but other than that it was simply the steady drone of the car tires on the highway as they headed to the place Pat didn't want to see.

It was the longest one hour drive Pat had ever taken in his life.

Even Penny was quiet riding in the backseat with Pat.

The trees that lined the streets that led to the funeral home were full of color. Autumn was Pat's favorite season, and it was also his dad's favorite, but Pat didn't want to think about that right now. Pat wasn't sure, but he started to get the feeling that autumn wouldn't be holding such a place of honor in his heart much longer after today.

He watched the passing trees from the backseat of the car as they rode to the funeral home where Pat would be able to see his dad for the last time.

Pat was captivated by the rich reddish and yellow hues that the decaying leaves on the large oaks and sugar maples were displaying for the world. They intermingled well with the last of the silver maple leaves that seemed to hold their brilliant green for at least a month past the oaks and ash trees. The grass in some spots was still pretty much green, and there were smatterings of leaves on the grass already.

The night before the actual funeral, was the Visitation. Delores wanted to have an open casket, which Pat couldn't understand. Funerals were already bad enough and a strange tradition for honoring the dead, Pat thought; but an open casket to actually see the dead person was a really an even stranger tradition that Pat didn't think he would be able to understand if he lived for all of eternity.

He did understand one thing about all of this madness…he would get to see his father one more time before they put him in the ground.

Pat and his family had a two hour window prior to the public viewing to spend time with their departed. The funeral director was an old friend of the family, and Pat liked him and his family very much. He had a daughter that was about Pat's age, and she looked very sad when he walked up the stairs on the outside of the funeral home.

As the director opened one of the double doors, Pat walked into the main lobby and was immediately assaulted by the scent of flowers…and a bunch of them by the mixed smells. The smell was almost cloying, and Pat couldn't understand how anyone could actually enjoy this onslaught of aromas on their nasal passages. It was so overly sentimental and sickly sweet that it made it hard for Pat to breathe.

Pat remembered walking up an aisle just like this a year ago when they buried Grandpa Al, and Pat looked up thinking he would spy Grandpa's profile over the edge of the open casket. His hand began to tremble when he noticed that the profile that he was seeing as he walked slowly up this long and terrible aisle was not that of his beloved Grandpa…

Try as hard as he could, Pat could not take his eyes off of the profile in that box before him. It just wasn't right. It just shouldn't be there. He wanted to scream at the top of his lungs that God made a mistake. His father should not, could not be in a coffin…not now, not ever.

He still needed his father.

What in the hell was God thinking doing this to a thirteen year old boy? Why couldn't God have picked out another, a different mechanic…surely his father wasn't the only truly great mechanic from whom God had to choose?

It wasn't fair, damn it. It wasn't fair that everyone Pat knew still had both of their parents, while Pat was forced to succumb to the fact that now he had only one...only one parent for the rest of his life.

It just wasn't fair.

Pat was left with a mom and a sister. Who was he to turn to with problems that he couldn't, he wouldn't bring up to his mom...even if his dad were still alive? Also, he no longer had Grandpa Al...

Pat and his family sat in the very front pew and Pat didn't think he'd ever be able to take his eyes off of his father lying in that light blue coffin that his mother said she picked out for her husband.

The funeral director came forward, offered his condolences, and spoke softly to his mother about something that Pat didn't understand, and wasn't sure if he wanted to understand.

Pat simply stared at the body in the box. His mind was trying to reveal to him that this was it; his father was really dead and laying *in* that box, but he just couldn't fathom it no matter how hard he tried.

His mother said something to Penny and Pat then rose to follow the director. Penny started to cry again, and asked her mother if she could stay with her. Delores agreed and then turned to Pat and said, "Will you be alright while Penny and I go with the director for a minute?"

Pat only nodded 'yes', unable to remove his eyes from his father.

Delores bent and gave Pat a kiss on the head and then, with Penny in tow, walked the aisle back to the entrance of the funeral home to meet with the director.

Pat sat there for a few minutes still trying to absorb what his eyes were displaying to him; that face in the box was so familiar, and yet so alien to him right now.

Before he even knew it, Pat was on his feet and walking slowly, timidly, even with a little trepidation towards the coffin that sat so prominently in the front of this chamber. There were huge bouquets of flowers sitting on small round tables at both ends of the coffin, and an even bigger one sitting on the ground right in front of the coffin. The colors that they presented were so bright they almost were hard to look at for a long period of time, Pat thought.

They were so brilliant and beautiful that it seemed that they tried to convey a sense of jubilation during a time of sorrow.

Pat was only a few steps from the coffin when he noticed that the body in there was wearing his dad's best suit. His dad only wore that when they went to weddings and…funerals.

Pat made it to this half open box holding this body prisoner. He looked inside and thought that the person lying in there was merely sleeping…had the look on his face like he was just about to open his eyes from a nap that was long over due.

He would open his eyes and be completely rested. He would *stretch*; turn his neck a couple of times to remove the kinks in it from sleeping at the wrong angle, and then cleanly and without much of an effort, step out of the box and walk down the aisle and out the front door.

Nothing to it…just as pretty as you please, he would leave behind this boy who just a minute ago was examining him with strange and curious eyes.

The face was so serene he just *had* to be only sleeping. He had to be…

The funeral director came up behind him so quietly that Pat didn't know he was there until he felt his hand on his right shoulder.

"You know, Pat," the director told him, "if you would like to touch your father; that would be OK. You have the right to touch your father one last time."

Pat looked up at the director who was giving him a reassuring nod. Then he turned his head back to the body in the coffin.

Did he just say that he could touch his father, Pat thought? That really was his father wearing his finest suit lying there in front of him, was it?

That wasn't his father.

Then Pat looked again only to realize that it really WAS his father, and he wasn't merely sleeping, was he?

He really was dead. He truly had died.

Huge, silent tears began to stream down Pat's face without him even noticing.

The director had turned and began to walk away without Pat even discerning his departure.

Pat lifted one trembling hand towards the box and let it come to rest on the lip. With the back of his other hand he wiped away most of his tears. The box was cold under his hand, and his finger tips felt the satin liner which was whisper soft and smooth. He stood there with his one hand resting on the lip, and his eyes never leaving the face of his father.

Pat's eyes scanned his father's face; he saw his glasses were clean, immaculate, and bright; looked at the way his tie was done so perfectly, so impeccably, that it had to have been completed by someone else because Pat remembered his father was all thumbs when it came to tying a neck tie.

The handkerchief in his breast pocket was a beautiful white with blue trim. It was folded in a tri-fold design, and somehow looked out of place on this man, Pat thought, but didn't know why.

There didn't appear to be a single dust particle on his suit jacket. Not a string or a single stray hair was out of place. It all looked so surreal, it just had to be.

Finally, after mustering up all the courage he felt he had, he lifted his hand from the lip and gently placed it upon the chest of his dead father.

Pat had expected the soft feel of his father's flesh beneath his waiting touch. What he felt was anything *but* comforting.

Pat instantly felt there was no difference between the lip of the coffin and the swell of his father's chest. Both were hard and cold. Touching his father's body was just like running his fingers over a bitter marble headstone in a cemetery that was ancient and forgotten.

Pat immediately pulled his hand back and absently wiped it on his suit pants as he started to back away from what he thought was his father, all the while his eyes remained on the body in the box.

Why did he do that? Why did he think that he would feel his father under his hand? Why didn't he realize that this was NOT his father, but all that remained of him?

Why did the director propose that Pat touch him?

What did the director think Pat would gain by doing such a horrible thing?

He backed away, little by little, still wiping his hand on his suit pants without even knowing that he was doing so, never taking his eyes from the open coffin before him.

He would never forgive the director for making that suggestion.

I

The weather outside when the funeral began was misty. The heavy rain that was expected hadn't started…yet.

People came from all around to visit with the McCray's in their time of mourning, and to view the deceased.

Pat turned his head, slowly, to capture all of the people sitting in this chamber with him and his family.

He saw people. He saw lots of people.

People that Pat knew: his Aunt Martha from Hanging Rock, and all of her children; his Uncle Bob from somewhere out in Washington. It had to be a long flight, Pat thought as he turned his attention to the next face.

His cousins, too numerous to mention, were all there.

The funeral home was fairly full with well-wishers. His father knew a great many people, and his family was fairly good sized, what with all the relatives that were in attendance.

There was a sign-in book in the front of the parlor in the foyer and when the funeral was all over his mother would see that there were over three hundred names in there.

Pastor Hartman came forward and began his sermon. His eyes scanned the congregation that was present. He looked very professional in his long white flowing robe with a violet colored ribbon that hung around his neck and down over his shoulders to don the front of his robe that decorated the outfit.

His voice was very serene and calming. It was very soft, soothing, almost…but on the point of being kind of creepy, Pat thought.

He spoke of better places to be, that the Lord our God was holding a spot for each and every one of us, that there was always room in God's heaven for his flock.

He spoke of how Howard was called to the service of the Lord, albeit, a little too soon; as the world did not learn the full prospective worth of Howard Raymond McCray. There was just too little time to discover what potential Howard had possessed.

He spoke of the surviving members of Howard's family. He spoke of holding on to what memories there were, to hold on until the time came for them to join their husband and father in *'the better place'*.

Pat listened to his words, but it seemed like they were only passing through as they went in one ear and simply out the other. The words held nothing to him as he stared at the now closed coffin in the front of the room, as it sat there, solemnly, with a huge bouquet of flowers on its top.

Pat could still see his fathers profile even though the cover was closed. He still had that awful feel on his hand from when he touched his dead father's chest. It was like touching the pew he was sitting on right now, and touching that hard pew didn't mean that much more to him than touching his father. Pastor Hartman rambled on and on about everything that God could do for us; but apparently, His life was way too hectic; or maybe He didn't give two shits about bringing Howard McCray back to his grieving family.

Maybe…and Pat was just spit balling here, maybe He was way too busy to attempt anything like that. He was waiting for all of us, He was willing to do great and wonderful things for us in the afterlife, but Pat silently wished that He would maybe consider getting off of His ass and doing something about his dead father in *this* life.

"How 'bout that, God," Pat thought to himself and then looked up at the ceiling? Was that a possibility, or was Pat just fooling himself into thinking God really, truly gave two shits…?

Pat looked over at his mother, her anguished face that looked twenty years older than she was, and wondered why a God would do that? Did He find some perverse pleasure in creating and then later destroying a life in a flash with no more thought than say…stepping on an ant?

Pat just couldn't help but question why a God, who everyone told him loved him and all of the human race so much, would be so willing to ruin Pat's life without even a second thought. It just didn't seem right. It just didn't seem reasonable or comprehendible.

Just like the buxom redhead holding the wrench in the Snap-On calendar at the Shell garage, Pat didn't buy it.

The sermon was over before Pat knew it, and everyone quietly headed outside following the coffin with his father inside, to their waiting vehicles so they could drive to the cemetery where his father had a place awaiting him. A place that was all green and deceiving. It was a place of grave and stifled screams where the grass grows thick over shattered dreams.

It was raining quite steady by the time everyone arrived at the cemetery. There was a burgundy-topped tent standing over the grave site, and about a dozen chairs for immediate family. It stood out in this landscape of marble and grass.

The rest of the well-wishers and rubberneckers had to stand out in the light rain.

Pat felt sorry for those who stood outside the canopy and silently waited for the ceremony to be finished. He almost felt an obligation to stand and let one of the women sit in his seat beside his mother. It was the right thing to do, but then again, it wasn't.

Pat searched the crowd for faces that were familiar to him. It seemed that everyone looked the same; everyone there were people that Pat simply just didn't know.

He would scan their faces. He would let his eyes fall on one face, study that face for a second or two, and then go on to the next face with little or no recognition of who it was that he had been looking at. They were all just nameless faces to him.

Why are you here, he wanted to scream at them.

It's raining outside, can't you see that? My father has died and is lying in that stupid box over there, and it's raining out.

Why are you HERE!!!

Pat turned back to his mother and saw that she had tears rolling down her cheeks again. Pat wondered if she would ever stop crying.

He reached out his hand and found hers. Delores turned and looked at her son and squeezed his hand, and then laid it gently within her hand back in her lap. They both turned their eyes back towards the waiting coffin.

Again Pastor Hartman spoke with a voice that was both soft and creepy, Pat thought.

Pat listened carefully to the Pastor's voice, but couldn't understand his words at all. He could have been speaking Russian, for all Pat knew, for the words held no meaning for him. They were simply words, and it was words of a different language that fell on Pat's ears.

Pat liked the Pastor, but was really starting to dislike his voice for some unknown reason.

Pat broke his gaze away from his father in the box and looked down. He noticed the green carpet that was laid for the mourners under the tent. It seemed that the carpet covered the ground for which all the chairs were placed, and surrounded the casket that held his father. It was a bright green carpet in contrast to the natural lawn that was in the cemetery. The cemetery grass was starting to turn, like the leaves, with the onset of autumn.

For some reason, this green grass-like carpet was just out of place here in the land of the dead. Dead leaves, dying grass, and dead people filled this place...save for the fake bright green grass that Pat sat upon right now. Pat kicked at the fake grass with the toe of his shoe. It seemed rather stiff and unmovable.

A curious crow landed in a branch of a tree just off to the right of the ceremony. Pat heard it caw and turned to look at it. It sat there, all black in an autumn color-filled tree and watched this service with its abysmal dark, unblinking eyes.

Pat wondered if the crow understood the Pastor's service any better than he did, and then he doubted the bird understood anything at all.

The crow continued to observe the service. Its dead eyes were as dark as a moonless night at midnight, void of anything that resembled a soul; they troubled Pat. He wanted to stand up and throw something at this sinister bird. At the very least, stand up and wave his hands in the air and scream at the crow...*'Get the hell out of here. This is a funeral...can't you see that? What are you, stupid? I am burying my father, in the rain; don't you realize that?*

He looked over at his mother again and noticed the tears were still flowing down her cheeks. Her expression never faltered, nor did it change, but the tears flowed nonetheless.

He turned back to the crow still sitting there on that dead branch. It appeared like it hadn't moved since it first arrived here.

What did this crow want? Was Pat losing his mind thinking that the crow actually *wanted* something from this sermon? Did this crow know something Pat didn't about death?

Was this crow a messenger of death? Was it here to take his father's soul away from this terrible place? Didn't Pat read somewhere that there was a bird that carried the souls of the departed from this world into the other world? Was it the crow, or was it a different bird?

Pat was pretty sure that this crow had some sort of semblance to something with death…but he couldn't put his finger on it, or his mind around it.

The crow stirred a little, cawed one more time as if to say *'good bye'* to whoever gave a shit, and off it flew…maybe carrying the soul of his departed father with it…maybe not.

Pat watched its flight.

It was just a stupid crow, that's all, Pat thought. It didn't take anything with it when it left here.

Pat turned his eyes back to the front. His father's casket was set upon a stand that held it in place until the service was over, and then the cemetery workers would lower his father into a cement holding area. Pat suspected the concrete holding area was necessary so people couldn't hear the dead trying to claw their way out back to the land of the living above them. The concrete holding vessel was built so the living couldn't hear the dead screaming from deep under the ground. It was built so the living wouldn't be able to hear the dead. Or, he reckoned, it was either that; or vise versa.

Pat would never look at cemeteries in the same light again.

Chapter 9

A couple of weeks had passed since they put Howard into a place that he would occupy for all of eternity. It was a place that would be covered by grass, come spring. A place that was as cold and emotionless as the body that occupied it. That was a place of shattered hopes, of dried tears and silent screams. Pat came to hate that place, save for his father being stuck there.

Pat wished he could go out to the cemetery and visit with his dad more often, whenever the time permitted, but it was so far away. He would get to visit with his dad whenever they were in Hargrove; but silently he didn't care for cemeteries anymore like he used to.

It seemed to Pat like everything in his life was changing for the worst.

It also occurred to Pat that everyone treated him differently these days: the kids in school, all of the teachers (even those of whom he didn't have classes, and probably with whom he never would have classes), the lady at the grocery store who always called him Patrick.

It was like, every time he came into a room, all eyes were immediately on him, all conversation would be silenced and one could hear the proverbial pin dropping as the silence filled the room.

Pat started to look at himself in the mirror to make sure he wasn't wearing a sign that held the caption: *"Depressed and Fatherless"; "Pity Me!!"* or *"Helpless Victim of an Untimely Death."*

Maybe he should tell these people that he was alright. They didn't need to be concerned about him, he was a survivor and he would be alright.

Maybe he should do just that.

Most people who did that sort of thing did it out of respect, Pat knew; but there were the few who did it for all the wrong reasons. The ones who always thought of Pat as a freak in their eyes before his father passed away, now thought of him as a freak that was now scarred for life due to an untimely death.

Some days Pat wanted to just walk up and slug those who treated him like a monstrosity. Punch them as hard as he could and scream in their faces, *"I am NOT a freak, you bastards."*

But, he wouldn't do that...couldn't do that even if he wanted to.

All Pat wanted, besides his father back in the land of the living and breathing, was to be a member of society; albeit with a damaged heart.

He did not want to be treated any differently than anyone else; he just wanted to fit in.

Pat would ride his bike past the Shell station after school for the first couple of days after the funeral, (he would be able to ride his bike for a few more weeks before the snow came with a fury) just in case it was all a mistake and he would see his dad's pick-up sitting outside. Pat would be able to burst into the garage, firmly hug his dad and never let him go.

But his hopes were extinguished as the nearer the station he got, the more empty his father's parking spot would be. He would park his bike and peek in through that dirty front window. He would never go past the front door threshold, nor would he ever step foot into the back room where the Snap-Op ladies were hanging above and behind the cluttered workbench.

He would stand there and look longingly in through that dirty, greasy window and watch the shadows of his deceased father float by him. He almost came to the point where he would knock on the glass to get that shadow to quit moving around, to come give his son a bear hug, and a kiss on the cheek...tell him that everything would be better from this day on.

Pat would go home wiping away the tears that he just could not hold back anymore, afraid to look anyone in the eye in case they decided to point and laugh at him as he flew by on his bicycle.

Pat went home and found his mother sitting on the couch, television off, just lost in her own thoughts. He tried to be as quiet as possible, but his mother heard him come in.

"Pat?" she asked with a voice that seemed so far away.

"Yes," Pat replied.

"Come in here, sweetheart."

Pat walked unhurriedly into the living room to meet his mother. Her face still held that look of defeat; a look of utter anguish that only time could ever remove.

Delores patted her hand on the couch next to her. "Sit down, please...would you?"

Pat did as he was told and sat down next to his mother. She immediately put her arm around his shoulders and pulled him closer to her.

"How are you doing, kiddo?" she asked him, looking straight ahead and not at him.

"I'm doing alright, mom," Pat replied. "How are you doing?"

"Oh, I'm handling it...I guess. I feel so tired most of the time, but...I'm handling it, the best I can, I guess."

Pat nodded and hugged his mother back. They stayed that way for awhile, safe and content to be in each others company.

Pat finally released his mother and stood up.

"I'm going to go upstairs and take a nap before supper," he told Delores.

"Maybe that's a good idea, Pat," she replied.

He knelt down and kissed his mother on the cheek, and then turned and walked upstairs with all of the enthusiasm of a condemned man walking up the steps of the waiting gallows.

Pat arrived in his room to find that it wasn't orderly as it usually was. He was quick to blame his sister for sabotaging his room, but then realized that the mess in question was purely of his own devise. The bed was heaping with clothing: some clean and folded, some soiled and in dire need of cleaning...as quickly as possible. He would have to remove both manner of clothing before he would be able to lie down for his nap.

He started gathering up the grubby clothing first, and walked to the hamper to unload it. Then he returned to get all of the fresh clothing and began putting it away in the closet and in his dresser.

He stripped out of his school clothing, pulled the shade on his window, and lay down on his newly cleaned bed.

It took all of a minute, and Pat was sound asleep...

I

...He was laying there when he had that weird, eerie feeling that someone was in the room with him. It was one of those, you think you hear a noise in order to make you wake up and look around to see what it was that made that noise, when there wasn't any noise at all. He sat up in his bed. He at least felt like he sat up in his bed to see what had or had not made that noise.

He wasn't sure he was even asleep, but it felt like he was; and it felt like he was wide awake.

There were faint wisps of smoke, or a misty fog rolling slowly and low in through his doorway. There was a white light, low and minuscule coming into his room with that mist/fog. Pat rubbed his eyes a little to try to aid his focus in the faint light that was in his bedroom. He looked over to his window and noticed that the shade was pulled down, and therefore, it was not allowing much ambient light into his room.

He looked back towards the doorway as the mist/fog was roiling close to the floor, and boiled upward ever so lightly. The light in question seemed to be coming from inside that fog/mist. The light seemed to pulse ever so slightly as the mist moved into his room as carefully as a cat creeping up on its unsuspecting prey. Further in the background, there was a shadowy image materializing there. It held the shape of a body. The closer this shadow came to the doorway, the more he could distinguish that it was someone. It was indeed the body of someone, and that someone was quite tall.

"Hello?" Pat said with a voice that wasn't really there. He figured that his throat was dry from sleeping, and he wasn't sure how long he had been sleeping...or if he was sleeping at all.

The dark figure that stood amid the wisps of fog/smoke in his door (Pat finally realized that it wasn't smoke because he couldn't smell it; but then his mind tried to wrap around the idea that there was a fog of some sort inside his bedroom, and his window was closed and the shade was pulled), didn't reply, nor did it come any closer when Pat spoke out.

"Hello? Who's there?" Pat said again.

The shadowy figure slowly began to move forward, silently, just a bit; and it finally made it all the way through the doorway and was standing inside Pat's bedroom. Pat squinted in the faint light to see if he could discern who was standing in his bedroom. And better yet, why *he was standing in Pat's bedroom!*

Pat look carefully, and then he noticed that the figure looked a great deal like his dad.

Pat gave this strange shadowy figure a double take, rubbed his eyes once more, and then refocused; that's when he saw that it really was his dad.

"Dad?" Pat said with hardly any voice at all. He thought he must be sleeping, because there was no way that his dead father was in his bedroom with him. Not now, not ever.

The shadowy figure moved forward and reached the foot of Pat's bed. It stopped, tilted its head slightly and looked towards the bedroom window like something on the outside was just calling its name, and only he could hear it. Satisfied with what he had heard, he slowly sat down.

The figure that looked like Pat's father turned back towards the window once more as if there was someone there. It stared at the window for a second, and then unhurriedly turned its head to look fully at Pat.

"Hi, Pat," this figure that looked like Howard McCray said to Pat with a voice that sounded as if it's throat were filled with gravel and water.

Goosebumps immediately sprang forth all over Pat's body; and the little hair on the back of his neck stood up as they didn't want to miss being part of the action.

"How are you?" this manifestation said to Pat as it laid one of its hands down on the bedcover. The sound of his voice scared Pat like he had never been scared before, and the sound of its voice would haunt his dreams from that day on for the rest of his life.

Pat stared at this apparition for a few seconds before he could shake his voice loose enough to answer its question.

"I'm good," Pat said with a shaky tone. "I'm good...fine, actually. I miss you, though."

"Yeah," the figure that held the resemblance of Howard McCray responded in his grim tone that reeked of the graveyard. "I kinda thought you were missing me. I miss

you as well. More than you could ever imagine. That's why I came back to you. I came back…for you, Pat."

Pat sat there, wide-eyed and not believing what he was seeing, and totally doubting what he was hearing. Pat fought the urge to reach out and touch this…this, thing sitting at the foot of his bed. If he did reach out to this…thing, would his hand feel substance, or would it go straight through it?

It looked like his dad, but it couldn't be his dad. He watched his dad get lowered into a hole in the ground at the cemetery. He went there just the other day to talk with him. Well, he went there to talk to his gravestone, anyway.

"What do you mean," Pat said to what looked like his father, "that you came back *for me? I don't understand."*

"Well," Howard McCray's figure said its voice so craggy and rough as if it were speaking through a long tube full of rocks and sand, "I have been missing you as well. I know it was hard on you for me to leave you. I know it has been hard for you, Pat.

"And…" the apparition turned its head and looked back towards the bedroom door from where it came, "…and I thought that maybe you would like to come with me; and we could be together…again." The figure then turned his face back towards Pat, and asked, "What do you say? Do you want to come with me, Pat?"

Pat stared at this dream…or apparition; he didn't know for sure which it was. Pat couldn't believe what he had just heard. He sat there dumbfounded. He felt the hot tears boil over the rims of his eyes and spill quietly and slowly down his cheeks. He didn't even try to rub them away.

Looking at this spirit, Pat suddenly was thinking that maybe this really wasn't his dad. There was something wrong with the way this ghost or spirit looked to Pat. There was something different. It sounded like his dad, and in a certain way, it appeared to be like his dad…but there was something amiss.

Pat struggled to find his voice. He couldn't believe what he had just been told by this…this, thing sitting on his bed beside him.

"Are you kidding me?" Pat said with ferocity in his tone that neither Pat nor the apparition would have expected. "You left me. *You realize that? You actually left me." The tears came with a heavy flood now, Pat did not care. He was furious. He curled his hands into tight little balls as they sat at his sides. He had a chance to vent his anger towards the man who had caused all of the pain and sorrow in his life for the past couple of days. He could direct all of his frustration back at the source.*

"I know there has been pain, Pat," the figure said to him and leaned forward closer

to him. *"I never intended this to happen the way it did…but, now I have come for you and we can be together again."*

Pat's body was racking with sobs and the tears flowed heavier than before. He could barely see the thing that occupied his bedroom with him due to the water in his eyes.

"There is nothing I would like better than to be with you again, dad," Pat said *through the sobs, "but I don't think I can do that. I mean…leave Penny and mom? Leave my friends? I don't think I can do that. I mean…I want to…part of me wants to be with you…but…I can't, dad…I just can't."*

Pat lowered his head and as his chin rested on his chest, the sobs became more intense.

"I sure wish you would change your mind, son," the apparition said with something *in its voice that could have been misconstrued as sorrow. "I really wish you would…but I doubt that you will."*

The figure that resembled Pat's dad stood up, without a sound, and turned away from his son. As he reached the doorway of the bedroom, he turned back, one last time, and said, "I love you, Pat. With all of my heart, I love you."

Then the apparition simply turned, and faded into the mist and was gone in a split second.

Pat fell back onto his pillow as the tears and sobs overtook him. He lay there with his eyes closed and cried for what felt like an eternity.

Was it too late to change his mind, Pat thought? Was it too late?

"Dad!" Pat screamed in his mind…

II

…He raised his head, rubbed away the tears that made his vision difficult, and noticed that the mist/fog and the apparition were both gone.

He immediately noticed that he was soaked with sweat.

He laid his head back down onto his pillow with only one thought running madly through his head and tears running silently down both cheeks:

What if I had said, 'yes', Pat thought?

Would there have been a chance that I would not have awoken from my sleep, if I had said, 'yes'?

Pat lifted his head again and looked towards his bedroom door. Did this really happen, or was it all just a very vivid dream?

Part of him wished his father would come back. There were so many things he wanted to say to his father before it was too late. Pat had forgotten to ask his father if he told him that he loved him. It was very important to Pat that his father knew that…and he failed to ask him that simple little question.

What if I had said, 'yes', Pat thought again. What would have happened if that word slipped out of my mouth?

Would I have died in my sleep, if I had said yes?

Pat laid his head back onto his pillow and stared up at his ceiling.

How long had I napped, Pat wondered?

Pat sat up and looked around at the strangely familiar area of his bedroom. He shook his head as if to clear his mind, but the dream was still there close enough in the front of his mind that it felt like he had just witnessed it.

Was it a dream? Pat wasn't really sure. It had all seemed so real.

What if I *had* said, 'yes', Pat thought to himself? Would I have even woke up after my nap, or would my mother have found me dead in my own bed?

Pat shivered a little with the thought of his mother finding him laying dead under his sheets in the morning, and then sleep overtook his mind.

Chapter 10

Pat sat on the edge of his bed and his clothes were soaked. He must have sweat a great deal while sleeping, he figured. He could not shake the dream from his fragile mind. It seemed more than a dream. He actually felt that his father was really in the room with him while he napped, but if he were to say that to anyone…anyone, they more than likely would gladly haul him away in a coat that wrapped the arms tightly around the wearers' body. It was a wonderful white jacket with brown leather straps that made it more fashionable, and practical; but was oh…so uncomfortable for the wearer.

Pat changed out of his wet clothes and slipped on something dry, went down stairs for supper and met his mother at the kitchen table.

"How'd you sleep," Delores asked him as she looked over her shoulder when she heard his approach. She had a hot cup of coffee sitting on the table in front of her, and the room was filled with the wonderful aroma of freshly made coffee.

"OK, I guess," Pat replied, and took a seat across the table from her.

They sat together in silence, both lost in their own thoughts.

"Mom?" Pat finally said as he watched the steam boil from her cup of coffee and remembered the mist/fog that rolled into his room during his dream/vision.

"Yes, honey," she replied and picked up her cup. She looked at him over the brim of the cup as she took a sip of her morning, and lately, her evening, 'waker-upper', as she called it.

"I had a dream while I was napping. At least, I think it was a dream…it seemed so real." He hesitated for a second, and then continued, "It involved dad. He came to me."

Delores set her cup down, not taking her eyes from off of Pat's face.

"What do you mean, *'he came to you?*'"

"Well, he came in through the bedroom door, sat down on my bed and asked me…well….he asked me to come with him."

Delores looked long and hard at Pat's face. Pat must have felt her eyes on him as he lifted his head and met her gaze from across the Formica table.

She held his eyes for a second and then said, "You mean you dreamt that your father came to see you…right?"

"Well, I think it was a dream," Pat answered her. "It just all seemed so *real.* I mean, dad came into my room, sat down on my bed and talked to me about being sorry he left, knowing that I missed him, and so on, and then he asked me to come with him."

Delores reached over and placed Pat's hand into hers.

Pat's eyes began to fill with tears without Pat even knowing that they were there.

"He asked me to come with him, Mom," Pat sobbed. "I didn't know what to say to him. I miss him so much, and…I just…didn't know what to say to him…but I told him, 'no'."

Tears now flowed down both cheeks as he continued to stare at her steaming coffee cup.

"He looked so sad when I answered him." Pat told his mother between gasps for air. "I was afraid that if I said yes…that maybe…I would have died; and you would have found me in my bed when I didn't come down for supper."

Delores squeezed her son's hand reassuringly, and kept her tongue still. She waited for him to get it all off of his chest, and then she would speak, if she needed to speak, that is.

"I know that this was all probably just a very vivid, very stupid dream," Pat told her as he raised his eyes from her cup to see his mother's face in front of his tear-stained view, "but he looked so sad, you know?

"It hurt me so much to see him look so sad." Pat said and looked back down at the table top again, trying to regain his composure.

"There was one thing that I remembered about all of this when I woke up. I thought there was something weird about how looked, besides being sad and all. It was just the way he *looked*... Then it came to me. Dad didn't have his glasses on."

Pat looked up after he said that and noticed that his mother had a catch in her breath. She had also released his hand and sat straight up when she heard his recollection.

"What did you say?" Delores asked with a hint of fear in her eyes.

"What's the matter, mom?" Pat asked her when he noticed her reaction.

"What did you just say, Pat?"

"I said that dad looked different, and then I realized that he wasn't wearing his glasses. I don't think I have seen him without his glasses for...well, I don't think I have ever seen him *without* his glasses."

"Pat..." Delores paused for a second, looked away from the table at the empty space in front of here as if looking for the correct words that just happened to be hanging out there in space; and then returned to his gaze, stared at him for a second or two and simply said, "Pat, your father was buried without his glasses."

Pat sat there and looked intently at his mother trying to understand what it was that she just told him.

"But, mom," Pat replied looked very concerned. "I remember seeing dad with his glasses on at the funeral."

"Yes, honey...he had his glasses on for the funeral," Delores told her son with as much composure as she could muster. "He had his glasses on for the visitation and funeral, but before they closed the casket and moved him out to the cemetery, I asked to keep his glasses."

Delores stared at Pat for a little while to see if he understood what she had just told him. Pat slowly shook his head as if that would help settle the disturbing information rattling around in his mind.

"Pat," Delores said, reaching out and grasping her son's hand once again, "honey, your father's glasses are in the safe. They are stuffed away in the safe in the den."

Pat looked at his mother while he absorbed what his mother just told him.

Could it have been possible? Could his father really have come for him?

Chapter 11

Pheasant hunting for Pat and the gang came and went. Pat went pheasant hunting with his friends almost everyday after school, and all day Saturdays and Sundays. They did OK for a group of young men walking along a river bank.

Deer hunting came and went. It was the first year Pat went without his father. He went with Elmer and Janet West and their family. It was fun, but it was the feeling deep in his stomach that Pat could not get over. The feeling like he was hungry. It was a deep empty feeling in the pit of his stomach, the very fiber of his soul that had ached so badly.

Although the West's did everything they could to make Pat feel at home with their family, it just felt weird to Pat not having his own father around for the hunting party.

Pat shot a small spike buck, and was pleased with his kill. Now his family would have venison for the winter, and beyond.

Pat was also saddened because his father did not witness the first buck Pat ever shot, or would ever shoot.

By the end of the hunting seasons, Pat had about 3 roosters in the fridge along with quite a few deer steaks and venison ring bologna.

Thanksgiving came and went. It was a quiet holiday as it was the first holiday that they celebrated without his father there. They had gone to Howard's mother's house. She set a very nice dinner, but the table was still empty, save for the tears, as there was a vacant seat at the far end of the table.

Christmas came…and so did the tears. Delores did the very best she could to get her children what they had asked for on their list. She tried to maintain her composure as they worked through the brightly wrapped packages that occupied the underside of the Christmas tree.

They had the family's traditional turkey dinner with oyster stew and pumpkin pie for dessert. There was not much for conversation while they ate; they simply ate and cleaned up after themselves. As soon as everything was completed to Delores' standards, they retired out into the living room for the opening of the presents.

Any other Christmas there would have been the constant chatter while devouring the turkey. The anticipation of opening the presents caused the children to not be able to sit still through the best meal of the year. They would have to be constantly told to settle down until everything was done: the meal, the cleaning up, and the putting away of any and all leftovers.

This year…all was quiet with a sense of gloom hanging over their heads like they were all inmates on death row consuming their last meal on earth before they take the long walk.

They cleaned up the kitchen in the same silence that held their meal.

"Are you kids sad that we didn't go to your Grandma's for Christmas this year?" Delores asked her children as they passed the threshold and entered the living room where a beautiful Christmas tree occupied one whole corner of the room.

"I kinda wanted to go," Penny said, "if only to see some of the cousins…but, I would much rather spend Christmas here in our house."

Delores put on her favorite Nat King Cole Christmas album on the small record player that she owned. Pat was asked to be the one who handed out the gifts this year, and right after Pat handed out everything to Penny, Delores and himself, they cried. There was no forewarning; it just hit all three of them as they sat there on the floor amid their gifts, and each one of them started out sobbing quietly, and then a bit more robust as the memories of past, joyful Christmas' came flooding into their minds.

They sat there sobbing, each in their own world until they joined in the center of the room for a group hug.

"You know," Delores said between sobs as she released her children from the group hug that they were in, "we are going to be alright. We have been blessed to be together as a family, and we shall grow stronger each day with the knowledge that we are still a family. Your father would be so proud of you kids for being as strong as you have been. I know in my heart that your father is watching us, and he is very proud of how we have been handling ourselves."

"I remember the first Christmas here in Wahkashen," Delores started out saying to her children as she stared out into the empty, quiet space of the living room as she slowly wiped away her tears. "Penny, you were almost two years old, and you Pat," she said and turned to face her children, "you were just a little over six months old. We moved into that little upstairs apartment…do you remember?"

The children sat there, teary eyed and nodded their heads.

"Pat used to love to go up into the attic of that old building, as I recall," she said and looked at him with a smile on her sorrowful face, "and I would beg Howard to make sure we had a gate up in order to stop him from trying to go up those stairs by himself. We had such wonderful neighbors in those years we lived there. I suppose we held about four Christmas' there in that small apartment."

Delores dropped her gaze to the floor before her and vaguely began to rub the right side of her temple.

"I remember your father bringing up the first Christmas tree in that apartment," she said, looking at her gifts spread out before her. "He was so very proud of that tree; as he bought it all on his own. It was a beautiful blue spruce," she continued and raised her eyes to meet those of her children, "if I recall and we decorated it that year with the eggs that we had blown out and put all four of our names on them."

The children immediately turned their heads to look at those very same eggs hanging on the tree. Penny had a hitch in her breath as she saw the one with her father's name on it and turned away from the tree and redirected her attention back on her mother.

"We would sit up late at night the night before Christmas Eve and wrap presents. Of course," Delores said, "that would be *after* your father played with all of the electronic gifts *first*."

Then she laughed, and it was a very real and hearty laugh as the memory had taken over her mind.

"Do you remember, Pat" she asked him and turned his way, "the electric tank that would shoot those rubber tipped darts from its cannon?"

"Yeah," Pat replied. "I really loved that tank."

"Well, your father and Elmer West sat on this very floor and played with that toy for a few hours. They chased the cat with it and tried to shoot the cat with those darts. I yelled at them, *'you boys stop that before you hurt the cat, or break that toy before Pat gets his chance with it'*. There they sat, cross legged on the floor and ran that damned tank for hours. I believe that they enjoyed that toy way more than you ever could have, Pat.

"That cat did not like your father much after that Christmas because of that stupid tank," she said, and then she smiled a solemn smile with the memory racing through her head like a runaway train.

"I remember that tank," Pat told her with a hint of nostalgia in his voice. "It was the coolest gift I got that year. I think it's still upstairs somewhere...but it hasn't worked for quite some time. I think I left the batteries in the controller too long and they bled and corroded the insides of the controller. It was a pretty cool toy, though."

"I remember one year," Penny said, still staring at her mother, "when we all went to The Hill on Christmas Day to go sledding. The Hill would take you all the way down onto the skating rink, remember? That was the year Pat almost ran into the light pole...you remember that, Pat?"

Penny turned to look at Pat as she wiped away the remnants of her tears with her sweater sleeve.

Pat laughed at the memory and replied, "Yeah. There was so much ice on the Hill's slope that year you could hardly control the runners. I think I remember had to bail from the sled before I piled right into that pole. I remember all four of us riding on that toboggan of dad's down the Hill that year as well. That was a lot of fun, too."

They all had a good laugh with that.

"I think your father did hit that pole that year," Delores said, and they had an even stronger laugh...a heartier laugh, than any of them had had in quite some time.

When the laughter died down a bit, all three of them sat on the floor and each appeared to be lost in their own thoughts, their own memories for a few minutes until Delores said, "Well, let's open up our gifts, and then we can have a piece of pumpkin pie…what do you say?"

The children nodded their acceptance to that statement.

"Pat, why don't you start?" Delores said and then ruffled his hair.

Pat really, truly despised it when his mom did that, but kept his mouth shut.

He reached over and grabbed the biggest box, as he always liked to start out with the biggest package first.

Pat opened his first package, very carefully, and found the CPO coat that he had wanted so badly lying inside.

He pulled it out amid the sighs of delight from both Penny and his mom. He laid it in his lap and sat there looking at it as if it were an odd curiosity.

Pat looked up from his prized possession with fresh tears in his eyes; tears so thick that he could barely discern his mother.

"Isn't that the one you wanted, sweetheart?" Delores asked him with tears welling up in her eyes as well.

"Oh, Mom…" Pat started, but could not finish his sentence as he flung himself into her arms.

They hugged for awhile and then Delores released her son.

"Your father and I went and bought that coat about three weeks after you and I saw it in that store," Delores said. "He was pretty excited about it…more so than me, and just the look on his face made it all worthwhile.

"He wanted you to have that coat so badly after I brought it up to him. He saved some money for a couple of weeks until he had enough to buy it. He agreed that you needed a new coat, so he wanted you to have the one that you sought after."

Pat looked back down at his prized possession. He had never been so happy and so sad at the same time in his entire life.

Chapter 12

Pat went back to school after the holiday break wearing his new CPO coat. He felt ten feet tall in that coat. Most of the kids that he passed gave him a double take as they saw the coat.

Pat felt proud for the first time in months. Pride strictly from a material object Pat didn't think was that great; however, it did not change the fact that Pat felt really good about coming back to school after the Christmas break.

Pat was heading to English when he heard his name being called from behind him. He turned around just in time to see Mike running down the hall towards him.

"Cool coat, man," Mike said and wrapped his arm around Pat's shoulder.

"Yeah, this is the one I was telling you about last summer," Pat replied with a huge Cheshire cat smile plastered on his face. "It is the exact coat I was telling you guys about." Pat's smile faded just a bit as he told Mike. "Turns out my dad bought it before he died so I could have it for Christmas."

"I hear ya, buddy," Mike said as he saw the hurt look in Pat's eyes. He figured he better start a new conversation to aid Pat in taking his mind off of his dead father. "We're going to get a hockey game going right after school down at the rink. You interested?"

"Yeah," Pat told him. "I don't have much for homework, so I should be able to get home, grab my gear and head down there. Who's all playing, anyway?"

"Well," Mike replied as he looked down the hall at a couple of passing girls from the ninth grade, "you, me, Chet, the Taylor boys, and probably the Grimm's…and a few more. Nice view, huh?" Mike nodded towards the ninth grade girls as they sauntered down the hall towards their next class.

Pat turned his head just in time before the girl's entered their next class. "Oh, yeah," Pat answered with a grin. "Hey, that looks like Julie Steege and Beth Donner, doesn't it?"

"You can tell who it is by just looking at the rear?" Mike asked Pat, and then gave him a lewd wink.

"Hell, yeah," Pat replied with a bawdy smile.

"That Julie is way too good looking, man," Mike said with a sneer.

"She ain't got shit on Alice, though," Pat replied and punched Mike in the arm and took off down the hall.

"Hey!" Mike cried out in surprise. "I'll get you for that, man," Mike called down the hall at his best friend before Mr. Saunders came out of his class room door with a look of disgust on his face.

"Mr. Schomer," Mr. Saunders said with a sneer on his face. "Must I always remind you to keep your voice down in the hallway? No one is allowed to yell in the hall. You will be disrupting other classes. Now get in here, as I am about to start today's lesson."

"Yes, Sir," Mike replied as he dropped his eyes and walked quickly past the teacher into the class room.

Mr. Saunders followed him into the room after he scanned the hallway both directions. Once satisfied that no other ruffians were left loose to wander the hallways unescorted, he closed the door to begin his class.

Pat arrived at the English class just before the bell rang indicating that everyone should be in their assigned class. It sure feels good to have friends, Pat thought as he found his seat and prepared for his favorite class.

Part Three

August 1972

Chapter 1

On the 16th of May, 1972, the Governor of Alabama, George Wallace, was shot and paralyzed by Arthur Herman Bremer, a 21-year-old bus boy and janitor from Milwaukee. He was making his third bid for the presidency, and after being hit four times by bullets, it more than sealed any future aspirations for being President.

On June 17, 1972 at the Democratic National Headquarters in Washington, D.C. in an office complex called 'Watergate'; there was a break-in. The men were arrested, and the attempted cover-up would seal the fate of then President Richard Nixon. This illegal action and other activities more than sealed any future aspirations for Nixon to remain President.

Now it was August, and it had been almost two years since Howard McCray died.

Two years had changed Pat from when his father was alive.

Two years had passed by, and Pat started to grow his hair out...much to the mortification of his mother.

"Mom," Pat said to her after a snide comment was made about the length of his hair, "it's nineteen seventy two. It's the fashion, that's all. It's not even that long."

It would be a debate for years to come, Pat figured. His mom didn't give up very easily...at least not without a fight.

Pat had been discovering that really, truly great music existed; and it wasn't being played on the Fairfield radio station that Pat listened to almost every summer day at the swimming pool.

Artists like David Bowie and his album 'The Rise and Fall of Ziggy Stardust'; Ten Years After and their album 'Rock and Roll Music to the World'; The Doors (after the demise of Jim Morrison who died of an overdose in 1971 before Pat had even heard of the band) posthumously produced 'L A Woman'.

The Moody Blues put out their seventh album, 'Seventh Sojourn', and later, in one year, a band named Pink Floyd, Pat's all-time favorite band, would release the biggest selling album of all-time, 'Dark Side of the Moon.'

Both Jimi Hendrix and Janis Joplin died in 1970, and Pat hadn't listened to them until they were dead. But boy, oh boy, was he listening to them now!!

The boys were out wandering the streets on this hot Wednesday night in August. Nothing more to do on a summer night at ten o'clock after watching the Wahkashen Legion Baseball team, lose…in extra innings.

On the way home, Mike told the gang of his big plan.

I

Mike told his friends to pay attention. He wanted the guys to listen carefully because this was going to be quite an adventure for the gang.

"We are going to grab my folks' tent," Mike started to tell the gang; "we'll pitch it in Cetanmila Park Friday morning. We'll go down on the north side of the skating rink, just off of the Snake road, over by the Gagelin shelter.

"There are lots of trees in that area, as you are all well aware, and it will be the perfect place to pitch a tent. We can roast hotdogs for lunch and supper, make campfire potatoes, have cereal for breakfast, go fishing and hopefully fry some of our catch, go swimming, and just hang out. I think it would be a great way to say 'So Long' to the summer, and 'Hello Again' to the start of another school year.

"What do you think?"

"Yeah, that's cool," was the only reply the boys could muster. It was all too good to be true.

"Count me in!" Lenny replied after smiling and thinking about it for the first few minutes.

"Oh, yeah…you can count me in, too," Pat said with the same enthusiasm. "I wanted to go camping lately. It's getting to be late in the year, so a camping trip before the start of school is OK with me. I guess if it has to be with you two…homos…well, then I guess it has to be."

"Homos?" Mike replied. "Just who in the hell are you calling a homo? You must be talking about Lenny, for it certainly can't be me. Hell, Karla and I are going out on a date this year, you wait and see." Mike then looked at Lenny with a smile.

"You two *are* the homos…homos," Lenny responded to both of them, and then pulled out a cigarette. "And besides, if anyone is taking Karla out on a date, it won't be a *homo* like you…"

Pat merely laughed at the possibility of either of them on a date with Karla. It was so terribly absurd. He would be taking her out, if anyone was taking her out.

"Wait a minute," Lenny interjected. "How long are you planning this camping trip?"

"I'm thinking from Friday morning to Sunday night," Mike replied with a grin and a puff of smoke. Mike liked his plan very much, and he was positive that the gang was more than ready, willing and able to attend.

After contemplating this for a second or two, Lenny told Mike, "I can do that." Then he looked over at Pat. "What about you, homo… You think you can get something like this approved?"

"I'm pretty sure," Pat returned to Lenny, and then looked over at Mike. "If I start with my mom tonight, I think I could actually pull it off."

"Then let's do it. My folks won't care if I use the tent. They haven't had it out in a couple of years, so my dad will want it aired out, anyway," Mike told them.

After a few more comments about each others sexuality, and a couple of cigarettes, it was agreed. The big adventure was set.

The boys started walking again with no particular destination in mind.

"Hold on," Pat said and came to a stop. "I was supposed to go to

Fairfield with mom and Penny this weekend for something or another," Pat said to the guys, "but I think I can get out of that."

"You really think she'll let you off of the hook?" Mike asked Pat.

Mike knew as well as Pat that the likelihood of Pat actually getting out of going to Fairfield with his mom and sister was just about as good as the Minnesota Vikings playing in Super Bowl VII this year. And that was pretty much…zilch. Hell, they lost Super Bowl IV 23 to 7. And, even Fran Tarkenton came back to the team this year.

"No, smartass," Pat replied with an air of sarcasm, "but I won't know unless I ask.

"Pat," Mike said and placed his hand on his shoulder, for comfort, "I hate to tell you this, but you really are a going to Fairfield with your Mom. And I only say that…because…it's true!!"

With that Pat slugged Mike in the shoulder.

"Thanks a lot, Pal," Pat told his friend with feigned anger in his voice.

"I don't mean to offend," Mike said rubbing his shoulder where Pat hit him. "I just want you to be a part of this grand adventure."

"Oh, I'll be there. You can count on it."

"Do you really think Karla would go on a date with me this year," Mike asked the guys with a straight face.

Lenny and Pat just looked at each other and started to laugh.

II

Mike had grabbed the family tent Friday morning after his folks said that they could go on a camping adventure. Mike told them that it would be just the three of them; Pat, Lenny and him. All they were going to do would be fishing, swimming at the pool, having camp fires, sleeping in the tent or outside looking up at the stars and talking well into the night.

It took a great deal of convincing on Pat's part to get his mom to agree to such an adventure, and she only did succumb under one condition: Pat had to check in every morning and report in to his mother. He had agreed to such a little thing in order to attend one of the greatest adventures in his young life. Besides, he would need to pick-up more supplies, anyway.

"I'm not so sure," Delores said looking at Pat, "Just you three boys? It scares me a little."

"The police drive through there on their routes all night long, Mom," Pat told his worried mother. "It will be alright. We will stay together at all time." And with that last statement, Delores turned and faced her son, eye to eye.

"I want for you to swear to me, Pat," Delores said to her son with serious conviction in her voice, "that you boys will always stay together, no matter what.

"I want to hear you swear that to me, Pat", she said again when he did not reply immediately.

"Shit, Mom...We will, I promise," Pat told her with a sinister smile on his face, not breaking away from her steely-eyed gaze.

"That is not at all what I meant, Pat," she said to him with a stern voice and a slight smile of her own. Her stare finally faded back to normality. "I guess Penny and I could go to Fairfield for an afternoon, just the two of us. She wanted to look at school clothes, anyway. You won't miss *not* shopping with your mother and sister, would you?"

"I think I'll survive the ordeal, Mom," Pat said to her as he rolled his eyes, and then Pat hugged her, hard.

When Delores felt certain that her son would do as they had agreed, she left the house to go bowling with her team. Pat called Mike right away after they closed the door.

"Well, I'm in," Pat said. "I have to check in with my mom in the mornings to prove I'm still alive, but that's all."

"I don't even have to do that," Mike bragged. "I have the tent out already, so you just pack a few things tonight and the rest in the morning and

I'll have my dad drag the tent down to the Park in the morning, and then we'll hook-up and get everything ready. Have you heard from Lenny, yet?"

"No," Pat told Mike. "Do you want me to call him?"

"Nah, he'll call me when he finds out. I'll see you in the morning."

"That's right. See ya in the morning."

Turns out Lenny didn't have any trouble with his folks. They were very understanding about young men needing time to spend with their friends. Lenny's parents were pretty cool, when you thought about it.

So the gangs little get-a-way was set-up, and all three boys would be starting on Friday morning, and ending on Sunday night.

The morning couldn't have come quick enough for Pat. He hardly slept at all with anticipation of the camp outing. It was going to be just the gang, no one else. What a blast this is going to be. Pat had set out everything he'd need to make the trip the best last night before he went to bed to get no sleep. He didn't want to waste any time trying to pull things together before he had to ride down to the park.

He looked at everything he had laid out.

Had he grabbed too many things for the trip? He didn't think so, but when he surveyed everything he had arranged, it sure looked like these boys were going to climb Mt. Everest, not just spend a couple of days and nights in Cetanmila Park.

He hoped he would be able to carry all of the necessities. If not, maybe Mike's dad would haul some it down there for him.

III

Pat was so excited he could barely sit still. He wrote out a list for the stuff he would need, and as he was re-reading the list and checking it against all of the gear he laid out to make sure that everything was in order, Pat recalled the last time he'd gone on a camping trip...

...his family had gone to Yellowstone three years ago, and had the best time ever, save for that black bear incident.

Actually, to call it an incident was making light of a very serious situation.

Dad was out collecting firewood right after breakfast on the third day of their trip. Although they had seen black bears in the area before, with their cubs in tow, they never had a female that came right into their camp site. On that morning of the third day, she decided that the time must have been right. She came straight into their site with an extremely hungry look in her eye.

She had two cubs with her, but they were occupied with climbing in and out of the large trash cans the park had provided. There were two trash cans strategically placed between two sites on one side of the road that were facing two other sites on the other side of the road. Those four sites would utilize those two cans.

Before the incident, Pat and Penny were tickled to death watching those cubs climbing all over fallen trees, up and down picnic tables and in and out of those trash cans. They were so adorable that Penny wanted to go give one a huge bear hug (pardon the pun) to which her dad had warned her about how cuddly they may look and how extremely terrible it would be to have them turn mean on you…or have the mother come charging at you in fear for her cubs' safety.

They had all just finished eating their breakfast which was camp style eggs and bacon, toast that Pat had made over the open fire with the wire handle holder in which he could do two slices at the same time, and washed it all down with fresh orange juice. His mom had made a huge batch of eggs and bacon, and Pat had eaten like a man who had just crawled on hands and knees through the Sahara for over six days.

The mother bear seemed to have forgotten all about her cubs for a second or so as apparently the smell of bacon and eggs was just too much to resist.

Delores was washing the dishes in a plastic basin as Pat and Penny were sitting on the picnic table watching the frolicking cubs. They didn't see the approaching mother black bear that had nothing on her mind but filling her empty stomach with Delores' fine cooking.

Delores had seen the bear's approach, and so she performed the mandatory, "Shoo," at the impending bear.

Delores had even used the perfunctory hand sweep thinking that that would be enough to make the bear think twice about furthering her forward momentum. I mean, she did use the magic word and the obligatory arm sweep. What more could a human do to help hinder the forward progress of a female carnivore?

The advance of the female did not deter with the active arm movements, nor did she falter at the voice of Delores; not only didn't she not stop, but she paid about as much attention to her and her ranting as the Nixon administration did to his cabinet.

All Delores thought about was to protect her children.

"You kids get into the car," Delores yelled to them, never taking her eyes from the

approaching bear, and breaking the children's attention they had on the playful cubs off of the side of the road. "And I mean, NOW!"

Penny and Pat turned their attention away from the playful cubs at the sound of their mother's voice to see the mother bear descending upon their campsite. They immediately did as their mother said and almost ran each other over trying to get to their car.

Delores looked around for anything she could use. Her only instinct was to grab the warm soapy water that was still in the basin on the picnic table she had used to wash the dishes.

"I told you to 'shoo'," Delores said to the bear while turning and reaching for the basin.

As quick as she could, Delores grabbed the basin and flung the warm soapy water directly into the bear's face.

The bear gave out a terrific howl, and turned and ran back towards the cubs. Within a second or so, the cubs joined their mother and retreated from the campground area.

Pat and Penny had witnessed all of this happen, wide-eyed, sitting inside their car with their faces glued to the car window. They were in awe at the heroics of their very own mother.

After the dust settled, so to speak, they exited the car and ran towards their mother. They both wrapped their arms around Delores' waist and hugged her as hard as they could, looking over their shoulder every now and again...just in case.

Howard came back with an armful of firewood he had collected and stood staring at the sight of his children and his wife in an embrace.

He had absolutely no idea as to what had just transpired.

IV

Pat checked his list, and just like that happy, white haired bearded gentlemen of the Christmas fame, checked it twice. Satisfied, he placed the list into his back pocket and then sat down to determine the best way to haul all of these necessities down to Cetanmila Park.

He was definitely going to need help from his Mike's dad. There was no way that he and his fellow gang members would ever be able to haul all of this shit down to the park on their bikes.

Smiling like the Cheshire cat, Pat went to call Mike about getting him and his Dad to haul this stuff for him.

This was going to be quite the adventure, Pat thought.

While he waited for Mike to answer the phone, his thoughts went to his dad…again. It seemed to Pat that whenever he had some spare time on his hands, his mind would pull memories of his dad out and shoot them across his brain.

Pat figured his memory of that camping trip to Yellowstone brought up his father.

He could still see the look on his dad's face when he returned to the campsite, after mom had fended off the bear with the basin of warm soapy water. He really had absolutely no idea what had just happened.

How long would these memories that came fleeting back to him in a random fashion happen to him, he didn't know. But Pat knew one thing for certain; the face of his father had started to fade, just a little, over the past twenty two months…

Chapter 2

There existed an organization known as: The International Organization of the Rainbow for Girls. This organization was established in 1922 by W. Mark Sexson, and is still going strong today; and has always been a positive influential society for young women, ages eleven to twenty, from all over the United States over the years.

It was, at that time and is today *"...a service-based organization for girls that provided leadership and character building opportunities..."*

That organizational statement sounded really rational and truly just for the parents; and for the participants as well. In fact, if it were not for the wording of the organizations statement, I doubt parents would have allowed their young blossoming daughters into such a club. Young women ages eleven to twenty had tremendous pressures to face on a daily basis, more so than boys of the same age; and to try to rope in the emotions that are changing along with the developing bodies through the introduction of puberty is like, well...it's a great deal like herding cats.

Providing leadership and developing character is a wonderful proposal. Providing an intellectual and cultural environment should prove to be another way to aid in establishing the leadership and developing character. At least that's what the director of the North Dakota organization had in mind in the summer of 1972 when the Rainbow Chapter took a group of these young women, from all over the state of North Dakota, on a week long retreat to Wahkashen.

The director had planned on the club leaving on Monday, and returning the girls back home on the following Sunday evening.

However, little did the director and his staff know that this was the summer of 1972; three years following Woodstock, and that 'free love' was still hovering in the air like so much dander from a dandelion at the lips of a three year old; also it presented a prime opportunity for some of these young women to build a little character of their own, albeit without the outside influence of their adult chaperones.

Three of these girls, three tie-dyed, clog and hip hugger wearing females, all from the small community of Garlton, ND, a stones throw away from the Canadian border, had plans of their own intellectual and cultural development. Linda Bjorne, Peggy Ramblith and Susan Sarandon (not the famous actress of the same name) came to Wahkashen looking for the opportunity to build leadership and enhance their character. But, with all three young women currently of the age of fifteen, and being budding, spiritual young hippie girls who lived in the articles written in the Rolling Stone magazines and abided by the 'free love' theorem of the late sixties and early seventies, they were looking forward to discovering more in Wahkashen than their director could even have imagined.

These three girls had all read 'The Sensuous Woman', by J, and had read most of 'Everything You wanted to know about Sex, but were Afraid to Ask', by Dr David Rueben, and were very eager to explore their spiritual meaning in a contemporary world. Or, as John Updike would write about in numerous novels about the times they lived in, these girls were, *"...trying to find meaning in a society spiritually empty and in a state of moral decay."*

It certainly went without saying, these young hippie girls were looking for love...

Chapter 3

The Rainbow girls got to Wahkashen on the Monday night prior to the boys witnessing the Wahkashen Legion baseball team lose, in extra innings; and it was there that they established their retreat at the local two year trade school that was reduced in both students and faculty during the summer months. The trade school had numerous dormitories to house the students throughout the school year. There were boy's dorms and a girl's dorm, and many smaller homes that housed all of the staff.

The school normally housed these students the entire year for schooling, and the students came from all over North Dakota, South Dakota, and Minnesota. Occasionally there would be students from other areas of the United States, but primarily it was local kids who attended this particular trade school.

For a nominal fee, the Rainbow organization would rent the dorms and all of the other classrooms for a week from the school. It was not very expensive, and with the parents' donations, it made the burden that much easier on the organization.

Once they got established, housed all of the girl's into separate dorms (they had to use some of the boy's dorms as well due to the large number of girl's that attended this year), the staff began to consolidate their training schedules to keep the girl's occupied.

The classes maintained the girls' activities for the full day, and most of the night. Linda, Peggy and Susan were dying to get away for a few hours and explore Wahkashen on their own. They knew that if they waited for this to happen, then it wouldn't.

So, they devised themselves a plan that would get them out for awhile, undetected, and then they could have a little fun on their own.

Friday night, after supper and all of the formal classes that they had to attend concluded, they would go to their rooms. When everyone was surely asleep after lights out, they would quietly and carefully meet in Linda's room, sneak out her window, and escape for a few hours.

That was the plan.

It worked to a tee.

So here were three hippie girls from Garlton, ND, running down the dark streets of Wahkashen looking for fun. They had no idea where they were going, and they were enjoying every step of the way.

They had been swimming at the pool in that park once or twice, and they enjoyed the serenity of the park, and seeing as how they were only a couple of blocks away and they didn't know where else to go, that was directly where they headed.

Three young hippie girls from Garlton, ND were heading off in the general direction of the Wahkashen Park on a Friday evening with aspirations of an adventure racing through their heads.

Chapter 4

Mike had a nice campfire going. He was quite the firebug, that's for sure, Pat thought. They had eaten a couple of walleyes that they had caught earlier that day. All they did was fillet them and fry them in a cast iron pan with butter. Lenny's mom would probably be mad later at Lenny for him *'borrowing'* it from her kitchen, but Lenny thought he should be able to get away with it.

He may get away with it, but Pat had his doubts. Moms are pretty picky about their appliances such as pots and pans. Dads were the same way whenever you decided to use their tools. Man, they would be furious if they found the wrench you were using to tweak your bike or something still laying on the garage floor when they got home.

Pat discovered that the hard way.

The boys were sitting around the camp fire, enjoying each others company, smoking a *'borrowed'* Camel that Mike had gotten from his dad (although Pat didn't think that Mike would return the smoked Camels), and the stars overhead, when Lenny heard what he said was girl's laughing.

"Shhhh," Lenny said to them after they told him that he was full of crap. "Don't you hear the laughing?"

Both Mike and Pat stopped talking and turned their heads to one side in a better attempt at listening to the sounds of the evening.

After staying that way for a few seconds, they all heard the soft chatter and a little giggling of what could only be female voices.

Looking up to the beginning of the Snake road, the boys could make out moving dark figures. There seemed to be three dark shadows moving towards them. The longer they watched, the closer they got, and the more visible they became.

They were just able to start making out what the moving figures were saying when they heard a voice say, very quietly, "...look, is that a fire?"

Another minute and the mysterious dark figures were just a few feet away from the gang's camp site, just outside the glow ring around the camp site from the fire.

"Hello there," said one of the dark figures. It was definitely a female voice, Pat knew. There was no mistaking that.

"Hi" Mike replied. "Who goes there?"

"Linda Bjorne. Who's that?"

"Mike Schomer," he replied, and then looking over his shoulder at the guys he whispered, "Who is Linda Bjorne?"

Pat and Lenny looked at Mike and both shrugged their shoulders. Then they turned their eyes back to the strangers who happened upon their camp site.

The girls didn't say anything else, but they didn't walk any closer. Pat could hear them talking quietly amongst themselves, and then they took a couple of hesitant steps closer to the camp fire.

Apparently unsure what they were going to do, the girls stood just outside the glow ring produced by the camp fire. Finally, after a few minutes they started to walk a little closer to the boys' campfire.

"May we join you?" one of the girls asked.

"I don't see why not," Mike replied, and the girls slowly, cautiously came into the circle of light. The boys then got their first glimpse of the three members of the North Dakota Chapter of Rainbow girls.

I

The boys had moved a couple of the parks picnic tables over to the vicinity of their camp site when they first arrived. Mike was sitting on the side of one of the tables closest to the fire, with Pat and Lenny sitting on the other side of the table, also facing the fire.

The girls came over to the fire and Pat noticed that all three girls were wearing blue jean hip huggers with the extra piece of cloth sewn in down at seem at the bottom by the jeans. The cloth which expanded the bellbottoms a bit more had various colors and flowers on it. Two of the girls were wearing t-shirts that must have depicted their favorite bands, Pat thought; and one girl was wearing a low cut light blue, almost a powder blue, pullover shirt that had the elastic around the collar area so that the wearer could slide the shirt down to below the shoulder line and the shirt would then come to rest just above the triceps.

Pat noticed that the bands depicted on the other two girls' shirts were *Led Zeppelin* and *Jimi Hendrix*. Nothing wrong with that, he conceded.

"Hi," the girl with the light blue shoulder shirt said. "I'm Linda Bjorne."

Pat noticed she had round cat-like eyes and short brown hair that accented her high cheekbones. Her hairdo curved around her face and really defined the roundness of her eyes. She was really cute, he thought. Somehow, he thought he had seen her before, but he wasn't sure where, or how.

Then she pointed to the girl in the *Led Zeppelin* shirt and told the boys, "This is Peggy Ramblith."

"Hi," Peggy said smiling sheepishly. She was a pretty girl in a different way. She had reddish hair and freckles. When she smiled her eyes tightened up so she looked almost Japanese.

"I'm Susan Sarandon," said the girl in the *Jimi Hendrix* shirt. Susan sported short blonde hair and a somewhat pudgy face. Not fat, but sort of pudgy, like with baby fat.

"Hello," the boys said together.

There was that moment of awkward silence where the girl's all just stood there. Everyone was kind of looking at each other, and then down at the fire, and then out into the darkness. That moment of awkward silence was finally broken by Lenny.

"Want to sit down?" Lenny said standing up and gestured to the vacant picnic table across from the fire.

"Sure," Peggy said and the girl's all took a seat on the same side of the vacant table facing the boys, and the fire.

The girl's all sat side-by-side and looked down at the fire not talking, just taking in the fire's collage of colors that accompany the snaps and crackles from the particles of water remaining in the firewood, as the flames engulfed the wood.

"Are you guys from town here?" Linda finally asked, looking up from the flames hypnotic vigor.

"Yeah," Mike replied still staring at the fire, "we are all from Wahkashen. Oh, by the way," he said as he sat up a little straighter and touched his chest, "I'm Mike Schomer and this here is Lenny Ermish." Lenny waved and smiled. "And that one over there is Pat McCray," he said as he pointed at Pat. Pat did the same exchange of smile and slight wave to the girls. Mike then turned and looked directly at Linda and said, "Where are you girls from?"

"We're from Garlton," Linda replied. "Do you know where that is?"

"Yeah," Lenny said and turned her way. "That's way up by the Canadian border, isn't it?"

"Yeah, that's right. That's pretty good as most people haven't even *heard* of Garlton, let alone know here it is."

Lenny smiled at that thinking it *was* pretty cool that he even knew.

"What brings you to Wahkashen?" Lenny asked them.

"We're Rainbow girls," Peggy said with a sense of pride in her voice.

"Rainbow girls?" Pat said. "What is that?"

"Rainbow girls are an organization similar to say…the Girl Scouts, and stuff like that. We get together once a month and they teach us stuff like: love, religion, nature, fidelity, patriotism…stuff like that. You see there are seven colors of the Rainbow, and each color has a specific representation to either: Love, Fidelity, Religion, Nature…and so on.

"We are on a week long retreat here in Wahkashen."

Mike looked down at his watch and saw that it was nearing ten thirty.

"They let you out this late?" Mike said with a mixture of sarcasm and curiosity in his voice. Not heavy sarcasm, because he didn't know these girls, but a little sarcasm, because that's the way Mike talked to most people.

"Well, no," Peggy replied, sounding a little embarrassed and self conscious as she looked down for a second. "We were getting bored and never got to go anywhere without an adult, and we wanted to get away and explore some; so, we snuck out for a little while."

The boys snickered a little to that bit of information.

"Cool," Lenny said, and the rest of the gang agreed.

All of them sat in silence for a little while enjoying the fire, *and* the company.

Pat kept sneaking glances at Linda. She was really cute, and he figured all three of the girls were probably the same age as him and the gang. At least, he *hoped* they were.

"You girls want a Pepsi?" Pat asked. "We have some in the cooler in the tent."

"You guys are camping out down here," Susan, who hadn't said very much since she introduced herself, asked.

"Oh, yeah," Lenny said and pointed back into the shadows behind them where they could barely make out a darkened shape of a tent.

"That is way cool," Linda spoke, and then said, "Sure, I'll have a Pepsi."

The other two girls had all agreed, as did Mike and Lenny.

Pat got up and walked into the shadows on the edge of the camp site, and everyone could hear him, not see him, raise the zipper of the tent and rummage around a bit.

They saw a light from a flashlight, and then they heard him return the zipper. He emerged from the shadows carrying a six-pack of Pepsis that he pulled from the cooler.

He started pulling them off, one by one, and handing one to each of the girls, and then he spread the rest out to the gang.

All three said 'thank you' as they accepted the ice cold Pepsi.

Once again the ever awkward silence descended upon the camp site as everyone was enjoying their Pepsi.

Mike broke the silence this time by lighting up a Camel from the pack he 'borrowed' from his dad.

"Do you have another one of those?" Linda asked Mike.

Mike looked over the fire at her, and said, "Sure...sure I do."

He got up, walked around the fire pit while shaking out a cigarette from the pack and offered it to her. Then, he reached into his pocket and produced a book of matches. He struck the match and held it for Linda in a cupped hand. Linda bent forward and touched the flame with the business end of the Camel. Pat looked up in time to see her face lightly illuminated by the flame of the match. She was very intriguing.

After she exhaled, she said, "Thank you. It's been awhile since I have had one of these."

"Not allowed to smoke in the Rainbow girls?" Mike said as he offered the pack to the other girls.

"Well, no," Linda replied. "And we never seem to get away long enough for us to even have a smoke."

Peggy accepted a cigarette and Mike lit hers as well. Susan turned down the offer.

"I don't smoke, but thanks, anyway" Susan said.

"We've been down in this park before," Linda said blowing out a puff of smoke. "We got to go swimming in the pool the other day."

Pat looked up at Linda after she made that statement, and then he wondered if he had seen her there and just didn't know it. But then again, he would have noticed a beautiful stranger like her…at least he thought he would be able to.

"And," Linda continued, "Seeing as how we knew this park, and that we are staying only a few blocks away, we figured we would come down here and hang out for a while."

"Where *are* you staying," Pat asked her.

"At the trade school," Linda replied. "I guess they let the organization rent out the place for the week."

Pat nodded his head and never took his eyes off of Linda. Finally, thinking maybe he would get busted, he looked away and back at the fire. He hated to get busted for staring.

"How long are you guys staying…ahhhh, camping down here?" Susan asked.

"Until Sunday," Lenny replied looking at her. "We got here this morning, and will pack everything up and go back home on Sunday."

"That's cool," Susan replied staring into the fire. "This is sure a nice park."

"Yeah," Lenny said, "we hang out here all the time. Hey, we're going fishing tomorrow morning. You guys wanna come with? I mean, if you aren't doing anything else."

Pat looked over at Lenny, but Lenny just kept his eyes on Susan. He didn't even acknowledge the *'I don't believe you just asked these girls to come fishing with us'* look from Pat.

"Where do you fish?" Linda asked looking over at Lenny and casually flicked her spent cigarette into the fire.

"Right over there," Lenny said and pointed in the general direction of the beach where the boys fish. "It's right along the banks of the Red River. We ate two walleyes for supper tonight that we caught."

"Cool," Susan said.

"Yeah," Mike replied. "It was very cool."

All three girls looked at each other, did a little conferring, and finally Linda spoke.

"Well, we have to do a big breakfast they planned for us in the morning, as a group, but then they said we were going to get some free time. We were going to go swimming in the afternoon."

The group thought about this for awhile, staring into the fire. Pat kept taking little glimpses at Linda sitting at the table.

"Well," Lenny finally suggested, "Why don't you do the breakfast thing, come down here and meet us for fishing, and bring your swimsuits with you and then we will all go swimming in the afternoon. Who knows...maybe we will catch enough fish and you guys can join us for supper?"

"That does sound like fun," Linda said. "Doesn't it guys?" she spoke and looked over at Peggy and Susan.

"Yeah, it sure does," Peggy said. And after a second or two she also said "Let's do it if we can."

"Alright, then," Mike said. "It's a date..."

"Yeah..." the girls said in unison.

A date, Pat thought? He'd never been on a date before. Not, like, an official date, anyway.

And although it was going to be the six of them together, he still considered it a date.

That was waaaaay cool.

Chapter 5

The girls stayed and talked for about two hours. It seemed like they would be able to talk all night. Typical girls, Pat thought. They could and would talk for hours, but tonight Pat didn't mind. Linda was really cute, bubbly and funny. He was truly enjoying her company.

But before it got too late, Linda suggested that they got back to the dorm before they got busted, and that would ruin tomorrow's plans.

So, they stood up and said 'good night' to the gang.

"Do you want us to walk with you," Pat asked, with great expectations. "It's kinda late, and you shouldn't be walking alone. It is only Wahkashen, but…."

"Nah," Linda replied. "We are only a few of blocks from here."

"It would be nice," Peggy replied and gave Linda a nudge in the ribs with her elbow.

"You know," Linda said after she took her hint, "it would be nice."

So, the boys all stood and they paired up to walk the girls back to their dorm room.

Mike walked with Peggy, Lenny walked with Susan, and Pat…well, Pat, he almost died because he got to walk with Linda, who Pat thought was *the* prettiest of the girls' gang.

They walked slowly up the Snake road that led back out of the park. Mike was in the lead with Peggy, Lenny and Susan were in the middle, and Pat and Linda took up the rear.

"So how long have you been in this Rainbow thing?" Pat asked and looked over at her. Although they were a ways away from the soft light of the fire, Pat imagined he could still make out her eyes in the dark; the way her hair surrounded her face giving it a semi-round appearance.

"I've been in it for three years now. My mom signed me up when I was twelve, along with Peggy. Susan started last year."

Wow, Pat thought…she is fifteen.

Cool.

"Do you like it?" Pat inquired as he shuffled along side her, hands in his pockets to try to stop them from trembling, wishing he could see her more clearly in the faint moonlight.

"Yeah, it's cool. I like the friends I have made so far, and some of the stuff we have learned is pretty interesting. Plus," she said and turned around so she was walking backwards beside him, "we get to go to cool places like this for a week."

"You think Wahkashen is cool?"

"Well, yeah. Way cooler than Garlton. You definitely have a much better park than we do. The pool is twice the size. We have a teeny tiny park with nothing in it but some old wooden picnic tables. You have duck ponds, shelters, and all kinds of cool stuff."

She then turned around again so she was walking forward with Pat.

Pat started to think about the park. She's right…it was a pretty cool park.

"Yeah, me and the guys hang out here a lot."

"You mean *'the gang and me'*, don't you?"

"Oh, yeah…you're right."

"I don't mean to correct you, but my dad does it to me all the time. So now I find myself doing the same thing. Weird, huh?"

"Nah, that's not weird at all. I should know better than to talk like a farmer. Unless, of course, you're a farmer, and then I would feel totally stupid for stating it like that."

"No, I'm not a farmer. I'm a city girl who lives in a small town."

Pat thought about what his dad always said to him. He thought about the mannerisms that his father always displayed…the 'Howard-isms' his mother called them. Like Pat's favorite Howard-ism whenever Penny or he was told to do something quickly, or else: "*They are going to have to perform a 2, 4, 6 on you.*"

When asked what that meant, Howard would reply, "*It will take two doctors, four hours to pull six inches of my boot out of your ass!*"

I

"So what else do you do besides hang with your friends?" Linda asked Pat.

"I play baseball; hockey in the winter."

"Really?" she replied. "Are you any good?"

"Not really."

"At baseball?"

"Neither of them," Pat said with a snicker.

Linda laughed at that and then said, "Well, at least you are honest. I like that in a man."

She has a cute laugh as well, Pat thought. I sure am glad I am walking next to Linda right now.

"How about you?" Pat asked Linda. "What do you do for fun when you are not chasing rainbows?

"Chasing rainbows…that's cute," she said and reached out and pushed him on the shoulder like a friend would do when you said something…well, something cute.

"I like to sew, and I go bowling every now and then. I ride my bike everywhere, and just hang out, you know, with my friends and stuff."

"That's cool," Pat replied.

"Hey," Linda said and grabbed Pat by the sleeve of his shirt, "you got a smoke?"

"Ahhh, no…but Mike should have some more.

"Hey, Mike!" Pat yelled out.

Mike stopped and turned around.

"What?"

"Wait up; I want to grab a couple of smokes."

"You wait here," Pat told Linda. I'll be right back."

"OK," Linda said, and then stopped in her tracks.

Pat ran past Lenny and Susan, who didn't seem to notice him anyway as they were engaged in a conversation about bands, which is about all Pat could decipher when he ran past them.

"Here you go, man," Mike said when Pat reached him and stopped. Mike handed Pat a couple of Camels. "You got fire?"

Pat reached into his pocket, rummaged around a bit, and then produced a pack of matches with the Shell symbol on them.

"Sure do, buddy," Pat told him. "Thanks."

Pat turned around and ran past Lenny and Susan, who still didn't seem to know he was even there, and returned to the place where he had left Linda.

When he got back to the spot, at least he thought he was at the spot, where he had left Linda to retrieve a couple of smokes, she wasn't there.

Pat's heart was racing. Where did she go?

"Linda?" Pat called out softly.

Pat waited a few moments. His heart was going to burst. Where could she have gone?

"Pat," Linda's voice replied back in the shadows of the trees on the side of the road, "I'm over here."

Pat turned to his left, squinted his eyes a bit in an attempt to see into the darkness that would allow him to see no more than ten inches from his face.

"Where?"

"Just follow my voice, silly."

Pat took a couple of steps off of the Snake road, and walked into an area of trees that were thick in this section of the park. Pat knew every little detail and area of the park, but with his racing heart and unable to see clearly in the dark, he was concerned that Linda would be too close to the duck pond and fall in, or something.

After he took a dozen or more steps he came upon a picnic table overlooking the duck pond. The moon was reflecting off of the water and it illuminated a little slice of the shoreline of the pond.

"Pretty, huh?" Linda asked as Pat made it over to the table, and sat down next to her.

"Yeah, it's really nice."

He handed Linda a cigarette, and then struck a match in a cupped hand, like Mike did earlier, and touched the end of Linda's cigarette, and then his, and then he threw the match towards the pond.

"You are pretty lucky to be able to sleep down here," Linda told him, and then turned her face towards his. "You have a girlfriend, Pat?"

Pat felt the red heat of embarrassment creeping up from under his collar. He thanked God that it was as dark as it was so Linda wouldn't see the redness on his face.

"Ahhh, well…," is all Pat could stammer out.

"I'm sorry," Linda said with a hint of apprehension in her voice, and turned her face away. "I shouldn't have asked you that."

"No, that's alright. You can ask me that."

Pat took a drag off of his cigarette and exhaled. "No, I don't have a girlfriend."

"Why not?" Linda inquired looking back at him. "You seem like a nice guy. You're kinda cute, too. I would think you'd have all kinds of girlfriends."

Pat turned and looked at her in the moonlight. She was facing him and she smiled, ever so slowly and softly. Pat's heart began to race once again inside his chest. He was afraid that Linda would be able to hear the hammering coming from the source. Try as he could, he just didn't seem able to slow his heart down to a normal rate. His hands were sweating and his heart was racing in his chest like a runaway train going down a steep mountain.

"Well, there aren't too many girls around here that I am at all interested in…right now, that is." Then his mind was filled with images of Karla, and how in love he was with her since he was a kid. He was interested in someone then who was way older than he was, and that was a love interest of sheer futility.

"And how about you," Pat asked her back. "Do you have a guy?"

"No, but it's not because I am not looking. I'm from a small town, and the pickings are quite limited."

"But," Pat said with a touch of hope in his voice, "you *are* looking, right?"

"Sort of, I guess…I don't know."

They sat and listened to the frogs sing their nightly songs, enjoyed their cigarettes and watched the moonlight strike the ripples in the water caused by ducks swimming across the water.

"So you've been to the park before…right?" Pat asked her.

"Yeah," Linda answered him while watching the ducks. "We got to come here one afternoon with the entire crew. There were lots of girls…"

"Did you spend the whole day here? What did you do?"

Linda turned to face Pat. "We had a *huge* BBQ and then got to go swimming. We walked through the zoo, which is really cool. We don't even have a zoo in Garland.

"We screwed around out in the playground for awhile and just kinda hung out, ya know? We had beautiful weather," she finished and then looked away.

"I hear ya," Pat said. "This is a pretty cool park with lots to do and see. I just love being down here, either alone or with my friends. If I'm not down here playing ball or hockey in the winter, I'm just walking around. It is so peaceful here.

"You know what," he said to her and she turned back to face him again, "we'd better get going, or we are going to end up walking back by ourselves."

"Yeah, I suppose you're right," Linda replied and flicked away her cigarette. "Besides, I want to come down here again in the morning and go fishing with you guys."

"That's right," Pat replied.

Pat and Linda caught up with the others at the entrance to the park. They were standing there talking softly just off to the side of one of the street lights.

"What took you so long? Where were you guys?" Peggy asked with apprehension.

"We were just looking at the pond," Linda replied.

"We'd better get moving or we will get busted for sure," Susan said and headed off in the direction of the school.

II

The boys had dropped the girls off without any incident and watched them as one by one they crawled back through a bedroom window.

They started back for the park and only got a few steps when Pat said, "Those girls are way cool."

"Oh, yeah...way cool," Mike agreed. "I am really digging Peggy. She has the greatest sense of humor and she is just awesome."

"Susan's nice, but I don't think she's very interested in me," Lenny said with a touch of humility in his tone. "I mean, we had a good conversation about music, and she really knows her music, but she also seemed very distant. She kept checking to see where everyone else was while we were walking, you know what I mean?"

"Maybe she's just a little insecure, that's all," Mike told him. "You'll see her again tomorrow, and then you can take another shot with her. Peggy's cool, and tough. She grew up with two older brothers and they taught her all kinds of stuff. She told me she got into a fight last year and really beat on this other girl. I guess it wasn't just a 'cat fight' of any type, because she knows how to use her fists."

Then Mike turned and looked at Pat and asked, "well, my man, you seemed to be hitting it off well with Linda."

"I think she's the coolest girl I have ever met," Pat told them. "I have never met anyone like her. She's smart, she's cute, she doesn't have a boyfriend and she's the same age as me."

They walked in silence for a minute. Pat had his head in the clouds and could not stop thinking about Linda.

The boys got back to the park at a little past one in the morning. They sat at the picnic table and had another smoke, then turned in for the night.

Pat lay in his sleeping bag and thought about Linda. He thought about how her smile had made his hands shake. He thought about the questions she had asked him about having a boyfriend. He thought about her laugh, and how she wasn't really afraid of anything.

She was definitely the coolest girl he knew.

"Pat, you asleep?" Mike asked him and snapped him out of his dream about Linda.

"No, I'm still awake. Why?"

"We are going to have to get more cigarettes tomorrow. I am almost out, and apparently the girls like to smoke, but don't have any of their own. So, you got any money?"

"Yeah, I still have some left from the money my dad gave me for the movie. We should be able to buy a few packs."

Mike rolled over to his right.

"Lenny, you up?" Mike asked and gave him a nudge.

"Yeah, yeah, I'm up listening to you two chickens pecking away over there," Lenny replied.

"You have any cash, smartass?" Mike asked him.

"Yeah, I have a couple of bucks."

"Do you think your sister will get some smokes for us?"

"Yeah, she'll do it."

"How about getting us some beer, too?"

"Yeah, she'd do that, too."

"Do you think the girls will drink beer with us on Saturday night?" Pat asked.

"Sure, the way they act, footloose and fancy free," Mike replied. "Besides, Peggy said she'd enjoy a couple of beers if I were to score some."

"Well," Pat said, "I have two dollars, so if I just buy the smokes that should get us at least six packs. Then, with the money you and Lenny have, it should buy us a couple of cases of beer, or so. That should be enough, huh?"

"Yeah, that should do it," Mike replied.

Man, Pat thought; tomorrow was going to be the best day of his life, and it hasn't even started yet.

Chapter 6

The morning came with a flurry of sunlight and bird songs. Pat didn't think he had slept at all, but he felt realty refreshed and prepared for the day. Pat heard the distant sounds of lawnmowers cutting grass in the vicinity of the ball fields. They had started early this morning, seeing as how it was Saturday.

Pat woke Lenny up and gave him all of his money for cigarettes and beer.

"Let's toss down some breakfast and then drive over and talk to your sister," Mike told Lenny as he rolled out of his sleeping bag. "Then we'll come back here and get stuff ready for the fishing trip. I'm not really sure when the girls will show up, but I would imagine it will either be right before, or right after lunch."

"I will run home quick to check-in with my mom and pick up so more supplies," Pat told Mike, "and then I will be back.

"Do you want me to stay here and wait for the girls while you guys are gone?" Pat asked Mike and Lenny.

"You may as well," Mike replied. "You can start making sandwiches and get all of that packed and ready. Lenny and I are going to get the money to his sister and get our order in. We'll have her deliver everything down to the fishing site. That way it will be out of sight, and we can get it all later in the evening. We will talk the girls into getting out again later in the evening."

Pat agreed to that, and set out to creating the best lunches he could with the limited resources that they had available. Maybe, after he checked in with his folks, he could grab a lot more stuff to make some really good lunches.

Mike was always the one the gang went to with questions or worries, and waited patiently for his opinion.

Mike was the unofficial leader of the gang, Pat thought…and he always had been. It probably was due to him being a year older than Lenny and Pat, and that he came from a family of two older brothers and a sister. Mike was the youngest in his family, but Mike was always the one that the gang went to with burning questions that needed immediate answers.

It seemed that no one in the gang did anything without talking to Mike first.

Pat remembered the time when it seemed Mike had become the unofficial leader. They were out on a baseball field a few years back. The neighborhood had built that field alongside the BN Railroad tracks and adjacent to old man Jefferson's house. Many times they would get about ten to sixteen kids together and play 'shirts and skins'.

Mike always chose Pat and Lenny to be on his team, and then whoever else rounded out the team, he didn't care. So that day they were playing a game when Lenny swung the bat, got a hold of the ball, hard; and hammered it foul right into Mr. Jefferson's south side upstairs bedroom window.

Every kid on the field split like so many cockroaches' when the lights were turned on. Lenny stood dumbfounded still clutching the bat in his hands when old man Jefferson came out of his house in a fury. Lenny finally remembered to drop the bat to the ground when he thought he was going to get the ass chewing of his life. Before anyone knew it or saw it coming, Mike stepped forward and claimed it was him who broke the window.

Pat and Lenny stood there with their mouths agape and their eyes wide. They just couldn't believe that Mike was willing to take the rap for the broken window. Old man Jefferson grabbed Mike by the ear and literally dragged him back to his house to call his parents.

Pat and Lenny stood on the ball field and watched for Mike's parents to come and get him. When they showed up, Mike's mom swore that the window would be repaired, turned and did the finger pointing thing lecturing Mike for something he didn't even do.

When Mike got into his family's car and drove away, Lenny turned to Pat and asked, "Why do you think he did that?"

"I don't know, Lenny," Pat replied watching the Schomer car driving away with Mike in tow. "I just don't know."

Pat and Lenny left the field and went home shaking their heads in disbelief.

Pat thought about it quite a bite that night, and when he talked with Mike the next day, Mike just shrugged his shoulders and said, "You guys would have done that for me, too…wouldn't you have?"

I

Pat finished the sandwiches just as the boys were making their way back to the park.

"How's the lunch building going?" Mike cried as he hopped off of his bike.

"I'm all done. I just now finished up." Pat replied. "You guys score?"

"Oh yeah," Lenny said, smiling. "It cost us a couple of extra bucks, but it was worth it. Lisa will drop off the beer right after supper."

"Are you sure she will?" Pat asked rather tentatively.

"Of course she will," Lenny blurted back with a hint of anger in his voice. "If she doesn't, she knows I will kick the crap out of her."

"I didn't mean anything by that, Lenny," Pat replied.

"She will," Mike said and grabbed Lenny by the shoulder to calm the waters a little.

"Yeah," Lenny said calming down…a tish. "She will."

"Lenny and I were thinking," Mike said to Pat after things were better, "that we'd go fishing for a little while, and then we'd go swimming. We'll send the girls back for supper, and then they can come down here again tonight. What do you think?"

Pat thought it over and finally said, "Sounds good to me. You know, we might even catch a fish or two. Maybe they'll want to stay for supper with us, if they can."

"I don't know," Mike replied. "They'll probably have to do the Rainbow thing, and then they'll sneak out. We'll just have to wait and see what they have to say when they get here"

"Yeah," Lenny added. "That's what Susan said to me last night. We'll see what happens when they get here."

"This is going to be the coolest day ever," Pat finally said, aloud, not fearing any ramifications from the guys.

"If they look as good during the day," Mike started to say, "as they did last night, we are the luckiest guys in Wahkashen, for sure. I can't wait to see Peggy in her swimsuit!"

"I'll bet Linda is just gorgeous in her suit," Pat said.

Pat's eyes took on a shine that the guys had never seen before.

Lenny finally added, "I don't know about you guys, but I am also looking forward to these girls from out of town getting into their suits, and *that's* a fact."

All three agreed, and laughingly they finished up with the lunches, and got ready for the girls of their dreams to finally appear.

The girls came to the park at a little past twelve. All three were wearing blue jean cutoffs, and were dressed in tie died shirts that sported a different band on each of their shirts. Linda looked absolutely beautiful, Pat thought as he walked over to greet her. Her face just gleamed. She was also wearing a pair of glasses. Pat didn't remember her wearing them last night. Even though he didn't remember, she was beautiful with or without the glasses.

"Hey," Pat said as he stepped forward. "Glad you could make it."

"I wouldn't have missed this for anything," Linda told him in a voice that seemed to sing in Pat's ears.

She smiled so broad and bright that Pat's heart just melted.

All six of them paired off, just like they were last night.

II

They talked for awhile about last night's adventure, and if they had gotten into trouble, in any fashion.

"Nah," Peggy said waving a nonchalant hand at the boys. "We were pretty sneaky last night. No one is the wiser, and that's a fact."

Peggy was wearing a Janis Joplin shirt today. She cutoff the sleeves of the shirt herself Pat saw, as there were telltale strings in various spots around the area where the sleeves had previously been housed. The morning sun made her red hair almost look like her head was on fire, and her freckles were a great deal more prominent. She even had freckles on the tops of her arms, and on her shoulders. She was very cute, Pat thought, but no where *near* as pretty as Linda was.

"We had everything planned perfectly," Peggy continued, boastfully. "Linda and I devised an almost perfect plan…and an excuse, in case we were captured."

"Spoken like a true soldier," Mike replied and was rewarded with fits of laughter from everyone.

Mike and Peggy started to walk towards a picnic table on the other side of the fire pit. Lenny and Susan sat down in a couple of old lawn chairs that Lenny had brought from home, which just happened to be located closer to the tent.

Pat and Linda just kind of milled away from the crowd towards the duck pond and found themselves a picnic table where they both sat down.

The sun was shining almost straight down on the duck pond and the rays broke up into a million sparkling reflections of light. It was almost too hard to look at without sunglasses on.

They unknowingly sat down on the very same picnic table that they had visited last night. There were about a dozen ducks and a few geese on the water, with more lying lazily on the banks of the pond just on the other side.

It was a beautiful August morning.

"Pat," Linda asked as she turned her face towards him after they reached the table and sat down, "do you have a cigarette?"

"Sure,'" Pat replied, feeling a slight tremble in his voice. He hoped that Linda didn't notice it or hear it as he fumbled for his cigarettes.

He handed her a Camel, and then started to dig through his pockets for some matches.

Linda's eyes never left Pat's face the whole time he was wrestling with his pockets to dig out those matches. She watched his face. She traced every line on Pat's face carefully.

After he lit Linda's cigarette, he fumbled out a smoke for himself.

Linda extended her smoke to him so he could light his from the lit end of hers.

"Thanks," Pat said after his cigarette was lit. He handed Linda's cigarette back to her.

"No," Linda replied as she blew out a breath of smoke, "thank you."

Pat smiled at her and took a drag from his smoke.

"Have you ever been fishing before?" Pat asked her, exhaling.

"I remember going once or twice when I was younger, I think with my Grandpa...but other than that...no, I haven't."

"You're going to like our little fishing spot. It's really quiet and solemn down there. The Red River moves really slowly down there by the oxbow, and every now and again a fish will jump. It's so peaceful and beautiful. I like going there sometimes just by myself to sit and...I don't know...reflect, I guess.

"It's pretty cool down there."

Linda looked at Pat for a second or two while Pat gazed out at the crew over where they were sitting and talking, and then Pat turned his head and for a split second their eyes met. In that split second, Pat feared he would be swallowed whole by the sheer depth and brilliance of her eyes.

Pat smiled at her.

"What?" Linda asked him.

"Nothing...you, you were looking at *me* like you had something to say," Pat replied with a sinister smile.

"It's just the way you talk; it makes me wonder about you."

"Talk? How do I talk?"

"I don't know...like you're older, or something."

Pat just smiled at that and turned away from Linda. He sat and looked out at the ducks on the pond for a minute, contemplating what Linda had just said to him. He watched the drake and his hen tooling around on the water with hardly a care, and with so much grace that the water hardly rippled at their efforts.

"Just how old do you think I am?" Pat turned back and asked her.

"I don't know…sixteen I suppose; maybe seventeen. You seem like you're older. It's just the way you talk, that's all. I like it."

Pat heard a touch of sincerity in her voice; and maybe some apprehension intermingled with it.

"I didn't mean anything by that," Pat said to her hoping he didn't make her upset. That would be the very *last* thing Pat would want right now! "I was just curious as to how old you thought I was…that's all. No offense."

Smiling at him, Linda said "that's OK, none taken."

They sat in silence enjoying their cigarettes for awhile.

Pat had so many things he wanted to say to Linda, so many things to say; and yet he was tongue-tied…for the moment.

"When do you have to go back to Garlton?" he finally spoke.

"Tomorrow…sometime," Linda replied. "Why?"

"Well," Pat stammered for a second, "I just wanted to know how long we would get to spend together…you know…hangin' out and all."

Linda smiled a genuine smile. She reached over and took hold of Pat's hand and gave it a squeeze.

"I like you too, Pat," Linda said to him looking straight into his eyes.

After about twenty minutes, Pat and Linda headed back to the camp site to join the rest of the gang.

"Let's get our stuff together and go fishing, boys," Pat said to the crew.

"Is it time?" Mike replied turning his eyes away from Peggy. "Already?"

"Yup, let's go," Pat replied and grabbed a handful of fishing gear. "The fish will not wait for any man."

The six of them reached the secret fishing spot after a fifteen minute walk through the ancient tangled oaks and maples that twisted their way along the path, and stopped by the boundary of the river banks at obstinate angles.

The mosquitoes and gnats buzzed softly and intermingled with a light breeze that manipulated the leaves of these trees that were silently reaching for the sky.

The Red River rolled by them as quiet and smooth as if a woman were moving a sheet of dark satin across a large mahogany table. Small eddies were created by the intermittent branch that hung over the undulating river and softly broke the surface of the water.

The girls each sat down on the strategically placed rocks and watched the boys place their lines into the water. After that task was completed, the boys returned to their prospective rocks to join the girl that occupied it.

They sat in silence and watched their lines for a few minutes.

"How long have you guys been friends," Susan asked and then nonchalantly swatted at something that flew past her ear.

The boys looked at each other as if the answer to her question was written on their foreheads.

Finally Mike spoke. "I think I met Lenny in Catholic grade school after he transferred from the public school."

"Yeah," Lenny replied, "and that's where I had met Pat, was the public school."

"I don't think I met Mike," Pat began, "until about a year ago or so. I have known Lenny for a lot longer than that."

"And, how about you girls?" Pat asked.

"Well," Linda said, brushing aside a strand of hair that dropped out of place on her forehead, "I met Peggy about ten years ago and Susan about seven or so, wouldn't you say, Susan?"

"Yeah," Susan replied. "That sounds about right."

"So you transferred into a Catholic school, Lenny?" Susan asked him.

"Yeah, after the first grade or second grade, I think," Lenny told her.

"Why'd ya do that?" Peggy asked him.

"My folks wanted me to get the 'proper' Catholic background, and so they transferred me before it was too late, I guess."

"Believe me, girls," Mike said. "It didn't help him at all."

That was received with great fits of laughter.

Pat handed out sandwiches to every one, and then broke open a bag of chips and passed it around.

They sat and ate their sandwiches, making small talk and laughing at the silly things that just happened to be mentioned at that time. They talked on about everything and nothing.

They sat and watched the river roll by slowly as the time they shared seemed to crawl at the same pace. The bugs buzzed, the crickets chirped and the sky was clear blue.

It couldn't have been a better day if they wanted it to be, Pat thought, and then he flicked his cigarette out into the river and watched the current pull it away from him in a spiraling motion.

"Let me tell you about the time, oh, a couple of years ago when I caught an eleven and a half inch walleye…right in this very spot," Pat began, "…using a gumdrop for bait."

After all of the caterwauling about their disbelief from the girls was over, he defended his story, and expounded upon it as well.

"Let me also tell you," Pat said as he was lighting another cigarette and looking directly at Linda, "that it was with a 'lemon' gumdrop…"

Chapter 7

The boys did their fishing, and bragging, which of course always ran hand-in-hand; then they carried back to their camp site a total of four large walleyes, which they would clean much to the terrified delight of their female guests.

It would make a fine supper tonight, Pat thought. He would steal an occasional glimpse at the girls while they were cleaning their prizes, and Pat was pretty sure that the girls were impressed with their forthcoming meal.

Once the fish were cleaned, they all decided to get some swimming in at the pool, so they left the camp site and walked over to the public pool.

As Pat walked into the doorway of the pool, he saw that Dan Meyer, was working solo behind the counter. Dan was a senior this year, so he was probably done the end of the summer and heading off to college…somewhere. When Linda wasn't looking, Dan slipped him the 'thumbs up' gesture after he spied Pat walking in with Linda. Pat was just beaming after Dan gave him the OK sign.

The boys changed clothes with a great deal of enthusiasm and chatter. They blasted in and out of the customary and required shower, and then, as quickly as the pool staff would allow, got out into the main pool area and waited for the girls.

The pool was fairly busy this afternoon, and the music blaring from the loudspeakers seemed to be in competition with the screaming children at the shallow end of the city's fifty meter pool.

The first girl out of the changing room was Susan. She was wearing a bright blue and yellow two piece suit. The color scheme looked really good on her, Pat thought, with her blonde hair. And, by the look on Lenny's and Mike's faces, it must have held the same impression on them.

Susan had fairly nice legs, and she filled out the suit quite nicely.

"Hi," Susan said, rather shyly, as she walked slowly towards the area where the boys had taken up occupancy.

The pattern on the suit looked almost like leaves or something to that effect. It was an interesting pattern, and the bright colors of the suit almost shimmered in the afternoon sun.

Linda and Peggy came out together, giggling and hanging onto each other as the water from their showers was still dripping off of them.

Peggy was wearing a tan-ish colored two piece which made her freckles a bit more prominent, and her red hair was radiant. Pat really enjoyed looking at her when she smiled as her whole face would light up, and her eyes would squint together so tight she almost closed them completely. She really was pretty, Pat thought.

Linda was wearing a lime green two piece that Pat had seen before, but it never looked like *that* on anyone else. She was absolutely gorgeous in that suit.

Her lean, tanned body was built exclusively *for* that suit. When she walked out of the women's changing area with Peggy, Pat noticed that many a male head had turned to witness her entrance. Her hair was wet and was plastered to one side of her face. Pat thought he had seen a picture like that in a certain magazine, but he thought the model in that picture was in no way better looking than Linda at that time.

When she smiled, her face absolutely glowed in the afternoon sun. Pat's heart filled with a sense of pride that he was actually getting to spend time with these fine young ladies. Never in his life could he have ever imagined that something like this would happen to him. Never.

"You look very nice," Pat said with a voice that hinted the excitement that he felt just looking at her.

"Why Thank You. You look pretty good, too," she replied.

Pat was wearing a blue pair of shorts which made his skinny legs look more like toothpicks than human legs, but they were quite tanned from all of the time spent here at the pool.

"Well," Pat said to her with a slight tone of embarrassment as he looked down at the aforementioned tan toothpicks. "I *could* have better legs. My legs look like branches from 'ol man Emerson's weeping willow tree.

"They don't look that skinny," Linda replied.

"Why, thank you very much," Pat said to her.

"Come on, then," Mike said to the crew. "Let's get wet!!"

And with that, he jumped (more like fell) into the water with a splash that showered the crew on the deck.

"Hey," Peggy cried, and then followed his lead with a giggle.

Susan and Lenny walked over to the small steps at the end of the pool and slowly entered the shallow end only to be immediately swallowed up by the numerous children playing in the water.

"Follow me," Pat told Linda, "I want to show you something." He then turned and walked towards the deep end of the pool.

Linda followed for a second, and then sped up so she was able to walk along side of him. She gazed out over the pool and had to squint as the sun reflected a thousand broken rays of sunshine off of the shimmering, boiling water that was in constant turmoil from the bathers that occupied it.

I

"Have a seat," Pat told Linda and gestured to the area where the sunbathers frequented once they reached the far end of the pool. He helped her lay out her towel, and then aided her by holding her hand as she eased herself onto the waiting towel.

"Now, watch this," Pat said raising his eye brows and then he gave her a wink.

Pat made sure that she had a front row seat to the diving boards, as Pat went to the second board, the one that was five feet above the water, stood in line and waited for his turn on the board.

He turned to look at Linda every now and again to ensure that he held her attention, at the very least until he completed his dive. Pat's heart was beating fiercely in his chest as he waited for the last two people to climb the four steps to the top of the diving board.

He watched as a boy of about six years old do a dive that looked almost painful when he hit the water. The next in line was a girl of about the same age. And, judging by the way the boy who had just completed the painful dive was egging her on, they were either brother and sister, or good friends.

All of his teasing did not go undone as she did a cannonball right next to his smiling, bobbing face. When she finally broke the surface, they were both laughing hard, and the boy had made a few coughing sounds as apparently some of the chlorinated water had found its way into his waiting mouth, and down his unexpected throat.

Pat was finally the next in line. After glancing over at Linda to make sure she was watching, he began to climb the steps. His heart was beating so fast and furious in his chest he felt like was going to pass out.

Thank God the music is so loud, Pat thought, *or else the whole pool might hear the hammering of my heart in my chest.*

Just before he began his walk to the end of the diving board to begin his dive, the music on the loudspeakers changed; it began to play, *"Long Cool Woman (in a Black Dress)"* by The Hollies.

Pat thought to himself, *I sure hope I don't screw this one up. She truly is one long cool woman…in a lime-green swim suit!*

He took one more look over to where Linda was sitting, and she was indeed watching him. Pat thought she was watching him very intently.

Pat also took one quick peek up at the lifeguard chair to see that Dan Meyer had replaced Candi and that he was currently occupying the chair.

He felt more confident to perform this dive in front of Dan instead of Candi…or, God forbid, Karla.

He walked to the end of the board, stood for a second with his hands to his sides, his heart feeling like so many horses running around unbridled inside his chest.

After a second or two, he raised his arms so that they were parallel with the waiting water below him, bounced one time, and then with everything he could muster, he kicked his feet straight out in front of him as the second bounce took him off of the board.

When he felt that he was perpendicular to the water below, he brought his knees in towards his chest and began to turn his body back towards the diving board. As he started his inward turn, he spied the diving board for a split second, and then the waiting water below as the turn made him see these things in a backward rotation. As he neared the full turn he needed, and after he was confident that he had indeed cleared the end of the diving board, he began to extend his feet out from his body so that he would be in a standing upright position as he entered the water.

When he felt the heels of both feet as they touched the water, he immediately pulled both arms down along his sides. He then entered the water like he was supposed to do, with the style and grace that makes the inward gainer such a pleasure to complete, and a delight to witness.

He was pretty sure that he didn't create much of a splash, either, as his entrance into the waiting water was nearly perfect.

Under the water he felt elation. He felt, after all of the times he tried this dive, after the one totally embarrassing failure in front of Karla and God, he finally completed this feat. He smiled under the water. He pumped his fist a couple of times under the water with jubilation. The smile was evident on his face; however, the smile in his heart only he and he alone would ever know existed.

Pat broke the surface of the water after the dive was completed, shook his head a couple of times to remove the excess water, and looked over at the lifeguard chair to see the smile on Dan Meyer's face.

"That was a good one, Pat," Dan yelled from the chair and gave him his second thumbs up for the day.

"Thanks," Pat replied, sheepishly, and began to swim over to the ladder where he pulled himself out of the water.

As Pat started to walk over to where Linda was sitting, he noticed that she was smiling. She held a *huge* smile on her face. The smile in his heart grew two times bigger.

She was also clapping very lightly…like the golf claps one saw on TV that the crowd gave to Jack Nicklaus or Arnold Palmer.

"That was terrific, Pat," Linda said to him with enthusiasm as he sat down next to her. "I didn't know you could do those kinds of things."

"Well..." Pat said, looking down at the cement upon which they were seated.

"That was like...really cool," she started in again.

Pat turned his face towards Linda's and simply said, "Thanks."

Pat stared into Linda's eyes for a split second, but he felt like he could stare into her eyes forever. He would forget about everything around him, as long as he had those beautiful eyes in which to loss himself.

Pat finally forced himself to break away from the entrancing spell her eyes had on him.

They sat for a second and watched as other people were trying this dive, or that dive. Some made really nice dives, while others made it look like that six year old boy did earlier...painful.

"Do you want to learn how to do it?" Pat asked her.

"Are you kidding me," Linda replied and grabbed a hold of his arm. "I would absolutely *kill* myself, Pat. I don't think I could even find the nerve to jump off of the high board."

"Sure you could," Pat told her, smiling. "OK, let's forget about the gainer. Let's focus on simply jumping from the high board. Let's go up and try it."

"No way."

"Come on...it's not that high. It just looks like its way up from down here. It's only about ten or twelve feet."

"It looks that high because it IS that high!"

"It really isn't. Come on...I'll go with you."

"Well I would certainly hope so, as I am not going up there alone."

II

So off they went after Pat held out his hand to her and helped her up from off of her towel. Linda was just chattering away all the way to the ladder which took you to the top of the board. Every now and then on the trip to the ladder, Linda would touch Pat's arm, or lay her soft hand on his shoulder in a fashion to aid her getting her point across. Pat heard every word, but he was so excited, he was practically beaming that she was with him, that most of her words fell on deaf ears.

Not only had Pat completed the dive in which he had worked so hard to master, he was now walking along side a very beautiful, highly sexy young woman who made heads turn as they passed.

When they finally got to the bottom of the ladder, Pat did a slight bow and extended his arm like a musketeer to Linda to show her that the ladder belonged to her. Laughingly, Linda grabbed hold of the railing on both sides of the ladder and cautiously began the climb to the top.

Pat had to use every ounce of fiber in his being to not look up and watch Linda's ascent up the ladder. It would be a totally, beautiful view, he told himself, but it would also be a very bad thing if he were caught looking at her ass as she climbed the ladder. It would really suck if Linda caught him looking at her ascending ass, or if anyone here in the pool caught him looking up when a girl was climbing the steps.

It just would be bad, anyway you sliced it, Pat thought.

So, he didn't look up.

He was extremely proud of himself for his self-restraint.

"Come on up, Pat," Linda cried from the top. "And hurry up."

"I'm coming," Pat replied and began his own ascent.

Pat arrived at the top to see Linda at the end of the board, tentatively gazing over the edge like an ancient explorer who had finally discovered the edge of the world truly *did* exist. And then, this explorer stood there, dumbfounded, looking over this edge at the world's end with wide-eyed disbelief at the unexpected abyss that lay below.

An explorer in a lime-green two piece swim suit that was absolutely the most beautiful explorer in the world, Pat thought.

"You are looking way too spooked, Linda," Pat said to her with a slight chuckle.

"This is like a mile high!" she retorted, and turned her face towards his. In her eyes, Pat did register a slight tint of fear.

"Maybe…maybe I should go first," Pat told her to try and ease the fear that she was so obviously displaying.

"That would be A-OK with me," she replied.

Pat started to walk towards the front of the board as Linda began to retreat back towards the ladder. They passed each other in the middle. Linda had her behind against one side of the boards railing, and Pat had his behind against the opposite side. As they slowly passed each other, Pat had his face very close to hers, and he could smell the perfume that she had applied as it intermingled with the chlorine from the pool, and the fear she wore like a coat.

Pat could smell her freshly washed hair as they passed each other as well. It was a wonderful clean scent that complimented her perfume.

They slid past each other, very slowly, and very close, and Pat could feel the softness of her golden skin as their legs and stomachs just barely brushed against each other. Pat had a moment there where he wanted desperately to reach out to her, grab her face in both hands and kiss her...hard. It took just as much of his inner fiber to resist *that* temptation as it did to follow her ascent up the ladder to this position.

"You aren't going to do one of those...one of those, dives...are you?" she asked with the fear in her voice highly prevalent.

Pat, although he had considered attempting the gainer at this level some time this summer, decided that he wouldn't challenge it at this exact time. Not in front of Linda, that is. He was proud that he made the last effort work, and therefore, he chose not to at this time. Besides, he was way too pleased with himself for completing the last one to ruin it with a screw up this time.

What with discretion, and all...

"No," Pat told her without looking over his shoulder as he faced to the front. "I will just jump off and show you how easy it really is."

With that said and not another word to follow, Pat simply stepped off of the edge of the diving board.

Linda leaned as far over the edge as she dared to watch his decent.

Pat hit the water without a sound, disappeared out of sight for a second or two, and then broke through the surface with a shake of his head.

He looked up to the top of the board and saw Linda leaning over and seeing the whole event.

"Come on," Pat said with the appropriate *'come on in, the water is fine'* gesture. "It's real easy."

"That's what *you* say," she yelled down to him while walking slowly to the edge, hanging onto the railing the whole way.

"It really is, Linda. Try not to think about it. Just step up to the edge and...jump!"

She took tentative, baby steps to the edge. Pat watched as she slowly looked over the edge and then he saw that her eyes got real wide. He couldn't help but chuckle softly to himself. Pat had never really, truly been afraid of much, so watching someone be tentative about a fear that they may harbor inside felt strange to him.

There was a young boy waiting back by the ladder's end at the top, watching Linda. He was pretty patient, but finally couldn't take it any longer.

"Hey, lady," the boy said, "can I go if you're not going to go?"

"Why sure," Linda told him. She turned, grabbed hold of the railing and walked slowly back to where the boy was waiting. "I'm just waiting for the right time to go, that's all."

"Sure thing, lady" the boy replied and ran to the end of the board. He decided to scare her a bit more, so he screamed loud and long all the way until he splashed in the water below.

Linda walked slowly to the edge once more, and spied Pat's smiling, reassuring face below.

"I don't think I can do this, Pat," Linda cried down to him.

"Sure you can," Pat replied, treading water. "It's easy, Linda. Trust me."

"Trust you?" she replied with the fear more and more apparent in her voice.

"Trust me," Pat said again smiling, still treading water. His arms were starting to get tired, but he would have stayed there for the whole day waiting for Linda if he had to. "I'm down here waiting for you. I wouldn't let anything bad happen to you. You just have to trust me."

Linda peeked over the edge once more.

"I can't believe I'm going to do this," she began.

And before Pat realized it, Linda was on her way down to the waiting water. She was screaming all the way.

III

Linda hit the water and disappeared. Pat swam over to her as quickly as he could and was there waiting for her as she emerged.

He was treading water while waiting for her to surface, smiling at the feat he had just witnessed.

"My top," she cried as she broke the surface of the water. She sounded a little frightened, and before Pat could get a word in, she disappeared under the water again.

Pat kept treading water while he waited for Linda to gather herself.

Linda came up again, a few seconds later, a bit more composed.

"I lost my top. I can't believe I lost my top when I hit the water," she said and then she began to swim to the side of the pool where there was a ladder to help you get out of the pool.

"What do you mean you 'lost' it? Did you lose it completely?" Pat asked her as he swam along side her.

"No," she said as she reached for the ladder. "It just came off, sort of over my head, when I hit the water. I had to go under and make an adjustment." She then gave Pat an awkward little smile that spoke chapters about the embarrassment she must have felt.

Pat immediately started to laugh, out loud, at the thought of Linda losing her top.

"It's not funny," she said and reached out and punched Pat in the arm. "It was kind of embarrassing," and then she looked around in case anyone had heard her.

She had begun to climb up the steps that led out of the pool.

"I don't mean to laugh, Linda," Pat said. "It just struck me as kind of funny, that's all. I lost my shorts one time."

"How'd you do *that?*" she asked him and stopped halfway out of the pool. She turned to face him and stood still on the ladder.

"I did a swan dive from that high board," he said trying not to stare at her while she pulled herself up the ladder. He did seem to be noticing everything about her with clear details. The way the water was running off of her wet body as she was half way out of the pool. The way her short hair stuck to one side of her head, while on the other side it was loose and water dripped from the ends of it.

"When I hit the water," he continued, "I realized that I had forgotten to tie the string in the waistband, and my shorts just kinda went...'*swoosh*'. They ended up right down at my ankles."

"Now *that's* funny," she said and finished climbing up the ladder, got out of the pool and headed for her towel.

Chapter 8

It was only three years after 'The Summer of Love' and it seemed that the love that was so highly evident at Woodstock was still abundant; it appeared to be in the air all through the summer of nineteen seventy two. The teachings of the Woodstock event lingered in the everyday business of life...even as far away as Wahkashen, ND.

Peace and harmony; patience and understanding with all things, and all people; and most importantly...Love.

These were the attributes that were so apparent and abundant during 'The Summer of Love'.

Pat felt it in his soul. It was all around him. It was in the trees. It was in every one of the birds that flew out from those trees. It was visible in everything that he touched. It seemed to have consumed him these past twenty four hours. He felt it. He knew it existed, although he could not see it. And, it had chosen him as its next participant.

Pat had never felt anything like this before. Not even over the past fifteen years (save for how he felt about his mother, father, and even his sister...a little, anyway). However, the past twenty four hours, and certainly this moment in time, he was quite sure of one thing: he was feeling this emotional tug in his heart. He knew he liked Linda a great deal. He liked everything about her. Her laugh, the way she carried and handled herself. He liked her with or without her glasses. He knew for sure that he definitely liked her in her lime green swim suit.

Was it love? He was not completely sure it was…but then again, he was not completely sure that it wasn't.

Pat sat next to Linda in the sunbather's area reveling in the feeling that flowed so freely and continuously through his body. He could not help but have a stupid *'cat that ate the canary'* smile on his face while he enjoyed this day; the very best day of his entire life.

He enjoyed everything about Linda. He enjoyed everything they did together. He enjoyed the small talk. He enjoyed the same talk. He enjoyed the no talk at all, as there never seemed to be an awkward moment of silence between them. They both seemed so comfortable together.

At least, that is how Pat felt about Linda and him.

Mike, Peggy, Lenny and Susan came and joined Pat and Linda about an hour after Pat made good on his promise to take care of Linda if she jumped from the high board. Linda was just giddy about the whole affair as she began to tell the whole tale to Peggy and Susan.

Pat couldn't wait to tell the gang that Linda had lost the top of her swimsuit when she finally did jump; but Linda beat him to it.

"So I finally get the courage to jump," she said to the girls, "and then I hit the water, and guess what!?"

"What, tell us?" both Peggy and Susan asked.

"I lose my top!!!"

"Get out of here" they screamed.

"I am so serious," Linda screamed back at them. "It was like as soon as I hit the water, my top slid up and almost completely over my head. Pat was so good about it and everything." Linda turned her eyes to Pat.

Mike and Lenny looked at Pat with eyes wide and the biggest shit eating grin on their faces.

"Hey, Man…" Mike leaned over to Pat and whispered. "How was the view?"

"I didn't get to see anything," Pat whispered back, a sense of sorrow in his voice. "She was still under the water when it happened, and I didn't hear or know anything about it until she told me about it."

"Too bad," Mike replied looking back at Linda. "Better luck next time."

"I wouldn't have minded seeing those," Lenny whispered to both of them and then stretched his neck over the tops of their heads to get a better view of Linda's chest.

It was agreed by the gang that a view like that would have made their afternoon, at the very least.

The gang sat and listened to the girls go on and on about how Linda had the courage to jump from *that* high up. They watched the remaining divers do their thing on all three boards.

Karla walked by and waved. All three sighed as quietly as possible.

Finally Lenny spoke up. "We should probably be getting going," he said, "if we want to eat supper anytime soon."

They arrived back at the camp site at about six o'clock. Immediately, Pat began to scrub potatoes so they could be wrapped into tin foil and placed into the fire that Mike had started about ten minutes ago. Lenny worked on the fish, and the girls were buttering bread to round out the meal.

This should prove to be a fine feast, Pat thought.

"We'd better go check in," Linda told the gang. "Then we'll tell them that we're going to the movies, or something, and then we'll come back down here."

"Yeah," Susan said, and she got up from the picnic table where she and Peggy were sitting. "We'd better go." Then she looked over at Peggy, who knew it was her turn to rise as well.

"I thought you were going to join us for supper," Pat said.

"No," Linda replied, "we'd better go back and eat with the girls."

"We can walk you back," Mike told them, "If you want us to."

"No," Peggy said, "you don't have to. You just make your own supper and then we'll come back. OK?"

Pat walked quickly over to Linda. "When do you think you'll be able to come back?" Pat asked Linda rather quietly.

"Oh," Linda started, "I imagine it will be in a couple of hours."

"Sounds good to me," Pat replied with an impish grin.

It was agreed all around that the boys would eat their catch of the day, and the girls would go have supper with the rest of their Organization, and then all would meet up later that night.

As the girls walked back up the Snake road, Pat couldn't help but feel a wanting inside. Something he had never felt before. It was a feeling that he didn't understand, yet; but it was also a feeling that he wanted to keep.

It's going to be a wonderful night, Pat was sure.

I

The boys ate in relative silence as the sounds of the swimming pool were done until seven o'clock when the pool would open again, and stay open until nine o'clock. The fish was really good, and Pat loved those potatoes that were baked in an open fire.

After the meal, they sat back and talked about the days events. Pat was enjoying his cigarette and couldn't stop thinking about Linda.

Eight o'clock would never get here soon enough. Pat thought he was going to explode while he waited for the girl's to show up. He checked his watch and it was only seven forty five.

Mike had a really nice fire going. The flames flickered and flared with the little breeze that was moving quietly and carefully through the trees that surrounded their little camp site. Every now and then the fire would crackle and pop as a water particle in the wood would explode from the heat of the flames. That was Pat's favorite part of camp fires; that and the multitude of colors that fires could create.

Pat checked his watch again and the time stood at eight fifteen.

The boys couldn't wait for the girls before they would crack open their first beer, so at about eight forty five, they decided to have a beer with their smoke. It was starting to get a little darker with dusk.

Old Milwaukee was an OK beer, but Pat had heard from someone in his class that Coors was supposed to be *the* best beer...if you could get your hands on it, that is. The way Pat figured it, any cold beer in his hand was the best beer in his hand.

"Remember, guys," Mike told them, "keep your eyes open on the Snake road for the cops. I would hate like hell to get busted drinking beer and smoking cigarettes down here tonight; or any night, for that matter."

They all agreed with Mike. After all, he was the unofficial leader…of the pack, so to speak.

They sat and watched the fire for awhile, each lost in their own thoughts. The breeze had let up a little and the smoke from the camp fire was rising practically straight up to the cloudless sky.

"I had a good time at the pool today," Lenny finally broke the silence and told the gang. "It was good to hang out with a good looking girl instead of you guys, for a little while."

"Yeah, yeah," Mike replied. "I love you, too, homo."

All three boys broke out in a fit of laughter.

Lenny was caught off guard with Mike's response and was taking a swallow of his beer when Mike did reply. As he began to laugh, beer was forced out through his nose.

"Ohhh, Man!" Lenny cried out. "Shit, that hurts. Don't do that when I'm taking a drink of beer, Man." Then, Lenny started to wipe the beer off of the front of his shirt.

"Don't take a drink of beer when I'm doing that," Mike replied and all three broke out in a good laugh again.

Yup, Pat thought…it is great to have friends, and then he took another swallow of the Old Mil in his hand.

II

The girls finally showed up at about ten minutes after nine. The boys heard them coming down the road, just like they did the night before. Giggling and chattering amongst themselves, the boys watched as their dark figures got closer and closer to the camp site.

"Hello in the camp," Linda cried out softly as they approached.

"Hello there," Mike replied.

They walked into the ring of light produced by the fire, and Pat's heart started to race in his chest…again.

Man, what is it about her, he thought?

"What took you so long?" Mike asked them.

"We had a small get together after supper," Peggy told him. "We were lucky we even got out of there when we did. We told them we had to get going or we were going to miss the nine o'clock movie."

The girls were dressed in rock-n-roll t-shirts and cut-offs…again.

Linda could have been wearing a potato sack for a shirt and she would have been fashionable, Pat thought. He was truly thinking that there was something really special about her that made him feel better about being a guy…especially tonight! Something special, or else Pat was just feeling a great deal like a horny fifteen year old boy.

That was probably it, Pat considered…but he sure liked what was in front of him.

"Yeah," Susan chimed in. "It's a good thing Linda remembered that that was what our excuse was going to be, or we would *still* be there." And with that being said, she sat down at the picnic table along side Lenny and gave him a big smile.

"Hey," Peggy exclaimed when she looked over at Mike, "where did you get the beer? And better yet, where is *mine*?"

"Oh, that," Mike stammered and lifted his beer to his lips and took another drink. "Oh, we have more of those. Pat, you want to grab a few beers for our guests?"

"Why certainly," Pat replied and headed for the tent.

"I'll help you carry some," Linda said and followed Pat to the tent.

As soon as Pat and Linda were out of the firelight, Linda caught up to Pat and grabbed a hold of his arm.

"Pat," she whispered. He slowed down and then turned around.

But before Pat had a chance to ask what she wanted, Linda came forward and gave Pat a kiss…hard, right on the lips.

The kiss seemed like it lasted for hours to Pat.

Linda finished the kiss, stepped back a bit, put her fingers to her lips in a motion that gave her an air of uncertainty, and made her look *damned* sexy, Pat thought. Then she said, "I've wanted to do that for quite some time now. I hope you didn't mind."

"Mind? You hoped I didn't mind? *Man*…," Pat said and stepped forward to return the kiss that he had just received.

Linda wrapped her arms around Pat's neck and Pat had his arms around her waist. They stayed like that for about ten seconds before they broke apart.

"We need to get some beer for the gang," Linda said, breathlessly, after she broke away from him. She ran her hands through her hair in an attempt to straighten out her composure. It was a very provocative move, Pat thought, but it probably was only meant to straighten out her hair, he figured.

"Yeah," Pat replied rather dazedly, "beer for the gang."

He stepped into the tent and opened the cooler. He started handing beer out through the door to Linda who was waiting outside. He was removing beer from the cooler with all the enthusiasm of a napping dog. His movements were like that of an archaic android in dire need of oil in all of its joints. His mind was ten billion miles away with the after effects of those kisses he had just received.

I definitely want more of those, Pat thought.

I'm pretty sure that I will be getting more of those, Pat also thought.

Once they had enough beer, Linda and Pat carried them back to the camp fire and distributed them to the gang.

They sat down at the open picnic table and cracked open their beers. Pat made a toast to everyone who in turn raised their beers and had a swallow.

After the toast was done, Pat turned and looked at Linda. The fire was reflecting off of the side of her face and gave her a glow he would not soon forget. She smiled at him and her smile was warm and sincere.

This was going to be a night to end all nights, Pat thought, and had another swallow of his beer.

Chapter 9

The gang sat around the fire and drank their beers. The night was unseasonably cool for August, and it stayed that way until morning. That made the fire a very fine place to be beside at this time. Every now and then a car would make its way down the Snake road, and they would quickly and carefully hide their beers until the car made its way past their camp site.

Only once did they notice that the car was the cops. They didn't stop, but the gang was a little concerned when they spotted the car coming down the road.

About ten thirty or so, Pat and Linda grabbed a six pack of beer and walked away, undetected, from the camp fire. They were walking hand-in-hand heading in the general direction of the playground. They really had no place in mind when they left the camp site, they just wanted to get away and be alone...together. The playground is where they ended up just because it happened to be on the general path in which they walked.

Their talk was mostly small, commenting on the beauty of the night, the cool glow of the camp fire when they looked back at it from where they were where, about one hundred feet away.

Pat enjoyed the feel of Linda's hand within his. She had very delicate hands, Pat thought; they were smooth, soft and subtle.

"You know," Pat said to Linda, "someone told me that this park was under water to the tune of fifteen to twenty feet back a few years." Pat looked around them and did a strange sort of pirouette with his arms out and chest high. "All around us right now was under water. I was just a kid, but I think it was my dad who told the flood of '65 had the Red crawl over her banks and spill out all over this area."

"You mean everything we see right now was under twenty feet of water? Red River water? Right here where we are standing?

"Yeah, that's what my dad said. I think I remember some of it, but I was pretty young then.

"He told me that just the very little peak of the warming house over there by the duck pond was sticking out of the water. They had to haul all of the animals out to some farmer's place and pen them up."

Linda turned her head around in an attempt to grasp what kind of impact all of that water would have had on everything in her vision.

It was hard for her to imagine.

"Let's walk over here, Linda," Pat said and turned towards the swing sets off on their right about ten feet away in the growing shadows of the large oaks.

Once they reached the swing sets area, Linda sat on one of the swings, and Pat pushed her for a little while. He watched her as she rose away from him and came back to him. She still had her beer in her hand and would take an occasional swallow when she was on the backward slide of the swing.

"Pat," Linda said as she was moving back and forth in front of him, "what do your parents do? For a living, I mean."

Pat found it interesting the way her voice got stronger when she was close to him, and how it would change in its timbre as she swung out away from him.

"Well," Pat answered her, "My mom works at the junior high school, in the kitchen, and my father was a mechanic...before he passed away."

"I'm sorry, Pat, I didn't know." Her voice was changing pitch by the *'now I'm here'* resonance and then the *'now I'm there'* quality as she was swinging back and forth. It sounded kind of cool to Pat.

"You don't need to apologize, Linda. You couldn't have possibly known."

"That is really sad, Pat. How old was your father?"

Pat watched her swing out and away and then back to him. He thought about his answer for a second, and finally said, very timidly but with a hint of sarcasm in his voice, "He was the ripe old age of thirty five."

Linda put her feet down and stopped so quickly that she almost came flying out of the swing.

"Are you shitting me?" she asked him and stared at him very intently.

"Not in the least," Pat answered her and then turned away from her gaze. He wasn't sure that he would start tearing up, as it were, but he didn't want her to see if he did...that's for sure.

"He was only thirty five years old, Linda" Pat said again.

"My God, Pat, that's awful." Linda said. "How old were you?"

"*Humph*, I was the ripe old age of thirteen," Pat replied with the same tone of sarcasm. He still had not turned around to look at her.

"So that was what...three years ago only?"

"Two...actually."

"So...you are...fifteen? I thought you were sixteen. I thought you said you were sixteen. Not that it matters, but you just seemed older than fifteen."

"Yup...I'm only fifteen," Pat said and turned to face Linda once again as he felt he had his feelings under control, for the time being that is.

He walked back towards Linda and began pushing her in the swing once more. "It seems like a long time ago, Linda," Pat said as he stood behind her and pushed her in the swing.

"It seems like a long time ago," he said once more.

"That must have hurt tremendously," Linda said as her voice was rising and falling.

"Yes...yes it did. But I am over it, for the most part, now," Pat replied.

But way back in the deepest regions of his mind Pat secretly wondered if that were a true statement.

"Hey," Linda said to Pat after she put her shoes down to the ground and stopped her swinging, "I have a great idea. Let's take a moonlight swim in the pool."

Chapter 10

Linda sat in the swing, not moving as Pat walked around from behind her and was now standing in front of her, staring at her with an uncertain look on his face. She smiled a slightly wicked smile waiting for a response.

"Are you serious," he asked and looked over his shoulder to the darkness that held the Wahkashen public pool.

"Of course I am," Linda said and stood up from the swing. She extended her hand out to him.

Pat stood there for a second contemplating the offer. He looked at Linda, and then over at the pool again. With a smile that began to spread across her lovely face, he understood that this was what he had been waiting for since they had met. He accepted Linda's waiting hand as she was going to lead him to their pre-determined destiny.

"Why not," he said and reached down and grabbed the plastic ring on the remaining beers that were sitting on the ground, and then took off running towards the pool.

"Hey," Linda called out to him as she reached for the disappearing beers, and missed. "Wait for me. Come on, Pat…It was my…*IDEA!!*"

Laughing, Pat ran ahead of her swinging the remaining beers at his side.

Linda ran as fast as she could to try to reach him. Linda was a fairly fast runner, and it took everything she could do to even get close to him at a dead run.

Linda finally caught up to him after a half minute of running. She was laughing and zigzagging along a path created by Pat as she followed Pat towards their waiting destination.

Pat could see fairly clearly with the moonlight. However, he was worried that Linda might run into something by running like she was.

"Be careful," Pat stopped suddenly, turned around, held his arms out to her and cried out. "I don't want you to trip or run into anything."

"Me," Linda said out of breath when she finally got along side of him, "I have night vision like a cat."

"You are a cat, silly," Pat said, and then meowed. "I just want to make sure you don't get hurt by running blindly into an area that you are not familiar with…that's all. Trees and picnic tables are very solid objects and react very sternly when in contact with unsuspecting flesh and bone."

Linda smiled at him and told him, "I just love the way you talk," and then giggled a little.

I

They arrived at one side of the dark pool, out of breath, but smiling and happy nonetheless. They had a pretty good buzz going, and this excitement just fed the fire a little. It was there that they then began to take a more stealthy position.

"OK," Pat whispered to Linda once they arrived by the bleachers that stood at the east end of the pool. "We have to be very quiet and careful. I would hate to get busted for this."

"I hear you." Linda whispered to him looking around to see if anyone was in the vicinity. "So, how do we get in there?" and then nodded towards the waiting pool area.

"Well," Pat said looking at her in the darkness of the shadows created by the bleachers, "we need to go to the other end, the west end where the kiddies' pool is located. They have a double gate set-up. They use a big chain and padlock to tie them together, but there is a gap big enough to scoot through…do you believe me?"

"I do believe you, Pat" she replied and then leaned close and gave him a warm kiss on the cheek. And then, with another wicked smile, she told him, "Lead the way, McDuffy."

"That's Mr. McDuffy to you," he replied and grabbed her by the hand to lead her towards the kiddie's pool entrance.

They snuck along the chain link fence that surrounded the Wahkashen public pool trying hard not to stick out for anyone to see them. They crouched at the waist and bent at the knees to resemble amateur cat burglars as they trod along the fence in the moonlight. Their shadows were bouncing and bobbing along the fence and on the concrete walkway that surrounded the pool.

It was a little difficult to be stealthy when you are crouched and sneaking along a chain link fence with gravel crunching beneath your shoes, but neither of them noticed those facts as their thoughts were on the destination at hand.

Once they reached the end of the fence, Pat stuck his head out around the corner, looked both left and right, up and down the main road that went past the pool.

Satisfied that there was no one in the immediate locale, he grabbed Linda's hand (it was so smooth, soft and warm, Pat thought) and ambled around the corner to the opening at the double gate. He crouched down and slid the four remaining beers through the opening in the fence where they waited for him on the other side. They sat on the concrete of the pool base, and cast tiny shadows of their own.

"OK, here's how this is going to work," he said in a whisper so low, Linda had to lean forward to understand his words. Pat could smell the fresh scent of her shampoo. He wanted nothing more than to shove his face deep into her hair at that moment and be lost in it for a few hours.

He came to his senses with a might he never knew existed inside him. Seeing as how his wits were getting duller and duller with the aid of the alcohol, he was amazed that he did not reach out, grab Linda, and very physically pull her close to him; bury his face into her hair, and well, just…inhale.

It would be hard to explain his actions to her when she questioned him about his antics, but he finally *came* to his dull senses, and was now preparing to go skinny dipping with her instead.

A fair exchange, Pat thought to himself…

II

"I will get inside and then help you in…OK?"

"OK," she replied and then giggled a little again.

"Are you ready?" Pat asked her with a sinister smile and a wiggling of his eyebrows.

"As ready as I'll ever be, I guess. This is so great!"

Pat smiled at her, and then grabbed her and gave her a kiss.

"Here we go."

Pat turned away from her, reached up and grabbed some of the links in the chain fence about head high. The links were cold under his fingers, and that made him smile even more, although he had no idea why. Maybe, he thought, it was because they were going to do something that was truly illegal, and that may end up getting them thrown in jail.

He then pulled himself up high enough to get his left foot on top of the thick chain that held the double gates together.

The fence rattled a bit at the weight that was applied to it.

"Shush," Linda said looking up at his ascent, and then giggled again.

Pat looked both ways up and down the road once more to ensure that no one had heard the rattling of the chain link fence. Content that they were not discovered, he then turned sideways and slid his body through the small opening. He was cautious to the sharp edges of the wires used to hold the chain link to the poles. He didn't want to snag anything, or rip his shirt or his skin.

Once he got past the opening and was standing on the chain on the inside of the fence, he simply jumped down and landed with a soft 'thud' on the concrete below.

"OK." He whispered to Linda, "do you think you can you pull

yourself up high enough to get your foot on that chain?" Pat pointed down to the chain in question that held the two sides of the gate together.

"I think so," Linda replied as quiet as a mouse.

"I will help you when you get towards the inside of the gate. And, be cautious of the wire ties. They have sharp edges."

"OK," she said and looked up at the opening. "Here goes."

With a slight grunt, Linda pulled herself up; and by using her feet against the fence in which she rattled it more than Pat had prior to her, her feet reached the chain that held the gates together.

She placed first her left foot, and then after a second or two she negotiated her right foot to meet the chain.

She stood, shakily, on the chain and then began to turn her body to slide through the opening.

Thank God we are as slender as we are, or we wouldn't have made it through that small of an opening, Pat thought; and then looked around once more to see if anyone heard her approach.

Pat reached up and grabbed Linda by the waist as she made it completely through. She placed her hands on the tops of his shoulders. He then helped her down to the waiting concrete below her, and the waiting arms of Pat.

They smiled at each other for the first part of their stealthy mission was completed. Then Pat bent down, picked up their waiting beers, and they both ran as quick as a bunny towards the dressing room building.

Once they reached the shadows of the building, Pat said, "OK. We made it this far. Now we need to get to the deep end of the pool, because any passing car will not see us in the water if we are in that end of the pool. OK?"

"Right," Linda said looking directly at Pat with a wide-eyed gaze that spoke of the excitement of their illicit escapade. Her eyes actually sparkled with the sheer thrill of their exploit.

"I'm thirsty," she told him. With that she pulled a beer from the plastic ring which held it in place. She carefully opened one of their stash. It opened with a slight '*gush*' and Pat cringed.

He immediately looked around, just in case. There was no one in the area, but...*Discretion* came to mind, and then he snickered.

"Sorry," Linda whispered, and then took a drink. She then offered the beer to Pat. He eagerly seized it and took a huge swallow.

"Thanks," he said to her and handed it back.

"Alright, now here is where we strip and get into the water," Pat said in an equally quiet tone. "That way our clothes are in the shadows and out of the way. No one will see our clothes over here and they won't get wet…and then we carefully sneak into the pool."

Pat looked at her. He smiled and she returned his smile. Pat reached for the open beer, had another swallow and handed it back.

When Linda grabbed the beer from his hand, Pat started to pull his shirt up over his head.

Linda watched as he started to remove his shirt, and then she set the beer down on the concrete. She walked a couple of feet to their right, away from Pat; and it was over there she began to take off her clothes.

"Oh, shit," Linda said in a low tone laced with sarcasm. She turned and looked at Pat. "I forgot…I don't have my swim suit on." She then smiled a wide, *'the cat that ate the canary'* smile that made Pat's heart sing in his chest.

It seemed that she held the ability to make Pat turn into so much putty in her hands with the mere smile that she possessed.

Pat smiled at that after his shirt cleared his head and whispered to her, "Neither do I," and then he gave her a seductive wink.

With that, he began to slide down the zipper of his shorts and pulled them down. The next thing was his underwear as Linda turned her head.

Linda had watched him undress, up to the point of him removing his underwear, and was amazed at how down-to-earth and unpretentious Pat was about the whole thing.

After Pat had removed all of his clothing, he was slowly tip-toeing towards the pool edge turning his head back and forth looking for any undetected eyes from people on the other side of the fence. Linda watched his bare butt as he walked cautiously towards the edge of the pool. She smiled at the sight.

Pat stepped easily and quietly into the water and began to swim towards the deep end where the diving boards were located. He barely made a sound as he entered the water and even less as he began to swim away from her.

Linda took a deep breath, and then pulled her shirt up over her head. She carefully laid it on top of Pat's discarded clothing, and then looked again at where Pat was in the water. Content that he was still swimming away from her, she quickly removed her shorts and underwear before she lost her nerve.

She didn't know why she was so suddenly feeling shy about skinny dipping with this cute boy. Maybe it was the beer, so she bent and picked up the open can and finished it in a couple of swallows.

The air was cool against her skin and she shivered, just a little. She quickly glanced down at her body and saw that her nipples had become hard.

Must be a little cold, Linda figured, and giggled again.

Linda literally ran to the edge of the pool on her tip-toes, and was just about to jump in when she came to a stop. She stuck her toe into the waiting water and realized just how cold the water really was.

As she grimaced and moaned a little, Pat stopped swimming and turned to face her.

Linda immediately wrapped her arms around her upper body to cover her exposed chest. Not realizing that she was completely naked in front of him, she only thought to cover her exposed breasts from his view.

As quietly as he could and loud enough for her to hear him, Pat said, as he treaded water, "Don't be such a coward and get in the water."

She turned towards his voice and spied the ladder at the beginning of the deep end where she climbed out just this afternoon. She walked quickly and with as much stealth as she could muster, being completely naked, towards the ladder that was about ten feet from her. She reached the ladder, turned her body and slowly lowered herself into the pool with a gasp and a groan.

Pat giggled at this and continued on towards the waiting diving boards.

Linda was in the water and started to swim towards where Pat was waiting. After a minute of two, she became used to the water, and actually thought that the water *was* warm.

III

Linda joined Pat at the deep end. He was hanging onto the lip of the pool, and he was smiling at her.

"Did you bring the beer with you?" Pat asked as she got closer to him, already knowing the answer.

"Ahhh, shit...no, I didn't," Linda replied and looked over her shoulder at the beer that was still over by their clothing.

Pat laughed at this and reached for her. Linda swam towards his hand, and when she was close enough to the edge, she grabbed a hold of it.

"Water too cold?" he asked her when she was next to him.

"Yeah, a little, but I'm getting used to it now." she said with slightly chattering teeth.

"The water is really warm, you know. It's the air that's cold." Pat said to her as he treaded water next to her.

Pat looked at her. She seemed so confident in the water with him. She was so completely cool with being naked in the water with him. Pat, on the other hand, was a little apprehensive. It would pass; he thought...he was sure of it.

Pat swam forward and then leaned towards her and gave her a kiss on the lips.

His lips were a little cold, and she snickered.

"What?" he asked as he leaned back.

"Nothing. Your lips were cold...that's all."

Pat swam to the front of her, and put his arms on either side of her. She could feel the skin of his legs against hers under the water. They played a little Indian leg wrestling under the water. She finally let go of the edge of the pool and wrapped her arms around his neck. She kissed him long and hard.

She pulled him closer to her. She felt his legs under the water against her skin and that made her even more excited. She immediately stuck her tongue through and past his lips and began exploring the inside of his mouth.

They stayed like that for what Pat thought was hours, and it was merely a couple of minutes.

They swam around in the deep end for a few minutes. They played an exotic game of tag, much to Pat's delight. It was so much better than playing tag with Dennis and the gang. Playing tag with a naked young hippy girl who had a pretty good buzz going beat any of the games of tag he had ever played, or ever will play, Pat thought.

They met in the middle of the deep end and both tread water for a second. Pat reached out for her and drew her close to him. He kissed her. She responded and immediately her tongue was in his mouth again. Pat thought he could get used to this.

When Pat broke away, he smiled at her and said with a slight lift in his voice. "Do you remember being here this afternoon and I got you to jump from the high board…above us?" Pat then looked up at the diving board in question.

Linda followed his gaze and then looked back at him. "Yeah," she said and gave him a sneaky smile. "So what's your point, Pat?"

"I think we need to play a game," he said with that same sneaky smile on his face. "I need a drink of beer, and the only way I am going to get it is to do my gainer off of the high board." He then moved his eyebrows up and down a couple of times.

"Pat!" Linda said with a quiet scream. "You can't do that tonight. Not now. Someone will see you…or at least hear you."

"Here's the deal," he replied swimming slowly around her like a shark circling its prey in the deepest of water. "We both jump off of the high board, together, and then swim over to the beers. And then we scram out of here before it's too late."

Linda never said a word as she continued to tread water and tried to follow him while he was leisurely circling her.

"Are you thirsty, or not?" He asked her.

She looked up tentatively at the high board.

"I can't jump off of that board at night, Pat. I could barely do it during the day!"

"Sure you can," Pat assured her still circling her. "I know you can. I watched you do it today, so I know you can do it.

He filled his mouth with pool water and spurt some at her. Linda turned her face away and splashed some water back at him with a laugh.

"Think about how cool it will be to jump out and into the darkness, knowing that there is water waiting below, even though you can't really *see* it. Think about how cool THAT will be."

Linda looked up at the board again.

"What if someone drives by when we are either on the top of that board, or just jumping into the water, Pat? What would we do then?"

Pat hesitated as he contemplated the question.

"Think of it as an adventure."

"An adventure?"

"Sure. Besides, I'm thirsty…aren't you?"

"Well, yeah," she replied tentatively, "but I don't think I can do that, Pat. Maybe we should just swim over and get the beer?"

"Come on," he told her swimming slowly to the edge of the pool. "You said you weren't going to jump this afternoon, too; and then you did it. Remember?"

"Pat," she whispered to him as he swam away and got closer to the edge. "Pat, someone will hear us hit the water."

Pat was crawling out of the pool, and Linda saw him stand there, naked as a jaybird, waving for her to join him.

Oh, shit, Linda thought, and started to swim towards Pat.

Chapter 11

Linda swam over to the edge of the pool where Pat was waiting. Pat reached down, extended his hand to her and helped Linda out of the water.

She came out easily with Pat's help.

There they stood on the concrete walkway, toe to toe; naked, sodden and smiling, two fifteen year old kids who were not at all anxious or uneasy about their nakedness, nor were they concerned with anything around them in that space of time.

One teenager, a hippy girl from out of town, looking for an adventure and love; the other, a typical hot-bloodied American male with the most amazing, wonderful opportunity standing directly in front of him...naked, slightly buzzed like he was, and grinning.

They were dripping with water from the pool, and it began to collect under their feet on the concrete where they were standing.

They were also dripping with adolescent innocence. It was simply exposed and pulled away from them all in one moment. It found its way to the puddle of water at their feet, and intermingled with that standing water. That puddle was growing slowly as the seconds flew by.

They were not embarrassed. They were not bashful or diffident with their bodies, and they were content to stand facing each other, completely out in the open to one another.

This was, after all, a few years after the *Summer of Love*, and apparently there was residue in the air...

No problems with that, Pat thought.

They stood there for a few seconds, beaming, letting their eyes roam a bit, as it were, as well as gazing into each others eyes as they contemplated the event that Pat had proposed in the pool.

The air was cooler than they expected with the water remains that lingered on their skin. Linda shuddered a little and Pat smiled. He could not take his eyes off of her. When he did, for a split second to scan their surroundings for unwarranted visitors, he would return his eyes to her.

Linda more or less wrapped her arms around herself as another shudder overtook her.

Pat didn't think she did this because she was apprehensive or shy at him looking at her, as it was her being a little chilled with the coolness of the outside temperature.

Linda finally stepped forward, unwrapped herself and placed her hands on both sides of Pat's face and kissed him hard and long.

Her hands then left his face and went down to the middle of his back as Pat's hands found her lower back. They clutched each other tighter.

Pat felt her wet skin against his. She was still warm, even in the coolness of the ambient air around them. The pleasure of her closeness to him, and because of her gentle, hot kiss, some excitement began stirring and waking up his groin. Pat figured he better step back for a second to compose himself, so he broke away before everything became too embarrassing for him.

"Come on," Pat whispered and looked around. "We need to do this and then exit the pool before we get busted."

Linda agreed and grabbed his hand as they headed towards the ladder that led to the high board deck.

"I will go first, and then I'll help you up," Pat whispered in her ear, and then gave her a little peck on her wet cheek, "just like when we broke into the pool. OK?"

Linda smiled at him, stopped him and squeezed his hand. "Thank you for doing this with me, Pat."

Pat smiled back and turned to the ladder and began his ascent.

The treads of the ladder were dark, and Pat had to go by feel to find his way; but he had been on this ladder many a time before, so he was quite confident that he could do it in the dark.

Once at the top he called down to Linda. She slowly began her own ascent in the darkness. She more or less used her hands and feet to tell her where she was going as she couldn't see much in front of her face.

Pat was waiting for her and grabbed her under the left arm when she reached the top rung of the ladder. His hand inadvertently brushed against her breast, but neither of them said anything about it.

The air seemed a bit cooler up here, Linda thought, and shuddered once more.

Immediately, Pat remembered being next to her this afternoon when they were in the same place. He remembered how she felt when she walked past him and brushed oh so lightly against him. He will remember how that felt for the rest of his life; how it felt, how she looked in that lime green two piece standing there with a look of fear clearly etched on her beautiful, tender face.

Now he was again, standing here next to her, and they were both naked…and slightly drunk.

"Isn't this great?" Pat asked her with an air of excitement in his voice.

"It's pretty exciting…and kind of scary, too," Linda replied in a quiet tone and looked over the edge of the railing that was on both sides of the high board deck.

"It's going to be OK, Linda. You do trust me, right?"

Linda turned and looked directly into his eyes, reached down and grabbed his hand, and placed it between her bare, wet breasts. She inhaled deeply and simply said, "Yes, Pat…I trust you, completely."

Pat smiled at her response.

"You ready?" Pat leaned forward and whispered into her ear.

She released his hand and said, "How are we going to do this?"

"I say we both walk forward to the end of the board, and on the count of three, you jump right, and I jump left."

Linda looked once more over the edge of the railing, then turned back to face Pat again.

"Oh, God…I don't know if can do this Pat…"

"We'll be alright, I promise."

Pat grabbed her left hand and tentatively led them to the edge of the diving board.

"Just hang onto my hand, and on three…we go for it."

"Oh…God…" is all she could say as Pat began to count, slowly and deliberately.

All Linda could hear was the word 'three' as she left the board and screamed…long and loud.

Chapter 12

They were back at the swings about twenty minutes later, still a little wet and still a little buzzed. They had one beer apiece left from their Midnight Swim.

A car came down the main road about ten minutes after they vacated the pool, and although Pat couldn't make out if it was a police cruiser or not, they both felt relieved that they were out of the pool before the car came around.

"That, my friend, was a total blast," Linda said to Pat while she sat on the very same swing she was on before her proposed midnight swimming quest. In her hand she held the last Old Mil, on her face she held a smile that was bright and beautiful.

"You know it," Pat replied and took a swallow from his beer.

"I have never done anything like that before, Pat…never. I will never forget that you and I actually did that."

Pat smiled at her and said, "I agree. That was the most fun I have had in a long time. To do something *illegal* like that. I mean sitting here with you and drinking beer is illegal enough, but the thrilling thing of actually breaking into the pool…It was very exciting, you know? What a great idea it was."

"Yeah," Linda replied and took another swallow of her beer. "It was *way* exciting."

Linda sat there and Pat stood for a while, both lost in their own thoughts for a couple of minutes. Pat imagined in his mind over and over the sight of Linda, wet and naked, standing there in front of him inside the empty pool. Man, how cool she was to be so free and open like that.

"Pat?" Linda asked which broke Pat out of his mental wandering. "Are you looking forward to going back to school?"

"Kinda, I guess," he replied. "How about you, Linda…are you getting excited about it starting all over again?"

"About the same. This has been a pretty good summer. Right now, I don't want it to end, you know?"

Pat turned on his heels and stepped in front of her while she remained on the seat, beer in her lap and a slight smile on her full lips. He got on his knees in front of her. He grabbed the chains that held the swing seat off of the ground just above where Linda's hands were placed.

"Linda," Pat said to her looking her straight in the eye, "you have made this summer the best summer I think I have ever had. I have never met a girl like you before. You're cute, *extremely* cute; funny, daring, smart, cute…I think I already mentioned that, and I really, truly dig hanging out with you. You are like, the most adventurous, the cutest girl I have ever met."

"I feel the same way about you, Pat," Linda replied giving him a huge smile. "It makes leaving here tomorrow really hard, you know?"

KABLAM!

There it was. There were the words Pat definitely did not want to hear. The world just came crashing down right on top of him, all with the utterance of a few simple words. All the jubilation he was feeling inside from his head down to his toes was voided from his body with three little words: *'leaving here tomorrow'*.

"Shit," Pat said and looked down at the ground in front of her, "I forgot that you are leaving here tomorrow. I'm never going to see you again, am I?" Pat asked her with a hint of sorrow in his voice and raising his eyes to meet hers.

"Hey," she replied and reached out to touch his hands that were holding onto the chains. "Don't talk like that. We are not that far away from each other. We can write to each other. We can still see each other, just not a great deal more; just not as much as you and I would like. But we can still *see* each other, if we truly want to." She was very sincere in her conviction, Pat thought.

He truly believed that she actually thought that she was right.

"There will be no way I will see you again," Pat told her with a heavy heart that was reflected in his voice. "I will never get to Garlton and you know it. *Shit!* Why couldn't we have met earlier in the week so we could have spent more time together? Damn…"

"Stop," she said and put her delicate fingers to his lips. "Just stop talking like that, Pat," she scolded him. "I'm serious here. I won't let you ruin a perfectly nice night for you and me because of negative thoughts about something that you and I have no control over. There is nothing we can do to change things when they are in motion, things that are destined to happen. I will not wallow in self-pity, nor will I allow you to do that either. We will see each other again and we will write to each other…right?"

Pat moaned something unrecognizable with his eyes to the ground, and Linda punched him in the arm.

"Right?" she said raising her voice a bit.

"Right," Pat replied with little conviction. His eyes never left the ground in front of his feet as if there were something hypnotic lying there; maybe a piece of an alien artifact that possessed his immediate and full attention.

Linda stood up. She grabbed Pat's hand and made him stand up with her and then she said, "Don't think about it, Pat." She lifted his chin so that she could look at his eyes. "Don't think about that at all. This night isn't over yet. And besides, I will not let you ever forget about me. You will never forget this night, or me, as long as you live. I promise you…you will never forget this night."

I

After Linda said that to him, she stepped closer and put her arms around his neck and kissed him again.

Pat responded by grabbing her around the waist and pulling her close to him. He wanted to pull her as close to him as humanly possible, without hurting her in the process.

The kiss was absolutely wonderful. Her kisses were absolutely perfect. Although he was no where near a master of the art of kissing (more than likely due to the fact that he did not possess the necessary components in which to practice…namely, those of the female persuasion), he nevertheless thought that Linda was perfect for kissing.

She slowly parted her lips and her soft tongue came out to find his and explore his mouth. Their tongues intermingled while the moans of an unknown ecstasy escaped from their young mouths. Her breath was a mixture of sweet tobacco and Old Mil. Pat enjoyed this creation of tastes very much.

Their bodies rubbed against one another. Linda ran her hands up and down Pat's back. They turned their heads from one side to the other, never letting their lips separate. Linda ran her fingers through Pat's hair and sometimes kissed him so hard it actually hurt…in a good way.

Pat's heart was beating like a freight train in his chest. He almost felt like he was going to pass out from the exertion of his over tasked heart. He decided if there ever was a time to do it, it was now. So, he was bound and determined that he would take a chance of a lifetime.

Ever so slowly Pat moved his right hand from around Linda's waist. He stroked the side of her hip gently. He felt the soft/rough texture of her blue jeans shorts. He felt the soft curve of her hip under his unstable, slightly vacillating hand.

Strengthening his courage with every passing second he moved his hand up the front of Linda's body and over the fabric of her t-shirt until it rested right below the swell of her breast.

Linda's moans increased and she arched her body forward exerting more pressure onto Pat's body. She kissed him even harder; her tongue roaming, exploring deep in his mouth. Pat took this response as her wanting him to fulfill his boyhood dream: cup a breast in his hand.

So, damning the torpedoes, Pat reached up and softly captured Linda's left breast with his hand.

'*The Eagle has landed*' raced through his mind.

It fit his hand perfectly, as if God had made her breast just for his hand. It fit like the proverbial glove. It fit like it was supposed to fit; like it was his all along, and it had been waiting in anticipation, just like he was, for this moment when it came to both of them.

There was no waste, as she gave Pat a complete hand full.

Linda wasn't wearing a bra this evening, Pat discovered, much to his delight; and the pliability, yet strange full firmness of her young breast was better than anything he had felt ever before in his young life. He tried to get his hand to quit trembling.

Maybe it never would, he thought.

He prayed that she wouldn't notice that his hand was quaking, or at the very least, that she wouldn't mind it.

She didn't resist his advance. She didn't push his hand away with disgust as he anticipated, and expected. If fact, she leaned into his wavering grasp with a hot intensity that he also never expected.

Pat could have remained in this position; kissing this beautiful girl, exploring each others mouths, chasing her tongue with his, cradling her wonderfully firm and warm breast carefully in his hand, forever and ever…Amen.

Linda finally broke away from their passionate embrace and absently used the back of her hand to delicately wipe her quivering lips. Her eyes held the wild-eyed stare of an impassioned animal when she looked at him.

Pat noticed that she was lightly trembling herself. He was pretty sure that it was not due to the coolness of the air.

Pat also noticed that her nipples were now quite hard, apparent and highly visible under her t-shirt. It could be the cool air, or it could be the intense passion that he was also feeling right now; a passion that they both felt, but neither of them could put a name to it.

She looked over her shoulder to the dark pavilion that stood tall, solid and confident in the shadowy background just beyond the playground.

Without a word, she grabbed his hand and led him towards that building on the other side of the quiet recreational area. They walked past a still merry-go-round. The moon shone through the silent bars of the carrousel and cast shadows on the ground before them. They stepped through those handle shapes created by the moon with out noticing, and without breaking up those moon shadows at all.

Their steps were crunchy on the small pea rock that was placed in the swing set area, and then became muffled by the soft dew-covered grass as they approached the pavilion.

Once inside the pavilion they found a dozen or more picnic tables lined up like so many soldiers in a formation.

It was a little darker inside the open pavilion, but not so dark whereas one could not discern objects. It only took a couple of seconds for their eyes to adjust to the dim light. It didn't seem to be much warmer inside here than outside due to the open construction of the building.

There was a smell in the air of the pavilion of ancient wood fires that emanated from the colossal stone fireplace at the far end of the building. It was a smell that was both dank and wonderful. The side walls of the building were only four feet high, and then were open to the roofline; held no windows or any type of screens but they supported large logs at specific intervals that held up the roof above them. The ceiling was also open and it was supported with fairly good sized logs. It was a beautiful, old and rustic building. Shadows hung thick and long on the east side of the pavilion. These shadows were created by ambient light that radiated from the old street lamp located along side the road on that side of the building.

Linda walked around a little inside and finally chose one of the picnic tables towards the middle of the pavilion and sat down on its table end facing him.

Pat could make out the features of her face and her body that he had known, even more intimately in the past hour or so. Her angelic face held slight shadows from the same light that gracefully streamed into the building from the open sides of the pavilion. She had such a tender face, Pat thought.

She stared at him with a wanting look in her eyes that was hard to ignore. She continued to stare at him with a haunting look and a slight smile on her face. Pat stood there, watching her every move, his heart beating loudly in his ears. She gently grabbed his hand, pulled him close and kissed him. Her tongue was once again on a quest in his mouth.

After their quiet caress, she tenderly pushed him back from her.

Pat didn't know what to say or do, so he stood there watching her.

Quietly, and not without a little nervous apprehension, Pat suspected, Linda simply pulled her shirt up and over her head. She turned at the waist and gently folded her shirt and then laid it on the table beside her. Turning and facing Pat once more, she sat there in the semi-darkness with her hands on the table at her sides, her inhibitions lying on the table like her neatly folded and evidently unnecessary t-shirt.

Her bottom lip was trembling ever so softly. It almost looked as if she was pouting, but he knew it was pure trepidation. He felt the same way.

His heart was racing so fast in his chest, Pat felt like it was going to jump right out his chest in front of Linda. It would simply leap from his chest and lay there in front of both of them...still beating rapidly.

Pat swore, at that time, he had never set eyes on a woman who looked so beautiful in his entire life. Not any of the women in the Playboy magazines were that enticing; not Alice, the lovely Alice with no inhibitions what so ever; not even Karla or Candi, nor the young Miss Daisy and her Patchouli overcoat.

Linda was the most beautiful woman Pat had ever seen.

"Linda..." Pat started to talk, but it was all he could get out before she 'shushed' him.

Wordlessly, she held out her hand to him.

Pat's whole body began to shudder. He swallowed hard with an inaudible click in his throat. He felt like he was sweating, and yet he wasn't. Absently, he wiped his dry palms on his pants thinking he was removing excess moisture. He was shaking so bad he felt that he may fall apart in front of her like he were made of so many Pick-up Sticks.

She sat there in front of Pat in the pale light from the street lamp outside, hand reaching out to him, exposed and calmly innocent, for the entire world to see. Except, the only one there to see her was Pat, and he was in full view.

He was in full view of her young beauty, and he was in awe.

He shuffled forward to her waiting hand, her waiting body, slowly, on shaky feet that didn't seem to want to listen to him. He felt as if he were hobbled for some strange reason. But he found a way; he discovered he had the strength to amble forward to her waiting embrace, to a night that Pat would never, ever forget as long as he lived.

Linda was right all along...

Chapter 13

About three weeks after Pat and Linda spent the night together; Pat was back in school...again. Three more years, and then he would be a graduate, and then he would go...well, he wasn't completely sure *where* he would go, but he was definitely getting the hell out of Wahkashen.

Pat received a letter from Linda around the second week of September. It was the first letter he received from her, and it was a welcomed sight. His hands were shaking, lightly, when he opened her letter.

It read:

Dearest Pat,

Well, the summer is officially over as I went and bought school clothes with my mom the other day. It seems my Mom won't allow school to start unless she physically takes me shopping for clothes. I wanted to buy some really cool tie-dyed T's, in fact I found a great one that was pink and blue with Jimi Hendrix on the front, and the Peace Symbol on the back; but my mom would have nothing to do with it. It was blouses and pullovers or nothing, she said. So, jokingly I asked her if she really intended for me to go to school topless!! You should have seen the look on her face.

You know, right after I said that to her, I thought of you and me at the swimming pool when I lost my top. I started to laugh aloud and mom asked me what was so funny. I didn't tell as I thought she wouldn't find the humor in it…you know what I mean?

I also thought about you and I when we went skinny dipping on our 'midnight adventure'. You know, I have never ever done anything like that before, and I am so glad that it was with you when I DID do it…

I hope the rest of your summer went well with you and the gang. I hope you have been practicing those dives…whatever you called them. You were really good at them. I hope you caught a great deal more fish down at your spot. By the way, thanks again for taking me there. I know a spot like that is very special to guys, and it was nice of you and the gang to share that with me and my friends.

Speaking of friends, Peggy got in trouble the other day. Her and a couple of other girls that I don't like to hang out with, went drinking on the gravel roads, and they hit a ditch and got stuck. They had to walk all the way back into town, and she got busted for being out after her curfew. She was grounded for a whole month!! Can you believe that? Susan and I thought that was a bit severe, but that's Peggy's dad for ya. He can be a real jerk at times.

I've been a good girl since I got home. I've been helping my Grandparents out more this summer than I ever have before. I go over and mow their lawn for them. I do this wearing my swim suit (I only say that because I know how much you appreciated my swim suit…right?) Ha ha.

Pat, I think about our last night together quite often. I think about it when I'm awake and I dream about it when I'm sleeping. I think about being in the playground with you and just talking…and kissing. I think about how sneaky we were to actually break into the pool and go skinny dipping…and get away with it!!! Oh, my!

It was a very special night for me…us. I think about how gentle you were with me, and how glad I am it was with you. I have to admit I was a bit nervous, but you have a very gentle way about you. That's what I noticed about you right away. That's what makes you so special in my heart.

I knew that about you when you showed me how patient you could be waiting for me to jump off of that high board at the pool. I have never done anything like that ever before in my life. You gave me the confidence to do that, and I love you for that.

I have no regrets for that night we shared, and I sure hope you don't have any either...I will never forget you or that special night, Pat.

Never.

I hope this letter finds you in good spirits and ready for the school year to start. I think I am going to take German this year (as I am mostly German descent, and my Grandmother and Grandfather would love me even more if I did!!).

I wish I could see you again. I wish we had a way to see each other again. But like my Grandmother says all the time, "if wishes were fishes, we'd have tuna for lunch every day." :o)

I miss you, Pat. Please take good care of yourself.
Write to me often, and I will write to you.

XOXO

Love,

Linda

Pat wrote back to her and made mostly small talk, answered some of her questions. It seemed like he just absently placed words to the page, stuffed the page into an envelope, sealed it and sent it to her. He didn't know what to say to her, nothing more than, say...spilling his guts with words like:

'I miss you so very much. I think of you constantly. You have truly touched my heart, and I do not think that my heart will ever be the same again.

I really, REALLY want to spend more time with you, because you are very special in my heart as well. You are a totally free woman and I think that is the best thing about you. I want to feel your touch again. I want to touch you again, and again...I want to be beside you walking through Cetanmila Park in the moonlight...'

...but he dared not actually say those words to her. He did not know why, he just couldn't bring himself to say that to her.

Did she actually say she loved me, Pat thought? He read that passage again, and again, and in a round-about way she really did, he guessed. That's kinda cool, he thought.

He supposed in his heart, that he felt love for her as well, but he could not confirm that as he never felt this way about a girl before. It probably was love that he felt for Linda, but he just wasn't sure...

Pat had not seen Linda for almost two months now, as October came rolling into Wahkashen with a cold furry. He had received only one letter from her, and could not get her out of his head, not even for a moment's peace. Although he wasn't bitching about constantly thinking about Linda, he wished he could see her one more time. Or, would that just make things worse and he would get greedy and want to see her and touch her more if that opportunity presented itself? Pat didn't know, but he did know that Linda was right in her summation that there was nothing either of them could do to change the outcome of things that were destined to happen.

He spent the first couple of months of school dreaming and wishing.

He wished he could be with Linda. He dreamt that they lived in the same town and they were a regular item that everyone envied. It seemed that Linda now occupied the space in his brain which Karla had a stranglehold on since time out of mind.

He suspected that Karla wouldn't mind, seeing as he had more of an intimate connection with Linda, and would not in this world, or the next, have that kind of opportunity with Karla, anyway

Pat thought about Linda a great deal these past few weeks. He dreamt of holding her in his arms again. He dreamt of her warm skin next to his.

How her eyes would light up every time he made her laugh, or how serious her face would become when she was ready to punch him in the arm...which she did quite often. He dreamt of thumb wrestling with her using their tongues instead of their thumbs.

He dreamt of cradling her breast; how warm, soft and full it felt in his hand. How long would it be before he actually had that chance again?

Would he ever get to *touch* Linda's breasts again? Would he ever get the chance to spend more time with Linda, at all?

Would he actually *see* her again?

He did not know the answer to any of those questions.

I

Pat did know one thing for sure, and that was he really, truly hated October, and dreaded that month for the past two years. It seemed bad things happened to him in October. It wouldn't be until he had grown and moved on that Octobers would be a better month for him; but for now, they pretty much sucked.

He thought about his dad more during October than any other time, he thought.

I suppose it had to do with the month of his death, Pat speculated.

He seemed to be spending more and more time thinking about his life, in general, as a confused fifteen year old in the seventies. He would reflect on his life and try to figure out just where he was going, even at this early age, but he felt that he just had no direction. He felt that there was no one in his life on which he could depend to aid him in steering his world into a more suitable, productive adult...with time.

There was no one in his life in which he could consult.

He had also discovered, with a huge delight, that he could find temporary solace in the arms of female companionship. Normally, this companionship would be found in the outlying towns, as the females in Wahkashen would not give him the time of day, let alone any type of comfort that was meant between a boy and a girl. That didn't bother him either, as Linda had proven. He discovered that he had merit; he had traits that girls had found, deep inside him, and had been able to bring those traits to the surface.

His life had literally been directed and driven by the female persuasion; both in his home with a mother and an older sister, and then by the females who were just as eager as he was to try and figure out life, and their place in it during the early seventies.

However, for the most part, he hated not knowing what was going to happen to him. He did discern that as soon as he graduated high school and moved on from here, he would be on familiar terms with what he was doing from one day to the next for the rest of his life.

He secretly hoped that he would once again see Linda.

He was positive of that fact...

Pat never saw Linda again.

Chapter 14

Pat walked aimlessly through the park one late October afternoon after school had let out for the day. He was alone, and he thought a great deal about what had happened to him this last summer. He thought about how things had turned out, with or without any outside influences and that he felt that he would be OK, now.

Pat felt less like a timid rabbit these days, which was a good thing to him.

He thought about Linda as he walked through the playground, saw the swing set where he had pushed her and talked about the end of the summer. He could still hear their conversation in his head, even though it had happened so long ago.

He would slowly recall their walk over to the pavilion, and as he stepped over the threshold and discovered that the tables had been moved into another configuration, he could still visualize Linda sitting at the end of the table, towards the middle of the pavilion. He could still see how her bottom lip trembled, oh so lightly, as she sat there naked from the waist up, and his heart broke.

Pat decided that this pavilion was not the place to be…and left as quickly as his feet would let him.

It seemed to Pat that there was some strange presence inside that pavilion that Pat could almost sense. Was it just a memory that he had, or was there some force from the past still hanging around there?

Pat didn't know. He did know however that it hurt him, deep in his soul, to be in there without Linda.

He wandered around the area where the gang had set-up their campsite that summer. He could recall everything that had transpired there with a clarity he never realized he had. He could still hear their laughter as they sat around the campfire the first night the girls showed up down there in the park. He remembered what the girls were wearing that night. He could still see their faces as they approached the gang's camp site that night, and timidly asked if they could join their fire. He could recall the conversations that Pat and Linda had those few days they were together.

His heart broke more and more with every passing, fleeting memory.

Pat needed to get away.

I

Pat had wandered over to the other side of the park and he had been sitting on the bleacher seats over by the swimming pool. These bleachers were in the vicinity of the infamous pavilion, and he was reminiscing on this late afternoon after school looking at the empty swimming pool. He was looking up at the high dive board and picturing Linda and him, naked, slightly drunk, and having the time of their lives when a girl from Flagstaff Falls, MN, which was located about twenty five miles from Bulliford, happened to be walking through the park. She stopped by the bleachers when she noticed Pat sitting alone.

"Hey," she said to Pat.

"Hey," Pat replied without looking back, and then turned around to look at her.

Pat was set back a bit when he discovered it was a girl that he didn't know.

"Oh...Sorry," Pat said to her with a slight smile that expressed his humiliation. "I thought you were someone else."

She was pretty; Pat thought and tightened up a bit in his posture. She had a nice smile and figure to go with it.

It had all started out as harmlessly as if she were merely asking for directions; actually, she had stopped and asked Pat if he had a cigarette.

"Sure...I do" Pat said and reached into his coat pocket and produced one for her.

She stepped forward and retrieved it from Pat's hand. Put it in her mouth and leaned forward for a light.

"Oh, sorry," Pat stammered out as he stood up and fished his Zippo out of his pants pocket. He struck the flint and the flame erupted. He reached out and lit the end of her cigarette.

"Thanks," she said and exhaled a long plume of smoke that more or less hung there in the cool autumn air.

"Do you mind?" she said and pointed to the area next to Pat on the bleachers.

Pat turned that way and looked down at the seat.

"Ahhh, no...no, I don't mind at all," Pat told her and then grabbed her hand to help her up to the level where he was sitting.

They sat and smoked and made small talk about the weather, the price of beer and cigarettes and everything else that they had no control over.

Well...one thing just led to another.

The very next thing Pat knew they were in her car, driving the back roads of Bulliford, drinking beer. She had left a ferret in her car when she walked over and met Pat. The ferret was named Leslie. Pat liked Leslie a great deal, and Leslie seemed to enjoy Pat as well. Leslie was very affectionate, so much like a cat; and, as it turned out, so much like her owner.

Pat took this woman from Flagstaff Falls to the swimming spot along the Otter Tail River, because she said she would rather just sit for awhile and enjoy the beer without having to manipulate the car at the same time.

It was there they spent a few hours of the evening together...trying to give Pat's life a sense of direction.

Pat kept doing the same thing in his mind while he was with her. He was comparing this woman to Linda. The way she kissed him; the way she felt under his hand. Her smell, her taste, everything...he compared her with Linda and discovered that there really wasn't any comparison.

Linda was his first, and would always remain his first. Nothing would ever change that. No woman would ever be able to change that fact no matter how many there were, and how hard Pat would compare them.

Linda was his first.

Period.

And so it was to be for the next few years, strange women turning up and trying, the very best they could, to console; to give Pat physical and spiritual guidance, blindly, but all along with good intentions in mind.

Apparently, these women saw something in Pat that made them eager to dig in deeper and discover more than what was on the surface.

This girl with her ferret named Leslie dropped Pat off at the park after a few beers and a couple of hours later.

He never did ask her what her name was...

II

Pat continued to work hard in school. He hung out with his friends, and had a few romantic encounters with girls from different towns. It didn't fill the empty void that was always so dominant in his heart, but it took his mind away from the pain he lived with for the time being. Hell, that was worth half the battle, and the dividends were fun, to say the least.

Pat discovered that there were things about him, parts you might say, that these girls found appealing: his smile; his laugh; his overall personality, and especially, his eyes. These girls thought his eyes were...how did they usually put it...*'deep'*? Some said to him that his eyes were, *'dreamy, and totally exposed his soul'*. He figured that they were mostly full of shit, but as soon as they *'stopped all that grinnin' and dropped all of their linen'* to console him, he figured that they reserved the right to say and think whatever they wanted.

It was all good to him.

He could find that he related to these girls fairly well, and it never took much of an effort to get them horizontal for an extended period of time. He had a heart that required the healing touch that they possessed, that they all held somewhere deep within.

It was his job to find that saving grace that they held.

Pat remembered one time when he was invited to a bonfire at someone's farm the summer of '74. He got a ride out there with somebody that he knew. Pat found out later that the guy had left after a couple minutes, apparently because his girlfriend was not anywhere to be found, and so Pat was stuck without a ride. He figured he would get one somewhere, sometime before the end of the party.

He was wandering around the farm yard, which held a huge bonfire about twenty feet in diameter, holding a plastic cup of keg beer. Somewhere, someone's car stereo was blasting out the White Witch album 'A Spiritual Greeting', and it sounded *really* good outside. That was when his eyes fell upon a girl he had never seen before.

She was a slight girl with smallish breasts, and a great ass. When she smiled at Pat, her smile was wide and warm. She was dressed in a white tank top style shirt and a nice pair of dark shorts. She started to give him the old once over with her eyes, and Pat figured '*Carpe Deim*'.

So, what the hell Pat thought. When this young lady looked back at him, he looked her directly in the eye and gave her the head nod that simply stated, '*follow me*'.

Much to Pat's delight, she did.

Pat turned away from the bon fire, walked a few paces, and then next thing he knew she was walking right beside him, smiling at him like she held a secret so luscious it was hard to contain.

Following Pat from the orange-red glow ring of the bonfire, Pat soon discovered she was from a small farming town about fifteen miles from Wahkashen. She had cat-like eyes, so much like Linda, and a beautiful smile.

Ten minutes later, Pat found himself standing next to a stream that meandered just past the farmstead and out of sight of the party. She was naked, just as he was, and she was standing there in front of him, calf deep in native grasses, her hands lightly touching his body; tracing his body was more like it.

It was all very erotic to Pat.

The sounds of White Witch coming from that car stereo were a little fainter this far from the party, but it intermingled well with the light gurgling sounds of the slow moving creek.

She came sauntering up to him. The next thing he knew he was rolling around on the ground with wild abandon in the arms of this girl who she showed him things. She showed him things, but never once told him her name.

She did things for him much more than he could have possibly anticipated. His heart was free for the hour or so they spent together. It was free and not weighed down with guilt, anger and sorrow.

Her touches, her kiss, her taste made everything disappear from his heart for the time being. It was as if her touch melted the gelid ice that encircled, encased his heart, and melted it away as easily as the sun does a forgotten and neglected Snow cone on the fairgrounds in July.

An hour later, he was standing back at the bonfire with another plastic cup of keg beer in his hand, still looking for a ride home. White Witch had been replaced by The Rolling Stones "Goats Head Soup' and that was alright with Pat.

III

Over the years Pat yearned for things to be different, but nothing he could do would change how his life had been altered by forces that he could not control. He was merely rolling with the punches, as it were. He had wished for more things over these past few years than he had ever wished for before in his entire life.

However, as time went on, Pat started to look at the life he was living like one of those Snap-On calendar models. He was always smiling at the camera, only exposing enough to the viewer to be appealing. He was making believe that he was really restoring a beautiful 1934 Chevy Coupe, when it was all a façade; he was living out a false life filled only with dreams and visions, smoke and mirrors.

He truly enjoyed the consultations and solace that were brought to him by the various women with no names. He had no complaints about any of that. That would be the last thing that Pat would ever want to change, or alter in any fashion; but the outcome of the past couple of years had truly been tough on his outlook on life.

He started to feel like a junkie when it came to those hot, quick, and emotionless, yet passion filled sessions that he found so easy to obtain in the early seventies. He just couldn't get enough. There was definitely an itch that needed scratching whenever the opportunity arose. He started to be aware of that fact that there was no end to his insatiable hunger, a hunger that he never even knew he had. There seemed to be an almost impossibility to satiate his need for future consultations.

He also felt like an alcoholic where one drink was not enough and one hundred drinks was never too many.

He speculated about these consultations, though. They were never a solution to his emptiness; and even though they did not make matters worse, they did not provide a resolution, either.

His life was nothing more than smoke and mirrors which no one was allowed to see past and these consultations were nothing than an emotional bandage to keep the wound from being exposed to the open air.

Pat knew these *'bumps in the night';* these poignant dressings were merely a sad form of escape from the pain and anger. They were a hard, gelid console found between warm, silky thighs, yet Pat didn't mind. No, he didn't mind that at all.

He never thought of his actions as degrading towards the women who offered these, these…carnal sessions. He thought of them more for the therapeutic effects that they held. Pat also figured that these women were gaining something with their shared interlude, even though he felt confident that most of these women were not falling in love with him anymore that he was falling in love with them.

They didn't want anything more from Pat than for him to scratch their itch, as well.

He found himself questioning life more and more these past days, months and years. He was questioning his religion and how profound *was* his belief these days. He had questioned God and his religious outlooks for quite some time, now; and so far the answers had evaded him. He had forgiven God over the past twenty four months, but he still hadn't forgotten the damage left by God's decision regarding his father.

Pat didn't think that his rolling from one woman to another would aid him in his search for enlightenment and wisdom; but then again, over the course of the past two and a half years he had met some very interesting people who gave him inspiration, and therefore, the will to continue.

So all was not lost on his quest for carnal solace, Pat figured as long as he could, and as much as he wanted.

As he searched thoroughly and examined everything in his life, and in his world, he found that solace by a young woman enthusiastic about trying to ascertain her place in this world when it came to love, life…and more importantly, sex; suited Pat…for the moment. That the time spent with a woman hungry for comfort and empty compassion, as was Pat, was a strange type of binding on Pat's heart. It was only a temporary repair, and Pat was well aware of that fact; but it seemed to ease his mind for a little while, and that was good enough.

Pat allowed himself time to heal from all of the wounds that had been inflicted upon him, and he seemed to be getting better and better each and every day. He was getting stronger with each and every carnal encounter.

He knew that he was a survivor, and so was his family.

Pat felt that he had lost God's faith, but he was positive that someday it would return. Pat simply wanted to fit in with the society around him any way he could.

He simply wanted…wanted to be somebody.

Pat sought, and knew, that he could be a productive member of this society; and all of the sensual interludes brought his passion for this outcome to the surface. He knew that spending time with these women would aid him in his quest to become a vital member in the world.

He wasn't positive…but he just knew.

Life had dealt the McCray family some really shitty cards, but they were making the best hand out of them that they could.

It seemed that that was all they were able to do...make the best hand out of shitty cards.

Epilogue
May 1975

There was an old saying in this world. There were many 'old sayings', Pat figured, but this was the one that caused him some introspection...to say the least.

They, according to a good friend who always wondered who 'they' were, said that, *"Time heals all wounds."*

Well now, if you thought about it, very carefully, you would have discovered that 'they' were pretty much...full of shit, Pat thought.

That expression was ten gallons of bullshit shoved into a five gallon Red Wing crock. It was shoved in so hard that it began overflowing and splashed on 'their' brightly polished shoes.

Now, if 'they' were speaking metaphorically about this topic when dealing with...let's say, a broken heart; a heart shattered by a lover who up and quit you immediately after you said *'I Love you'* to that person. Then, as you are standing by in awe, they pulled out this vital organ, lay it on the ground right before your eyes, and began grinding out a cigarette on it with the heel of their shoe; then that may work in this sayings favor. You may, I reiterate, you *may* recover from that ordeal with Time's aid and assistance.

Time will assist you. Time will hold your hand, so to speak, figuratively, as you suffer the indignity of watching someone scraping the remnants of your heart from off of the bottom of their shoe, with the assistance of a busted dirty twig found discarded and lying in a deserted parking lot, somewhere.

However, Time does nothing to 'heal' any wound. Time is not a remedy, a bandage, a drug or an instant cure-all that one would find on any commercial on TV or an advertisement in a magazine. Time is not a constant, it is relative and a continuum which lacks spatial dimensions; and therefore, does nothing to repair an injury sustained through a life altering tragedy; such as death. You cannot expect any Band-Aid type items, either large or small, to be placed on that wound to give support in the recovery.

Time will not be able to suture a wound of the heart.

A wound suffered by someone, like the death of a parent, or the death of a child or a good friend, is a deep, jagged wound inflicted upon that person's heart and soul that no medicine in the modern world can possibly cure. That kind of wound will rankle, become puffy over time and red with a long-term infection of spirit. The wound is so cavernous that not even the most potent of hydrogen peroxides will bring that infection to the surface.

It is a well know fact that that type of wound will fester for a good deal of time and then remain an open gash for all eternity. A large piece of the person's heart will be missing due to this type of wound, and, consequently, that wound will never scab over and become normal...albeit with a normal scar.

It just will not happen.

All time does is work on the person's memory; fade the remembrance of the existence of the loved one lost. As time passes, so do the recollections; the pictures in one's mind begin to die away, as it were, and before one knows it, the pictures are so fuzzy in the brain that the deceased person may not have existed at all.

That is all time does to 'heal' any and all wounds.

And, that is all hypothetical, anyway.

So if 'they' were speaking hypothetically, well then 'they' could pucker up and hypothetically kiss Pat's skinny white ass.

Because, he wasn't buying any of it.

I

It had been almost five years now, and Pat had healed…a little. So apparently, time had done its job, Pat suspected. He still missed his father tremendously, and he was positive that he always would; and he still wished that he were here with him today. Pat thought about all of the things that his dad had already missed: the baseball games on TV (not the ones Pat never played in for the Wahkashen team); the school dances and the proms, the drive-in movies, and his first girlfriend (not Linda, although Pat really missed her, as well)…

He did not get to see the excitement on Pat's face when his first girlfriend taught him how to drive a car. It was a '64 Rambler with what they called 'rape seats' in it. The front seats both folded down completely to make the whole inside of the little car a bed, as it were.

The transmission in that car was a three speed manual with the stick on the column. Pat had a little trouble negotiating between the clutch and the gas…but just like sex, the more he worked at it, the better he got.

Or at the very least, he thought he got better at it. That was better at driving; and also with sex, of course…

His first steady girlfriend, Paula was her name, was very patient with Pat as he tried to maneuver the car and get a feel for the clutch. She did chuckle, much to the vexation of Pat, but made up for it in other ways, much to the delight of Pat.

She was also very patient with him the first time that he tried to maneuver her bra, and get a feel for her body as well, and then they had made love.

Pat believed that she was a virgin when they first got together, in the Rambler, of course.

They had rape seats…

He never did tell Paula that he had done this before.

Discretion and all…

There were so many things, events and mistakes that his father had, and would miss throughout Pat's lifetime…

...the time when Penny, Mom and he were raking leaves just two years ago and Pat got a wild hair up his ass to jump off of the garage roof into a huge pile of raked leaves.

He landed in those leaves with a soft 'thud' and a great belly laugh. He really felt great that morning. Nothing would be able to change how Pat felt that day.

Not to be out done, Penny decided to try it, much to the angst of their mother, as she placed her hands to her face and meekly tried to cover her eyes. Penny landed quite hard at an odd angle, and she sprained her ankle real bad, almost to the point of breaking it. It was but pure luck that it didn't snap, according to Delores.

It was great! Pat wanted to do it again, but Delores screamed that she almost had a coronary thrombosis the last time and that if he valued his life, he better think twice about even attempting a stunt like that again; and then she went back to caring for Penny and her hurt ankle.

Pat laughed, Penny cried and Delores yelled.

It was a great day.

It was a great memory for Pat; one that Pat would have been willing to share with someone special, like his dead father.

II

As it were, Howard didn't get to be there for Pat when he finally *did* learn how to drive, when he failed his first driver's test, much to the amusement of Penny. He wasn't there for Pat when Pat had no one to whom he could divulge about the evening he spent with Linda, and how he felt about it; and how he continued to feel about her. And to this day, he had still not spoken to anyone about it; and probably never would.

Howard missed the day Pat shot that huge buck a couple of years ago. Pat saw that deer running hell bent for leather through the hills of the Badlands, and when he finally got the stag to settle down for a second or so, Howard also missed the spectacular shot Pat made to drop that beast.

Howard would miss the day Pat graduated; the day when Pat would eventually get married and start a life with his own family. He would miss out on picking up and holding his grandchildren...

His dad would not be there to talk to him about his addiction to the fairer sex, and the mindless animalistic lust that came with every encounter.

Pat reflected on all of the things that his father would miss out on in his family's life. He would always think about that whenever a life altering change would happen to Pat, his sister, or his mom (who would eventually remarry).

Pat thought about how his life had been spent these last five years.

Would his father have been proud of him?

Would his father have been disappointed in him?

Would he even have had the opportunity to have met Linda had his father been alive?

There isn't anything Pat could do no matter how hard he prayed, no matter how much he wished; to change the fact that his father was dead and had been dead for nearly five years now.

Pat remembered a conversation he had with his mom a week before graduation about the years that have gone by since the funeral. They were sitting at the kitchen table.

"Do you think dad would have been proud of me, Mom" he asker her. "Would he have been proud of me graduating?"

Delores reached across the table and grabbed hold of Pat's hand. She gave it a squeeze, and then another, a little harder than the first one.

"Pat," she began with a faint and warm smile on her face. "Your father would have been extremely proud of everything you have accomplished." She looked him directly in the eyes and gave him a warm smile. "In fact," she continued, "I am quite certain he is smiling down on us right now, beaming with that pride."

Pat looked down at the tabletop and thought for a few seconds. When he lifted up his face to look at his mother again, Delores could tell that the pain had not fully subsided in her son. Not fully, yet.

"I sure hope that he is," he told her with tears welling up a bit. "I just wish I could be sure that he is that's all."

"I am more than positive that he is, sweetheart," Delores said and then got up from her chair. As she walked over to Pat's side of the table, Pat got up and they hugged.

They remained in that safe embrace for a few minutes, not talking; just enjoying the gentle embrace that only a mother can have with her son...and vise versa.

"I'm sure he is, Pat," Delores whispered into her son's ear.

III

The time had finally arrived. Graduation day...

He had made it.

Lenny had made it. Mike had also made it...they were done with high school. Now it was up to them to decide what they were going to do with their lives. All three would walk across the stage in the high school gymnasium and accept their well deserved diplomas. They would say their *'thank you'* to everyone who gave them graduation gifts; attend the graduation parties and listen to their classmates brag about what they were or were not going to attempt in their lives.

The gang had made it through high school and they were not damaged by the experience.

Lenny started taking college classes while they were finishing their senior year and had done well with mathematics and chemistry; Mike was going to go to work in the area and Pat...well, Pat was going to go attend the trade school in Wahkashen where Linda and the Rainbow girls stayed...almost three years ago.

Three years ago, and it seemed more like three decades.

IV

The year that had really changed Pat's life was nineteen seventy. It had turned Pat's world completely on its ear. It tested the very fiber of his character. It scarred Pat for all eternity and yet it also helped shape Pat's temperament in a sad and strange sort of way.

The year that had helped contour Pat's undefined life, so to speak, was nineteen seventy two. That was the year that he discovered that he really had importance, in the eyes of someone else. That someone saw something special enough inside his broken heart worthy of aiding him in a special way.

That he was a worthy person fit to be in this world. That there were people, of the female persuasion, who would discover that he, was a laudable person.

He would prove to everyone else that he was a survivor, and worthy to be a member of this planet. That no matter what he attempted in this life, he would never fail, because at least he had tried.

Now it was nineteen seventy five, and Pat's whole life was laid out in front of him like so much virgin carpet waiting for his steps on it to explore and test the texture of the fabric. He had so many things he wanted to explore, so many dreams he wanted to fulfill, and so many places and people he wanted to go and see.

Pat had last heard that Brian Osterman was serving time in the state penitentiary for assault and battery. That was fitting as he always seemed to have something to prove, to himself; and now, in Pat's mind, there should be plenty of opportunity in the pen for Brian to prove his manliness, Pat thought.

Pat had learned the difference between 'assault' and 'battery' when he watched two guys fighting over a girl at a barn dance in the fall of '74. The police had been called and one boy was charged with 'assault' because he had swung at the other boy, but didn't make contact. However, the other boy was charged with 'assault' AND 'battery' because he swung, AND made contact.

He knocked out a couple of the other kids' teeth.

Pat stood by with the curious crowd as the boys tussled with each other, and he watched the girl in question during the fight. She was stunning, to say the least, but Pat couldn't understand how two guys could do that to each other over a girl who looked like she was totally bored with the whole event.

Pat almost went over to talk to her about a secret consultation that he was feeling the need to acquire from her; or, by her, but then Discretion once again raised its intelligent head…

…There was also another saying in this cold and frightening world that went, *'That which does not kill you, makes you stronger'.*

Pat wasn't sure if 'they' had given the world that saying, but it really was fitting when reflecting back on the life that Pat had been given.

Pat looked back at all of the events of the past five years and wondered; wondered what would have happened to him had his father survived. Would he be on his way to the Shell station to work beside his father until the end of time?

Would he even have met Linda, had his dad been alive in 1972?

Would he have had the opportunities to get together with all of the women by which he'd had the pleasure (all puns intended) to meet these last couple of years. Would there have been the time to explore with them, had his father been alive? Would there even have been reasons to find solace in their open arms, and open legs?

Way too many things may or may not have changed the course of Pat's life had his father lived.

He did not know the answer to these questions that had followed him for the past five years. He would search and search, but the answers would always lie just out of his reach.

However, he did know one thing: Pat had lived to tell the tale of death's destructive, life altering force. He had survived in Death's shadow for the past five years, and he had suffered and became experienced as he walked along the path that was his long journey into to a life.

He had endured the Brian Ostermans, the bullies who forever had the taste of fear on their tongues. They did not alarm him anymore. They could no longer inflict their will upon him anymore. He simply refused to let it happen. He found out that he was a very tolerant person, a highly assiduous person, and that these bullies would not affect his life anymore. Mike assured him of that fact the day that they broke Brian's nose.

Pat was no longer one of the timid rabbits of the world; the cautious robin on the ground looking for the stray worm to appear while constantly being on the alert for the predator. He had overcome that portion of his life. He had learned to control his fear; although, he was still quite cautious because *Discretion*…

He had great friends in Lenny and Mike…lifelong friends who would always be there for him; as he would always be there for them.

Good friends did have to work to keep their friendships *great,* Pat always thought. And for Mike and Lenny, it really wasn't work…it really wasn't even an exertion at all; it was merely an unconscious effort for friends that one would kill for; or die for, that's all.

Yes, Pat thought: *'that which does not kill you indeed makes you stronger'.*
Pat would choose to live with that motto from this day forward.

He had survived the metaphorical and hypothetical healing of a broken heart and gouged soul, and he felt that he was now a much stronger person because of it.